LP
WRIGHT   Wright, Jaime Jo,
CURSE   The Curse of Misty Wayfair
            DISCARDED
        Huron Public Library

THE CURSE OF MISTY WAYFAIR

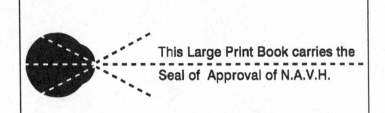

This Large Print Book carries the
Seal of Approval of N.A.V.H.

THE CURSE OF MISTY WAYFAIR

JAIME JO WRIGHT

THORNDIKE PRESS
A part of Gale, a Cengage Company

Farmington Hills, Mich • San Francisco • New York • Waterville, Maine
Meriden, Conn • Mason, Ohio • Chicago

HURON PUBLIC LIBRARY
521 DAKOTA AVE S
HURON, SD 57350-2797

Copyright © 2019 by Jaime Sundsmo.
Scripture quotations are from the King James Version of the Bible.
Thorndike Press, a part of Gale, a Cengage Company.

ALL RIGHTS RESERVED
This is a work of fiction. Names, characters, incidents and dialogues are products of the author's imagination and are not to be construed as real. Any resemblance to actual events or persons, living or dead, is entirely coincidental.
Thorndike Press® Large Print Christian Mystery.
The text of this Large Print edition is unabridged.
Other aspects of the book may vary from the original edition.
Set in 16 pt. Plantin.

LIBRARY OF CONGRESS CIP DATA ON FILE.
CATALOGUING IN PUBLICATION FOR THIS BOOK
IS AVAILABLE FROM THE LIBRARY OF CONGRESS

ISBN-13: 978-1-4328-6247-3 (hardcover)

Published in 2019 by arrangement with Bethany House Publishers, a division of Baker Publishing Group

Printed in the United States of America
1 2 3 4 5 6 7 23 22 21 20 19

HURON PUBLIC LIBRARY
521 DAKOTA AVE S
HURON, SD 57350-2797

To my littles, CoCo and Peter Pan . . .

*May you find your identity not in your
past, your present, or your future.*

*May you find your purpose not in
yourself, your family, or those
who surround you.*

*May you know you were designed by a
Creator, with great attention to detail.*

*May you know Him, and by doing so,
know yourself.*

But here let me say one thing: From the moment I entered the insane ward on the Island, I made no attempt to keep up the assumed role of insanity. I talked and acted just as I do in ordinary life. Yet strange to say, the more sanely I talked and acted the crazier I was thought to be. . . .

Nellie Bly,
Ten Days in a Mad-House

CHAPTER 1

THEA REED

Pleasant Valley
Northwoods of Wisconsin, 1908

Melancholy was a condition of the spirit and the soul, but also of the mind. Still, she'd never seen melancholy claim a life and be the cause of a body laid to rest in permanent sleep. At peace? One hoped. Prayed, if they were of that bent. Regardless, as she positioned herself beside the corpse, boxlike camera clutched to her chest, Thea Reed found melancholy fascinating. For its persistent grip and the power it held even unto death. That it could claim a life was a horrifying mystery.

Memento mori was becoming less prominent in the photographer's world, but the tradition still gripped those of sentimental pandering. Rose Coyle was one of those. A photograph to hold tight to as she posed beside her deceased sister, frozen in time as if they both still lived. Though tears welled in Rose's eyes, her shoulders remained stalwart.

Thea tucked away the ever-present nudge of guilt. The idea she benefited monetarily from others' grief. It was a morbid career she'd fallen into as a girl. A traveling photographer and his wife needed a helper, the orphanage mistress had told Thea. A decade later, she was now the photographer while her benefactors were dead. But what choice did she have? Only a leftover letter with miniscule clues gave Thea any hint of her past. While the enticements of who Thea Reed might really be had brought her here, to this town, Thea knew dreams of a future were something women with roots and ancestry concocted. Orphans played the hand they were dealt, even if that hand was ghastly at its best.

Thea cast Rose a glance from the corner of her eye as she carefully collected her photographic equipment. Rose was not far in age from Thea, perhaps only a few years older. Well, if one surmised merely by the porcelain complexion, the unlined corners of the brilliant blue eyes, and the crow black hair that swooped into a lustrous silken crown on Rose's head. Thea shifted her gaze toward the other model, giving Rose her distance and allowing her the privacy to dab her eyes with a handkerchief bordered by purple tatting.

Thea flipped open the lid of the velvet-lined case that housed her camera. She paused before lowering her precious camera into its box. The deceased woman — Mary Coyle — was nowhere near as striking as her older sister. Mary was simple by comparison, and even in death, one could see that in life she'd been pasty next to Rose. Ash blond hair, dull due to the lack of life. Her lips a muted pink, her nose dotted with freckles that now had no hope of ever disappearing. Her body lay limp, propped into an upright position by the aid of Thea's metal hanger that cuffed to the corpse's arms and neck and helped her to stand like a mannequin one might see in Miss Flannahan's Boutique four towns over.

A sniffle jerked Thea's attention back to the living and squelched the thoughts that made her mind spin like five children's metal tops whirling across a wooden floor.

"I'm so sorry." Rose blinked quickly, yet the moisture on her lashes only made her blue eyes larger and more iridescent. Thea engaged in a twinge of inadequacy herself, but then she ignored it like the little devil it

11

was. Her brown eyes and honey brown hair might be uninspiring next to Rose, but she had life, whereas — Thea finally rested her camera in the box — whereas Rose had grief.

"There's nothing to apologize for." Thea had no struggle infusing empathy into her voice. The entire afternoon had been dreadful for Rose Coyle.

"But the photograph . . ." Rose's voice dwindled in a muted whimper.

Thea buckled the camera case. "The photograph will be fine, I promise."

She hoped. Rose had been so fidgety that keeping her expression stoic for the time it took for the lens to expose to light and capture the image made it almost definite the photograph would turn out blurry. But, compared to a corpse, any live human being would seem fidgety.

Thea swallowed her observation. She was used to the morbid, the dead, but then the strange questions would come during heightened times of distress and mostly when she was disturbed. When ghosts lingered in the air, their skeletal-like fingers stroking the back of Thea's neck. A taunt, mingling with a subtle dare to find them. Catch them. If only Thea could. Ghosts were never captured, or they would be

12

entrapped in tombs with their bodies. No, their spirits roamed free, Thea had been taught. Some good, some desperate, and some — the worst sort — wicked and evil.

"Tea?"

"Pardon?" Thea's head snapped up from her frozen state over her camera case. But her eyes didn't meet with Rose's. Instead, her gaze settled again on Mary Coyle, knowing she would need to detach her from the frame.

"I wondered if you would stay for tea?" Rose had summoned strength from deep within herself, it appeared. Tears had dissipated, though every ounce of composure could not hide the shadows that lingered under her eyes.

Thea nodded before she could consider, sympathy gaining the better hand over sound judgment.

"Yes. Please." She bit her tongue. *No. Thank you.* Never mingle with a customer. It had been her benefactor, Mr. Mendelsohn's instruction, and his wife's sternly supported conviction. Thea usually heeded it.

Rose had already exited the parlor with a murmur. It was too late and too rude to decline now. Thea should have finished here, laid the burdensome body back on its

13

temporary cot before the undertaker came to prepare Mary Coyle for her final rest and position her in a coffin. But now, tea it would be, Thea supposed, which only meant squelching the curiosity of Mary, her life, and subsequently her death, would be more difficult.

It took time, but eventually Thea had freed Mary from the trap of the photographic frame that held her prisoner. Laid and covered, Thea stepped back.

"I'm sorry life was such despair," Thea whispered.

Mary did not answer.

Drawing in a deep breath and then expelling it slowly between her lips, Thea gathered her equipment. She moved to the parlor door, but that niggling sense — that *feeling* — gave her pause. She looked over her shoulder. Mary hadn't moved. Of course she hadn't. Nor had she spoken.

But oddly the black crepe shroud that covered a photograph of Mary when she was very much alive had slipped down the piano, onto its bench, and gathered in a filmy pile on the floor. Thea stared at the photograph. Not one sibling but two flanked Mary Coyle. All three of them smiling. All three children in adolescence.

Thea nodded. She understood now.

14

Mary had been happy once.

Before death had come to play.

Rose was kind — and chatty. Likely to avoid the suffocating weight of grief. Thea tried to be vague in her answers.

Yes, she was new to town. Yes, traveling photographers sometimes knocked on doors to inquire if a service was needed. No, she wasn't here to visit any family. No, she'd never been this far north in Wisconsin before.

Thea cringed inwardly. It wasn't particularly true. She may have been. As a youngster, before memories became firm images in a person's mind. Just vague shadows. It was why she'd come north, wasn't it? To clear the fog away from those blurred recollections?

Of course, she'd not tell Rose that. Thea preferred anonymity. For no other reason than that she was used to it, it was comfortable, and if asked to define who she was, she really had nothing substantial to offer.

Thea dabbed the cloth napkin against her lips. Rose met her curious gaze over the rim of her teacup. Sadness still lingered there, but Rose's dark brow winged upward in question. Inviting and warm.

Thea accepted the unspoken invite. It was

15

time to divert Rose's polite curiosity with some of her own.

"I couldn't help but wonder, I noticed you had a brother." She didn't reference the photograph she had re-shrouded before leaving the parlor.

Rose lowered her teacup. "We still have a brother."

We. Poor Rose. Like Mary were still alive. There was no past tense.

"Simeon." The name caressed from Rose's lips gently, with a deep fondness that Thea couldn't relate to.

Rose smiled one of those bittersweet smiles as she ran her fingertip around the edge of her teacup. "Simeon is my younger brother, between Mary and I. He is . . . special."

Her interest more than piqued; Thea was also equally as anticipatory of escaping the gloomy atmosphere and driving away on her horse-led box wagon. She shifted on the hard wooden chair. The lace tablecloth caught under her leg and drew taut, making the china rattle. Thea made it her excuse for escape.

"Thank you so much for the tea." Thea summoned every manner Mrs. Mendelsohn had taught her in their short years together.

Rose drew a breath, shuddering only a

16

tad. "And the photograph?"

Oh yes. Business. Thea gave Rose an approximate date. She would need to find a satisfactory place to develop the plates. Her wagon was equipped, but barely. Finding an established portrait studio she could partner with was a better option. She wasn't certain if that was normal, but it had been Mr. Mendelsohn's way of doing business, and Thea was well versed in it.

Rose led Thea to the front door, the wool carpet runner beneath her feet silencing the footsteps that would have otherwise echoed on the scuffed walnut floors. Always observant, Thea noted the wallpaper was more faded by the entryway than in the hall, which made sense considering the windows that flanked the front door. Sunlight was sure to drain color from the paper roses. Thea drew her attention back to her client. Life had drained color from Rose Coyle. Only the sapphire of her eyes and the coal black of her hair and lashes saved her from being ghostly.

"My brother will give you your partial payment." Rose hesitated, and her voice dropped into a wispy tone. "He's good with numbers."

"And I shall find him where?" Thea ventured.

Rose's fingers flew to her neckline, fidgeting with the lace at her throat. The only bit of adornment on her otherwise black silk mourning dress. She seemed taken aback by the question.

"Your brother — Simeon?" Thea pressed.

"Yes." Rose gave her head a little shake, but her eyes grew dull and vacant. She dropped her hand from her throat. "Simeon will be in his workshop."

An uneasy sensation coursed through Thea. Not unlike the one in the parlor. As if they were being watched — as if *Mary* watched them. A common superstition but one Thea found immensely hard to shake.

She nodded, grappling for the doorknob. She wished to leave now. She had no more courage left to cast a final glance into the parlor, where Mary Coyle lay, and no bravery to investigate Rose's sorrowing face again.

Thea's fingers brushed Rose's as they'd already turned the knob and opened the door. She snatched her hand away and edged past Rose, catching a whiff of perfume. Thea turned to bid Rose farewell, but Rose was already closing the front door, her face slowly disappearing as the crack between the door and frame shut.

Tiny bumps raised on Thea's arms. She

18

observed her horse and wagon. She could just leave. Avoid the *special* Simeon Coyle — whatever that inferred — and be rid of this creepy house and its inhabitants. There had been a tiny glimpse of fear in Rose's eyes just as the door closed. Fear of her brother perhaps? Or something greater and more threatening than the melancholy that had wasted away Mary Coyle?

She needed the money. With that determination, Thea made her way over a stone path through flower gardens of summer growth. Chives with bristly purple blossoms, lavender bushes lending a distinct scent in the air, both calming and pungent, and a mishmash of wildflowers waving in the slight breeze. The path passed through a gate and then it was gone. Only dirt and patchy grass led Thea to the door of the shed, Simeon Coyle's workshop.

Thea knocked firmly on the door. A sparrow fluttered above her and landed on the peak of the roof. It cocked its head to the right and danced a fidgety little waltz across the ridgepole. Thea met the beady eyes and didn't miss the sparrow's quick nod before it fluttered away.

Mr. Mendelsohn had believed spirits sometimes took the form of other creatures. Perhaps it was Mary Coyle giving her approval to stand before her brother's place of work. Or, Thea blinked as the door began to open, superstitions shouldn't be taken so far. Thea knew little of God, but Mrs. Mendelsohn had argued with her husband many times that a human simply did not return as an animal. It was ungodly and sacrilegious.

Much as Rose had closed the door, Simeon Coyle opened his. With a nervous suspicion in squinting gray eyes. Brown hair the color of tree bark straggled over his forehead in straight strands parted down the middle. He eyed Thea. Perhaps he'd not seen a stranger in his entire life? His eyes looked her up and down, until finally he opened the door enough for her to see his whole body.

Simeon Coyle did not step from his shed. Nor did he speak. His jaw was square, his shoulders lean with suspenders spanning over them, and he was only slightly taller than she. There was nothing remarkable about him. Nothing at all.

They stared at each other.

Simeon, waiting.

Thea, tongue-tied.

There was something about Simeon Coyle. His sharp, observant gaze conflicted with the hollow expression on his face.

She cleared her throat, trying to find her voice.

He blinked.

Thea stumbled back a step. She was losing her senses, surely! Yet she would vow there was an instant tugging of souls between her and Simeon Coyle, with inexplicable reason other than an innate comprehension that they shared something unspoken. Something yet to be defined — if they gave it opportunity.

"I've come only for money." Thea's words bridged the space between them. Words that eliminated the invisible thread between them that made no logical sense.

Simeon blinked, his face pulled into a scowl, making his one eye close like he was winking. But Thea was certain he wasn't. Just as quickly, his muscles relaxed, and his expression returned to a quiet study of her. A movement caught her attention, and Simeon's hand stretched forward. In his grip, a coin in half payment for the photograph. Thea reached for it, and he released the money.

Without another word, Simeon Coyle closed the door. The latch clicked quietly as he reentered his shed. But, Thea could not chase away the feeling that a door had also opened into the secret places inside of her,

and Simeon Coyle had unassumingly
walked right in.

Chapter 2

Heidi Lane

Pleasant Valley
Northwoods of Wisconsin, Present Day

A mortuary had more appeal than the cluttered aisle of the antique store. Heidi Lane edged around a dresser circa 1889 with a mottled mirror that returned to her a distorted image of herself. She paused, staring back at her eyes. Brown with edges of black. Monkey-fur eyes. That was what her older sister, Vicki, had called them, along with her childhood nickname *Monkey.* Perhaps one of the few semi-fond memories she had of her younger years.

The letter burned in her back pocket. She'd stuffed it there when she'd left Chicago for the drive north. Nine hours later, including a few stops for gas, pizza-flavored Combos, and La Croix water, and she was here. In a town new to her, but her parents'

HURON PUBLIC LIBRARY
521 DAKOTA AVE S
HURON SD 57350-2797

and older sister's home for the last several years. Heidi had never visited. Never desired to visit. Until the letter arrived.

She blinked, breaking her catatonic stare into the old looking glass. Mirrors made her nervous. Antique shops intrigued her, yet they also could be unsettling. At least in a mortuary, things stayed dead — presumably — but in places like this? Ghosts loitered in corners, under furniture, were released when one uncapped a cardboard hatbox, or reflected in old mirrors — like this one.

Heidi turned away. She reached for a teacup with a scalloped handle, a pink rose hand-painted down its ceramic side, and a little ledge built inside the cup to protect a man's mustache.

"It's a lovely cup." The unexpected voice beside her gave Heidi pause, but didn't make her nervous like the mirror had. She welcomed the sound, the company. It was pleasant to be around strangers rather than close family. People who didn't know her, didn't judge her, and didn't care that Heidi covered her anxiety and lack of confidence with recklessness and impulse.

"The hand-painted roses are beautiful!" Heidi infused her customary friendliness into her response and squelched the uneasiness that had riddled its unwelcome path

HURON PUBLIC LIBRARY
521 DAKOTA AVE S
HURON SD 57350-2797

into her spirit. "It's a mustache cup."

A smaller woman stood beside her, hair cut in a wedge a bit too young for the age that labeled her face at approximately — Heidi considered, then took a guess — late fifties. She was classy, in a simple, small town, northern Wisconsin sort of way. In other words, blue jeans and a floral button-up blouse. But she seemed warm and welcoming. Unjaded by the bustling world of expectations beyond the North-woods.

The woman studied Heidi with an authentic smile and a bit of surprise. "Not many people know that's a mustache cup."

"No?" Heidi tried to ignore the feeling that this woman was exactly what she would have wanted for a mother. One couldn't make a judgment like that at first sight. Not to mention, she had a mother, albeit a much older one who'd done her best but still misunderstood every nuance that was Heidi. The letter burned a hole in her back pocket.

"I have a plate in the same pattern as the cup, if you're interested." The woman pressed into Heidi's thoughts.

"Oh, no. No, thank you." Heidi replaced the cup on the shelf. She'd ducked into the antique shop to avoid her sister, Vicki, who'd been striding down the sidewalk toward her. Heidi wasn't ready for Vicki to know she was in town. Not yet. The sky would fall soon enough. Why not avoid it for a blissful extra thirty minutes?

"I'm not really shopping, just browsing. I have some time to kill."

The woman reached out and patted Heidi's arm. "Ahh. Well, let me know if you need anything."

Heidi let her eyes graze where the hand had touched her. How long had it been since she'd been touched in a platonic gesture of motherly kindness? As a child she'd craved protective snuggles and cuddles, the kind a little one received from a nurturing mother or doting grandmother. Instead, she'd received a list of dos and don'ts, and the ever-cautious eye of a carefully guarded parent.

"Oh, wait!" Heidi snapped her fingers, the flash of her *Fly Free* tattoo on the inside of her left wrist reminding her to prepare for Vicki's condescension when they finally met up. The feathered words wove between and wrapped their green-inked way up the inside of her thumb.

"Yes?" The woman turned.

"Do you have photograph albums?"

"Of course!" The shopkeeper brightened and waved Heidi toward her. "Come this way." She hip-hugged between two counters with mint-green pottery and china dogs on top. "I'm so sorry for the close quarters." The words were tossed over her shoulder. "I keep telling my husband to ease up on the estate sales, but he loves our weekend jaunts."

Heidi gave her a reassuring smile before grabbing at a wooden rolling pin that began its descent off the edge of a porcelain wood stove pushed against the wall.

"I'm Connie, by the way." Connie edged around a rocking horse.

There was no rhyme or reason to the store. Heidi flicked at the horse's rope-hair mane.

"And you are?" Connie paused beside another bureau, this one mirrorless.

"Heidi." No reason to provide Connie with her last name. She'd instantly connect her to Vicki, even if Vicki's married name was McCoy. The family lodge and cabin resort on the lake was, after all, *Lane Landings,* the only getaway in Pleasant Valley.

"Well, Heidi. Here are the albums I have on hand for now." Connie ran her palm over the worn velvet cover of one of the old albums. "Most people aren't too interested in buying these, so my husband and I are less likely to pick them up. This one, and"

— she reached for another album with a hinged clasp that held the cover closed — "this one, we bought at a garage sale here in town."

Heidi nodded.

"Well, I'll leave you to it, then." Connie matched Heidi's smile. "Let me know if you need anything."

The next several minutes, Heidi flipped thick paper page after page. They were at least two millimeters in depth, with the cardboard pictures mounted beneath crumbling paper-framed edges. She wasn't sure why she'd asked for photograph albums. Maybe because in a place like this, Heidi's own sense of restlessness came to the fore. Piles of household belongings, once common everyday articles, were now displayed and on sale like artifacts of yesteryear. They didn't belong anywhere. It was a feeling Heidi was all too familiar with. Looking at the photographs gave the antiques in the room purpose. It connected them to people who, now long dead, had once loved. Like hearkening an old-fashioned fairy tale, not of romance but of belonging. Identity.

Heidi turned the page and ran a finger across the face of a young man, his hair parted in the middle, clean-shaven, a boy really. His jacket was cut like a soldier's.

Impossible to tell the true color, but dark like a Yankee's maybe? With big military buttons. Another page revealed a family photograph. Man, woman, two sons, a baby in a long, white nightgown, its sex impossible to tell since both boys and girls in that era wore dresses until toddler years.

It was as though the photographs sucked her into them. A time machine of sorts. Heidi's heartbeat lessened in pace, her shoulders relaxed, and she tucked her blond hair behind her ears. Maybe she'd purchase this album. Carry with her the spirits of the dead and revive them in the moments when Heidi couldn't find anything else to cover up her restless nature.

One more page. One more and then she'd buy the album and make Connie a sale. She'd return to her car, give Vicki a call, and let her sister know she was in town. Then she'd brace herself to listen as Vicki lectured her on how she should have come years ago. When was she going to grow up? She was thirty now. Thirty. They needed her to be responsible. Yadda, yadda yadda . . .

And the letter in her back pocket would explain why she'd come. An explanation Heidi had no intention of telling Vicki.

The page fell with a *thud* that might've sounded like thunder to a mouse but was a whisper to the ear of a human. The impact of its fall, the whiff of musty paper that slammed into Heidi's attention, was a moment that stole her breath. Her gaze collided with another set of familiar eyes.

"What . . . ?" Her unasked question drifted down the overpacked aisle of the antique store. She stared until a coldness filled her stomach, edging its way up into her chest, until finally Heidi expelled her held breath. She touched the woman's face. Pale and lifeless, but eyes open with an awkward droop to the lids. Painted-on eyes. Dead eyes. The woman was deceased at the time the photograph had been taken, and someone had taken a paintbrush to try to make her appear alive.

She yanked the open album off the bureau and hugged it against her chest. Looking around, Heidi maneuvered her way through the mess toward the front of the store.

There. Connie.

Heidi wished for another human's presence now. Preferably a *living* presence. She dropped the album onto the wooden checkout counter with an unintentional firm clap. Connie startled, lifting blue eyes, her graying blond hair feathered around her chin.

"Is everything all right?" Her concerned expression roved Heidi's face.

"Would you tell me what you see in this picture?" Heidi rested her finger on the face of the corpse's photograph.

Connie frowned, studying Heidi's face before dropping her gaze to the picture. "I don't understand," she murmured. "Did something — oh!" Surprised eyes flew up and met Heidi's.

"You see it too?" Heidi pressed. A cold sensation came over her, not unlike a skeletal hand curling around her throat and starting to squeeze. She swallowed, feeling the pressure from the unseen hand. A ticklish curdle in her stomach. The one that hinted of panic before the actual panic set in.

Heidi swallowed again, this time accompanying it with a big breath. She faked a flippant smile to fool not only Connie but herself.

"This isn't something you find every day in an antique store!" She framed it with a chuckle, but Connie's eyes narrowed, her attention still on the photograph.

"Well, I'll be." She reached and turned the album. Connie leaned closer to the photograph, then pulled back. Her voice held the same disbelief that Heidi had coursing through her body.

"That is remarkable."

"She looks like me," Heidi breathed.

"*Exactly* like you," Connie echoed her affirmation.

Their eyes met over the photograph. It wasn't much different, Heidi assumed, than the fictional stories of time travel, having your photograph snapped, and then discovering it when you landed back in present time. Evidence of your time machine, your jaunts into the past, and the manipulation of the future by visiting days gone by.

Heidi closed the album. "I'll take it."

She had to. She possessed no such time machine. Heidi hadn't traveled to the past and yet — she dug in her leather shoulder bag for her wallet — there she was, in the sepia-toned picture, complete with the tiny mole above the corner of her lip.

Connie took the credit card Heidi offered her. Silent, she wrapped the old album in tissue paper before sliding it into a brown paper gift bag.

Heidi slipped her fingers through the bag's handles as Connie gave it to her.

A ghost had risen from the album's pages, beckoned to her, and begged to have her story told.

"Here's your room." Vicki flicked on a light even as she raked fingers through her thick, straight blond hair and expelled a sigh that rivaled the exasperation of a mother of twelve. Only she wasn't a mother and seemed perfectly content in her choice.

Heidi gave Vicki a sideways glance as she edged past her older sister. She hugged the antique photo album to her chest almost as a shield, but she was long past needing armor against Vicki. Or the rest of the family, for that matter. She could deflect the negativity by sheer talent now. At least she wanted to believe she could.

"Thanks," she muttered. Vicki had a way of stealing joy, spontaneity, and outright *life* from a moment. Like someone sucking the air from a room. Heidi gently laid the album on the twin-size bed with its red bandanna patchwork quilt. Vicki was not going to steal her momentum.

Fly free.

The reminder flashed on her tattoo as Heidi waggled her wrist at her sister with a smile she hoped was both confident and impish at the same time.

"Love it here!" She spun with her arms stretched out, ignoring the momentary pang she felt at the look of disgust on Vicki's face at the tattoo. Better to get it all out in the open right away, absorb the censure, and move on. "The room is legit."

Actually, it was Northwoods all the way,

which was a complete one-eighty from Heidi's décor preferences. Quilt already accounted for, it had an unstained pinewood trim that went halfway up the wall and was bordered by stenciled forest-green pine trees. Black-and-white photos of the forest were framed and hung on the wall — regardless that looking out the window gave you the same view — and the furniture was also pine. Brad, Vicki's husband, crafted furniture. He probably made the dresser, the bed, and the bench her luggage was already piled on.

"Thank you." Vicki's voice was tight. Her baseball T-shirt with gray body and red sleeves was casual, as were her jeans, though they didn't match her uptight personality.

Heidi gave her sister a crooked grin. "So, I have another one too." She flashed the *Free Spirit* tattoo on the other wrist like a brazen sixteen-year-old rebel.

Guess not much has changed.

Vicki raised one eyebrow, slightly darker than her hair. "I suppose there's one on your lower back. And your inner thigh. What? Eagle wings or Chinese symbols?"

Neither, but Heidi nodded with a grin she was sure stretched off her face. She neared her sister and fingered hair on Vicki's shoulder. "We should get one together.

Sister tattoos."

Heidi was kidding, but if Vicki were to surprise her and agree, Heidi would jump at the chance. She'd always craved Vicki's approval — no, more than that — her acceptance.

Vicki huffed and spun on her heel. "For heaven's sake, Heidi." She stalked down the hallway of the main lodge house. The upper level served as the bed-and-breakfast and the bottom level as the main living quarters.

Heidi danced after her sister's shadow. Okay then. So, no sister tattoos. Might as well make the best of it.

"So. Where is Bradley?"

"*Brad* is at work." Vicki's voice remained tight. She rounded a corner.

Heidi followed. "Is he still working as a mechanic?"

"Yes."

Well, Vicki was chatty today. "And he still makes furniture on the side?"

"Correct."

They rounded another corner and walked through the lower level's family room. More wooden furniture with navy blue cushions. "So, how's the resort doing?"

"Fine." Vicki opened a door that led into the kitchen.

"Could I by any chance have a Dr Pepper?"

"Oh, stop it!" Vicki jerked to a halt and spun on her heel.

Heidi bit the inside of her upper lip to keep from smiling. She hadn't lost her ability to get under Vicki's skin in 10.5 seconds. She should feel guilty, but she didn't. If being separated from her family the past several years had taught her anything, it was that she owed them nothing. She shouldn't change who she was for them. She shouldn't cease *living* just because Dad had, and she shouldn't stagnate today just because Mom was losing her memories. Brad and Vicki had taken on the gargantuan task of running a lakefront resort with cabins and a lodge house in the economically deprived Northwoods of Wisconsin. None of it was her fault, and none of it should be killjoy enough to make life this undeniable pain in the rear.

Vicki's glare softened a bit — not much but enough to make Heidi feel a tad guilty. Tired lines winged from the corners of her sister's eyes. An age spot was peeking through any attempt with concealer to hide it. Vicki was forty-five. Vicki was . . . exhausted.

A pang of guilt made Heidi's flippant

smile dwindle. Okay. So maybe she was being a tad over the top and insensitive.

Breath blew from between Vicki's lips. "I'm sorry. I'm not being very welcoming."

Ouch. Heidi felt even guiltier now. She searched her mind trying to recall the last time she'd ever heard Vicki apologize.

Vicki gave her an honest stare. "I know you don't want to be here, Heidi, which is why I'm also equally as confused as to why you *are* here. You've never come, never visited. Even when Dad — well, apparently funerals aren't your thing. But, since you came, we need you. *I* need you. I need you to be with the family and do your part. I can't run this place, take care of Mom, be a wife, and be a nurse four days a week at the clinic."

Heidi didn't say anything. She'd be a complete fool if she did. Once she'd graduated high school, she really had left them all behind. It'd been twelve years. She'd seen Mom and Dad twice when they'd journeyed to Chicago to visit her. She'd had distant conversations with Vicki on the phone. One or two visits when Brad and Vicki made it south and Heidi had the stamina to meet them halfway and tolerate a weekend with them. Christmases were phone calls, Face-Time, and a few visits from Mom after Dad died suddenly.

If Heidi were honest, Vicki may be uptight and no fun, but she was also a loyal daughter, predictable, dependable, and everything Heidi wasn't.

Vicki ran her fingers through hair that looked like she'd washed it maybe yesterday morning. "Mom isn't getting any better." Tears glistened in her eyes. She blinked them away so fast, Heidi wasn't sure she'd seen them.

"I know." Heidi softened her voice. All glibness aside, Heidi understood this perhaps more than Vicki realized she did. Mom had dementia. Full-on dementia with a prognosis of life that went on for years, but with a mind that was shutting down, and fast. It would hurt Vicki more than it would hurt her. Her relationship with their mother had been rocky. She was the surprise child. The one who came late in life and sort of ruined the happy middle-age years.

Vicki moved to the kitchen counter and opened the fridge, pulling out a Dr Pepper.

Of course. Vicki would know Heidi's favorite drink and stock the fridge to accommodate her. It was what she did. Notice the details, adhere to expectations. Heidi wanted to feel something — anything — that resembled being touched by Vicki's thoughtfulness. But taking care of people was what Vicki did. Because it was her job.

Heidi took the bottle of Dr Pepper, but Vicki held on to it for a second, forcing Heidi to look her in the eye. Dark brown eyes like Heidi's. Like the dead woman in the photograph.

Heidi shivered.

Vicki held her gaze, her exhausted eyes sharpening to a stern squint. "For our sake, Heidi, step up."

Heidi tugged on the bottle and drew it toward her. Stepping up wasn't on her list of talents.

CHAPTER 3

THEA

The tired, little northern town ran juxtaposed to its name. Pleasant Valley. It was neither pleasant, nor was it in a valley. It wasn't unlike a funeral pall that had lowered itself over the town like a thick fog across an open countryside after a warm rain and a chilly night.

Thea was shaken from her visit to the Coyles. A simple knock on the door inquiring if anyone needed a family portrait, a memento mori, or even a single portrait for a lover. Traveling photography sales. Just as Mr. Mendelsohn had trained her to do. But the emotion of the afternoon was so raw, so very exposing, that it left Thea feeling unsettled.

Perhaps the Coyles were unsettling, but Pleasant Valley had its own oddities too. The one main street that split Pleasant Valley into two sides was just as peculiar.

"It's the Protestant side," the boarding-house mistress, Mrs. Agatha Brummel, said and gestured toward the west. "And that is the Catholic side." Her index finger tilted east.

Thea couldn't help but raise her brows. The woman's pointed chin jutted out from the froufrou of ruffles at the neck of her otherwise sturdy black dress.

"We're all on good terms, you see," Mrs. Brummel continued as she hitched up her skirts and beckoned Thea to follow her up a very narrow staircase made more claustro-phobic by the walls on either side. "But, everyone knows a Protestant and a Catholic dining together over Sunday dinner are sure to argue. Doctrine and all, you see?"

Thea didn't. But she allowed Mrs. Brummel to go on chattering in her reedy voice about the Virgin Mary, the Sacraments, and something to do with whether one baptized a soul as an infant or submerged the person in the nearby river as an adult.

The door to the room Thea was renting opened as Mrs. Brummel twisted the glass knob. It was tiny, with a lone window across the room overlooking the Catholic side of the street. Thea blinked to clear the idea from her mind. She wasn't bothered by any predilection of association, so much as

41

wished they'd all agree so she could make sense of how to determine her own eternal destination.

A bed extended out into the middle of the room. A small bureau, a writing desk, and a straight-backed chair were the only other pieces of furniture. A watercolor painting of a cow beneath a maple tree hung over the bed — the only warm spot in a room otherwise clinical and undefined.

Mrs. Brummel crossed the room, the heels of her sensible high-button shoes echoing on the rugless wood floor. She pushed aside plain curtains, her back to Thea. "Don't let the Catholics intimidate you now."

Thea bit her bottom lip. It would be funny if it wasn't so very pathetic. "I've been exposed to them before," she goaded Mrs. Brummel with her serious tone, as if it had been a traumatic experience when in fact it had all been quite pleasant.

Mrs. Brummel turned, her thin, mousy eyebrows raised over eyes holding little color other than gray. "Well, you know what I mean then." She gave a curt nod.

Thea blinked away any humor that might have entered her expression and gave Mrs. Brummel back a very comforting, very conjured smile of shared opinion.

Mrs. Brummel returned to the doorway

while Thea edged to the side, clutching her camera box in front of her. The woman eyed it, then lifted her gaze to Thea. "I assume you have a trunk?"

"I do." Thea nodded. "My belongings are at the blacksmith's in my wagon."

"Ah yes." Another curt nod of comprehension. "And rented a stable, I assume, for your horse. Smart young lady, you are. All these newfangled motorcars. Whoever thought it? A lot of good they are around these parts. Roads with ruts the size of valleys. Very well then. I'll send someone to retrieve your belongings for you."

"Thank you." Thea offered a smile. The blacksmith was . . . she thought for a moment . . . oh yes, he would be on the Catholic side. Her curiosity got the better of her. "Pardon me, Mrs. Brummel, but may I ask what caused the town to divide into religious sects?"

Mrs. Brummel tilted her head to assess whether Thea was serious or not. Her lips pursed. "Pleasant Valley is the child community of the original logging camp that settled here in the late thirties. Before the war and most certainly before any of us knew who Lincoln was." She waved a hand as if to silence her own wayward chattiness. "When Mathilda Kramer married Fergus

Coyle, well, it was all rather a mess. Mathilda was the daughter of the man who owned the logging camp. Coyle was a laborer and very Irish Catholic. Kramer, being quite wealthy, preferred his daughter wed someone more suitable, but the business wasn't stable enough at the time to risk an insult to his employees if a fuss were to be raised over societal standing and bank accounts. Kramer claimed it was all because Mathilda, who was very German Protestant, married an Irish Catholic. In any event, it still had poor effects on his employees and the town."

Thea rested her camera box on the floor. "So, it has nothing to do with religion, but the fact that a wealthy man's daughter wed an Irish pauper."

The logic gave Mrs. Brummel pause, but then she nodded. "I suppose it does have little to do with the Catholics per se." She waved her hand in the air again, dismissing the thought. "Either way, the town has always been on tentative terms and —" Mrs. Brummel cast a glance toward the window, then back at Thea, her eyes serious and penetrating with their stark sincerity — "and that is why the entirety of Pleasant Valley avoids the Coyles to this day."

Thea reached up to pull the hatpin from

her hat. "Fifty-some years later, Pleasant Valley is still punishing the Coyles on Kramer Logging's behalf?" Her mention of the logging company brought a spark of admiration to Mrs. Brummel's eyes.

"Well, not only that, I suppose. But also what happened *after* the marriage and throughout the years that makes us keep the Coyles at arm's length."

Thea rested her hat on the writing desk. "And that is?"

Mrs. Brummel's lips stretched in a wan smile, and her eyes grew a bit colder, as if something awful had snuffed the warmth from the room. She lowered her voice to a hiss-like whisper.

"It's the deaths, Miss Reed. All the strange dying the Coyles have had over the years. A stroke of bad luck, the superstitious say. Now, poor Mary. Poor, sweet Mary. We all know the truth."

Thea swallowed, recalling vividly the Coyle home and the very recent passing of Mary Coyle. Funny how chance would have led her to their door, of all doors, to solicit photography services.

"A spirit haunts these woods, Miss Reed." Mrs. Brummel raised an eyebrow that winged over her left eye like a crow's beak. "Every time a Coyle passes, the spirit wails throughout Pleasant Valley the evening prior to their death. Half the time, no one even understands why they die, they just . . . pass away. Like poor Mary, God rest her soul."

Mrs. Brummel walked through the bedroom doorway into the hall. She paused and offered Thea a grim smile. "They call the wailing woman Misty Wayfair."

"W-Who is Misty Wayfair?" Thea couldn't control the fearful stutter in her voice.

Mrs. Brummel's mouth turned up on one corner in a sideways smile reminiscent of someone who knew a secret. "She's the woman Fergus Coyle was meant to marry, but didn't. They found her body in a well the morning after his first night with his new wife, Kramer's daughter. Misty Wayfair had been strangled, they say, but that may just be the old story." Mrs. Brummel's smile dissipated. "Still, I would avoid the woods in the nighttime hours. Misty Wayfair likes to wander there."

A grim nod. A lowered chin. A stern eye.

"And she is not a friendly spirit," Mrs. Brummel concluded.

She wasn't entirely sure how, but Thea found herself awake the following morning, dressed in her darkest gown of deep gray, and positioned on the buckboard of Mrs.

Brummel's carriage. The wheels carted them outside of Pleasant Valley, its springs bouncing them on the seat until Thea wanted to rub her backside.

Today was Mary Coyle's funeral, Mrs. Brummel had announced that morning as she served Thea a bowl of oatmeal with a puddle of maple syrup in the middle. Very few from town would attend, she'd stated, being that Mary *was* a Coyle. Still, Mrs. Brummel had wiped her hands on her apron. It was Christian duty, after all.

Thea hadn't denied Mrs. Brummel her company, although now she questioned the wisdom of it. Part of her had been convinced when they started out that a return visit would erase the unwelcome shiver that ran through her at the memory of yesterday. Of the dead Mary, the grieving Rose, and the indecipherable Simeon.

Now, as they neared the farmhouse, its narrow frame void of any angles or gables, Thea knew how very wrong she'd been to come. Her heartbeat quickened, her palms grew clammy, and for some reason every memory, both bad and worse, filtered unbidden through her mind.

Mrs. Brummel hustled toward the front door, which was perched open for visitors. There was no backward glance over her shoulder toward Thea, and it appeared she was content to let Thea fend for herself. "Miss?"

The deep voice just behind Thea's left shoulder caused her to intake a quick breath as she spun. A tall man stood behind her, trussed up in a black suit, with a tie, a watch fob, and a bowler hat. His mustache drooped on either side of his mouth, his brown eyes sharp, with a bit of a John Wilkes Booth look about him. Thea figured that was not a complimentary comparison.

"Are you going in?" He extended his arm to encourage her to proceed.

"Yes." A quick nod and Thea moved with hurried steps toward the house.

The man followed and was mere inches behind her as she slowed and crossed the threshold.

"Dr. Earl Ackerman," he muttered in her ear.

Thea shifted aside and away from him. She met his gaze. It wasn't inappropriate or overly bold, yet she was still uneasy. She refrained from granting him her name and nodded instead. Acknowledgment coupled with subtle indifference.

Mr. Mendelsohn would have been proud of her.

Thea entered the parlor, so familiar from

yesterday. Mrs. Brummel stood to the side with two other women, their faces pinched, hands held by their lips as they murmured quietly to one another. She shifted her gaze to the casket. To Mary. Even paler than the day prior, the body now fully prepared for burial. Her hands crossed over her bosom. Her hair arranged in a curled pile on top of her head.

"You came." A soft voice interrupted Thea's perusal of Mary Coyle. "Bless you," it continued.

Thea met Rose Coyle's eyes. A sheen of moisture covered them, pooling in the corners. Rose dabbed at the tears with an embroidered handkerchief.

"Is it wrong that I-I will be rather thankful when this is behind us?" Rose's admission might have shocked anyone else, but it echoed the very thoughts Thea had entertained many times over while learning the postmortem photography trade from Mr. Mendelsohn.

Thea gave Rose a reassuring smile. "I don't believe it is wrong. I believe it is natural."

Rose bit her bottom lip. Her eyes shifted about the room, timid of those who'd come to pay their respects. She leaned into Thea. "They all believe something is amiss. It's why they're here. Curiosity. As if we were a mystery to solve."

"Are you?" Thea asked, before she stopped to think. She covered her mouth with her fingers. "I'm so sorry," she breathed.

"I don't know." Rose's voice was watery, with a wary edge to it as she glanced toward Dr. Ackerman, who stood over Mary, hat in hands. "We are Coyles, and Coyles have always been . . . cursed, I suppose."

"Not cursed." Dr. Ackerman had somehow overheard. He neared them, his eyes fixed on Rose's face with familiarity. "You are a story that people cannot leave unread, when it is simply none of their business to begin with."

For a moment, Thea's opinion of the man swayed toward appreciation. He sounded appropriately offended by the guests milling about, sampling Rose's plated baked goods, and whispering.

"There is no story but sadness and grief." Rose's lip trembled. She looked between Thea and Dr. Ackerman. "It is a dark and desperate world that Mary lived in."

CHAPTER 4

She had to leave, to get away. The walls were closing in on her with a suffocating persistence.

"Take the pictures," Mr. Mendelsohn had always instructed, *"and then leave."*

Get away. Before you become a part of the deceased's story, tied to the family with emotional threads that became more entangled the longer you mingled.

Thea pushed past a couple entering the Coyle home, curiosity etched onto their faces with the boldness of an onlooker visiting a circus. Here to ponder the freaks, the objects of rumor and mystery. There was no grief, no empathy, and certainly no genuine condolences. The Coyles were alone.

Tears were not what Thea battled as she hurried down the stone path between the lavender and the wildflowers. It was an ache, sharp and dull at the same moment. Poignant right now, but a foe she'd long held hands with and grown used to its insistent throb. It was the emptiness forged from the moment she'd watched her mother walk away, never to return. Those persistent questions *Who am I? Why am I alone?* that dogged her soul. Watching anyone aimless and unclaimed, staring after a person who'd left them, upon whom they'd relied, loved, *needed* —

The collision was hard. Hard enough to cause him to stumble backward, instinctively reaching for her arms but slamming them against his shed. Thea's body pressed against his, stunned by the impact of running into Simeon Coyle with the force of a woman fleeing her own demons.

It was a long moment, silent and strange. His narrowed gray eyes searching deep into hers, the edges crinkled in study as though he wasn't surprised by the collision at all. His hands embraced her upper arms with a firm grip, and he made no motion to push her from him, from the breadth of his chest, from the wisp of air that separated their faces.

"You're not all right," Simeon Coyle observed. The low tone of his voice, rusty and rarely used, sent shivers down her spine even as Thea sensed herself meld even closer to him.

She was dizzy.

Caught off guard.

She was hypnotized by a man who hibernated in a shed. Locked away like someone with no senses.

"I'm fine," Thea breathed.

Simeon Coyle blinked. Long lashes dusted his chiseled cheekbones before raising again.

"You're shaking," he stated, studying her face.

"Yes. No — I'm fine." Warmth spread through her. The curiosity of leaning against a man's chest, smelling the cinnamon on his breath, stunned her. Now, reality began to penetrate her stupor, and she struggled to push away from him.

He released her.

"I'm sorry." Thea smoothed her dress, staring down at her shoes in embarrassment and not much different had they been caught stealing kisses behind a woodshed.

There was no answer, but she could hear him breathe.

"I'm sorry also for your loss," she added, lifting her eyes.

He offered an awkward, sad smile, as if unsure how to accept condolences. His eyes shifted toward the house, toward the gawkers come to stare at his dead sister's body.

Thea backed away another step.

Simeon didn't follow her. Instead, he seemed to consider the house, the funeral, and all it implied. His hand reached for the door to his shed, and he opened it.

Before Thea could react, before she could say a word to keep him before her, to offer her companionship to the house or express more condolences, Simeon disappeared into the shed.

The door closed.

Firm.

It was a stunning shift from the concerned man who'd held her against him just moments before to a man whose lost expression was a perfect mirror of her own.

The letter stared up at her, the scrolling penmanship staggered and wavy, indicative of the author's shaky hand. Thea was already more than a bit disturbed by Mrs. Brummel's ghost story of yesterday — this Misty Wayfair, a wandering spirit — and her discomforting time at Mary Coyle's funeral. Why she tortured herself by slipping the well-read letter from her valise and opening it, Thea couldn't explain. It was a repeated torture, almost addictive in its picking at the pain while reviving a thin splinter of hope. There would be no comfort in the words, no solace. Only fuel to continue the slow, ever-present coals smoldering in her soul.

"You were twelve."

Those three words split Thea's life into two broken halves. Life before the Mendelsohns and life after. She perched on the edge of the bed in the stark boardinghouse room, her weight causing the mattress to sag.

"It was our Christian duty to take you."

Her eyes skimmed the words. At twelve, the Mendelsohns had whisked her from the only home she could recall, and her new life had begun.

A nervous prick traversed with rapidity up Thea's spine as she folded the last letter from Mrs. Mendelsohn — a letter she'd found after the woman died — and jammed it back into her valise. Her breaths coming in short, quick sniffs, Thea bolted from the bed to the washbasin on the stand by the bureau. Lifting the heavy, white crock, she poured tepid water into the matching bowl.

She splashed water on her face. The wetness jolted Thea from thoughts that trapped her in a spiral of remembrances. Tugging her downward, threatening to become more alive than Misty Wayfair's spirit. More alive than her own rapidly throbbing heart.

Thea turned to the mirror on the bureau,

its edges blackened with age, the oak frame that held it in place scrolled and swooped around it. Water dripped down her cheeks. Deep, brown eyes stared back at her. She was Dorothea Reed. That was, for the most part, all she knew. Thea reached up and pushed light brown hair away from her face. Straight hair, unimpressive and mousy, barely held in place by pins.

Mrs. Brummel might be worried that Thea would unintentionally encounter Misty Wayfair in the forest. But Thea knew the only one whose soul she ever questioned was that of a woman who shared her features. A vague, blurry image in Thea's mind. A feminine voice with no distinguishable tone. Perhaps kind, perhaps not. But the one who'd given Thea her name, *Dorothea*, and left her on the steps of the orphan home. She was why Thea had come to Pleasant Valley, after all. To find her, or to lay her to rest for good.

Most people did not wish their mother dead. But Thea did. More than anything she'd ever wanted. She wished to lay the woman to rest along with the questions, the betrayal, and worst of all, the series of circumstances her mother had put into play the day she left a little girl to sit on a stair and then walked away.

CHAPTER 5

HEIDI

The lodge house for Lane Landings rose two stories, was built of log, and had as many angles and crevices as a creative architect could draw into its blueprints. Heidi padded across the wood floor and into the kitchen. The expanse of three broad windows over the sink revealed a view of the lake, bordered by pine and oak trees with maples and poplar dotting in and out amongst them. She paused for a moment to take it all in before turning to the Bunn coffeemaker and tugging the pot from its warmer.

Heidi liked her coffee black, though something about the Northwoods brought out the cozy in her. She adjusted a red-and-navy plaid blanket she'd wrapped around her shoulders like a shawl and retrieved heavy whipping cream from the stainless-steel fridge. Creamy goodness swirled in the

Costa Rican blend, and as she lifted the pottery mug to her lips, Heidi wondered briefly if Heaven might be a little bit like this.

She slid onto a barstool. Taking another sip of her coffee, she tugged the letter from her flannel pajama bottom's pocket.

The handwriting was shaky across the front of the envelope. Heidi ran a finger across it, as if somehow by doing so it would revive old memories long repressed. Memories she would *want* to remember, instead of the ones she tried to forget.

Heidi Loretta Lane.

Her name in the address field was formal, and she could remember hearing her mother call it with that stern edge in her voice. Loretta Lane. The woman she was named after. Heidi stared at the *Return to* corner of the envelope.

L. L.
Briar Ridge Memory Care
Pleasant Valley, WI

Years with barely a word from her, and then the letter had shown up in Heidi's mailbox. Cryptic. Almost desperate.

"Please. You must come."

So she had. Out of obligation, some concern, and definitely curiosity. Why

58

dementia-ridden Loretta Lane wanted her here in Pleasant Valley was a mystery.

"I'm heading into town." Vicki's strident voice matched the pace of her march into the kitchen.

Flustered, Heidi jammed the envelope and its contents back into her pocket.

Vicki didn't seem to notice Heidi's sneaky gestures as her hand burrowed in a blue canvas tote on the counter that was crammed with junk mail, rubber bands, odds and ends, and — interesting — Vicki pulled out a ring of keys. It was an unorganized place for her typically systematic sister.

Heidi quirked an eyebrow at her frazzled sibling. Vicki jammed the keys into her purse and shot a stern look toward Heidi.

"We've got new boarders for Cabin Two coming in at ten a.m. for early check-in. Brad cleaned it last night, but I need you to take towels over there. Four bath, two hand, and two washcloths."

Heidi took a sip of her coffee and watched her sister over the rim of the mug.

Vicki continued as she swiped some renegade papers from the opposite counter and stuffed them in her purse. "The boarders upstairs in the main lodge will need new towels. I typically deliver them after lunch and pull the dirty ones. Think you can handle that?"

Heidi bit back a smile and raised her mug. "Towel duty. Got it."

Vicki froze and eyed her. The assessment was accompanied by a sigh through her nose. "You should visit Mom too."

"I will." Infusing a chipper nonchalance into her voice was what Heidi did best.

Vicki blinked. "When I get back tonight, I'll take you through the ins and outs of running day-to-day chores for the lodge."

"Capeesh." Heidi sipped more coffee, leaning against the counter on her elbows and staring out the windows at the view.

Vicki paused, eyed Heidi once more for good measure, and frowned.

"Go!" Heidi smiled, trying to add warmth to her eyes, anything to get her sister to feel reassured enough to leave. "I've got the towels."

"Fine." Vicki spun and headed out of the open kitchen to the front door. She paused, her hand on the knob, and attempted a smile. "Mom will be happy to see you, you know."

"I know." Heidi nodded.

The door closed.

If Mom remembered her. Heidi blinked fast to push back renegade moisture in her eyes. She didn't want to be here. To be with family, to run a lodge, to be reminded whether by frank words or inference that she always fell just short. Like the prodigal son compared to his perfect older brother.

Heidi cleared her throat, her voice echoing in the empty room. She needed to get busy so she didn't think too much. Easy morning chores for Vicki and then she'd reread the letter Mom had penned to her. Every single nonsensical word that ended with her plea for Heidi to come.

Returning to her room, she slipped on a pair of black leggings and a buffalo-checked flannel shirt. Socks, knee-high wine-colored boots to offset the red-and-black shirt, and she felt her confidence growing. A few minutes in the bathroom fixed her face, lip gloss, mascara, and a bit of chocolate eyeliner to emphasize her eyes. Hair? Check. It was straight and colored golden blond with the tips dipped in royal blue. She'd seen Vicki eyeing her hair last night. It was well dyed, professional and classy, but the blue? Heidi ran a brush through it before fingering in some styling paste to give it texture. Vicki probably wasn't a fan of the blue any more than she was a fan of the tattoos.

Heidi exited the attached bathroom and

grabbed her cellphone from the nightstand. She hesitated. The photo album beneath her phone stared up at her and seemed to beg to be opened again. A small shiver wrestled Heidi's body. What was normally compelling now gave her pause. Then again — Heidi reached for the album — maybe she'd overreacted yesterday. Maybe Connie Crawford had as well. A postmortem photograph from the early 1900s couldn't possibly be her mirror image. Not if one really looked close.

She sank onto a chair and opened the musty volume. The moment she did, Heidi could almost sense the souls of the dead rising from the pages, whispering in her ear, floating about the room, pleading to have their lives rediscovered.

"Stay dead," Heidi whispered, then laughed at herself. She wasn't superstitious. Being raised in a very Christian home, with Dad being a pastor and Mom a church secretary, there wasn't much room for considering ghosts as legit human spirits. Still . . . Heidi ran fingers over the two-toned photograph of a middle-aged woman in starched silk. Still, they had stories. At one time, they had lived, hoped, dreamed, wept, and laughed. Moments lost in the funnel of time. Tiny granules of sand that fell and were lost.

She turned to the page with her supposed doppelgänger. Again, as before, Heidi's breath was snatched away. She sucked in more oxygen as she studied the photograph. There were actually two women in the picture, though Heidi had been so distracted yesterday she'd hardly looked at the one. The woman to the left — who was very obviously alive by the life in her eyes — was a raven-haired beauty. Thick lashes, perfectly curved lips, iridescent eyes. Beside her, the dead woman with painted-on eyes.

There was no mistaking the similarities. Heidi studied it, even reaching for her cellphone and flicking on its flashlight, though her bedroom was already filled with daylight. Yes. The hair appeared to be the same color as hers, sans hair dye, a mousier blond. The eyes, a perfect almond-shaped imitation. A heart-shaped face with high cheekbones, narrow chin, and full lips. The mole. Heidi leaned closer. It was . . . phenomenal. She really *was* the woman in that picture! Minus the lifeless face, of course, the pasty skin, and the slightly tilted head that gave her a bit of a zombie-like aura.

Heidi reached between the delicate paper-page frame that held the cardboard photograph in place. She gently tugged it out. The photograph's footer was simple, the words scrolled in antique print.

Amos Bros. Photography
Pleasant Valley, WI, 1908

Interesting. It was a local photograph. Heidi scrunched her face, recalling the conversation with Connie Crawford. Yes, she'd mentioned going to estate and garage sales.

Heidi flipped the photo over. A feminine script was scrawled on the back of it, as if whoever had owned the photograph saw fit to record details in the event time attempted to erase them.

Dorothea Reed — photographer
Misty Wayfair

She ran her index finger over the faded ink. Misty Wayfair. Perhaps the name of the dead woman in the photograph? Or the living? Misty was a rather odd name for the turn of the century, but then what did she know? Heidi turned the picture back so she could stare into the dead features of her Edwardian look-alike.

"Are you Misty?" Her whisper broke the silence.

Heidi waited, even though she knew the woman wouldn't answer. Wouldn't say "yes" with applause for being identified, or shriek in protest and deny the name as hers.

There was no answer.

Only the ticking of the wall clock, the sound of a dehumidifier in the hall kicking in, and —

Heidi's eyes lifted. Sensing she was being watched. The hairs on her arms prickled. A coolness settled over her, chilled from the awareness of being very alone and yet, not alone at all. She cast glances into the corners of the bedroom, as if an apparition might appear and renounce everything Heidi had ever believed about the nonexistence of ghosts.

She tucked the photograph between the pages, not bothering to insert it back into its paper frame. The album closed with a *thud.* Heidi stood, clutching it.

Where are you?

She glanced toward her open bedroom door. The hallway was lit, and daylight was not a friend to ghosts. And yet Heidi knew she was not alone. She took a step forward, then froze.

The window.

A woman at the window with massive dark eyes hollowed further by huge shadows beneath them. Her head tilted to the side, watching. Watching her.

Heidi's scream ripped from her throat, gargled like she was being strangled. Not unlike waking from a nightmare mid-scream and clawing at the air to rake fingernails across the face of an imaginary foe.

The album dropped from her hands.

It was all in slow motion. The album falling to the floor. The photograph floating from its pages and sliding across the carpet. Heidi's second attempt at a scream. And suddenly, it was all over.

The woman had vanished, as though she'd never been there.

Heidi stood shaking in the middle of the room, her arms wrapped around her body.

She looked down. Down at the lifeless woman in the photograph. The woman who looked just like her. The woman who had stood outside her window, soulless eyes peering in.

Heidi pressed the gas pedal down as she pulled away from the lodge. She glanced behind her, thoroughly convinced the woman in the window was chasing her down the curved driveway, screaming with a gaping mouth in a chasm so large an unsuspecting victim could fall into it and never return. Thick forest rose on either side of the drive, unwelcoming to the sunlight that tried to pierce through and warm the earth. She paused only a moment at the end of the drive before turning toward town.

A mile down the road, the *clunk-clunk* sound coming from a back rear tire alerted Heidi to more problems.

"For all that's holy and sane and great dane!" Heidi had learned creative cussing from her father, who thought *darn* was enough to blacklist a person's soul. She pulled the car onto the shoulder and switched on her hazard lights. Heidi jumped out of the vehicle and rounded it. She couldn't see anything at the back — at least nothing obvious to indicate the source of the clunking sound. Hopping back in, she unhooked her iPhone from its clip on the dash and speed-dialed.

She'd seen her brother-in-law, Brad, for all of five minutes last night. Good thing he liked her and was a mechanic. After an assurance either he or someone would be out to meet her to take a look and give her a tow if needed, Heidi settled in her car to wait.

Alone.

On the side of the road.

She flicked the locks.

On retrospect, she should have called the cops. But then the woman had vanished. Completely. She'd simply been there one moment and evaporated the next. You couldn't call the police on a ghost, and, assuming logic prevailed and it wasn't a ghost, the woman had done nothing wrong besides peek in her window.

Heidi blew a breath through her lips. It was probably a lodge guest. Wondering where their towels were. The ones Heidi hadn't bothered to swap out in her mad dash to leave it all behind.

She glanced into the woods through the passenger side window, then through the driver's side window at the woods on the other side of the road. Maybe this was why she preferred Chicago. A person could *see* there. Buildings, public transportation, huge billboards, and lights. It was occupied by humanity. Here, it was just trees and trees and more trees, with patches of small fields in between them. Like little glimmers of openings before being suffocated by woods again.

Movement at the corner of her eye startled her. Heidi stiffened, staring into the trees. She sagged with relief. A tawny doe stepped from the woods, her eyes huge. Behind her, a gangly fawn, spots dotting its fur like a paintbrush had slapped on white paint. Heidi shifted in her seat, and the doe caught sight of her movement. With a bound, she darted across the road, her fawn scampering behind her, long legs tripping and skidding as it went.

More silence, and then finally, ahead in the distance, a pickup truck heading her way. Heidi was sure it was Brad, until it came closer into view. A gray Silverado, its front fender rusted where it was dented. It pulled to the side of the road, the hood of the truck nose to nose with the hood of Heidi's much smaller Honda Civic.

The man in the driver's seat was not her brother-in-law. Heidi rechecked the locks as she surveyed the forms through the truck's windshield. Odd. A yellow tabby cat perched on the dash, more of a kitten really, its yellow eyes studying her as intently as Heidi studied it. The driver's side door opened, and before the human could descend from the vehicle, a dog leaped out. A long-haired mutt that looked to be a cross between a collie and maybe a German shepherd?

Oh heavens. The dog was missing an eye!

Heidi sank lower in the seat. What was wrong with this place? Ever since she'd set foot in Pleasant Valley, everything was just off.

A man stepped out from the truck. Work boots, greasy jeans, a black T-shirt with a dingy gray flannel shirt left unbuttoned over it. Baseball cap so filthy it looked like he'd dipped it in an oilcan before putting it on his mahogany-brown hair. Stubble all over his unkempt face, and eyes — oy! The steel gray eyes — Heidi didn't know whether to melt or be terrified. The man could be no less than six-foot-two with the build of a logger. There was no smile on his face. He was impassive.

Heidi yelped as his fingers rapped on her window. He bent at the waist and peered in. She peered back.

"How about you open your window?" His bland statement was more of a *no-duh* command. He didn't seem amused.

Heidi turned her car key so the battery sprang to life and she could roll down her window an inch. Just an inch.

"Are you Brad's sister-in-law?"

Oh, thank God.

Heidi nodded. "Yes. I am. Where is he?"

"Busy." The man moved back a few feet and raised his brows to indicate she should realize she was safe and to step out of the car.

No way.

One, she was from Chicago and wasn't

70

stupid. Two, he could kill her with one swipe of that permanently grease-stained hand. Three, she'd already had the fright of her life this morning, and for all sakes and purposes maybe he was a ghost too.

Heidi avoided asking him if he was dead. That probably wouldn't come across as friendly.

"It's my back tire. It's making clunking sounds."

He blinked.

Heidi tried again. "Over there. The back tire? On the passenger side."

He just stood there. The dog meandered over to his side and sat down, staring at her from its one good eye. Heidi shot a glance at the truck. Yep. The cat was still watching her too.

"Did Brad send you?" Heidi yelled through the crack in the window, even though the conversation they'd already had sort of made that obvious.

The man nodded. His arms were crossed over a very broad chest.

"Okay, soooooo . . ." She dragged out her words. He didn't move. "My tire?"

The man blinked and then, with a barely concealed sigh, rounded the car. She watched him in the side mirror. He squatted next to the tire, bent and looked under the vehicle. Grabbing at something, he tugged and pulled and then stood, apparently finished with whatever he'd found.

He rounded the car, dog at his heels. Bending, the man's mouth descended to the crack in the window. Heavens, his lips looked like they'd been carved from clay and hardened beneath the hands of Michelangelo himself.

Heidi looked away.

"A stick."

"A what?"

"You had a stick wedged between the muffler and the chassis."

"Oh." Heidi mustered a smile and shrugged, embracing her ignorance. "Well, I thought maybe it was the tie rod."

"That's on the front wheels." His correction was disinterested. "You all good then?"

He really was Brad's ministering angel. Although, Heidi frowned, *angel* wasn't exactly a proper description. She rolled her eyes at her own heightened sense of erratic caution. Overreacting and assuming everyone was out to assault her was a bit ludicrous. She unlocked the car and opened the driver's door.

"I'm sorry." She draped her arms over the door, making sure her rear end could take a quick drop and land back onto the driver's seat if necessary. "I didn't mean to be rude. I just — well, a girl's gotta be cautious."

The man eyed her for a second, then muttered, "Then I wouldn't have opened your door." He turned on his heel and headed back toward his truck, dog marching beside him.

"Hey!" Heidi hollered after him. His retort had stung. She wasn't used to acquaintances — *strangers* — reprimanding her, let alone allowing it to bother her. But for some reason, his rebuke did. Maybe because it made sense.

He turned, question in his eyes.

"What do I owe you?"

"Nothing." He opened his door. "Just watch out for sticks next time."

His words were delivered with zero humor.

"What a — wow," Heidi mumbled with a frown as the man stepped aside to let the dog hop into the truck. "What's your name?" she ventured. Not that she cared. But if Brad asked her later about the man he'd sent, it'd help to refer to the guy by name.

The man tugged at the brim of his soiled hat. "Rhett. Rhett Crawford." He climbed into the cab and slammed the door.

Heidi watched him back up and then spin the truck around and head back toward

Pleasant Valley. She was fast regretting ever coming here. And, she hadn't even seen her ailing mother yet.

She slid back in the driver's seat and shut the door. It was best to follow Rhett Crawford back into town. Not because she wanted to follow *him,* but because she needed population. People who breathed and could form a smile. She needed warmth, spontaneity, fun. Anything to get her mind off the ghostly vision at her window, the dead woman, and the idea that Pleasant Valley wasn't pleasant at all. It was a grave that had somehow opened and was planning to exhume all its secrets. Secrets no one even knew it had.

CHAPTER 6

"Hi, Mom."

The greeting sounded inane to Heidi's ears. She sank onto a chair opposite the gray-haired woman, slumped in a wheelchair, organizing buttons into piles on the tray in front of her.

This was going to be harder than she'd expected. Heidi knew seeing her mother for the first time since she was diagnosed with dementia would be tense, but the envelope she held between her fingers made it even more so. Questions of whether Loretta Lane would even recall the words she'd penned or be able to explain what she'd meant by them was yet to be seen.

Heidi watched her mother's long finger move a brown button into a pile of blue. She offered Heidi a small smile, with no sign of recognition, and dropped her gaze to the buttons. She was a shell. There was no familiar scrutiny of Heidi. No familiarity

75

at all. Heidi hadn't expected the twang of bittersweet regret to build a lump in her throat.

"Mom?" she tried again.

This time, Loretta Lane lifted cloudy blue eyes, her gray brows furrowed in concentration. A tiny smile touched her dry, chapped lips. "Ohhh! It's *you*!"

Heidi nodded, reaching out to take her aging mother's hand. "I'm here."

She didn't know what to say. Which was sort of funny. Her father had always said Heidi could sing and dance her way out of a hostage situation. Now? She was tongue-tied. She set the envelope on the table between them. Maybe her mother would notice it, say something about it.

Loretta ignored it and reached out, patting the top of Heidi's hand. "Good girl," she crooned.

Her palm was cool, the skin almost translucent. She was seventy-six. Heidi only thirty. In some ways, it didn't seem fair she was losing her mother before she was barely out of her twenties. And this? The hand pat, and now the way her mother's fingers folded around hers? This was a gentle side of her mother she'd not often seen. Mothers were supposed to live — forever — even if you didn't really like them. Loretta had just always been there. Always. Heidi could look back to her early years and recall vague moments of fondness. A mother who'd nurtured her. But as she grew, things changed. Her parents trusted her less, faith became rule-bound, and Heidi had pulled away.

A twinge caught her. *She* had pulled away. Sometimes finding her own blame in the distance between her and family was painful — too painful — to focus on.

"How's that young man treating you?" Loretta's words broke Heidi's train of thought. The older woman's expression showed concern with a hint of criticism.

Heidi drew in a deep breath and let it out slowly. "No young man, Mom. Just me." She flicked the edge of the envelope, hoping to draw subtle attention to it.

"Oh good." Loretta gave a curt nod and raised her gray eyebrows sternly. "I never liked him. Not a spiritual bone in his body."

Heidi had no idea who her mother thought she was talking about. She lifted the envelope. Time for a more direct tack.

"I got your letter."

Loretta tilted her head to the right, looking down at the envelope. A pause. Finally she reached for it and read the address. There was a little sound in her throat, one of surprise, and then she lifted her eyes to Heidi.

"That girl. That girl." She shook her head and handed the envelope back to Heidi. "She likes bluebirds. Did I tell you that?"

It was true. Heidi had always loved bluebirds. An uncomfortable sensation filled her as she realized her mother was speaking to someone else entirely. She didn't recognize her. Didn't recognize the letter.

"So much trouble. But so tender too." The woman's eyes grew distant. A thick knot formed in Heidi's throat.

"Mom?" Heidi pressed gently.

"What, child?" Loretta tilted her head in the other direction. Studying. Eyeing Heidi with a clouded gaze. "Oh!" Her hand fluttered to her throat, and she leaned forward. "You came!"

Heidi wasn't sure who her mother thought she was now. "I did. Yes. You asked me to."

"I did, didn't I?" Loretta had a bit of clarity in her vision now. She nodded thoughtfully, her eyes narrowing, deepening the wrinkles at the corners. She squeezed Heidi's hand.

"It was my fault. I — I had to see you." There was a desperation in her mother's voice. Loretta glanced at the envelope and released Heidi's hand, reaching for it again.

78

"I'm here," Heidi whispered.

"This." Loretta tapped the envelope on the table. "Vicki doesn't know I wrote to you."

"I assumed she didn't," Heidi responded.

Loretta bit her chapped bottom lip. She looked away and up, then back to the table. When she raised her eyes, there was confusion in them again. Loretta's throat bobbed as she swallowed hard.

"You're really here?" There was wonderment on her face now. Confused wonderment. Her eyes were wide, staring at Heidi as if she were looking at a ghost.

"Yeah, Mom. I'm here." Heidi mustered a smile.

The woman blinked several times to clear her vision. She patted the sides of her short gray bob and shook her head as if to unclog her thoughts.

"Well, then," Loretta breathed. "I thought you were dead."

Fast-growing darkness suffocated the car, squeezing Heidi's conscience like a vise. She pushed the gas pedal down further, urging the car forward with an unwise increase in acceleration.

Dead. Her mother thought she was dead. She'd recognized her in the end, hadn't she?

Or was she lost in a world of her own making? The letter written by her mother was discarded on the passenger-side seat. Worthless words with no explanation.

She'd come to Pleasant Valley at the pleading of a mother who didn't even know who Heidi was.

Trees whizzed by on either side of the road, the center line a blur. Heidi flicked her headlights on to offset the dusk. Her mother's words repeated over and over in her mind, creating a familiar and very unwanted weakness in Heidi's stomach. Her breaths came short and quick.

"I thought you were dead."

Heidi knew it was her mother's dementia speaking. But still, she'd vocalized Heidi's worst, most innate fear about her family. That one day they would disown her. The misfit child who never measured up and was no longer worth their efforts.

"I thought you were dead."

Heidi squeezed her eyes shut, then opened them just as fast. Driving wasn't a great time to try to erase the memories, but the gut-clenching anxiety of the day was giving panic far more power over reason. So many memories flooded her mind, shortening her breaths. They whirled out of order, chaotic, suffocating any ability to coherently process them. Just memories in a jumble, embraced by dread.

Her pastor dad lecturing her twelve-year-old self about how listening to the secular music radio station wasn't glorifying God and certainly wasn't helping with her spiritual development. Images of her mother sitting on the edge of Heidi's bed when she was fifteen and curled into a ball of tears, inexplicable emotions coursing through her, and hearing her mother coach her that she needed to work on her faith. Daily devotions, prayer, all of that would make this unreasonable sense of panic leave her.

What more likely than not was meant to be some sort of loving instruction had instead made Heidi feel *less than.* She wasn't enough spiritually, she didn't have enough faith, she didn't read the Bible enough . . . so that by the end of high school, Heidi had had enough.

"Oh my — !" Heidi jerked back to reality as a dog darted into the road. She slammed on the brakes, the tires screeching their resistance to the sudden attempt to stop. The rear end of the car fishtailed left, then right, and then that sickening sensation when the left side of her bumper slammed into the creature.

A yelp.

A scream.

Heidi tried to compensate for the erratic movement of the car, but she'd been going too fast. The nose of her vehicle aimed for and careened into a grassy ditch. The crash shot Heidi's body forward, but thankfully her seat belt locked and held her back. The impact wasn't great enough to inspire the airbag to deploy, but regardless, the jolting stop left her stunned.

Everything fell silent with the exception that she could hear her breaths, her heart pounding in her already throbbing head. Heidi fumbled for the car door. It opened without issue, and she unhooked her seat belt, stumbling from the vehicle.

Bewildered, she stood in the long grasses of the ditch.

A keening wail pierced through Heidi, shaking her to her core. She wiped her hand over her eyes, blinking rapidly. Tears burned their way down her face, and Heidi swiped at them.

The figure of a young woman running down the sloped yard from a house set up and away from the road jerked Heidi's attention from her own dizzying state of mind to the dog she had just hit.

Oh dear God.

Heidi stumbled forward. She wasn't a dog

fanatic, but she had no desire to hurt one, let alone a family pet!

The dog was whimpering, its front legs pawing at the asphalt. It was a stocky white pit bull with a tan mask. The fading daylight didn't help Heidi's assessment, but if she were placing bets, the dog's rear leg had to be broken.

Another wail, this time coming from the side of the road, yanked Heidi's attention from the wounded animal to the woman. She was at best in her early twenties. Her slight frame looked as if it could blow away in the wind. When she reached the road's edge, she froze as if an invisible wall were there. Her forearms rotated in an aggravated circular motion, and her body rocked as she wept.

Heidi held out her palm. "Stay there! Please." The last thing she needed was a frantic pet owner rushing to the dog's side and being bit due to the animal's instinctive defense mechanism. Or worse, being hit by another idiot driver like herself.

The young woman didn't answer. She was fixated on the dog, and her weeping had contorted her face into one of sheer agony.

Heidi squinted into the diminishing light, trapped between rescuing the dog she'd hit or hurrying to the emotional aid of an obviously distraught human being. Not to mention, it was getting more difficult to see. Curse the dusk! It was so empty. She hated this. Hated being alone and solely responsible. Hated being confronted with the reality of the day's events from a ghostlike face at her window, to her mother. Now this?

The woods were closing in on her. Their branches reached for her, even though they bordered the mowed lawn of the country residence. Heidi's sense of reason whirled faster and faster in her mind, like a carousel on hyperdrive. She couldn't pause it, couldn't grab hold of it to slow it down, to make sense of anything.

Heidi sank to the road, still caught between the woman and her dog. She needed escape, not unlike the agitated owner who continued to rock in grief. Heidi's body shook from nerves, her hands quivered, and her fingers clawed at her jeans in a rhythmic tic. She couldn't control it. Couldn't stop it. She was drowning . . .

Headlights blinded her.

No!

Heidi scrambled to her feet, drawing in quick shuddered breaths. She held out her hands, and if she had the superpower to stop the truck that was approaching, she would. It slowed, then pulled off into the driveway, just shy of where the dog lay. Tires crunched on gravel as the vehicle pulled to a stop. A door opened, then slammed shut. Flashlight. A large form.

"Emma!" The gravelly voice sliced through the tense air. The man ignored the dog and sprinted to the woman's side. He squatted down in front of her so they were eye to eye. He didn't reach for her. His hands perched on his knees.

"Emma. Emma, everything is all right. Let's breathe."

It was Rhett Crawford, the mechanic.

He took a deep breath. He let it out. Emma imitated. They breathed in, breathed out, breathed in, breathed out. Heidi noticed she was breathing with them. Her anxiety that threatened to immobilize waned now into a more controllable distress.

Rhett reached into the pocket of his tan Carhartt jacket. He pulled out a red ball, big enough for a hand to comfortably wrap around. He handed it to Emma, who took it.

"Squeeze it, baby girl."

She did.

"There you go." He stepped away from her.

Emma calmed, and even though her upper body still rocked, she was in control of herself now. Rhett snatched his phone from the back pocket of his jeans and sent a quick text. Once done, he turned back to Emma.

"I texted Mom. She'll be down in a sec, okay?"

A nod from the young woman, large eyes searching Rhett's and finding stability there.

Rhett shifted from her and stepped toward Heidi. His eyes brushed over her, then settled on the dog. She heard him curse under his breath.

"You all right?" His words were tossed at her as he neared the dog.

"I'll live." Her response was flippant, but it was all she could think to say.

He knelt by the animal, who lifted its head and whimpered. Rhett mumbled something to the dog, running a hand down its spine, its leg. The dog whined.

Rhett stood and motioned for Heidi. "Stand over here."

She moved toward him, casting an unsure glance at Emma. He followed her gaze.

"She'll be okay. I need to run to my truck."

Heidi stood over the dog as Rhett ran to the tailgate of the pickup. He came back carrying a piece of scrap plywood.

Kneeling by the dog, he looked up at Heidi. She stood there helpless.

"We need to get Ducie onto this plywood

and off the road," he instructed. "Can you help?"

"Ducie?"

"The dog?" His voice had a hint of irritation.

"Oh." Heidi knelt next to Ducie. Big chestnut-brown eyes stared up at her, begging for help.

This was her fault. All her fault.

It was now her turn for medical attention. One hour later, that is. Heidi was still shaking, although she'd done a decent job of hiding that fact by fabricating her special, nonchalant smile, often called upon in moments when she was certain the Apocalypse was all of sixty seconds from beginning. She sat on the edge of a kitchen chair, in the house from where the dog had run and Emma had followed. To her surprise, Emma's mother was none other than the antique owner, Connie, who'd sold her that awful photo album with the doppelgänger dead woman. Apparently, Connie was Rhett's mother too.

Rhett had removed his jacket and also the flannel shirt that hung loose over his T-shirt. The greasy baseball cap was still secured on his head. He didn't give her nearly the same attention as he'd given the dog. Rhett was pouring coffee into a mug as though driving one's car through an animal into a ditch was just another day at the — well, not the office — *the shop?*

Heidi blinked rapidly to do away with the white spots that often affected her sight when she was warding off panic.

"Nothing's broke?" Rhett inquired, his voice even.

"My car might need surgery," she quipped, but it came out a bit snappy. Even conversation directed toward her felt overwhelming. Trying to segregate the elements of the messy day was like trying to sort a bag full of macaroni noodles into a baby-food jar.

"I meant you." There was no humor in Rhett's voice. He didn't sound irritated either. Just a straight shooter.

"No, I'm fine." She wasn't. She never was. But she lied to herself about it every day, so lying to a stranger was simple.

"K." He didn't even ask what happened, or why she'd hit Ducie, the dog, or what she was planning on doing with her car half buried in his parents' ditch.

Rhett turned toward her, coffee mug in his hand. "Cream? Sugar?"

"Huh?" Heidi blinked.

"Cream or sugar?"

Oh. Wow. He was prolific with his words. Heidi blinked several times and then shook her head. "Black."

He raised an appreciative brow and handed her the mug.

Connie Crawford breezed into the room, easing out of her sweater and hanging it on a wood-stenciled row of coat pegs by the door. She patted her son's shoulder as she passed him on her way to the coffeemaker.

"Emma is fine," she reassured them. Connie's brief sweep of the room with her soft smile included Heidi.

"I'm so sorry," Heidi breathed.

"I'm sorry you've had to sit in that chair while we all hustled around you the last hour!"

"Oh no, no. I mean, what can I do? Can I pay the vet bill? Anything."

And please don't sue me. She could feel the anxiety crowding her throat, burning tears behind her eyes. It was here. Full on. She'd be lucky not to throw up.

"Heavens no!" Connie leaned against the counter, holding the warm mug between her hands. Her eyes were warm, if not downright apologetic. "Ducie is Emma's service dog. We have insurance for him, so it will cover the vet bills. My husband just called from the vet with Ducie." She glanced at Rhett. "It looks like a clean break of the tibia. They're casting it now."

Heidi sucked in a shaky breath. "I'm so sorry," she said again.

"We got that part." Rhett had an edge to his voice. Either he was irritated she'd repeated herself, or he was irritated at her. Probably both. She could see the tension in his shoulders, around his jaw, and the corners of his eyes.

"Rhett." Connie said his name as a mother might veil a slight scolding to her adult child.

Rhett pushed off the opposite counter. "Not much we can do about your car tonight." He avoided Heidi's eyes. "I'll send someone tomorrow with a tow truck."

Connie moved past her hulk of a son, who only needed green skin and a raging growl to complete the persona. She seemed to read Heidi's face, her pasted-on smile, and her stiff shoulders. She pulled out a chair at the table beside her, leaning forward on her elbows, hands still cupping the coffee mug.

Heidi looked down at her coffee, un-sipped and perched in her hands. The liquid tremored a bit as her hands shook.

Connie narrowed her eyes. "Are you truly all right?"

"I am." Heidi consciously made her shoulders drop. She softened her smile and met Connie's eyes. Eye contact was always good. It helped people believe you were telling the truth. But the way Connie searched hers told Heidi that the woman was not one to be fooled.

"Really. I just feel awful." She did. Inside and out.

"Accidents happen." Connie gave her a reassuring smile. "The only reason Ducie even ran into the road was that Emma had the dog out for their evening walk and Emma's scarf blew off her neck. Ducie was attempting to retrieve it. He was unleashed and ran out into the road. So it was our fault."

"You don't leash service dogs at home." Rhett growled like one as he crossed his arms.

Connie shot him a stern glare. "You do in some circumstances."

He harrumphed and stalked from the room.

"Ignore Rhett." His mother waved him away. "He's insatiably protective of his sister. You could be Winnie the Pooh and he'd still glare at you if he thought you'd put Emma or her dog in any danger."

That was — reassuring?

Heidi sipped her coffee for something to

do. To keep herself from crying. She hated this uncontrollable part of her. The kind that ran away with her logic and self-confidence and left a quivering mess behind.

"Anyway," Connie finished. "Emma has autism. She's high-functioning, but routine is important and this will obviously be a setback for her. Rhett is a natural-born rescuer and fixer."

And she was a natural-born screw-up. Heidi winced. They'd get along fabulously.

Connie tipped her head and studied Heidi. "Did you ever find out if you're related to that woman in the photograph?"

Change of subject. Connie was adept at calming nerves. Normally, Heidi would have allowed herself to be sidetracked, but that particular question revived events from earlier in the day.

"Um, no," Heidi answered.

"I'd be curious to know if you are. I'd love to help you find out, if you ever want to."

The sound of work boots clomping on the hardwood floor brought both women's heads up. Rhett marched back into the room, snatching up his keys from a key-ring hook on the side of one of the cabinets.

"Let's go." He stood over Heidi.

"Go?" Heidi craned her neck to look up at the superhero wannabe with serious personality issues.

He stared down at her with the thunderous scowl of the Hulk.

Connie interceded. "That's Rhett's refined way of saying he'll take you home."

Heidi smirked — she had to — at Connie's unveiled dig at her son's manners. She supposed being driven home by Rhett wasn't the worst thing in the world, but it was the Hulk in him that kept Heidi from thinking Rhett Crawford was even remotely a superhero.

CHAPTER 7

THEA

A tiny bell tinkled out a melody as Thea pushed open the door to the only portrait studio in Pleasant Valley. That they even *had* a studio was perhaps a miracle in and of itself, as a town based solely on the collection of lumber certainly didn't have enough population to support an entire year's worth of salary for a photographer. Still, if she had learned enough from Mr. Mendelsohn, they would be partners by end of day. As a traveling photographer, he'd made it his art not only to garner sales door to door, but also engage the temporary comradeship of others established in the field. Thea hoped to garner the same results.

Now, her shoes clapped along the floorboards as she gave the small studio a quick once-over. *Amos Bros. Photography* had been painted on the front window in stenciled letters with scrollwork beneath it. Each wall in the room appeared decorated to be a different room in an actual home. One of the walls was cream with emerald green bordering and hand-painted bouquets. A velvet-covered chair, a white pillar of four feet or so, a few plants, and an easel were positioned strategically. In the chair, an orange cat was curled up and watching her through slits for eyes, its tail twitching up and down.

"May I help you?" The booming voice jolted Thea from her observations. A man of medium height and build entered the room from a doorway near the wall opposite the front entrance. His long mustache draped along the edges of his mouth, thoroughly and completely white. His hair was parted in the middle, yet it was hardly worth the effort, for there wasn't much left atop his head to part at all.

Thea composed her wits and ceased her meticulous perusal of the room. She cleared her throat. "Dorothea Reed." She extended a gloved hand, and the elderly man eyed it. Seemingly unused to palming a lady's hand, he took it gingerly, fingertip to fingertip, then released it.

"Martin Amos."

"Nice to meet you, Mr. Amos. I am a photographer — a traveling photographer

— and I have settled in Pleasant Valley for the time being."

His eyebrow lifted. Not unfriendly, more like he waited before he drew any sort of conclusion about her.

Thea swallowed. "I've no intention of setting up competitive services, I only wondered if I might be able to garner employment with you. For an interim period and a small sum, offset by allowing me use of your development room. I have a small black room in my wagon to create the negative plates, but for transfer to paper I need a more suitable work space."

"My development room?" Mr. Amos coughed.

It wasn't as though she'd requested entrance into his private living quarters.

Thea nodded. It was never easy asserting herself now that Mr. Mendelsohn was gone.

"Employment?" He cleared his throat again.

"For a small sum. I must be able to cover my own living expenses. But I'm not looking for extravagance, Mr. Amos. I would appreciate the freedom to develop my photographs when I take them on my own time, outside of town."

Mr. Amos blinked. Finally, he crossed his arms, his gray wool suit coat stretching taut against thin shoulders. "You're proposing I allow a traveling photographer entrance to my business and interaction with my clientele, so you can develop photographs that you took of your own accord and therefore stealing from me potential business?"

Well, she had bungled this up well and good, hadn't she? Thea opened the satchel she gripped tightly in one hand. "Please. I'm quite good at assisting accomplished photographers such as yourself. For pay, I would help you here in the studio. And as for my own work, if you take a look at it, you'll understand. I've a very special type of photograph. . . ." She didn't bother to mention that she also took the normal portraitures. Instead, she made a silent promise to stay honest and only photograph what she represented to Mr. Amos now.

"Ah. Memorial photographs." He spoke over her shoulder as she pulled out samples. Thea looked up and noticed his eyes fixed on the photographs that were pasted to thick paperboard.

"Yes," Thea nodded. "It's a privilege to help family members capture the final pose of their loved ones who have passed on. I've all the equipment. Backdrops, framework, even sewing kits to assist with preparing the body if needed. I only do not have a decent place to develop the photographs."

The man waved her pictures away. "That's — disturbing."

"So, you don't offer memorial photographic services?" she asked innocently, knowing full well there was the possibility he did not, and hoping it was true. While it was traditional to take photographs with the newly passed on, many photographers still found it unsettling. Why wouldn't they? In small towns such as these, they often knew personally those who had passed on and so collecting their last image was rife with memories, superstitions, and even for some, grief.

"When I must." He crossed his arms over his chest again. "I wouldn't deny the last memento to a grieving family."

"However, you don't travel to find them?" Thea pressed forward, borrowing confidence from the fact she'd heard Mr. Mendelsohn use this same line of reasoning before.

"Door to door?" He sniffed. "Certainly not."

"There is business there," she cajoled.

He narrowed his eyes. "I refuse to monopolize on another's grief. What? Would you have me knock on every door and ask if someone may have recently died there?"

Thea nodded, hoping to keep her expression both pleasant and helpful. "Yes, and to inquire if someone is near passing over. Sometimes the person is too ill, so we must wait until they're at eternal peace. But many find it a blessing not to have to seek out the services of a photographer. Many often wished they had, only it's too late. You cannot exhume a body for memorial's sake, of course."

The man blanched, and his eyes widened. "Why, you are a spit of a —"

"I believe you called me a 'traveler,' " Thea provided, offering him a delightful smile.

He blustered.

Thea snapped her valise shut. "You are one of the Amos brothers, as the window implies?"

He nodded, lost for words.

"Well, Mr. Amos, shall we start?"

Thea had exhausted all her gumption cajoling her way into attaining Mr. Amos's tentative agreement. In the hours of the morning after she'd arrived, Thea had learned Mr. Amos was a happily married man. He and his wife, Greta, had three grown children, all daughters, all married, and all moved away. There were no grandchildren. His brother had passed away six years prior, leaving Mr. Amos sole proprietorship.

One of the rooms in the secluded area of the studio had a small table and chairs in it, a countertop, and several photograph albums. A back door had a draft slipping through a gap at the floor, but it brought into the room fresh air and an early summer scent of life. Now, the most permanent resident of the studio, Pip the orange tabby cat, sauntered in, chin lifted in complete ownership of the place, and brushed by Thea's legs.

"Cheeky little fellow," she muttered after him.

Pip trilled a tiny meow in response.

Thea familiarized herself with Mr. Amos's work and had to admit he was a very fine photographer. She ran her finger across the border of one of his photographs, the fleur-de-lis a beautiful brass color, and the woman in its frame, young with coiffed hair that waved and flowed with such perfection that Thea could only stare. At times, she wished she were beautiful. That the camera would capture her image and convince her she was worth looking at. Convince her she was worth — *something*.

Thea slammed the album shut, hiding the beautiful woman from her view.

The instant the photo album clapped its pages together, the back door jerked open. Thea jolted, startled as a form burst into the room, completely unaware of her presence. His head was bent toward the floor, a bulky camera stand under one arm, while the hand of the same arm gripped a wooden camera box. In the grasp of his left hand was an album, and he blustered ahead, dropping it onto the table. The camera stand clattered against the counter as he balanced it there, and at the same time he bent and rested the case on the floor. Pip scampered from the room, leaving the mess behind in a whisk of fur and tail.

Thea blinked. She'd not expected this. Not anticipated that Mr. Amos already had an associate. Why then would he have even entertained the possibility of adding another?

The man turned. Gray eyes lifted, squinting in deep contemplation. Straight hair fell on either side of his forehead, not combed or styled, just haphazard and thoughtless.

Simeon Coyle.

They stared at each other for a moment, both caught by surprise. A distinct, unsettled air fell over the room, as if neither were supposed to be there at all, and both were afraid the other might tell. Simeon was the first to break the stare. He ducked his head, fumbling at his back pocket and yanking forth a cap that he tugged onto his head and over his eyes. He held his face away from her, so Thea only had the privilege of seeing the left side of his profile.

His shoulder lifted upward in an odd little jerk, then settled.

Thea frowned.

He noticed.

"Pardon me." Simeon ducked away and turned on his heel toward the open back door.

"Wait!" Thea collected herself. She hurried after him, but Simeon was walking at a pace reflective of a man attempting to escape, but also trying not to run and bring attention upon himself.

"Mr. Coyle!" Thea tried again, grasping the doorframe and leaning out into the daylight.

Simeon stuffed his hands in his coat pockets, his shoulders hunched, and rounded a corner out of view.

Thea blinked a few times. She'd not expected to see him, and obviously he'd felt the same about her. His retreat didn't carry with it the feeling of fear. Rather, in that moment, it was as if she'd once again run into him, they had touched, and a spark like a cannon cracker had ignited. It seemed Simeon Coyle knew less what to do with that feeling than she did.

Mr. Amos's voice filtered from the front, drawing her away from contemplating Simeon and why he'd been here in the first place. There was a potential client in the front. Something about a family photograph. Mr. Amos was speaking with a woman.

Will they be able to keep the child still?

The mother gave a short response. He'd unintentionally insulted her child.

Is Grandma going to pose with the family?

An insinuation the elderly woman might be a problem.

Thea knew the best way to solidify her very tenuous position with Mr. Amos was to make herself known in the conversation and earn the approval and even the need of the female customer. He would hardly be able to not pay her even a little if a customer preferred her feminine presence.

But her attention was captivated by the album Simeon Coyle had dropped on the table. It had flopped open, revealing pages with paper frames but no photographs inserted behind them. She moved to it, reaching out and tipping the cover closed. A soft, chestnut velvet covered the outside of the album, with gold-and-bronze-embossed flowers and a brass clip that held the pages shut — had it been clipped properly.

She turned a few pages. Only four held photographs. The rest of the album was empty. But once her eyes locked with the woman's in the first portrait, all warmth left her face. A soulful horror filled her, the kind that left Thea grasping for the edge of the table to keep her upright, her knees from buckling.

The woman who stared back had frozen eyes. But unlike the deceased Thea was accustomed to photographing, this woman was alive. She could tell by the shadows that indicated a natural flush in the cheeks, the tip of the head, and a tiny downward quirk to her lips. As if the subject wanted to smile but couldn't get her mouth to cooperate. As if the hidden terrors in her soul dragged her face down into depths of misery.

Dark ringlets fell to her shoulders, the sides drawn up in a tight knot. Her left shoulder slouched lower than her right, and her chin jutted out as if she were unaware how to pose, what posture was, and even how her appendages should align with her body. She was awkward, detached, and —

"What are you doing?" A man's hand slammed the album shut and yanked it away from Thea.

Thea yelped, leaping back, even as she lifted startled eyes to Mr. Amos's.

"I'm s-sorry, I —"

Mr. Amos turned on his heel, the album tucked under his arm, and then he spun around and glowered at her. "Was Simeon here?" he barked.

Thea gave a wordless nod.

Mr. Amos searched her face as though trying to determine whether to send her packing or tolerate her for no good reason, which he already had. His eyes narrowed.

"Leave Simeon alone, you hear?"

Thea gave a quick nod. If she were four, she couldn't have felt more reprimanded, more mortified at being caught looking at something she was not allowed to see.

"And don't you tell anyone — *anyone* — he was here. Understand?"

"Yes. Yes, I understand." Thea nodded again. "But I —"

"No." Mr. Amos glared at her. "If you're to work here and assist me, I will entertain no questions about Simeon Coyle. He is off-limits."

"Yes, sir." Thea hadn't missed the insinuation that Mr. Amos was considering employing her.

"All right then." His tone softened some.

105

"You are welcome to stay for a bit. I'll assess your abilities. I'd like to see your plates. Your equipment."

Mr. Mendelsohn's equipment, Thea mentally corrected.

"Must be the Lord's timing, bringing you here. I'm getting old. Help isn't a bad idea."

He might be curmudgeonly, but Mr. Amos's brown eyes grew misty, as if he'd warred against growing old once, but had since accepted his fate. Perhaps that was why postmortem photography bothered him. One day it would be him in the photograph.

Thea offered him a gentle smile. "I'm not sure what the Lord has to do with it, but luck is a wonderful thing."

Mr. Amos paused and raised a bushy white brow. "The Lord has everything to do with it. Luck is just a passing fancy." He marched from the room, not offended but with a firm step that stated he didn't want his belief questioned.

Thea stared after him. Mrs. Mendelsohn would have agreed, but somehow she would have stated it ominously. The "Lord" had brought her here, and His club of judgment was barely restrained. Mr. Amos, on the other hand, made it sound as though God cared.

She shook her head. Perhaps He did. But never about her. And certainly not about those poor souls in Simeon Coyle's album. The images were imprinted in her memory. Outlined with an ink so permanent, so indelible, Thea knew she would never forget them. What she'd seen — what that woman was — was someone not dead, and yet not really alive either. It was almost as though Simeon Coyle had somehow captured a soul suspended between two worlds, trapped somewhere in the middle, and imprisoned like a slave who could not break their chains.

CHAPTER 8

She hadn't expected a dinner invitation to the Amos home, but apparently Mrs. Amos held a lot of clout over Mr. Amos and his crusty exterior. Still, Thea sat at the table set for three, thankful for the cloth napkin on her lap that she could fidget with. Tea with Rose Coyle had already pressed her abilities at fostering etiquette and acquaintances. Now she must dine with a man she'd all but pushed her way into working alongside, while also enduring the genuine sweet graces that were Mrs. Amos.

"Now, dear, you must tell us all about yourself." Mrs. Amos eased her plump body onto her chair after setting dessert plates in front of Thea and Mr. Amos. Fine slices of vanilla cake, along with a side sauce made from canned peaches.

Precisely the comments Thea preferred to avoid. Nonetheless, she mustered a smile, flattening the napkin on her lap with a few strokes of her nervous hands.

"She won't tell you a thing, that one," Mr. Amos grumbled around a forkful of cake. Apparently he'd drawn a conclusion after only one day. Thea could hardly blame him, and she was a bit taken aback by his astute assessment of her. Here she thought she'd wheedled quite a lot from him without revealing much of herself at all, but in fact she'd exposed her penchant for remaining unreadable.

Bother.

"Now, now." Mrs. Amos reached out and patted her husband's hand. The simple gray cotton of her dress softened the wrinkles in her face. A pretty woman, aged with soft white curls pulled back, and green eyes that twinkled.

She directed that gaze at Thea. "Mr. Amos is a bit grouchy, and I've grown quite used to it. You will too, I'm sure."

Thea offered a smile and no words. What could one say in response to that?

"A blessing you are. I was just telling Mr. Amos yesterday that it was time to consider an apprentice. And then, a few prayers, and you appear." She smiled. "An answer if I ever saw one."

Thea stared at the elderly woman. She'd never been called an answer to prayer. A burden, a child who must be righted, a worker, but never that.

Mrs. Amos took a bite of cake, chewed, swallowed, and tilted her fork down for more. "Oh, child, you do need some good home care, don't you? I can see it in your eyes."

Once more, Thea had nothing to say.

"I suppose you met Pip." Mrs. Amos chattered away. Her cheeks grew rosier, if that were possible, and a smile never left the corners of her eyes. "That cat found his way to the back door and never left. Seven years later, I think the cat could probably do all the work himself if Mr. Amos would let him."

"He's too lazy," Mr. Amos grumbled.

"He's old. Like you, dear," Mrs. Amos countered.

Thea didn't miss their exchange of looks. But unlike the usual negative glares she was accustomed to, having grown up beneath the care of the Mendelsohns, this one was laced with humor and a bit of love.

"You're not from around here, are you?" Mrs. Amos took a sip of her tea.

Cake stuck in her throat. Thea wasn't trying to hide who she was. Not really. But talking about who she was would never be easy — or simple. In fact, her mind drifted to Mrs. Mendelsohn's letter, her mother, and the faded memories of her four-year-old younger self. She would need to begin asking questions, revealing bit by bit why she was here. It was why she'd come to Pleasant Valley in the first place. Still, the years of Mr. Mendelsohn lecturing her on how to maintain a distance from all clients and working associates made loosening her tongue difficult. There were other things to hide, other elements of life, the behind-closed-doors part that Thea couldn't tell. Would never tell. It was all a tricky balance.

"No." She swallowed, finally answering Mrs. Amos. "I'm from several hours south of here. Toward the Illinois border. Although, we traveled quite a bit."

"Drifters." Mr. Amos coughed and reached for his coffee.

"Mr. Amos!" his wife chided.

Thea barely caught the wry smile that touched the older man's lips. So he was trying to goad her? To be funny? Or to catch her off guard?

Thea chose to engage him in his silly little game, whatever it was. She offered him a warm, manufactured smile. "I do so enjoy the drifting life. Free, answering to no one, simply being true to oneself."

"Oh yes!" Mrs. Amos clapped, stunning

Thea for a moment and apparently Mr. Amos also, if his sharp look meant anything. The woman folded her hands. "I too have always had a bit of wanderlust. To see different places, meet new people. Still" — she gave Mr. Amos a loving look — "I do so love this old man, so I've stayed at his side."

She smiled.

Mr. Amos harrumphed.

"And there are days I've questioned my choices," Mrs. Amos tossed in at the last moment.

Mr. Amos choked on his coffee.

"There, there." His wife patted his hand. "Just always remember, you won. Even my heart, you crotchety old thing."

Thea bit back a real smile. He'd been had by his own wife.

"I'm not really a drifter." Thea gingerly cut a tiny bite of cake with her fork. "Actually, I was taken in by an older couple when I was twelve. Mr. Mendelsohn was a photographer, and we traveled as a means to offer portraiture services home to home."

"How delightful." Mrs. Amos was clueless.

Mr. Amos raised a bushy eyebrow. "Taking photographs of the deceased, Greta." He saw the need to educate his wife.

Her expression dimmed a bit, but not in

judgment of anyone. "Oh, how sad, but how thoughtful too. Poor families having lost loved ones. It's not always foremost on one's mind to search out a photographer, is it?"

Thea bit the inside of her cheek. It was almost exactly what she'd said to Mr. Amos when acquiring the agreement of her employment. To be honest, she felt a bit validated.

Mr. Amos glowered at her.

Thea couldn't help it. Her smile released in full genuine satisfaction at having bested him. For a moment, she thought his eyes twinkled with a hint of respect, but it was so fleeting, Thea determined she might have imagined it.

"Took you in, eh?" Mrs. Amos continued as though they'd never been sidetracked. "What a nice couple."

Nice. Thea focused on her plate, on the cake, anything but the memories. The frightening tales of superstitions and ghosts from Mr. Mendelsohn that left her quivering, and the pious judgment from Mrs. Mendelsohn, who stated that anyone who believed such would see the fiery wrath of God. It seemed she'd been quite all right with that being her husband's supposed eternal demise.

Thea wished for neither. Neither ghosts

nor the blazes of Hell. But anyone had yet to offer an alternative.

"So, you've traveled here simply for photographic purposes?" Mrs. Amos was relentless in her innocent inquisition.

Thea concentrated on chewing and swallowing, then gave a small shrug. "Not entirely. M-My mother, supposedly, was from the area originally. I'm . . ." She hesitated, then decided there was no point in withholding. It was why she had come. It was only frightening to venture forth and begin. "I'm attempting to find her."

There was no need to add that she hoped to find out her mother was dead, so she could finally lay to rest her deep sense of inadequacy as a daughter, as an unwanted child, and the bitterness that came from remembering a blurry face and hand that waved farewell.

"Oh, my dear . . ." Mrs. Amos stared at Thea in empathy. "What a lovely thing to do. A reunion perhaps?" She looked between Mr. Amos, who seemed vaguely interested, and Thea, who urged herself to stay with the conversation and not retreat.

"Perhaps," Thea answered. *Perhaps not.* A gravestone would be resolution. The period at the end of a sentence, so to speak.

"Well, Mr. Amos and I have lived here in

Pleasant Valley for well on to thirty years now. Perhaps we knew your mother, if she were from these parts."

"I'm not certain she was from Pleasant Valley specifically." Although, this was the name of the town Mrs. Mendelsohn had mentioned in her letters.

"What was her name?" Mrs. Amos inquired, her tea forgotten, her eyes sparking with interest.

Therein lay a portion of the problem.

Thea pushed her dessert plate away from her, the cake barely touched.

"I'm not entirely certain," she admitted. "The orphanage, where I spent much of my younger years, listed me under my name of Dorothea Reed. But according to — well, the records — my mother was listed by the same surname with only the initials *P. A.* at the front."

"P. A.?" Mrs. Amos spoke the initials as if chewing on them to determine their origins. "P. A. Reed. Hmmm. Mr. Amos, are you familiar with that name?"

Mr. Amos scraped the last bit of crumbs from his plate. "Not at all."

"Nor am I," Mrs. Amos sighed. She shook her head in thoughtful consternation. "I would think I'd recognize the name of Reed, but I do not."

Thea tried to ignore the twinge of disappointment. It would have been far too simple to stumble upon someone who'd coincidentally known her mother, and so fast on Thea's arrival in Pleasant Valley.

"Perhaps . . ." Mrs. Amos's voice rose in pitch, like she had a grand idea. She looked to her husband. "What if she were from — ?"

"I do believe that was good cake," Mr. Amos interrupted, pushing back on his chair, the legs scraping against the floor.

Mrs. Amos appeared bewildered at his sudden movement, and perhaps his compliment.

"Well, I — thank you, dear. As I was saying —"

Mr. Amos leaned over and planted a kiss at the base of Mrs. Amos's ear. Thea could have sworn that he also whispered something. Whatever it was, Mrs. Amos's brows raised and her expression grew shuttered, as though she understood — didn't like, but understood — whatever the man had to say.

As he shuffled from the room, Mrs. Amos watched him leave before turning a lovely smile on Thea. "Oh, the old man and his gout. Now, let me tell you about my hobby. Quilting. Do you quilt, Miss Reed?"

It was apparent the personal inquisition was over.

A fog had settled over the rooftops of the buildings in Pleasant Valley, and there was a gray blue pallor that never seemed to lift. It was made more emphatic by the midnight blue tones of the trees that bordered the town. Thea could hear the river, its muted riffles as it rolled over rocks and dead trees. She paused, her skirts hitched in her hands, her foot tentatively hovering over the rutted dirt street, ready to step from the boardwalk and cross onto the Protestant side of Pleasant Valley. Bringing her toe back, Thea planted it once again on the walkway.

Pleasant Valley was eerily silent. It was only seven p.m. and dusk had settled. She'd declined Mr. Amos's offered escort home at least three times before the couple reluctantly agreed. Now she questioned the wisdom of that. There were no sounds of a piano from a whiskey bar, no wagons rolling past as loggers returned to town to join their families, no Wednesday night prayer meeting lighting up the white clapboard church on the Protestant hillside, and no one out for a stroll. It was only her.

The reminder of the letter in her room at Mrs. Brummel's, and that its contents had been the inspiration to bring her to Pleasant Valley, made a shiver ripple down her spine. Thea had a feeling that people were watching her, ducking out of view behind a pushed-back curtain or darkened window. As if they were asking, *Why has this strange young woman come to town?* A woman who photographed the dead and was neither Catholic nor Protestant but tended to believe in unsettled souls hovering between earth and eternity.

Thea shifted directions. She hurried down the walk, away from the portrait studio, past darkened doorways of random little shops she didn't bother to identify. The boardwalk ran out where an alley sliced between it and the blacksmith's shop. She veered to the right, down the alleyway. In the distance ran the river. It sliced a shimmering gray swath through the woods on its far side, the uneven downward slope of the hill and the road that led out of town. Something about the river called to her, and Thea didn't understand why.

She ventured from the road, and her feet found the earth beneath them rocky and hard. The soil was a thick clay. Muddy when permeated by rainwater, but today, unwilling to bow beneath her steps and allow even a footprint. She leveraged her body toward the hillside as she sidestepped down the embankment until she stopped at the river's edge. Boulders dotted the shoreline, and truthfully there wasn't much of a shore to be found. It was a bank, cut and jutted by the waters, probably during flooding. A downed oak tree exposed its broad root base toward the town above them, while its trunk and dead branches splayed into the river, daring the water to best its great strength and sweep it away.

She halted, the toes of her shoes extending precariously over the edge. Drawing her navy blue cloak around her, Thea stared down into the roiling waters as they collided with rocks and fell over miniature waterfalls into calm pools before swirling in their tempestuous journey forward.

"It makes you want to jump, doesn't it?"

A soft gasp escaped her, and Thea teetered forward when a hand gripped her shoulder and held her steady. She tilted her head to look at the fingers curled over her arm. Her eyes lifted to meet eyes the color of the gray river-water foam. "I wasn't considering diving in," Thea answered, her tone soft, even though she highly suspected Simeon Coyle hadn't been looking for one. A warm flush covered her face.

The wind lifted straight hair from his

119

forehead, tossing it into a disheveled mess. His shoulders were just slightly higher than hers as he stood beside her, hands now slid into trouser pockets. Suspenders wrapped over his torso like two bands imprisoning him from flying away. His mouth twitched.

"You wouldn't drown. Not here. It's not as deep as it looks." Simeon's words lingered as he dropped to the edge of the bank and slipped over, his shoes landing in a splash. Water swirled around his ankles, and he bent, plunging his hand into the river.

"What are you doing?" Thea leaned forward gingerly.

He didn't respond, only fished around with his hand before swishing it in the water as he brought it up to the air. In his palm Simeon held pebbles. River pebbles, smoothed by the water. Black, gray, marbled, and some copper in tone. He bounced them in his palm a few times, making a clattering sound. Simeon's fist closed around the pebbles, and he slipped them into his pocket. Within seconds he'd grasped the bank by Thea's feet and jumped up beside her. Droplets of water from his sudden movement spattered Thea's skirt.

Simeon wiped his hands on his pants as he stood. Without a word, he started forward, toward the road and away from Thea.

"Wait!" Thea spun around. The man was going to just leave? With nothing said but an awkward rhetorical question?

Again, Simeon's shoulders were hunched, though this time she realized it was not from timidity. He had some physical malady that caused his body to twitch, to seize, and even to momentarily disfigure his face. It did so now, contorting his features as he ducked his head away.

"Simeon Coyle!" Thea shouted.

The man stopped. He looked over his shoulder at her without turning his body.

Thea lifted her hand to hold hair from her face. "What will you do with the pebbles?"

It wasn't what she'd expected herself to ask. The question just spilled out. Inane and meaningless.

A slight quirk tilted the corner of his mouth, but other than that hint of emotion, his face was placid. Until it wasn't. His right cheek seized upward, closing his eye and tilting his head. Simeon seemed to accept the tic, and when it eased, he shrugged.

"I'm going to give them meaning."

At her bewildered frown, Simeon hunched against the wind and hiked toward town, leaving Thea at the edge of the river.

Give them meaning? The man was more

bewildering than a pig hitched up to a wagon.

A splash in the river snagged Thea's attention. She spun back to the water but saw nothing. Just the same tempestuous waters that were hypnotic in their journey. Her eyes skimmed the breadth of it, then lifted to study the opposite side of the river. The woods, the shadows, the long trunks of oak and pine, with some poplars a stark white against the deeper hues. The miles of forest that stretched beyond, hiding wildlife and . . .

Thea squinted. A flash of light, or . . . Curious, she stepped forward, but her foot dangled over the edge. She yanked it back, balancing as she focused on the diminishing light.

There.

Another wisp of white. Filmy and loose, like a long sash of material waving in the wind. It seemed to float through the trees until . . .

Thea covered her mouth with her hand, stifling her intake of breath.

Long, bare legs with bare feet. She could see them moving slowly, her eyes following their form up until the rest of the body disappeared behind undergrowth and shadows.

No.

There.

A being came into full view. For a moment it stopped. The sheer white of a gown, thin and almost translucent against the black forest. Long hair, wavy, so dark it was almost black. And her face —

Thea blinked, the instinct of her body against the force of the breeze that sprang tears into her eyes and pressed her skirts against her legs. Thea wiped frantically at her unbidden tears, cursing the blurring of her eyes.

The vision was gone.

Left behind was the forest, the willful river water, and Thea. Trapped between a town shrouded in silence, a ghostly apparition dancing along its borders, and a strange man with pebbles in his pockets who made her insides as weak as Mrs. Brummel's coffee.

CHAPTER 9

HEIDI

Lane Lodge's windows were illuminated from the top floor to the bottom, private quarters. Every window was brilliant, the front door opened wide, and two police cars parked at an angle in front.

"What on earth?" Heidi leaned forward, ignoring Rhett's dog that sat between them in the pickup truck — Rüger was its name.

Archie, the very lively tabby cat, leapt off her lap onto the dashboard, his long tail feathering her face. Rhett's truck seemed to be a mobile home for the one-eyed dog and ratty cat.

Rüger growled deep in his throat, and the third male of the car — Heidi glanced at him — still had no visible reaction. The man was chiseled out of granite. He'd been silent the entire trip back to Lane Lodge. She'd been okay with that. Heidi needed the time, the silence, to attempt to drag herself from the quagmire of her unease.

"Get out." Rhett's command wasn't brutish. It was just that. A plain and simple command.

Heidi obeyed, albeit shooting him a pursed-lip glance of derision. A little warmth infused in his voice might help him not seem as unlikable.

"There you are!" Vicki's voice was high, laced with stress and about as warm as standing in a swimsuit on an iceberg. She stalked toward them, and Heidi took a step backward, closer to Rhett. For now, she'd take the cranky superhero knock-off over Vicki.

Heidi shot a look at Rhett. Vicki paused when she saw him, glanced between him and Heidi and then back at Rhett. She wiped her hand over her cheek in a gesture that was swift but telling. She'd been crying.

"There was a break-in. I got home, the basement door was wide open. We're lucky nothing was stolen from our guests on the second floor."

"No one was hurt?" Rhett's body language shifted to one of concern again.

"No, thankfully." Vicki crossed her arms over her chest. She tipped her head back toward the lodge. "Brad is in there now talking to the cops."

"I'll head in."

Heidi eyed Rhett's tall, broad form as he hiked toward the lodge, but she sensed Vicki's disapproval sparking through the air. She stifled her shaking breath. Tried to ignore the nausea in her stomach and the ravenous disquiet that continued to eat at her nerves.

"Where were you?" Vicki almost hissed, though Heidi saw tears in her eyes. Sparkling, frustrated tears of exhaustion.

Heidi hated confrontation, yet she couldn't escape it.

"I went to see Mom." She left out the part about hitting Emma's dog with the car. If she mentioned that, she'd probably begin to cry too. That would be the end of everything. Specifically, her last thread of emotional control.

"All day?" Vicki tipped her head, wrapping her arms tighter around her body.

"No. I-I wandered around town a bit. Got some coffee and lunch. I needed to clear my thoughts." Clear her thoughts and erase the image of the woman peering through her window.

Vicki interrupted, "And so you didn't restock the towels, assist the guests, nothing? Gosh! It's like you're sixteen years old and just don't think! Now this!" She waved her arm in a sweep of the lodge. "What *did* you do?"

The question ended in a quieter plea. The tone hurt and exasperated, as if Heidi could just give her sister a logical, responsible answer, then everything would at least make sense.

Heidi mirrored her sister and crossed her arms. "What do you mean, 'what did I do'?"

Vicki dropped her arms to her sides. "Someone broke in. Your room is ransacked, completely ransacked."

"What?" A chill started at the base of Heidi's spine. She looked over Vicki's shoulder toward the lodge. "Just my room?"

"Yes." Vicki nodded. "Nothing else was touched, thank God, but the police want to talk with you, and I too want to hear what you have to say."

Heidi pushed past Vicki. There was nothing in her room to find. Nothing to steal. She sensed Vicki was close behind her as she hurried through the house. Voices filtered from the main living area. Heidi dodged down a back hall to avoid what she assumed was the police. Her bedroom door was open, lights on, and it was empty of people.

"Heidi, wait!" Vicki commanded. "I don't

know if the police are —"

Her words cut off. Probably because Heidi had already seen it. There. On her mirror. Written in thick, red smears of lipstick.

Madness.

The one word was terrifying. It meant nothing to Heidi, and yet it was like a cheesy omen from a horror movie right before some masked intruder exited the closet with a machete. Heidi glanced at the closet. The doors were already open and it was empty.

"What does — what is that supposed to mean?" Heidi couldn't help but ask the incredulous question.

"We're hoping you have the answer to that." Vicki crossed her arms again. "The cops want to talk to you. Now." Her words were pointed and meaningful, but Heidi didn't move.

She reached out to touch the lipstick word, then drew her hand back. "I don't know what happened, Vicki, honestly I don't."

Madness.

"You don't have someone out there you owe money to or something? This wasn't random, Heidi."

"No." Bewilderment mixed with apprehension lodged in Heidi's chest. "No, I-I don't."

Vicki drew in a deep breath, then blew it out.

Heidi muttered, "It makes no sense."

Madness.

"Doesn't it?" Vicki's question was loaded with insinuation.

Heidi's gaze flew to meet her sister's. Vicki sniffed and wiped her eyes. Her tone was accusatory when she finished her thought aloud.

"I think it makes all the sense in the world."

The initial commotion on Heidi's return had settled. No one had yet to ask why Rhett was with her and where her car was. Of course, considering there had been a break-in, it kind of made an absentee car with a perfectly healthy sister little cause for concern by comparison.

Heidi jammed her hands in the pockets of her jeans and leaned against the living room wall, noting with preoccupied recognition that her waistband was the same height as the green-plaid wallpaper border. She could hear Vicki in the kitchen turning on water, a pot banging on the stovetop. Tea. Vicki's calming go-to had never changed. Heidi would place bets on her life that it was straight-up green tea, no sweetener added.

Two police officers stood in the circle of couches and coffee table. Brad, with his curly, tousled dark hair and broad shoulders, looked almost puny next to Rhett, who topped her brother-in-law by about four inches and far more brawn. All four men appeared to know each other, and if it hadn't been for a quick eye from Brad, Heidi would have just escaped to — well, somewhere other than here.

Images of the face in the window this morning had revived with a stark coldness that encouraged Heidi to remain in the presence of the four northern-woodsy men. Female independence and warrior women aside, Heidi couldn't argue that sometimes — darn it all — it was nice to have a man around. She'd never admit it out loud, however.

"Heidi?" Brad waved her over. His fingertips were grease-stained, much like she'd noticed with Rhett's. His T-shirt was untucked from his jeans and stretched across his chest. Warmth emanated from his hazel eyes, which tonight hued yellow because of the amber tones of his shirt.

She pushed herself off the wall and neared the group.

"Hello, Ms. Lane. I'm Detective Davidson, and this is Officer Tate. We just have a few questions to ask you." Davidson's statement was so rhetorical, Heidi didn't even bother to smile.

She glanced at Brad, who gave her a brotherly nod of encouragement, then to Rhett, whose gray eyes reflected — well, she didn't know what. He was the master of the poker face. Why was he still here anyway? This was really none of his business.

Detective Davidson was speaking, and Heidi blinked to queue herself into the conversation. The questions came like rapid-fire gunshots.

"Where were you today? Do you know of any reason why your room specifically would be targeted? An ex perhaps?"

Oh! Interesting. There was a flicker in Rhett's eyes at the mention of a possible ex-boyfriend. Heidi bit her lip to hide her smile — and her nerves. This wasn't the time. She cleared her throat. "No, Officer. I've no ex to pester me. I'm woefully single."

She shot a glance at Rhett, who again seemed unaffected. Detective Davidson wasn't, though, and he gave a chuckle.

"Well, we have to explore all options." He shifted his attention back to Brad. "We've checked for prints. We'll run them against the database and rule out all of yours. Odds are the intruder was smart enough to wear gloves or something. We checked around the house — no foot impressions, no broken windows, no blood."

"Blood?" Brad's eyebrow zinged upward.

"Like if someone busted a window and nicked themselves crawling through," Officer Tate interjected.

"Oh," Brad nodded.

Detective Davidson answered with a nod of his own. "Yes. So, point of entry appears to be the entry door. It wasn't jimmied or anything, and Vicki said it was ajar when she got home." Detective Davidson looked back at Heidi. "Do you recall if you locked it when you left?"

Nope. Nope. She hadn't. Vicki hadn't gifted her with a key to get back in. Heidi shook her head and tucked an escaped tendril of blue-tipped hair behind her ear. "I didn't. I recall not locking it because it seemed weird to leave a door unlocked. I'm from Chicago, so a lot of us have bars on our windows, unless you're in the suburbs."

"We don't normally worry about locking up," Brad said on Heidi's behalf. "We have guests come into the main foyer where the reception desk is. The inner door from there into the main living quarters is usually locked, but" — he glanced at Heidi with an apologetic look in his eyes — "I guess Vicki

132

hadn't expected Heidi to go anywhere."

Yes. Trapped in the prison of the Lane Lodge, fulfilling her family duty. Heidi winced inwardly.

"One more question." Detective Davidson exchanged looks with his partner, Officer Tate.

"Yes?" Heidi tried to infuse warmth into her voice. Her defenses were crumbling. There was no appropriate time to interject humor, act impulsively, change the subject, and she had nothing to war against the rising angst.

"The word written on the mirror . . ." He paused, studying her reaction.

Heidi glanced at Rhett, who studied her too.

Brad did likewise.

Heidi waited.

"Do you have any idea what it means?"

The bombshell question. The insinuation from Vicki just minutes before. It all made sense, didn't it? Heidi's throat started closing. Black shields seemed to draw over her peripheral vision, as if she were going to black out. But it wasn't fainting, it was more. So very much more.

A hand on her upper arm steadied her. Its pressure was gentle but firm, coaching her to breathe deep, to take a moment, to not give in. Heidi looked up, and her eyes collided with Rhett's. He blinked. Long lashes framing his eyes.

This was unexpected.

"Take your time." His words were toneless, but Heidi appreciated that. There was no infusion of accusation, or suspicion, or even impatience.

Heidi locked gazes with him, for no other reason than to keep from going under. When she answered Detective Davidson, she stayed focused on Rhett.

"I don't know why anyone would specifically write that to me." Her voice was a whisper.

It wasn't entirely true. Vicki could have — though she seemed too shocked and horrified to make Heidi believe she had. If Vicki had written it, it would have been a cruel accusation from a spiteful sibling.

You're going crazy, Heidi!

Heidi remembered the first time Vicki had told her that when she was fourteen, and Vicki found her rocking in a corner, arms wrapped around her knees.

But anxiety — unaccounted fear — didn't imply madness. Not in today's world. It just bespoke of social fears, or PTSD, or, in Heidi's diagnosed case, hormonal imbalances and an iron deficiency that needed supplements and the aid of a prescription. And she was blessed! Not everyone could find a reason for their struggles. They were just there. Persistent demons that never went away.

"Heidi?" Brad's voice yanked her from her stare into Rhett's firm, unblinking focus.

She broke the gaze and drew a deep breath as she redirected to Brad. "Yeah?"

"Is there anything else you can think of that might be of help to the police? Anything you might know, might *have* that would be worth targeting your room for?"

"Yes," Detective Davidson nodded. "Nothing of value was taken that Brad or Vicki have noticed, but we'll still need you to check your room in a minute here. So far, it seems the break-in had a different goal in mind. We need to know what it was."

Heidi squeezed her eyes shut and then opened them, raking her fingers through her hair. They for sure would think she was mad if she brought up what had happened that morning. The old photograph of a woman who looked just like her. A very dead woman. The fact that that same dead woman had appeared at her bedroom window, staring in at Heidi like a wandering soul determining its intent where Heidi was concerned. That same face had vanished as quickly as it'd come and . . .

"There weren't any footprints outside?" Heidi asked before she could stop herself.

A light of interest sparked in Detective Davidson's eyes. "No. Why?"

No footprints?

So perhaps not a mere human peering in her window? A person with a soul would have almost made Heidi feel better.

"What is it?" Brad pressed.

Heidi heard a movement behind her, and she turned. Vicki stood there, her arms crossed, balancing a cup of green tea in her hand. Her stormy eyes were sharp, insistent. She knew Heidi well enough to know that Heidi wasn't being up-front.

Fine.

She wasn't one to run from a challenge, avoid risk, or take the easy road. Heidi blew a deep breath from her lips and gave her head a tip, shoving nervousness away like a person shoved a dresser in front of a door so it couldn't be opened.

This time it worked.

For now.

"I thought I saw a woman this morning," she admitted.

"A woman?" Detective Davidson raised his eyebrows.

Heidi nodded. "Staring in my window.

But, I looked away for a second and when I turned back, she was gone."

"For heaven's sake." Vicki sighed and rolled her eyes.

Brad held his palm toward his wife to shush her. "Did you get a good look at her? What did she look like?"

Oh boy. Heidi shrugged. "It was almost — she was a ghost."

She saw the officers exchange glances.

"I mean, it was that fast. It was creepy and I — I was freaked out. So, I left. I wanted to see my mom in town, and I had things to do anyway."

"You didn't call the police?" Officer Tate asked, no accusation in his voice, just a curious quirk to his mouth.

"Call them for what?" Heidi responded. "There wasn't anyone there."

"Did you check?" Detective Davidson asked.

"You mean look out the window?" Heidi saw Vicki take a step forward. She could sense the warmth from Rhett's arm. He'd long since dropped his grip, but he hadn't moved away. "No. I mean, sure I looked out the window. But I didn't go around the lodge to confront anyone. I figured —"

Nope. Best to stop there. One mention that Heidi had even entertained the idea that it had been a spirit, a ghost or apparition in the midmorning light, and Vicki would want Heidi to see her psychologist again. This had nothing to do with her mind, but everything to do with that blasted doppelgänger from the photo that had Heidi seeing sideways.

"You think it could be —" Officer Tate's question was cut off by Detective Davidson, who held his hand up and stopped the man mid-sentence.

"Could be what?" Heidi asked.

Detective Davidson side-eyed his partner, and his lips pressed together as if he didn't believe a word of what he was about to say. "It's nothing, Ms. Lane. Just an old legend in the area about a woman from way back when that supposedly haunted these parts."

"What? That Misty Wayfair legend?" Vicki rolled her eyes and gave an exasperated sigh.

"Misty Wayfair?" Heidi shot a glance at Brad, then at Rhett. For the first time, a tiny smile tipped Rhett's mouth. Or maybe not. As quick as she'd thought she'd seen it, it was gone. Like the image at her window. "Who's Misty Wayfair?"

She remembered the name, scrawled on the back of the photograph. Now it made her skin crawl.

Detective Davidson leveled an irritated

glare at Officer Tate. "It's nothing to be concerned about. Ghosts don't toss a room and leave threatening messages on mirrors. Well, perhaps a poltergeist, but . . ." He gave his head a quick shake as if he was losing it and rubbed his eyes. "So, here's what needs to happen. Doors should be locked. Alarm systems won't work here 'cause you're too far out for Wi-Fi, right?"

Brad nodded.

Detective Davidson responded with his own. "Thought so. You may want to consider putting in one based off your landline. Of course, this whole thing may have been a prank by some local kids. Who knows? Definitely keep your doors locked from now on, windows too. We'll keep an eye out on the place, ask around, see if there's anything else we can find. But for now, the best thing to do is just be sure the place is as secure as you can make it."

"*Who* is Misty Wayfair?" Heidi demanded.

The room fell silent. Well, it *should* fall silent, Heidi figured, because her voice had come out shrill and adamant. Even Vicki had stalled the lifting of her teacup halfway to her mouth.

When no one jumped to answer, Officer Tate gave his partner a hesitant look before responding. It seemed he was the more superstitious of the two.

"She was murdered back in the late 1800s. Story has it, Misty Wayfair is seen from time to time these last hundred years or so. She runs barefoot in the woods, looking for a way out. It's like she's trying to escape."

"Escape? Escape from where?" Heidi took in the faces around the room. None of them seemed to believe the story, and yet no one would look her in the eye.

Except for Rhett.

He answered her with the blunt honesty she'd both wanted and feared.

"The asylum."

"The asylum?" Heidi responded in disbelief.

Officer Tate had found his voice again. "There used to be an asylum in these parts. Way back when. They say Misty Wayfair's ghost somehow got locked up with the patients after she was murdered. When the asylum closed, and the patients were dispersed back in the twenties, Misty's spirit got trapped there. She never left."

"So they say," Heidi finished for him, an icy chill traveling down her spine.

"So they say," Officer Tate affirmed.

CHAPTER 10

THEA

"Did you hear the wailing last night?"

Mrs. Brummel's question made the spoon freeze halfway to Thea's mouth. She stared over the silver at the woman pouring her a glass of milk for breakfast. The boarding-house matron didn't seem bothered or unnerved. It had been all Thea could do to keep her wits about her after returning to her room last night. She'd tried to convince herself that she'd been caught between that foggy world of the river and the forest, and that the vision she'd seen across the river had been a mistake. An illusion.

But she hadn't heard wailing.

"No. I didn't."

"Oh, you lucky thing!" Mrs. Brummel paused, milk pitcher hoisted in midair, her right hand propped on her hip. She reviewed Thea with her sharp gaze, and the neckline of her black dress rose so high and so tight around her throat, it seemed as if it would choke the woman if she even tried to swallow. "That ridiculous cat." She shook her head and clucked her tongue.

Thea brought her spoon back down to rest on the edge of her bowl of oatmeal, Mrs. Brummel's only breakfast option at the boardinghouse so far.

"A cat?" she choked out.

Mrs. Brummel's thin eyebrow jaunted upward, and her lips pursed. "Martin Amos's cat, Pip. I daresay, that thing could raise the dead with its caterwauling. He's looking for a female cat, no doubt."

A hot blush flooded Thea's face. She pushed the bowl away from her and tossed the napkin from her lap onto the tabletop. "I've much to do today."

"Oh?" Mrs. Brummel was nosy.

"At the portrait studio." Thea supplied an answer, though she didn't need to. What seemed like moments later, Thea had gathered her belongings for the day and made haste from the boardinghouse. She was more than capable of chitchat when it served a purpose, but discussing the romantic adventures of a feline was not something Thea wanted or could focus her attention on.

She shuddered as the toe of her shoe

ventured onto the road that split the main street of town. A large wagon rumbled past, with a wave of a brawny hand from the logger sitting high atop the wagon seat. This street really was, for all sakes and purposes, the only street of interest to the public. But she couldn't help her vision straying to the borders of the forest across the river. The bare legs and feet, the obscure face, the long, dark hair . . . no. She had seen *someone* in the woods. It had been no illusion. She couldn't shake the suspicions that she'd caught a glimpse of Mrs. Brummel's Misty Wayfair ghost. The murdered woman who haunted the Coyles after Mathilda Kramer had married Misty's lover, Fergus Coyle. Was it for revenge that she haunted them? A hatred for anyone bearing the Coyle name? Thea couldn't shake the story from her mind.

"A spirit searching is a horrible thing. They haunt until they find rest. Some never do. If there's something unsettld between them and another, they'll wander for eternity."

Mr. Mendelsohn's words still raked a cold set of fingers up Thea's spine. This awareness of the afterlife was something she wished she had not been educated in. She'd never seen evidence to support Mr. Mendelsohn's suspicions. Never a whisper in the night, never a thump or a thud. No articles moved when no one was around. Nothing but the eerie coldness a person felt when they *sensed* something — *someone.*

Mrs. Mendelsohn had countered that Thea would position herself on the wrong side of God were she to take up a study of the spirits. That God had banished King Saul for no less, and it was sheer witchery.

Reaching the corner, Thea moved to round it and head toward the back entrance of the studio. It would be unlocked by seven-thirty promptly each morning, Mr. Amos had instructed. The front door, not until nine.

A movement startled Thea, and she palmed the side of the building, freezing in her steps. The lean frame of Simeon Coyle emerged from the studio. He paused and nodded, speaking to someone — more likely than not, Mr. Amos. His left hand clutched a black satchel, worn with scuffed leather at the corners. Large enough to carry his photograph album, or perhaps photographs on cards Mr. Amos had already developed and set.

She blinked. Simeon lifted his hand in a slight wave and turned toward the river. Not toward town, as one might assume, although he was probably not well received there. But neither did he go in the direction of the Coyle home, which was located almost halfway to the main base of the Kramer Logging post.

After a moment's hesitation, Thea decided to follow him. Regardless of the uneasiness that spread through her at the sight of him dodging the edge of town and heading toward the one-lane bridge that spanned the river, Thea couldn't put aside the questions rising in her mind. The Coyles were, as Mrs. Brummell had stated, a strange family, and now only two of them remained. If they *were* being haunted by a ghost, was this why Simeon darted around as though trying to avoid attention? And, she couldn't just *ask* Mr. Amos what Simeon did, or about his coming and going from the portrait studio. The old man had made it quite clear the first day that his association with Simeon Coyle was to remain unquestioned and unspoken of.

But remembering Mary Coyle's face as she'd stared at it through the lens of her camera, and seeing the peculiar photographs Simeon had in his album, Thea had to know more. If there was one thing she did share with Mr. Mendelsohn, it was the deep sensing that someone was trying to speak, to surface.

Perhaps, in an odd way, Misty Wayfair had tried to gain Thea's attention last night. Before vanishing and making Thea half believe she was losing her mind.

Something did not match up.

Not Simeon Coyle. Most definitely not the death of his sister. Not for the last time did Thea frown at the idea that one simply did not die from being melancholy.

She froze in mid-step as she reached the bridge.

Melancholy. A strange memory assaulted her. One that hadn't risen before. She'd been little, and her mother had seemed so large. Crawling onto her lap, her dress tangling around her feet, Thea recalled reaching for her mother's face. Staring into empty eyes. Eyes that had lost their life. As a child, she didn't know why. Melancholic eyes.

"Mama?"

No response.

"Mama, I'm hungry."

Still nothing.

Thea reached for her mother's face. Small hands cupping both cheeks, turning it, until her mother seemed to awaken for a moment.

"I'm sorry," her mother had breathed. A fingertip touched Thea's nose. "Your mama is sad. So very sad."

"Why?" Thea asked.

Her mother shook her head. "I don't know why. I never know why."

Thea gripped the rail of the bridge. Simeon's form moved farther ahead of her.

She should turn back. Back to the portrait studio and Mr. Amos. She'd told him she would assist a sitting later that morning. A family with three small children — and a dog, no less. But what did a soul do when its very core churned with the unsettled motion of the river that flowed beneath this very bridge?

Simeon's long strides took him down the narrow dirt lane and into the woods. Bluish hues painted a thickly wooded picture ahead of her. A place that in fairy tales would hearken images of the gingerbread house and the witch that ate little children for dinner. She glanced over her shoulder, toward Pleasant Valley. The steeple of the Methodist church and the cross at its tip seemed to cry for her to go back, to retreat.

But she couldn't.

It was as if the Pied Piper had begun to play his tune, and Thea could only follow.

CHAPTER 11

It rose from the middle of the forest like a solitary prison only a mile or so out of town. Three stories in a rectangular form, made of brick with no embellishments other than an iron-rail fence bordering its yard. Cut from the woods, the clearing was remarkable, and the trees butted up not far from the fence line as though they wanted to grow over and into the yard but dared not. Moss and mold had turned some of the brickwork dark green with age. Windows lined all three stories. Ten across and three down. They were glass-plated with four panes each, the grid a simple cross of dark lines. Behind them, inside, were bars. Horizontal lines that silently said if one were to enter, one would not leave by way of a window. The roof was shingled and dark. Everything about the building was dark.

Thea's feet grew heavy, and she stopped her subtle trail of Simeon Coyle. She rested her left palm against the trunk of an oak tree that rose high above her. Old leaves blanketed the forest floor, along with pine needles. There was some underbrush, but mostly the carcasses of rotting logs long fallen from their woodsy sentinel. A pungent smell filled Thea's senses, like the mixture of damp, fresh air and the mold of fallen autumn leaves. But she ignored the eerie beauty of the woods and the imposing simplicity of the building in front of her.

It was Simeon she watched.

He reached the gates, which rose at least a foot above his head. They opened to his touch, the sound of iron hinges groaning their protest. His steps were slow but not intimidated. He seemed neither anticipatory to enter nor frightened to leave. Rather, Thea saw the downward slope of his shoulders and it reminded her of resignation.

Simeon closed the gates behind him, latching them shut. There was no key turned into the gate lock, Thea noted. She could follow, if she wished.

So she did.

Tiptoeing forward, she strained to make out words painted on a green sign that hung over the double doors of the building's front entrance. She noticed that Simeon turned right and away from them, his steps leading him across the lawn toward an outbuilding in the distance. When she arrived at the gates, Thea reached out. The instant her gloveless hand curled around the iron bar, something inside of her recoiled. She dropped her hand.

An invisible sort of weight settled on her chest and made it hard to breathe. Thea stared through the bars, narrowing her eyes to make out the sign's thin script, written in dark brown lettering almost impossible to read against the green background.

Valley Heights Asylum.

She squeezed her eyes shut and then opened them, only to read the words again. An asylum? In the woods outside of Pleasant Valley? But Mrs. Brummell had said nothing of it, and wouldn't that have been of far more import than a street dividing the town into denominational sections?

Thea took a step back. She would not enter. No. She'd heard of sanatoriums. Places where —

"It's a place for the mentally insane."

Thea's mouth dropped open in a silent scream. She spun on her heels at the voice behind her.

"Rose!" She snapped her mouth shut as she took in the woman who, it seemed, had followed her as she had Simeon. Only Rose wasn't secretive in her approach. Her eyes were gentle, questioning, with a slight raise of her dark eyebrows. A lucid but sad glow in her sapphire eyes.

"Were you following my brother?" she asked. There wasn't accusation in her voice, and, if she didn't appear so pale and worn from grief, Thea would almost have wondered if a small laugh had tilted her lips.

"No!" Thea denied. Then she thought better of it. "Well, I — perhaps."

Rose looked beyond her, at the asylum, her eyes taking in the breadth of it. "When family brings a relative here," she murmured, "they don't intend on returning for visits or pleasantries."

She wanted to ask why Simeon was here, and even more so, why Rose. Instead, Thea turned and followed Rose's line of sight. The building was a prison then. Of the worst sort perhaps. She glanced back at Rose.

Rose sniffed and adjusted her grip on the handbag she clutched. Her hands were gloved in black, and the black dress she wore was simple but made her features stand out so beautifully, so pale and etched, that Thea could hardly look away.

"Simeon is the groundskeeper," Rose explained. "Among other things." Then a tiny laugh did escape her, but not one that entertained any sort of humor. "It's the only work he could find. Pleasant Valley is . . ."

"Yes," Thea finished for Rose. There was no need for the woman to explain. She'd experienced enough of Pleasant Valley already to understand why the woman let her sentence hang.

Rose sucked in a deep breath. The determined sort that matched the squaring of her shoulders and the upward tilt of her chin. "This is where Dr. Ackerman works."

The name sounded vaguely familiar.

Rose met Thea's questioning eyes.

"You met him at — my sister's funeral."

Oh! Yes. Thea remembered now.

"Would you like to come in with me? The hospital doesn't approve of random visitors, but they'll let you in if you know me." Rose invited her almost as if one would offer entrance into one's home.

Thea didn't miss a tiny flicker in Rose's eyes. Hesitation perhaps, or shyness. She wasn't sure. She certainly wasn't going to ask why Rose had earned the right to enter.

While she had no innate desire to pass through those iron gates and walk the stone path to the front door of this place, another thought festered in the back of Thea's mind. A memory of her dinner at the Amos house when Mrs. Amos had inquired of Thea's mother and Mr. Amos had abruptly changed the subject just as his wife was about to offer a suggestion.

Perhaps this was it. Mrs. Amos's suggestion. Her mother, not known by a longtime citizen of Pleasant Valley, was perhaps . . .

"Please." Rose's voice had lessened to just above a whisper. "Do come in."

Thea forced herself to remember why she'd come to Pleasant Valley in the first place. To bring closure to the remembrance of a woman she wanted to forget. A mother who had shirked not only her responsibility but, more importantly, turned a stiff back to love.

She swept a searching look over the rectangular windows on the third floor. Like a row of tombs that, when one was granted entrance, all memory of them in the live world faded. A place where minds were stirred by uncontrolled thoughts, where actions were spurred by irrational behaviors that could be described in no other way than — insane.

No. No, she didn't want to enter. She didn't want to consider or even suggest that her mother might have once crossed the threshold of this place. If she did, it changed all of Thea's already turbulent emotions about the woman. It wasn't clean, nor was it a firmly closed matter like it would be if Thea found her mother's name engraved on a tombstone.

Sometimes death was more welcoming an ending to a story. It was final, and the lives left behind could grieve, if needed, but then move on.

But a home for the mentally insane?

Thea saw the faces of the photographs in Simeon's albums. The suspension between life and death. Eyes neither alive nor dead. Minds neither aware nor empty.

It was a horrible, terrifying trail to follow, and Thea would need more answers before she was willing to walk it.

She left Rose there, alone, at the gates of Valley Heights Asylum, shrouded in its canopy of towering trees. She hadn't even said farewell, nor had she turned at the sound of Rose's concerned cry.

Instead, Thea had run.

When Mrs. Amos opened the door, a surprised look on her round, wrinkled face, Thea wasted no time with pleasantries.

"Last evening," she began, breathing heavily. Catching her breath after her harried pace back to town would have been a clever idea if she'd stopped to think first. "You were going to mention something — an idea — about my mother. Mr. Amos stopped you. Why?"

Mrs. Amos opened the door further. "Oh dear. Do come in."

Thea nodded. The warmth of the home, coupled with the smell of freshly baked bread, covered her with an unexpected sense of calm as she entered. Her spirit grappled for it. Like a lifeline.

Mrs. Amos motioned Thea into a small parlor. Two stuffed chairs, arms covered with doilies and the seat cushions worn, bordered a fireplace. There were coals in it.

"Please sit," Mrs. Amos instructed.

Without argument, Thea relaxed into one. Mrs. Amos took the opposite seat, sank onto it, and adjusted the folds of her dark blue skirt. Her blouse was full over her broad bosom, and her waist was almost indiscernible as it met her hips. The roundness of Mrs. Amos reminded Thea of the perfect grandmother. Soft, cozy, and safe.

"Now . . ." Mrs. Amos smiled gently. "Mr. Amos was expecting you at work, wasn't he?"

Oh yes. Thea bit her lip. She'd been foolhardy.

"Posh." The old woman waved her hand. "He'll live to see another day regardless. It seems you have far more depths to explore than a portrait."

Thea winced. The woman read her well.

"To answer your question" — Mrs. Amos straightened the doily that had been brushed askew on the arm of her chair — "as we chatted last evening, I was reminded of a hospital we have just outside of town."

"The asylum?" Thea interrupted.

"You know of it, then?" Mrs. Amos appeared surprised.

"I just recently found out."

"Yes. Well, it was uncalled for. I must apologize. Sometimes this old mind of mine goes to places where proper manners don't follow. My father used to call me a curious cat when I was a little girl. Regardless, Mr. Amos stopped me before I finished. Forgive me for the implication your mother may have been, or might be, a patient there. I meant absolutely no insult!"

Thea was anything but offended. In fact, to a degree she related even more to Mrs. Amos. She told Mrs. Amos so and watched relief fill the old woman's faded eyes.

"I have vague memories," Thea admitted, and the kindly look on Mrs. Amos's face was all the coercion Thea needed. "Most of them leave me bereft and not endeared to my mother at all."

Mrs. Amos nodded, her lips rolling together in an empathetic frown.

"I've no reason — no reason at all — to believe your mere suggestion has any merit. Yet, now that I am here in Pleasant Valley, there are so many . . ."

"Oddities?" Mrs. Amos supplied.

"Yes!" Thea gave her the sort of exasperated sigh she more than likely would have squelched in front of anyone else. "Mrs. Brummel has told me stories and —"

"Mrs. Brummel has a wagging tongue, and it bodes no good for anyone. Especially for Christian charity." Mrs. Amos tapped her finger on the chair. Her blue eyes sharpened. "I suppose she went on about how the town is split, Catholic and Protestant?"

"Yes."

"And how it all started when Mathilda Kramer married Fergus Coyle?"

"Precisely." Thea sagged into the chair, a bit relieved that Mrs. Amos didn't appear as intense or disturbed by the stories as Mrs. Brummel had made them out to be.

Mrs. Amos gave her fingers a little wave. The lace at her sleeve was haphazardly tucked into the bottom of her cuff, but she didn't seem to notice.

"Mr. Amos and I knew Mathilda Coyle.

The stories have haunted that poor family for years, and all because she wished to wed the one she loved. My goodness! I would have done quite the same as she did."

"So, Mrs. Brummel's story is true?"

"Which one?" Mrs. Amos shrugged. "All of them have merit to one degree or another. Mathilda's father did disown her because she converted to the Catholic Church."

"And that's a mortal sin?" Thea didn't know, and she truly wondered.

Mrs. Amos's lips tightened. She toyed with the lace at her cuff and pulled it out from where it'd been tucked. "All I'll say is, the Christian church has been divided on many grounds and for many reasons and for many years. The heart of the matter, I believe, isn't to do with the name on the door but the God within."

Thea blinked. It made some sense. She wished to ask more but didn't want to sidetrack away from the main topic of conversation. "And Misty Wayfair?"

"Misty Wayfair." Mrs. Amos shook her head sadly, her white cap well attached in place over her white hair. "She is a story. That is all. A rumor."

"You don't believe in ghosts? In curses?" Thea surmised.

Mrs. Amos smiled wanly. "Well, if I let my

imagination go wild, I'm quite adept at being taken in by it all. The Coyles have had a sad and tragic series of passings. But because Misty caused them? Oh, so doubtful. For what could a wandering spirit really do, if it truly existed? They don't hold the power of God over life and death, do they?"

Thea wasn't sure if she was supposed to answer that. And if she was, she didn't know the answer.

Mrs. Amos continued, her wobbly and aged voice musing aloud. "I thought when Mr. Kramer's nephew, Mr. Fortune, inherited the logging company, things might be set to rights. But I'm afraid Mr. Fortune has turned a blind eye toward his cousins the Coyles. Regardless, it is what is."

Thea leaned forward. "What type of passings?"

"Hmm?" Mrs. Amos tilted her head as if she didn't understand.

"You mentioned the Coyles had a series of unfortunate deaths . . ."

"Oh yes. They did. They have. When Simeon and Rose were in adolescence, they lost their father. A most horrific accident. He fell from the loft onto his pitchfork, no less. It was then the rumor began that someone had seen the ghost of Misty Wayfair the night before. She'd been singing and dancing through the woods."

A chill riddled through Thea. The memory of the vision the night before was ripe in her mind.

"Then their mother passed not long after. She passed away . . ." Mrs. Amos hesitated, as if warring with herself. "She died due to melancholia. She was never the same after her husband's death."

"Melancholia," Thea repeated.

Mrs. Amos gave her a knowing glance. She lifted her index finger. "This is where Mr. Amos would tell me to bite my tongue. But I see in your eyes you think as I do."

"How does one die of sadness?"

"Yes!" Mrs. Amos leaned back, a bit satisfied. "How *does* one? Wasting away, I understand. Becoming reclusive, failing to get proper nourishment, yes. But then, if one does die, isn't that because one contracts an illness because of a poor state of mind? So then wouldn't she have died of pneumonia? Or perhaps the fever? But to call it melancholia . . ."

As Mrs. Amos let her sentence drift away, her eyes met Thea's.

Thea nodded. "And that is why people believe in Misty Wayfair's curse."

"Yes," Mrs. Amos nodded. "Mr. Coyle falls on a pitchfork. Mrs. Coyle dies of sadness? And then Mathilda herself? She passed away in her sleep. Poor Mary, of most recent times, just like her mother? It is all very unexplained. Especially in the wake of the fact that Misty Wayfair died such a violent death. Strangulation, so the story goes."

Mrs. Amos didn't appear mortified. For an elderly woman, she seemed a bit too intrigued. Had Thea unwittingly opened the door to Mrs. Amos's age-long curiosity?

"The story goes that on the night of Mathilda and Fergus Coyle's wedding, Misty Wayfair was strangled and thrown into a well. The rumors state she was — *involved* with Fergus." Mrs. Amos touched her lips with her fingertips as though by doing so it would lessen the shock of her story.

Thea waited. She'd already heard something similar from Mrs. Brummel, but perhaps Mrs. Amos would add more detail.

Mrs. Amos busied herself by picking at a wayward thread on her sleeve. "Mathilda would never speak of it. Only to defend Fergus's honor and that he was never involved with the woman."

"Who was Misty Wayfair?" Thea breathed.

Mrs. Amos's eyes flew up to meet hers. "She was — a woman. Who kept guests from the camp."

Thea blushed.

Mrs. Amos nodded. "The entirety of the story is sad. On all accounts. But, not more than twenty years ago, Mr. Kramer — who was very old by then and on his way out of this world shortly after — built the asylum. Valley Heights, they called it. With room for a handful of patients."

Thea collected her thoughts. The story of Misty Wayfair, the origins of the asylum, it all had nothing to do with her mother. And yet the story of the Coyles and the logging company so permeated every facet of Pleasant Valley, it seemed hard to disassociate them.

"And you think maybe my mother was one of the patients there?"

Mrs. Amos's eyes grew tender. She leaned forward, reaching for Thea's hand. Thea gave it to her and welcomed the warmth of the old woman's grasp.

"Many strange things happen here. Mrs. Brummel will blame it on superstitious lore. I contend, if someone would merely speak the truth, it would all make sense. But as for your mother, I can only surmise. If you've been told she was from Pleasant Valley, I would have known of her. So, to not know of her means only that she must have been *there*. At the hospital. So much of life is a mystery, and so often it is left unsolved."

Thea swallowed back a sudden rush of tears. Ones that demanded she be honest and ones that surprised her with their poignancy.

"I wished my mother to be dead," Thea admitted.

Mrs. Amos's hand tightened in understanding.

Thea swiped at a tear. "Now, hearing the story of the Coyles, Kramer Logging, of Misty Wayfair and whatever it was she suffered . . . now I wish my mother were alive. That she wasn't touched by this cursed place."

"Oh, my dear," Mrs. Amos breathed. "This place isn't cursed. No more than any other. It is a wilderness of people wanting to understand where they belong. To build a life, to live it, and to one day pass on to glory should they be firm in their faith and knowledge of their Creator's saving grace."

Her words left Thea empty.

"I have none of that." Thea swallowed again as the lump in her throat grew tighter. "No family. No life. No . . . eternity. I don't even know who I am."

Mrs. Amos reached forward with her other hand and took both of Thea's in hers. Her firm grasp and steady gaze captured Thea in a way no one ever had.

"You are created to be an image of your Creator, my dear. That is a great honor. To be designed as Thea Reed, and signed by the mark of the Artist himself. You are a work of genius. But until you know that, your name, your roots, your past, and your future will be what you chase after. Like a leaf that blows in the wind. I would bid you all the best in catching it, only, if you do, it won't satisfy. You will still wonder who Thea Reed is, long after your primary questions have been answered."

CHAPTER 12

HEIDI

When she was a kid, she'd had a pet frog. Heidi remembered her father bringing home crickets from the pet store, and she'd dropped a few into the aquarium only to flinch as the long, sticky tongue of the amphibian shot out and snatched the insect. Legs kicked as it lodged in the frog's mouth. The worst part, besides the gruesome sight, was the small container of crickets beside the tank. Unsuspecting little creatures, rubbing their hind legs together in a spring chorus of conversation as a vicious predator loomed beside them, separated by a plate of glass — and Heidi's mercy. She'd released the crickets the next day and insisted her father take the frog to a nearby pond and release it too. Circle of life aside, Heidi had no intention of committing such offenses against living creatures.

It was how she felt all too often.

Not that her parents had intentions of eating her, but more so, that they were always there, and Heidi never knew when they would pounce if she spoke, or sang, or danced just wrong. There were legalities of the faith to follow. To them, the lines were clearly drawn. To Heidi, they'd been the plastic container she was trapped in. A container she'd escaped shortly after high school. College had been her playground, but even there, Heidi felt as if she had a tiny parent perched on each shoulder, both censuring her actions. So, for the most part, she'd been a good girl. But along with that came the very real drifting away from her family, until her career took over, life became easier alone, and distance made family more tolerable.

Heidi jerked her head up as Vicki accidentally dropped a stainless-steel pan into the sink. Her sister's face almost reflected how Heidi felt. For a moment, she wondered if Vicki had ever felt trapped too? She always assumed Vicki aligned herself with their parents out of personal choice. But what if — ?

"The dishwasher is broken," Vicki muttered. Maybe to her, but Heidi didn't respond. Vicki retrieved the pan, turned on the water, and grabbed a scouring pad.

Heidi sat on a stool at the kitchen bar, her elbows propped on the granite countertop, hands splayed on both sides of her head. She hadn't slept last night — at all. The couch was hard, and she certainly wasn't going to sleep in her bedroom. Vicki might have scoured the mirror and removed the lipstick message with Windex, but she couldn't scour the vision of the dead doppelgänger, or worse, the resurrected doppelgänger staring at her through her bedroom window.

Legend, ghost, or real, Heidi was not a fan of this Misty Wayfair woman. Or people who broke into houses and didn't bother to do anything but completely scare the occupants.

She studied Vicki, who applied as much elbow grease to cleaning the pan as she had to cleaning the mirror last night.

"Thanks for getting that message off the glass," Heidi ventured.

Vicki paused, her head coming up to give her sister a surprised look. A slight smile touched her lips. Heidi realized she probably hadn't offered much in the way of gratitude to her sister. That was something she did need to take personal responsibility for. As people said, when you point your finger, there's still three pointing back at you. Heidi preferred not to dwell on what she may have contributed to the family dysfunction.

Vicki returned to scrubbing. "Well, I just think it's ridiculous the police can't do anything." Her words were a mix of irritation and worry.

"Yeah." Heidi's response was absent. She ran a finger over a marble pattern on the counter. "So . . . this asylum . . ."

"What?" Vicki put the pot on the drainboard and submerged her hand to unplug the drain for the dishwater.

Heidi infused more assertiveness into her voice. Images of the photo album with the dead woman replaying in her mind. "This asylum the police mentioned last night? The Misty Wayfair character. What do you know about it?"

Vicki wiped down the sink. "As Mom would say, it's 'stuff and nonsense.' You know there's no such thing as ghosts."

One of the few things Heidi was prone to agree with her sister on. And still . . .

"But, there was a woman looking in my window. Was it a guest maybe? Of the lodge?"

Vicki dried her hands on a towel. Her blond hair was pulled back in its typically low ponytail, a few strands framing her face.

Her eyes weren't as hard and bitter this morning. Heidi wished she looked like this more often. She was more approachable, more — *human.*

"Doubtful. It's only May, so school hasn't ended in most places. Our guests right now are all older, not young enough to match your description."

Heidi nodded. So much for that idea. She debated showing the photo album to Vicki, but then Vicki continued.

"As for the asylum, it's abandoned. It's out in the woods down Briar Road about a half mile after you cross the bridge over the river. I don't think it's even safe to explore, from what I've heard. The foundation is a mess. But, I've never actually been out there."

"When did it shut down?" Heidi folded her hands in front of her, and her gaze trailed the green of her tattoos. *Fly Free.*

She'd been trying to her entire life.

Vicki leaned against the sink and crossed her arms. "I don't know. I don't know much about it or this Misty Wayfair story. She's just folklore really, again from what I've heard."

Vicki wasn't going to be much help. At least not with local history. Still . . . family history? Maybe. After all, Heidi *did* find that

169

photo album with her look-alike dead woman in the local antique shop run by Connie Crawford. If she was related to the woman in the picture — the woman looking in her window — then how did it end up in Pleasant Valley when they hailed from Minnesota originally?

"So, how much do you know about our ancestry?" Heidi asked.

Vicki shifted and crossed her ankles, then leaned back against the sink again. "I don't know what you mean."

It really wasn't that hard to understand. Heidi tried again. "Grandparents, great-grandparents, where our family comes from. Germans, Vikings, Celts?"

"Oh." Vicki's face turned expressionless, and Heidi couldn't tell if it was because she knew something and didn't want to say, or because she had no interest and had never entertained the question before.

"You'd have to ask Mom. I don't know anything," she answered, her words a bit clipped.

"You think Mom will even remember?" Mom. The woman had thought she was dead, for goodness' sake. How would she even have an ounce of memory for ancestral history?

Vicki shrugged and pushed off the counter. "I doubt it. Why do you want to know anyway? I'd rather find out who broke into this house. I've got damage control to do with the guests. They're all unnerved, and rightfully so. It won't surprise me if some of them check out early." Her armor was back on, and Heidi squelched a sigh. Vicki grabbed a pile of used dish towels to take them to the laundry room. She paused and gave Heidi a poignant look. "If they do check out, we'll lose money having to refund the days they didn't stay."

Heidi tilted her head and gave Vicki a raised brow. "And that's my fault?"

Vicki shrugged. "Not necessarily. But it was your room, your mirror. I don't know what you've been doing the last several years, but . . ."

The dropped sentence was rife with implications.

Heidi owed her sister no explanation, but old instincts to defend her decisions still ran thick through her. "I've been waitressing, okay? That's it. And working some administrative temp jobs."

Vicki gave her a look that indicated she either didn't believe her or that it was no shocking surprise Heidi had developed into nothing much worth talking about.

And that was the look Heidi had lived with

all her life, in this cricket-container world that some people called a family.

Connie Crawford opened the front door. Her smile stretched across her face and reached her warm, brown eyes.

"Heidi!"

Heidi stalled for a moment and then responded with an equally friendly smile. Gosh, she could really enjoy Connie's company! It was a breath of fresh air over Vicki's, and there was an instantaneous nurturing air about the woman that made Heidi wonder, briefly, if she'd been lucky enough to have been Connie's daughter, would the woman be proud of her — for being her?

Heidi glanced over Connie's shoulder. "I was wanting to check on Emma, and the dog."

And appease her own conscience for slamming into the canine with her car that was, interestingly enough, no longer in the ditch and also nowhere to be seen.

"Oh, you're so kind! And you walked all the way here? That's at least three miles!"

The walk had done her good. Cleared her head, her thoughts from the mind-numbing depths of all things dark and suspicious. Circumstances might not have changed, but she was rising from the quagmire of last night's desperation.

It'd also given her time to relive her conversation with her mom. To reconsider the letter she'd received and maybe even reason it away as her mother losing her mental faculties rather than a sincere cry for help, cloaked with strange statements that made no sense.

Connie opened the door wider. "Come on in."

She led the way through the kitchen. "I have a part-timer running the store today," she explained over her shoulder, even though Heidi hadn't asked. "Both dog and owner are fine, but Emma needs a bit more assistance at the moment."

Heidi winced. That was for certain her fault.

Connie led her through a doorway into the family room. She paused and smiled at Heidi with a reassuring pat on her shoulder. "It's really all right, Heidi. Emma is a trooper, and she'll adjust. It might be slow, though. The finding of that new routine can cause much anxiety. She's not used to not having Ducie at her beck and call."

Emma looked up and smiled a quick flash of a smile as they approached.

"Hi." She lifted a hand in a wave. Far

more relaxed than the previous night, Emma sat intent at a table with a board game of Risk. She was setting it up.

"Risk!" Heidi grinned. "Now *that* is my type of game!"

Emma didn't respond. Her hand went to the infinity scarf around her neck.

Connie chuckled. "Emma always wins, and I find it quite disheartening."

"It's strategy." There wasn't much emotion in Emma's tone, and she tugged at her scarf again. Heidi realized it was probably a gesture of comfort for Emma.

The young woman was dividing armies.

"Forty armies for two players, right?" Heidi welcomed the sense of pleasure that coursed through her at the sight of the game. It was a beginner question, but it broke the ice between her and the woman whose dog she'd almost killed.

"Yes." Emma nodded but stayed hunched over the board.

"I'd like to play," Heidi ventured. She really would. Get her mind off everything even more than the walk had.

"Sure." Emma pushed a pile of cards in Heidi's direction. "We need neutral territories."

"For two players, that's how it's done," Connie explained, watching.

"I remember." Heidi sat in a chair opposite Emma. A thumping sound grabbed her attention, and she looked down at the floor by Emma's feet. Ducie lay there on a dog bed, his hind leg in a cast. She'd not seen him there when she'd come in, but now Heidi could tell that although the dog might be incapacitated, he had no intention of leaving his mistress's side.

No wonder Emma was calm.

Heidi smiled. This might be the first moment since she'd arrived in Pleasant Valley that she could draw a deep breath and feel at peace. At least for a second or two.

"Rhett had your vehicle towed to the shop," Connie broke into Heidi's thoughts.

"That was kind." She watched Emma arranging the cards. It was also presuming of him.

"Your brother-in-law, Brad, called this morning to make sure it was taken care of. Rhett was on it right away."

Oh. Brad. Heidi had eventually explained her own evening's accident, which somehow seemed to pale in comparison to squad cars, cryptic lipstick messages, and rumors of ghosts.

"That's why you came, isn't it?" Connie's inquiry caused Heidi to snap from her mental picture of Vicki's heavy sigh from

175

the night before as Heidi had admitted to almost killing Emma Crawford's service dog.

"Huh?" Heidi blinked.

Even Emma paused to watch her.

"Your car? That's why you stopped by?" Connie pressed.

"Oh!" *Pull it together, Lane.* Heidi nodded her head, pushing strands of blue-tipped hair behind her ear. "Well, yes, but I also wanted to check in on Emma here, and of course the dog."

"Ducie," Emma supplied.

"Yes, Ducie." Heidi accepted the correction.

"It was a bit of a traumatic night," Connie admitted. She reached out and pushed on Emma's shoulder. A firm grip and an applied pressure. Emma smiled at her mother, a quiet expulsion of breath that seemed to squeeze any uninvited anxiety from Emma's body.

Heidi could comprehend a little of how Emma felt. Pent-up anxiety was awful, sometimes paralyzing. "I really am sorry. I didn't realize how fast I was going, and I was distracted."

"You should concentrate harder." Emma lifted large brown eyes set in a fine-boned face to Heidi. There was kindness in her expression, in spite of the abrupt correction. As though it were obvious, and Heidi should know this naturally.

Heidi swallowed and choked. "Yes. I probably should."

A smile quirked Connie's lips. The older woman pushed back a strand of graying blond hair. "Emma is very honest."

"Honesty is wise." Heidi affirmed Emma.

Connie redirected her attention to her daughter. "Emma, are you fine if I go call Dad?"

Emma nodded and leaned over to scratch Ducie behind the ear.

"He was supposed to be home today to be with Emma, but he was called in." Connie's voice lowered. "Murphy works at Kramer's, and sometimes they can't do without him."

"Kramer's?" Heidi inquired, sidestepping the emotional twinge of guilt that Emma's routine had been so obviously disrupted, and it was all Heidi's fault.

"The logging and lumber company," Connie explained.

"They were founded in 1838." Emma's insertion was matter-of-fact. "By Lewis Kramer. His parents were immigrants from Stuttgart, Germany, when he was five years old. He came to Pleasant Valley in the summer of 1831, and seven years later, Kramer Logging was formed."

Heidi couldn't help but allow a small, impressed laugh to escape her lips. "Emma Crawford, that's phenomenal date retention."

Emma smiled. A thin, wan smile that communicated she appreciated Heidi's words but wasn't sure why she was impressed.

Connie left the room to go place her call. Heidi sat down opposite of Emma and began to prepare for a game of Risk. It wasn't what she should be doing, yet she couldn't shake her uneasy and aimless feeling. One that could almost drift away sitting opposite of Emma and in the presence of Connie Crawford.

"I used to play Risk on Friday nights when I lived in Minnesota and I was in high school. But that was a long time ago." Heidi picked up the instructions. Emma seemed to ignore her, and Ducie released a heavy dog sigh from his place on the bed.

Heidi kept rambling.

"My friends and I would conquer the world. We split into teams of two since there were several of us. We'd make hot cocoa, have popcorn, and make a real game of it. And I" — Heidi tossed an infantryman into the air, then caught it in her palm — "usually dominated the board."

Emma reached for the infantryman.

Heidi drew her hand back and gave her counterpart a teasing grin. "Ah ah ah! You'll have to seize India to get this guy!" She made a flourish of stationing the piece on India.

"No." Emma shook her head, drawing in a shaky breath. "No. There are rules." She slid her chair back and cast a nervous glance at Ducie. It was as if she wanted to leave the room but hadn't the heart to leave Ducie with Heidi. She began to tug at her scarf.

Something had just gone dreadfully wrong. Heidi stood and reached toward Emma. "I'm sorry. I didn't mean to upset you."

"You don't throw the infantryman!" Emma jerked away and gave Heidi an offended glare, emphasized by a yank on her scarf.

"Emma, I —"

"You can leave now." A definitive male voice sliced through the air.

Heidi's eyes collided with the commanding expression of a very protective older brother. There was nothing else to do but agree.

CHAPTER 13

"So, what's it like working for my brother-in-law?" Heidi's attempt at conversation fell flat.

Rhett didn't respond. He didn't even blink.

Heidi had boggled everything. From her attempts at smoothing things over with Emma to her awkward exit from the Crawford home after Rhett told her — in no uncertain terms — he would drive her to the repair shop to get her car that had been mended to the point of being drivable.

Rhett's truck bounced over a pothole as he drove her into town. Hopefully, Brad had supervised the repairs to her car, because if Rhett had worked on it, Heidi couldn't be sure the man wouldn't sabotage something and make it careen off a cliff just to be rid of her.

Sheesh! Heidi bit back a sigh and looked out the window at the trees whizzing by as the truck made its way toward town. This was why she wanted to avoid Pleasant Valley and her family — people like Rhett Crawford. She became a very pronounced King Midas, but instead of everything she touched turning to gold, it all turned into chaos. It'd happened several times during her preteen years, and those incidents seemed to set the stage for her future. Mom had gotten her a job at the church, volunteer of course, but helping stuff church bulletins and manage the little library. The time she'd put the books back on the shelves by alphabetization instead of some numeric system was bad enough. It'd sent the other elderly volunteer lady into a complete tailspin of disorganization. Worse was the time Heidi had inadvertently stuffed the church bulletins with half-sheet copies of the invitations for a surprise birthday party for the head deacon and ruined the surprise when he opened the bulletin Sunday morning along with everyone else. The actual half-sheet announcement page she'd stuffed in the church members' mailboxes. Hey, at least they'd gotten the weekly activities. Yet the head deacon hadn't gotten his surprise birthday. They were both minor mishaps in the scheme of preteen life, but Heidi could still remember the look of frustration and disappointment in her mother's eyes. The shake of her head. The "When will you start taking things seriously?" question.

Now? Here she was. Years later. In a town her family called home but she had never been to. Perched on the front seat of a beat-up truck next to a man who had every right not to trust her — or like her. Heidi could only think of one way to try to smooth it over, and that was to talk her way out of it. Like she did most everything. Infuse the situation with humor and warmth and hope she could crack the hard shell of the person opposite her. Outside of wit, she didn't have much else to offer.

Heidi stole a glance at Rhett. His baseball cap was firmly squashed onto his head, and his square jaw was so sharp she wondered if he was clenching his teeth. Riding next to the gargantuan mechanic was like trying to become BFFs with the Incredible Hulk.

"I'm glad Brad had you get my car towed and fixed. I tried changing my oil once," she rambled, hoping to garner a smile, a blink, a nod, really anything from the man. "That was an epic fail. I ended up with oil all over the carport, and my landlord was not happy. But, I tried. Right? Bonus points for trying?"

She gave her head a fun-loving little toss.

No response.

Archie the cat stared at her from his well-balanced-and-yet-precarious position on the deep dash of the truck. Rüger sat beside her, his nose tipped up and staring forward as if to perfectly imitate his master.

"So, do you sing?" Heidi leaned forward and flipped the knob on the radio. A classic rock song warbled through awful speakers.

Oh, there was a reaction. Rhett reached out and switched the music off.

She eyed him.

"Sometimes," Heidi goaded, "sometimes I wish I had a pocketful of glitter I could pull out and just toss into the air when I'm around people like you. You need a little sparkle in your life, Mr. Rhett Crawford."

Sideways glance.

The truck bounced again, and Heidi lurched upward, grabbing for something to hold on to.

She grabbed his arm.

And released it.

He might as well have been made of hot lava, which wouldn't make sense 'cause his arm was as hard as a rock.

"You don't like glitter, I suppose." This was exhausting. *He* was exhausting. Pleasant Valley was the epitome of exhausting, as it made her oh so aware of how inept she was at anything real or deep in life.

"What do you do for fun? I like to sing karaoke. Do you have a karaoke bar? We should sing together." Heidi did a little mime-jive to an imaginary song.

God help her. She was annoying herself.

She slouched back against the truck's seat. "Why are you named Rhett? Your mom go all *Gone With the Wind* on you?"

Rhett's knuckles whitened on the steering wheel. His chest rose in a deep breath.

"Oh, for the love of Pete, say something!" Heidi rolled her eyes at the man.

He glanced at her. "What do you want me to say?"

Finally. He had a voice.

"Anything. Answer any of my questions."

He reached up and adjusted the brim of his cap. "I don't work for your brother-in-law. No bonus points for trying to change your own oil. If you didn't know how, it was dumb to try. No, I don't sing. Glitter can go to the lake of fire. I work for fun. We do have a karaoke bar. My mother named me Rhett because it was my grandfather's name. I've no clue what *Gone With the Wind* is."

Rhett's lips closed. Tight.

Rüger gave Heidi's elbow a nudge. She lifted her hand and set it on the dog's head,

184

scratching behind his ear. Every ounce of ambition to save herself, the moment, and her time here in this town deflated as quickly as if Rhett had reached out and stuck a needle into a balloon.

She couldn't help the shaky breath that escaped her. Heidi turned her head toward the window. A gas station. A run-down billboard for Kramer Logging. An old Methodist church that looked as though it'd been built in the late nineteenth century, with a wing added on in the 1940s.

Rhett coughed.

Archie's feline tail lifted from his perch on the dash and then laid as soft and soundless as a feather dropping onto the floor.

Rüger rested his nose on Heidi's leg.

At least the dog liked her. And, even better, she hadn't tried to kill this one.

The absurdity of her first thirty-six hours in Pleasant Valley was as ironic as the name of the historic logging town.

"Emma has autism."

Rhett's words ripped through the cab's silence. He waved to someone on the sidewalk by the post office.

"Your mom told me last night." Heidi left her response at that. There really wasn't much else to say without getting herself into a deeper hole.

"She's adapted well and can hold her own alongside any of us."

Heidi nodded. It was the safest thing to do.

Rhett gave her a sideways look. "But routine and processes are important. So is not talking a mile a minute about random crap."

Got it.

No talking.

Heidi bit the inside of her bottom lip and widened her eyes at Archie, who stared at her with yellow orbs as if trying to read her mind.

She decided to try another approach.

"I'm sorry." The words came out in a whisper. Mostly because those pesky emotions crowded her throat and didn't let her voice it louder.

Rhett steered the truck down a side street. "I get that you feel bad, but . . ."

The word hung between them.

But.

But, we don't know you.

But, you just had your room busted into and graffitied.

But, you're irresponsible.

But, you're reckless.

But, you have no life.

Heidi looked out the windshield as they

pulled into the lot of the repair shop.

Rhett's Auto Shop.

She shrank into her seat. And there was the rotten cherry on top of old, frosted ice cream. She thought Rhett worked for her brother-in-law, Brad. Apparently it was the other way around.

Heidi gave her head a subtle shake as she reached for the door handle. It would be best to get out of the truck now. Away from Rhett Crawford.

Heck. It would be best to get out of Pleasant Valley.

Heidi stopped at the local grocery store, Vicki's list on an app in her phone. Basics like bananas, eggs, milk, and the main staple of all Wisconsin refrigerators, cheddar cheese. She eyed the front dented fender of her car as she rounded it and headed for the store. Apparently, Rhett hadn't charged her labor for the repairs — which was odd considering he didn't like her — and he'd allowed Brad to fix it at cost for parts. But he'd also made it clear that body work wasn't going to be part of any deal. Not that she had the cash to pay for it. She'd tossed the invoice for the parts onto the front passenger seat. It stared up at her with its big, black numbers. A couple hundred dollars too much to begin with, and with the deductible on her insurance, that wasn't going to be her saving grace.

Inside the store, she began piling the items into a grocery cart. Vicki might have given her a list, but she hadn't given her cash or a credit card. Apparently, this was to be one of Heidi's contributions for staying at Lane Lodge.

This and the texted reminder to: *Stop and see Mom again today. I can't make it, and we try to visit her daily.*

Heidi reached for a group of organic bananas, then thought better of it and opted for the cheaper bananas that probably had been doused in pesticides.

No one will talk to me, Mom's letter had read. *It's time. The thoughts are driving me mad.*

This from a woman who, according to Vicki, received daily visits? Heidi's breath quivered as she sucked it in and rolled her cart beyond the bananas.

Mad. The handwriting on her mirror was an ironic and disturbing follow-up to the letter from her mother, which had compelled her to come to Pleasant Valley in the first place. If the woman wasn't kept in a memory-care facility with locked doors and around-the-clock surveillance, a strange part of Heidi would be suspicious that *Mom* had broken into the lodge and lipstick-wrote on her mirror.

But to what end? And why the recurring theme of madness — so not a politically correct term anymore, by any means — and, if Heidi were being honest, insulting.

She gripped the handle of the cart tighter to quell the tremble in her hands. She looked around for the self-checkout but only saw six aisles with three of them manned by cashiers. One of them was an older woman, with permed gray hair and wire-framed glasses. She smiled and waved Heidi over. Solid, small-town friendliness.

"Hello, dear!" she greeted, reaching for the dozen eggs Heidi put on the belt.

Heidi nodded and continued unloading her items.

"You're new here. I've not met you before."

Heidi mustered a smile. This was a good distraction. If only her family were half as welcoming. "Heidi Lane. My sister owns —"

"Lane Lodge! Yes! Brad and Vicki! Such lovely people. We go to church together. You'll have to tell them Jean said hi."

"I will," Heidi nodded. *Lovely people.* The description didn't match Vicki. Brad, sure

— he'd always been nice. But Vicki?

"Mylanta." Jean clucked her tongue as she *bleep*ed the UPC printed on a loaf of bread. "It has sure been a rough one this past year. What with your mom, Loretta, and all? You never know how fast dementia is going to take one's memories." She bleeped a bottle of ketchup. "I know it's just about eaten your sister alive. How are you handling things, dear?"

Heidi reached behind her head and pulled her hair back into a ponytail minus the hair band, then released it to fall in blond-and-blue strands. She wasn't sure how to respond.

"Never mind." Jean waved her off and hit a button on the register. "I've no filter. I'm sure it's been just as hard for you."

She quoted the total, and Heidi looked for the chip reader on the credit-card terminal.

"Just swipe it, honey. We don't have those newfangled things yet."

Heidi did so.

"Anyways," Jean chattered on, "are you here for good or just short term?"

Heidi waited for her receipt to print. "I'm — not sure."

"Makes sense." Jean nodded, even though it really didn't. She ripped the receipt from its feeder. "Well, you need to take some time and make sure you see the sights too. I know Pleasant Valley isn't all that much, but Vicki will keep you occupied with stuff to do until the good Lord comes, if you're not careful."

Heidi laughed out loud this time. "That she will."

Jean gave her a knowing smile. "Yes. So, you make sure you see our three sites of interest. There are the Copper Falls about forty minutes north of here. Beautiful waterfalls and a nice, easy hike along the trails. You'll want to see Statue Park. An old resident of Pleasant Valley made metal statues with all sorts of recycled bits of things. Sort of artsy-fartsy, I guess you'd say. And then, Valley Heights Asylum." Jean nodded and gave Heidi a mysterious grin. "That place is as haunted as they come. Have you heard the story of Misty Wayfair?"

"I've heard of her." Heidi reached for the plastic handles on the grocery bags and lowered them into the cart. "But, I'm not real familiar with her, or the asylum."

Even so, she was interested. Very interested. She hadn't been in Pleasant Valley for more than three full days and Misty Wayfair's name was popping up everywhere, and now the second mention of the asylum.

"Oh!" Jean gave Heidi a wave of her hand.

"Well, then, before you go snooping around the asylum's remains, you need to see if Connie Crawford — have you met the Crawfords yet? — will have you over to meet her daughter, Emma. That girl knows all things about the asylum and Misty Wayfair. She has a mind like a bear trap, that girl. Brilliant young woman. She'll tell you all you need to know, if you're interested in that sort of thing."

Emma Crawford.

Heidi wheeled the cart out of the store. She was definitely interested, but going back to visit Emma would more than likely induce Rhett to charge her for the labor on her car.

She reached for her keys and hit the unlock button on the fob.

Heidi stopped.

Someone had slipped a small, white note card under her windshield wiper.

She looked around. There wasn't anyone in the lot other than a young mother pushing two screaming toddlers in a grocery cart.

Heidi grabbed the note and flipped it over. Her keys slipped from her fingers and clattered to the asphalt. She stared at the handwriting. Shaky, almost like an elementary student just learning their letters had written it with a pencil.

Are you as mad as I?

That wicked curling of weight around Heidi's chest made her fall against her car. Her heart pounded in her ears, and she took two, three, four quick breaths. Heidi ran her palm across her cheek and raked agitated fingers through her hair. She rammed the note card into her purse.

She wasn't mad. She never had been. *Never.*

But the furious pounding in her chest and the spots dancing in her eyes made Heidi question herself. It was why she was here, after all, wasn't it? The anxiety, the debilitating sense of helpless panic that had spiraled her into losing job after job, leaving behind an unfinished college education, and bringing her to her sister's to stand in the shadow of her critical eye?

No, she wasn't crazy, or insane, or any other demeaning term.

She was just Heidi Lane. An anxiety-ridden woman who hid behind a façade of "You only have one life to live." Her excuse for her failures.

Jean's words echoed in her mind. The asylum. A place for people who had lost their minds and couldn't function in the real world. For a moment, such a place actually sounded like a reprieve. An escape from having to pretend that some days, just functioning with a logical, coherent thought was an exercise of tenacity in and of itself.

Heidi stared at the note card that peeked up at her from her purse.

Was she mad?

Someone else seemed to think and imply she was. Someone unknown. As unknown but also as eerily familiar as the woman who'd stared through her window. Someone who looked like her. Heidi swallowed a knot in her throat. Someone who looked like the dead woman in the photograph.

Heidi's thoughts twisted and turned in her head. They were chaotic and overwhelming as she pondered them.

Maybe the woman had never really been there after all.

Maybe if she were to look harder at the picture, the woman wouldn't resemble her so much anymore.

Perhaps . . . whoever had left the note card knew something Heidi didn't. That she *was* mad. That these panic attacks felt like a sheer loss of mental control, even though logically Heidi knew they weren't.

So, she did what she did every other time it became too much to process, too suffocating to manage through, and too dark to see beyond. Heidi ran. She dropped her purse,

left her keys, her car, and the groceries. And
Heidi ran.

left her keys, her car, and the shoe rack. And Heidi ran.

CHAPTER 14

THEA

Her room was cold. The chilling type of cold that seeped into her bones and her muscles. Damp aching that lingered long after she had snuffed out the lamp and settled beneath the sheet and light blanket provided by Mrs. Brummel in her boarding-house bed. Thea tossed and turned, the bedding coming untucked and tangled around her body. She needed peace, even a precarious peace. For all her fascination and curiosity with the lives and stories of others, hers was one she often wished could be tossed on a pile of banned literature and begun again. The asylum loomed large in the back of her mind. The question of her mother and if she were in any way related to that dark place. And Mrs. Amos's counsel had left her questioning. If she found herself, would she still be lost somehow? A conundrum that seemed spiritual and elusive at the same time. Was one's purpose defined by knowing who they were, where they were from, or by something — Someone — greater?

Coming back to her room at night brought little peace and comfort. There was a darkness here, in Pleasant Valley. A spirit that lingered in the air, embracing its inhabitants, sinking into one's soul like an uninvited guest entered a home and refused to leave. Something was out of place, and the people of Pleasant Valley seemed to know it. Keeping to themselves, smiling little, separated by a street, a history, and worst of all, a legend.

Misty Wayfair.

The name seemed to whisper into Thea's dreams. She was awake, and yet Thea wasn't entirely sure she wasn't dreaming at the same time. In the night's stillness, she twisted herself free from the blankets, swinging her legs over the side of the bed and resting her bare feet on the wood floor. She lifted her face to the lone window. The moon shone through, patterns of shadows from the curtains dancing on the floor and across Thea's skin. She watched them, mesmerized for a moment, reaching out to touch the shadow on the back of her hand. As if a ghost had entered her room, kissing her skin with a chilled touch, a shadowy spell, calling to her.

Misty Wayfair.

Thea rose, her white nightgown falling around her ankles. She moved to the window, reaching out to push the curtain aside. The street was silent, the buildings dark forms in the moonlight. Beyond the street and the deserted workplaces, the river flowed in the distance. Its waters glistened and called to Thea with a restless abandonment. Beyond lay the forest — the *asylum's* forest.

She heard it again. So small, so soft that Thea blinked, trying to awaken herself fully. Trying to convince herself she wasn't dreaming.

Misty Wayfair.

Her gaze drifted back to the river, to the stable, the blacksmith's shop, down the empty street toward the portrait studio, and the whitewashed post office.

"Misty Wayfair." The words were Thea's own whisper this time.

For she saw her now.

Alone in the street, the lithe figure of a woman floated. Her feet touched the ground, but it seemed that, in the moonlight, she was transparent, glowing in white. Her gown fluttered around her legs as she gave a slow turn in the empty street, her arms stretched out as though attempting to fly away on the clouds of death. Hair the color of burnt embers floated around her shoulders, the strands thick and filmy.

Thea's breath held in her chest, stopped by a heavy weight, unable to lift, to breathe around the pressure. The windowpane felt cool against her forehead as she strained to peer up the street where the woman twirled again, as if waltzing to an unknown sonata. Around and around she twirled, her head tipping back, her face lifting to the night sky like a bird set free.

Thea pressed the palm of her left hand against the glass. The vision was mesmerizing. Not only in her midnight beauty, but with the grace in which she traveled down the road. The rocks, the sticks, the animal droppings, and the rubble did not seem to affect her feet. Nighttime was her friend, embracing her with a welcome she received from no one else.

"Misty . . ." Thea whispered. Her breath fogged the windowpane.

Below the boardinghouse, Misty froze. Startled. Her dancing ceased and was traded instead for the stiffening of her shoulders. Her hands lowered to her sides. She stared up the street from where she'd come, afraid, as if someone were hunting her.

Thea watched, her throbbing heart louder than the tiny breaths that escaped her nose.

Misty clutched the front of her nightgown, pulling it into her chest and up her legs in a frantic, frightened gesture. Her legs were thin and pale, almost inhumanly so.

In that moment, Thea sensed it too. An imminent danger. The form of fear a prey might feel as an owl swooped from the branches, its claws fully extended to skewer through skin, lift the body, and carry it away. The deep horror a person could sense in their soul, when a foreboding came over them, oppressive and dark. The knowing it was coming. *It* being defined as the circumstance that would grasp hold of a being's peace and squeeze it until it shattered into shards of irreparable glass.

"Run." The word filtered through Thea's lips, through the glass, and somehow . . . Misty Wayfair heard it.

She lifted her face, shadowed as the moon cowered behind a cloud as one would cover one's face from the sight of something horrible. Misty's eyes were deep and dark, though it was impossible to make out specific features in the night. Her cheeks were gaunt, as hollows in the face of one who rarely eats. But etched into every nuance of her form, every shadow on her face, was fear. A stiffening, immobilizing fear.

Thea's gaze locked onto the phantom-like sight. Her throat tightened. It was time. Time to catapult this vision from her frigid state.

"Run," Thea urged. Her voice was just above a whisper, but she palmed the glass, rattling the panes in its frame. "Run."

A questioning look from the shadowy being.

She lingered there, a moment of time positioned between peace and fear, a connection of souls, and then . . .

Misty Wayfair ran.

"We'll need a fern."

Thea startled and juggled a vase she'd lifted from a shelf. It tossed in the air and fell to its demise on the wood floor, shattering in shards of blue ceramic. Pip hissed, arched his back, and glared at her with judgmental eyes.

"For all that's holy!" Mr. Amos blustered past her, snatching up a broom that leaned against the wall. "I asked for a fern. What're you so jumpy for?"

"I'm sorry." Thea stepped aside as he swept the shards into the corner. She couldn't shake the darkness from the night before. The sight she'd seen, or *thought* she'd seen. So surreal she questioned if she had perhaps been dreaming.

Mr. Amos looked up at her, clouded blue eyes under bushy eyebrows of gray. A moment's study and then he shook his head. "Never mind. I didn't like that vase anyway." He leaned the broom against the wall again, then skewered her with a look. "Your mind's not with it today."

Thea swallowed a nervous lump in her throat. If she told the old man about Misty Wayfair, he'd only mock her. A man of faith, he wouldn't believe she'd seen the ghost — the legendary ghost — who haunted the Coyles in retribution for thwarted love.

A shaft of sunlight spread through the window and across the floor. Thea stepped into it. Anything light, anything pure was calming to her frayed nerves.

"Well?" Mr. Amos barked.

Thea blinked. "Pardon?"

"Never mind." Mr. Amos turned his eyes to the ceiling. "I already live with a woman with her head in the clouds, what's the difference if I work with one too?"

His words were cutting, but then Thea noticed the twitch of his mustache and quick wink as he brushed past her.

Thea offered him a weak smile. No. She couldn't explain last night. Misty Wayfair, her shadowed features that Thea couldn't even remember the details of, and the odd dance down the main street of town. She'd had a dream once as a child that Mrs. Mendelsohn had been angry with her. When Thea had asked Mrs. Mendelsohn, the older woman had told her she'd not been angry and they'd never argued. A dream. But so real of a dream.

Perhaps that explained Misty Wayfair. Perhaps the unsettling visit to the asylum, following Simeon Coyle through the woods, the vision across the river of a bare-legged woman — perhaps all of it compounded with each other until they became half-real, half-imagined circumstances.

Mr. Amos was right. Her mind wasn't with it today.

Thea straightened her shoulders and drew in a steadying breath. Mr. Amos groused in the corner, fumbling with equipment. The man's shoulders appeared more hunched today, perhaps borrowing from some unknown stress. Simeon perhaps. She'd seen him exit the portrait studio again, early this morning. This time, Mr. Amos had walked with him, toward the asylum, and had not returned for over two hours. That she'd gained entrance to the studio was made possible because of a note Mr. Amos had left her, and the fact he apparently trusted her and the town enough to leave the door unlocked.

Thea determined to busy herself with work she'd been doing before the vase had shattered and she'd turned into an immobilized statue herself. She scooted a waist-high podium, Greek in style, wood made to look like marble, a few feet to the right. Bending, she hoisted a potted fern onto its platform.

Mr. Amos coughed, the hacking rattle of an old man, as he dragged a chair next to the plant. He stood back, hands at his waist. "That'll do."

"The photograph is of a family?" Thea inquired. He'd told her earlier, but she'd forgotten in her preoccupation with forgetting everything else.

His lips pursed. "No."

It was more than apparent that the photographer was not welcoming the forthcoming visitor. Thea gave him a studious look. Mr. Amos ignored her.

"Who is it, then?" she finally asked when it became obvious Mr. Amos was not going to offer it.

"Kramer Logging's Mr. Edward Fortune,"

Mr. Amos supplied.

The memory of Mrs. Amos's brief history about the nephew who'd inherited Kramer Logging instead of the Coyles came to mind. Thea raised a thin eyebrow. "*The* Mr. Fortune?"

"That's what I said, didn't I?" Mr. Amos readjusted the plant on its stand.

"Why does he need his portrait taken?" Thea tipped her head in question, struggling to come to terms with the idea that in a few moments she would be meeting the man who had come into the Coyles' rightful inheritance.

"How should I know?" Mr. Amos strode past her and headed toward the back room. Thea followed, curiosity getting the better of her good sense and by no means stilling her tongue.

"And he was Mr. Kramer's nephew?" She tried to let Mrs. Brummel's gossipy sketch of the Coyle family history fall into place in her mind.

Mr. Amos made a pretense of raising a sandwich to gobble before Mr. Fortune came for his sitting. He nodded, his mustache twitching as he took a bite, chewed, and swallowed. "Nephew by marriage. When things turned sour with Kramer's daughter, Mathilda, and after the whole

Misty Wayfair debacle, Edward stepped up to help. But don't be fooled. He's no saint. Everything about that family is a shame. That logging company shoulda been Simeon's."

The final words were a muttered growl.

Thea hesitated, but then dared to ask, "Would Simeon have wanted it?"

Mr. Amos's head shot up. "Who knows? But he wasn't given the chance, now, was he? Suffered for the sins of his grandparents — sins or choices, doesn't matter."

"Does Mr. Fortune seem at all apologetic to the Coyles?" Thea crossed her arms over her chest and watched as Mr. Amos fiddled with his napkin.

He groused under his breath, but finally answered. "Doubtful. He took over the company before Simeon was born. Never seemed to try to set things to right. Maybe he doesn't even know exactly what happened. It was all a mess."

An idea came to Thea's mind. It was so simple, almost strange to consider. "So, Simeon would have been a logging baron if his grandmother Mathilda Kramer hadn't —"

"Hadn't married Fergus Coyle?" Mr. Amos stopped and gave Thea a direct stare. "Yes." His eyes dimmed, and he looked toward the back window in the direction of the asylum. "Time changes what one values. And with Simeon's sister, Mary, just passed on . . . it's not as though a pair of orphaned siblings even care about a logging company anymore."

Mr. Amos sniffed, then turned back and gave Thea an honest nod. "Simeon and Rose have only each other. The last of the Coyles. The last of the Kramers, for that matter. Half the town wants to blame Misty Wayfair for that. No one points a finger at Edward Fortune. He got the lucky end of the whole sordid tale."

Mr. Amos cleared his throat, breaking himself from his musings. He waved her off, although Thea said nothing.

"Simeon and Rose, they haven't much future really. Death has a way of dealing its hand when you least expect it. I rather believe it's all poppycock, but folks say Misty will come to claim them too. It's just the way of it with the Coyles. Misty Wayfair won't be at rest until every last one of them has passed on and joined her."

CHAPTER 15

Mr. Edward Fortune was indeed a debonair and cultured man who seemed misplaced in the small backwoods town of Pleasant Valley. He wasn't unkind; rather he was indifferent. As indifferent to Thea as she was to the fern that framed Mr. Fortune in the photograph. That the owner of Kramer Logging was accustomed to getting his way was apparent by the simple fact he all but told Mr. Amos where he would stand, how he would position himself, and at what angle he wished the portrait to be taken.

Mr. Amos blustered about. He was perturbed — annoyed even — and he was barely concealing it.

"This plant needs removing, if you will." Mr. Fortune gave a haphazard wave of his hand. "Ridiculous greenery is completely unnecessary."

Mr. Amos gave Thea a silent glare, and she hurried to do Mr. Fortune's bidding.

She wished she could exchange places with Mr. Amos and take the photograph herself. Although she wouldn't mind a postmortem of Mr. Fortune.

Thea hid her wince.

That was unkind.

Yet, as she removed the plant, she couldn't help but picture the entitled logging baron hoisted on her metal frame, gray and unmoving. It wasn't the most awful thing she'd conjured in her mind, though she had no intentions of driving the man to his death. Still, it seemed highly unfair that, for whatever reason, Misty Wayfair found it necessary to haunt the Coyles when really Mr. Fortune was the one who had inadvertently ruined it for all them.

"Very good."

The approval of Mr. Fortune did nothing for Thea's ego, and she wasn't interested in what Mr. Fortune might or might not think of her. She was itching to stand where Mr. Amos stood, behind the camera, peering through the lens and calculating the overall schematic appeal.

"I do have meetings to attend to, so if we could take this portrait posthaste," Mr. Fortune announced to the room with a pointed, blue-eyed stare beneath a crown of gray hair.

"Certainly," Thea murmured when Mr. Amos made no effort to respond.

"And," Mr. Fortune continued, now having an audience, "I would like to have the portrait developed and delivered as soon as possible. It is a gift for my wife."

"Mr. Fortune, I must ask that you stop talking." Mr. Amos stood behind the tripod, having slipped a plate into its slot. His mouth quirked in an irritated scowl. Thea knew he was soon ready to uncap the lens. The light would filter through and the picture collide with the wet chemical on the plate. Lack of movement was a must.

"My apologies," Mr. Fortune muttered without sincerity.

Thea tried to fathom how this man was a distant relative to the Coyles. But it was impossible. They were so different.

Mr. Fortune's expression changed from posed to alarm.

Thea spun as she heard Mr. Amos's gargling cry. He grabbed at his arm, staggered, and crumpled to the floor in a heap. His legs tangled with the legs of the tripod, which wobbled and toppled to the floor in a wild shatter of wood and glass.

"Mr. Amos!" Thea raced to his side, dropping beside him on the floor. His eyes were closed, his face a grayish hue that boded no good.

"Go fetch the doctor!" she shouted over her shoulder at Mr. Fortune.

"Mr. Amos." Thea patted his cheek, whiskers rough beneath her palm. He was unresponsive, and she hadn't a clue what to do. When Mr. Mendelsohn had dropped dead not long ago, she'd merely stood beside his form, staring down in utter shock and — ashamedly — relief. But there was an urgency in her blood now. The kind that came from the tiny roots of affection that had formed for the cranky old photographer.

"Please!" she begged Mr. Fortune.

The logging baron seemed frozen in place. In shock perhaps, or maybe from sheer bewilderment at the sudden shift of events and inconvenience to his day.

There was a scuffling. The back-room door yanked open and slammed against the wall. Footsteps pounded across the wooden floor. A person knelt beside her. The instant waft of cedarwood and sawdust met her nose, and Thea's shoulder was brushed by another's.

Simeon.

"For all that's holy — !" Mr. Fortune

exclaimed on seeing his much-younger cousin.

Simeon ignored the man, and while fumbling to loosen Mr. Amos's tie, he commanded Thea's attention with his eyes. His face gave a severe twist, and she had to focus on his words to understand him.

"The doctor is four blocks down toward the boardinghouse. Turn right at the corner and head for the white two-story building next to the tannery."

Thea nodded.

"Go," he insisted.

Thea scampered to her feet. The toe of her shoe stepped on her hem, tripping her. She grabbed at Simeon's shoulder to steady herself and keep from falling atop Mr. Amos.

Simeon's warm hand encased hers, stabilizing her as she rose. Thea felt calluses on his palm. The heat of his fingers wrapped tight around hers. One more concerned look from him, as if unsure whether she was capable of fetching the doctor, and then he dropped his grip.

Thea raced for the door, sidestepping the shattered remnants of Mr. Amos's camera. She ignored the burning sensation of a tear as it whisked down her cheek. The sound of her shoes clomping along the boardwalk.

Dodging a few townsfolk who eyed her with question as she increased her pace to a sprint.

Mr. Amos.

This wasn't about the past, not even about the future. It was right now. The present.

But for some reason, the old photographer's words from earlier resonated like a horrific echo in Thea's ears.

"Death has a way of dealing its hand when you least expect it."

Thea rounded the corner and saw the two-story building as Simeon had described. Yes. Death was stealthy and swift, and when Death bit, it left a wake of unfinished business in its path. It touched them all, and apparently it would touch them again today.

The interior was as dim as Thea's emotions. A lone lantern flickered on the middle of the table in the back room of Amos Bros. Photography. Crickets chirruped their consistent warble outside, conflicting with the pattern her fingers drummed on the table. She sucked in a deep breath, staring down at the photograph she held in her other hand. The faces of Rose and Mary Coyle stared back at her. She'd mounted it on cardboard this afternoon with shaking insides and a mind preoccupied with a crotchety old photographer clinging to life. Since she couldn't very well sit at Mr. Amos's bedside, she'd returned to the studio to clean up the shattered remains of the camera and to try to calm herself.

Mr. Amos hadn't died. Yet. Thea ran her thumb over the image of Mary's face. So cold, so lifeless. God save her from having to take his postmortem photograph!

What was this place, Pleasant Valley? Yes, she had traveled with the Mendelsohns, finding economics where others drowned in sorrow. Yes, she had convinced herself that offering photographs such as these would bring comfort — and they would — to the families left behind. But never had she allowed herself to learn their stories.

She cared for Mr. Amos. If even just a little. Watching a man grapple for breath, clutch at his chest, and then lay in the pre-pallor of a deceased condition was traumatic. It was why she hid here — hid from the ghost of Misty Wayfair, from the vague memory of her mother. Mr. Amos's collapse was an illustration of life itself. It would all be brought to a sudden end . . . and then what?

Thea startled as the back door opened. The sound of the river flowing in the distance was accompanied by a swatch of moonlight.

Simeon entered, saying nothing, and shut the door behind him.

For some reason, she wasn't surprised he'd found her here. There was some unspoken thread between them, something that defined them, as though they were walking a parallel journey that intersected, if just for a moment, in life.

He neared the table, removed his hat, and set it down next to the lantern. The chair's legs scraped against the floor as he tugged it out and sat. He seemed at peace, for now. There was no tic in his face, his shoulders were level, and his body calm. Still, Simeon said nothing. He sat opposite her, his hands folded on the tabletop.

Silence.

Thea heard him breathe softly, matching hers breath for breath. Each of her hands held a corner of the Coyle sisters' photograph. Now was hardly the time to slip it across the table to him. Not with Mr. Amos's condition hovering over the shop. She did it anyway.

Faces up, Thea pushed the cardboard rectangle across the table.

Simeon stared at it in the dim lantern light.

She watched his face. It was resigned. He

didn't lift the photograph, nor did he touch it.

Instead, he said, "It will be touch and go for a while. Mr. Amos is not well." Simeon's thumbs tapped together as his fingers interlocked with each other and his hands rested on the table. "There are services he renders to the asylum." His eyes raised to meet hers. "If you're willing, your help would be a kindness."

"What kind of services?" Thea ventured, though she thought she already knew.

Simeon dropped his gaze back to his folded hands. His right hand twitched upward, then relaxed. His cheek muscle jumped.

The photograph lay between them, like a third being in the room, daring them to speak of it.

Simeon cleared his throat. "There are patients — record keeping hasn't been good. Dr. Ackerman requested we take photographs of each patient, so we can log their names, dates of admission, and —"

"Dates of departure?" Thea understood. Departure meant death. No one was admitted to a hospital with a troubled mind and left renewed and healed.

Simeon gave a short nod. "Yes."

"Are they the ones in your album?"

He studied her face for a moment. "They are."

Thea sucked in a small breath, blowing it through her nose softly in a stifled sigh. She looked at the wall, just above Simeon's shoulder. "Does no one come to visit?"

"The patients?" Simeon's voice rose a tad, enough to call Thea's attention back to his face. It was scrunched in a scowl, then fell back into place. "No," he replied. "No one visits."

Thea nodded, taking in the short answer weighted with such depth, such pain that she sensed the agony in the core of her being. She had no desire to return to Valley Heights Asylum. Not to the gates, and certainly not beyond them.

But a distinct memory traversed her mind, and the words of Mrs. Amos, indicative that her mother very well might be tied to that place, were unforgettable. Her mother. She'd been wearing a dark cloak that day. It was worn on the hemline, with tiny threads trailing along the walk as she'd left Thea on the orphanage steps. Like a tiny trail of tears as the bond between mother and daughter permanently ripped apart.

"Do you know — was there ever a woman by the name of Reed at the asylum?"

At her question, Simeon reached out and

drew the photograph of his sisters toward him. In that gesture, he seemed to acknowledge her own loss along with his. That tragedy of unanswered questions that lingered and was never resolved.

Why did melancholy claim his sister's last breath?

Why did her mother leave her behind?

"I've not worked at the asylum very long." Simeon shook his head. He turned the photograph over, to the blank side of the cardboard. "I know of none living there by that name."

His thumb rubbed over handwriting that Thea had forgotten she'd penned on the back of the picture's cardboard setting.

Misty Wayfair.

She blanched. She shouldn't have written it while she pondered the implications of the ghost and the Coyles' relationship. It was an absent-minded, grief-induced action she'd meant to correct before handing the photograph to its owners.

Simeon turned the picture over, not seeming stirred by his sister's death titled with their curse's name.

"None living?" Thea frowned, turning her attention to his denial of knowing her mother. His words implied death.

Simeon pushed back in his chair. He left

the photograph on the table and reached for his hat. Thea stood with him, matching his movements. He was finished with the conversation. She had made him uncomfortable, and he was preparing to take his customary flight.

"Simeon, please." Thea rounded the table quickly, without thought, and placed her hand on his arm. The touch commanded his attention. But, to her surprise, his wrist turned, and his fingers enclosed her forearm.

They stood in the dusky room, warmth of their hands spread through the thin sleeves of their clothing. Eyes locked. Chests rising and falling in the quiet breathing so carefully controlled and revealing tempestuous emotion beneath.

Simeon's hand tightened on her arm just as she lost her grip on his. He pulled, drawing her closer, secretively, as if even the walls would listen to his words. Long lashes framed his eyes, and as he blinked, they swept over cheeks that hinted at strength, in spite of the muscle that jumped in his jaw.

She could feel the warmth from his face as they stood shoulder to shoulder. A mere breath separated her from him, and in the space of that quiet moment, a lingering, a *yearning* passed between them.

He spoke, and she couldn't help but watch his mouth move.

"When they pass, they are unremembered," Simeon whispered. His carved lips moved with a gentle certainty that emphasized his words. "No one wishes to remember."

He looked past her to the table, to the photograph of his sister, Mary, then brought his eyes back to hers. "You have immortalized her on paper. Help me bring life to the others."

A stirring shifted within Thea. She closed her eyes, because the pleading in his was too much for her soul. Desperation. Too many souls lost in the shadows of the asylum, in the legends of Pleasant Valley, in the line of the Coyles. Too many stories never finished. A chapter just cut off, with no ending to bring resolution to the life of a person who had been born but whose life held no purpose.

"I do not want to find my mother there." Even as the words escaped her lips, Thea could almost see the truth of them suspended between Simeon's face and her own.

A whisper between them.

Simeon's eyes narrowed with feeling. He swallowed. His hand released her forearm and yet Thea stood rooted to the spot, her shoulder touching his, their faces turned toward each other.

"I know." His response was fraught with meaning, and Thea understood.

The stories she would uncover behind the walls of Valley Heights would not end pleasantly. For there were no happily-ever-afters in an asylum.

"What a shame. What a dreadful shame." Coffee poured from the kettle's spout as Mrs. Brummel filled Thea's cup. She was joined at breakfast by another boarder. A gentleman of smaller stature with a balding head and a mole just to the left of his nose. Mrs. Brummel moved to his cup and poured more of the dark liquid.

"Mr. Amos," she explained to the new-comer. "Dropped before Miss Reed's very eyes, he did." Mrs. Brummel hustled back toward the kitchen, chattering over her shoulder, "I saw Dr. Kowalski yesterday. He was quick to say it'll be touch and go for a bit. Poor Mrs. Amos, what with her arthritis and all."

Thea stirred some honey into her oatmeal. She would visit Mrs. Amos. Be sure the old woman was cared for. Maybe even attempt to help her clean or — or something. They couldn't be left on their own, with grown children miles away. They were too elderly, and Mr. Amos — his portrait studio would need tending. Perhaps that was how she could best help the couple who had, in a relatively short period of time, wheedled their way into her affections.

The man to the right of her spooned a bite into his mouth and said nothing, staring ahead as if reading something on the table. Only there was nothing to read.

Mrs. Brummel returned, her black skirts rustling on the floor as she sat down in front of her own meal. Thea questioned whether it was customary for a boardinghouse matron to eat along with her guests. But apparently, for Mrs. Brummel, she ran things however she pleased.

She reached for the small silver vessel of honey. Her sharp eyes swept over both Thea and the new guest. "Mr. Fritz," she goaded with a *click* of her tongue, "did you sleep well?"

"Yes, thank you," he mumbled politely, dipping his spoon for another bite.

"I'm sure you're wondering why all the bother about Mr. Amos." Mrs. Brummel scooped some raisins from a bowl and dropped them in her oatmeal.

Mr. Fritz's head came up, a bewildered expression on his face. Thea bit her lip to hide her smile. She was sure he wasn't wondering at all.

"While we're all horribly upset about Mr. Amos," Mrs. Brummel continued while shoveling her spoon into her bowl, "word has it that Edward Fortune was quite put out. Especially with the appearance of Simeon Coyle, who came to Mr. Amos's assistance."

Mrs. Brummel skewered Thea with a very direct look. "We're all quite confused as to why he was even there in the first place."

Thea's oatmeal went down her throat like a square block.

"Who is 'we'?" she countered, aware she sounded quite rude.

It earned her an appreciative glance from Mr. Fritz, and pursed lips from Mrs. Brummel.

"Why was Simeon Coyle there? Mr. Fortune stated he was quite unwelcome, and that in his malady Mr. Amos even tried to wave the man off."

"No!" Thea's spoon clattered to the saucer beside her bowl. "That isn't true. Simeon works —" She bit her tongue.

Mrs. Brummel's eyebrow had risen over her left eye, accentuating her angular features. Mr. Fritz had even stopped to look between them, now apparently interested in the little drama unfolding.

"Yes?" Mrs. Brummel prodded.

Thea folded her hands in her lap. This was all going very badly. "Simeon — was needed."

"Simeon." Mrs. Brummel clucked her tongue and shook her head. She waved her spoon in Thea's direction. "Do be careful, my dear. I'm not certain why you would be on such personal terms with any of the Coyles, and it is disturbing, to say the least, that it seems Mr. Amos has business with them. We all know the detriment that can bring."

"Detriment?" This time it was Mr. Fritz who inserted a question. He took a swallow of coffee. "I don't believe I understand."

"You wouldn't." Mrs. Brummel gave a sniff that indicated she would take it upon herself to inform him, even if it was distasteful to recall.

Thea wished to excuse herself but something rooted her in place.

The woman laid down her spoon and folded her hands primly. "The Coyles do not have a pleasant history. With luck or blessing." She shifted her eyes to Thea. "Their father passed several years ago. A freak accident when he fell from the loft in their barn and landed on a pitchfork."

Mr. Fritz blanched.

Mrs. Brummel continued the story of the Coyles just as though it were a story bandied about like common folklore. "Their mother passed, and not long after, so did the grandmother, Mathilda, leaving behind the three younger Coyles."

"And then Mary," Thea whispered without thinking.

Mrs. Brummel gave a quick nod. "Precisely. And as I told you when you first arrived, before any Coyle passes, Misty Wayfair is always spotted."

For added measure, Mrs. Brummel gave Mr. Fritz a thin smile. "She was murdered, Misty Wayfair was. She dares anyone to befriend the Coyles. Apparently wants to thwart them of love and friendship as she was. Very few have tried, and those who do either flee Pleasant Valley or . . ." She raised her brows pointedly. "Or they die. A shame really. One should never befriend a Coyle." She gave Thea a long look. "Be careful, Miss Reed. I would hate to see you follow in Mr. Amos's fate."

Thea rested her spoon beside her oatmeal. The feel of Simeon's breath on her face as he'd pulled her close. The realization she had already fallen into some sort of kinship with the Coyles, if for no other reason than

225

on Mr. Amos's behalf. And then came the vision of Misty Wayfair, dancing down the street, far less a ghostly vengeance and more a frightened spirit.

"Excuse me." Thea pushed back her chair and moved to exit the room.

"Well!" Mrs. Brummel's voice followed her. "Too late for that one, I'm afraid. Simeon Coyle has cast his spell, and mark my words, Misty Wayfair is sure to follow."

CHAPTER 16

HEIDI

It had been a week since her anxiety attack in the grocery store parking lot. A week since Brad had found her at the park down by the river, staring across it and into the forest beyond. A week since she'd pocketed the mysterious note and said nothing — to anyone. A week since Vicki had loaded her down with so many chores around the lodge, she hadn't time to consider anything but laundry, cleaning floors, checking in new guests, and retrieving extra TP on request. In a way, she was grateful. It was a distraction from the whirling what-ifs in her mind.

Heidi hadn't visited her mother once. She'd refused to open the old photo album. The mysterious note left on her windshield was still stuffed in the pocket of her jeans from that day. Maybe she should've called Detective Davidson or Officer Tate. Involved the police somehow. But, in the end, Heidi didn't want answers. She wanted to forget about it. To move on. Besides, she'd heard once that fingerprints were difficult to pull from paper, so what could the police even do?

Heidi snapped open a bedsheet and let the white cotton fall over the twin bed mattress. The cabin had been cleaned from top to bottom, and all that was left to do was put fresh linens on the bed and fluff pillows cased in red patchwork shams. It was the last cabin to be cleaned since the guests had checked out earlier in the morning. It was Sunday, and Brad and Vicki had gone to church. Heidi opted out. She wasn't sure her attending church would do anything but exacerbate old, hard feelings rather than bring the hope it espoused. She knew it was somewhat of an excuse, but for now, that niggling nausea of barely controlled worries in her stomach told her she couldn't afford more.

The sound of crunching gravel and a vehicle's engine stirred Heidi's attention. She gave the end of the bedsheet a quick tuck and fold under the mattress before moving to the window of the tiny cabin's kitchen.

Rhett Crawford and Emma.

Heidi studied the handsome profile of the mechanic. He really was something. Impressive, confident, commanding . . . and outright unlikable. But in a weird way, Heidi admired that about him. His unlikable nature was due to his protective guard over his sister, so it had merit. Heidi eyed him briefly before reaching for the door. If her family had shown an ounce of the loyalty Rhett showed Emma, how different might her life have been? She hesitated. If she'd shown any loyalty to her family . . .

She pushed open the screen door, the squeaking of its hinges drawing Rhett's attention from the front entrance to the lodge.

"Not churchgoers?" Heidi teased as she made her way across the circular drive. She hoped her smile more than made up for the way her heart picked up speed when Rhett looked her direction. Rüger, the dog, sniffed the ground and the grass by Rhett's feet.

Heidi focused on Emma, whose sideswept bangs and shoulder-length straight hair framed a face that was the feminine version of her brother's.

"We go to church." Emma's expression matched the sincerity behind her words. "Every Sunday. From eight in the morning till ten."

Heidi gave Emma a smile that welcomed

her as an equal. The younger woman could probably run circles of intelligence around her, and yet some people were determined to treat those with autism as different. She wouldn't be one of those people.

"Church is over, then?" Heidi gave Rhett a flicker of a smile but addressed Emma. That probably meant Brad and Vicki were on their way home.

"Don't you go to church?" Emma asked, her gaze direct and honest.

Heidi probably wouldn't have even squirmed at the question if Rhett hadn't been standing there, staring at her with an element of disinterest and vague suspicion all at the same time.

"I haven't been in a while," Heidi admitted to Emma, an apologetic nod accompanying it. She reached down and scratched Rüger's brown-and-tan fur that flopped between his eyes as he nudged her leg.

"You should come with us next week." Emma turned to Rhett. "We can give her a ride?"

Rhett shoved his hands in his pants' pockets. "If she wants to come, I'm sure Heidi can drive herself."

His words reminded Heidi of the car accident. She hid the twang of hurt at Rhett's snub and turned a bright smile on Emma,

230

changing the subject. "How is Ducie?"

Emma returned the smile. "He is good. His leg is healing."

Heidi couldn't help but feel relieved. "Wonderful!"

She kept her tone even, her words short. Regardless of how she felt about Rhett, his comment that too much chatter would be overwhelming for Emma had stuck in Heidi's memory. She wanted Emma to like her. For some reason, she longed for Emma's approval. Probably because she'd almost taken from the woman the one creature that brought her comfort. Heidi could relate. She almost wished she had a dog for a companion.

Heidi bent to give Rüger a healthy rub-down, relishing the feel of his longer hair, the warmth of his body. Yes, a dog might be just another creature to some, but Heidi could understand why they played such a vital role in people's lives. They were your friend — unconditionally.

"What brings you to Lane Lodge?" This time Heidi didn't try to avoid Rhett's eyes. In fact, she felt her chin tilt up and a tiny smile tease her lips. Almost challenging him to make her feel inferior or stupid.

He did neither. Just gave her a shrug instead. "Emma wanted to see you to ask if you'll play a game of Risk with her again sometime."

Warmth spread through Heidi. She reached out to give Emma's arm the lightest touch, but then drew back, unsure how Emma would respond to physical expression coming from someone other than family. "Thank you." She captured Emma's gaze. "I really mean that."

For a brief second, something passed between her and Emma. An understanding of sorts. A realization that for all their differences, they were also very similar.

Emma's eyes lit up, and she tugged at the scarf around her neck. "Can you come to my house? Tomorrow? Dad is going to be at work, and Mom was going to stay home, but I'd like you to come instead. Then Mom can go to work." She turned to Rhett, who looked completely caught off guard. "I'll be fine if Heidi is there."

For a man of few words, Rhett appeared to have misplaced the remaining bits of his vocabulary. He stared at Emma. Heidi could only assume it wasn't her usual behavior to trust someone she didn't know so quickly. Especially someone as prone to accidents as Heidi was, and the one responsible for turning Emma's ordered world upside down.

Feeling a bit daring and rather enjoying

the idea of stirring the pot, Heidi jumped in before he could formulate an excuse. "I would really enjoy that, Emma. I've no plans tomorrow."

She did actually, but she could catch up on the lodge's laundry after she got home.

"We'll see," Rhett finally said. It was a noncommittal response for Emma, and an obvious no for Heidi. What had seemed a gesture of reconciliation from Rhett to bring Emma here proved to fall short when faced with the reality of Emma's request coming to fruition.

"Seriously, I'm fine with helping out," Heidi pressed, not caring how Rhett felt. She owed the Crawfords — owed Emma — that much and more.

"We don't usually —" Rhett broke off when Emma interrupted, surprise registering in his eyes.

"I'll ask Mom." Emma spoke, and it was so.

Rhett worked his jaw back and forth and gave a little nod, his granite expression locked with hers, and Heidi saw the distrust in his eyes. Every particle of Heidi's being rose to the challenge. Just as she had when she was younger and her parents — Vicki — implied she was incapable or inadequate.

Sometimes the best way to counteract her

anxiety was outright, reckless stubbornness.

And if the title of Most Stubborn was at stake here, then Rhett Crawford had a war on his hands.

Heidi couldn't blame Connie for being reticent about leaving her alone with Emma. The fact of the matter was, they didn't really know her well, and leaving Emma with someone untrained to help care for her was a bit of a question as to how Emma might react once the familiar and trusted elements were removed. But, Emma had been adamant that Heidi come, Connie had stated on the phone. Adamant that she wanted Heidi there. To play Risk. So, day one had been a test day. Connie hadn't gone to work as Emma had suggested she could, but instead she worked outside in the yard in case anything was needed. The second day, on invite from Emma because she wanted a repeat, Connie had ventured to work. She had also snuck home three times to make sure things were going well. Heidi couldn't take offense to it. She wasn't a mother, but she was sure she'd have done the same thing. The last time home, Connie's shoulders visibly relaxed. They were fine. Emma was fine.

Heidi shifted in her seat again. It was the

third day in a row she had come, but she hadn't the heart to refuse, nor did she want to. Emma's company was refreshing. The game of Risk, however, was progressing well — for Emma. The board game was completely covered by her players, and Heidi was on the verge of surrendering Brazil. They hadn't done much beyond labor over the game, and they had reached a companionable silence. Ducie, with his cast-encased leg, was resting on the floor beside Emma, always eyeing Heidi with suspicion. Not unlike Rhett.

Heidi was growing restless. Sitting for hours playing a board game had been a blessed diversion at the start, yet she'd never been one to sit still for too long. Now that she'd come as well to collect her emotions and quell her anxiety, Heidi couldn't help but revisit her mother's letter.

She'd reread it that morning before coming to the Crawfords'.

We lived in a house of ghosts, the letter had said. *Unspoken voices. The past and the present colliding with such force, we could only survive by ignoring it.*

Please come.

Heidi, you are the reason the voices are never heard.

"Your move." Emma's voice split through

Heidi's subconscious.

"Oh!" Heidi hesitated. Jean, the cashier, had implied that Emma knew all sorts of old history about Pleasant Valley. The asylum, for starters. Was it coincidence her mother spoke of madness at the same time someone had seen fit to leave Heidi their creepy calling card? Officer Tate, the night of the break-in, hadn't seemed to dismiss Heidi's claim of seeing a woman looking through her window.

Misty Wayfair.

The name scrawled on the back of the antique photograph.

"Emma," she spoke before thinking it through, "do you know anything about the legend of Misty Wayfair?"

Emma blinked, then pulled on both sides of her infinity scarf, patterned with tiny little yellow dogs on a blue background. "Yes."

That's right. Closed-ended questions got a closed answer. Heidi restructured her question for Emma. "Would you tell me what you know about Misty Wayfair?"

Emma leaned back in her chair and draped her hand over the arm to brush the broad forehead of Ducie.

"Misty Wayfair died in 1851. She was the rumored lover of Fergus Coyle, who married Mathilda Kramer the day before Misty died."

Heidi frowned. "Kramer? As in Kramer Logging?"

Emma nodded, a proud smile touching her lips. "Dad has worked for Kramer Logging since 1985. Rhett was born a year later."

Emma's penchant for recalling dates was remarkable.

Heidi leaned forward, her elbow brushing a few infantrymen on the board, which toppled in their home space of Western Australia. "How is Misty Wayfair linked to the old asylum?"

Officer Tate had alluded to the ghost story the night of the break-in, but Heidi wanted Emma's factual interpretation of this lore, minus any personal superstition.

Emma thought for a moment, her eyes narrowing. She studied Heidi before reciting what she knew. "Some people say when she died, her spirit was trapped in the asylum and never released. Some say she wandered the forest and danced in the streets at night. But" — Emma's expression grew serious, stern almost, as if people's misinterpretation of the legend was offensive to her — "Misty Wayfair was always seen before a Coyle died."

Heidi frowned. Coyle. Fergus Coyle who'd married Mathilda Kramer.

"Who exactly are the Coyles?"

Emma smiled. "People who lived in Pleasant Valley."

A literal explanation for a generic question. Heidi tried again. "But, what are the Coyles remembered for?"

Emma's eyes brightened. "For Misty Wayfair."

It was a circular conversation. Without knowing what she was trying to uncover exactly, Heidi couldn't ask questions that would help her to understand more.

"Have you ever been to the asylum ruins?" Heidi ventured.

Emma gave her a long look. "No."

"Oh." Heidi readjusted her focus to the Risk board. She needed to drop the subject.

"We could go." Emma's suggestion sliced through Heidi. It'd been what she was thinking, but also what she was questioning as a good idea. She'd not mentioned anything to Connie about taking Emma from the house.

"Mmm, probably not wise." Heidi had a challenging time focusing on the game now.

"Rhett told me he'd take me someday," Emma stated flatly.

Heidi looked up at the young woman

whose pretty eyes were directed at her troops on the board. "And he hasn't?"

"No."

Wondering why made it clearer to Heidi she should probably avoid it herself. "Maybe I'll ask your mom when she comes home. If she says it's all right, we could go tomorrow."

"You could text my mom now."

True. She could. Heidi leaned back in her chair. Emma gave her a direct stare and blinked. Waiting.

Yes. She would text Connie. She and Emma both needed a diversion from the board game.

She hadn't heard back from Connie, but by the time she'd texted her, Emma had already gone outside and was waiting in the passenger seat of Heidi's car. Connie would respond, and if she said no, Heidi figured she had enough time to turn the car around and head back to the house.

Now, Heidi's car crossed the bridge over the river, leaving the boundary of city limits — "city" being an exaggeration — and onto a rural road that curved into the thick forest. A few small homes breezed by, set back into the trees, and then it almost seemed they'd entered something like a state park.

Habitation dwindled, and the side roads turned to gravel with small, white signs and arrows in black to guide you in the right direction.

"What road is the asylum on?" Heidi peered ahead with squinted eyes, maintaining her speed of thirty miles per hour so she could read the signs.

"Briar Road," Emma replied. She kneaded her scarf as she looked out the window.

Heidi glanced at the screen on her phone. No text yet. A part of her thought of turning back, but Emma's focus was so intense and set on the road ahead of them, she could sense the woman's interest. Emma would be fine.

Maybe she should have maneuvered Ducie into the car, just for security. Heidi gave Emma a sideways glance. Emma's hands had dropped to her lap and were calm. She was calm. Heidi warred with the niggling sense of not having heard back from Connie and the desire to keep going. Having Emma with her at the asylum might open a world of information. Information that might help Heidi make sense of . . . whatever there was to make sense of.

A sign for Briar Road was on their left. Heidi slowed and turned the vehicle. The tires rolled onto gravel, and Heidi winced at the deep ruts in the road that appeared wide enough for one vehicle. Apparently the asylum wasn't the tourist destination Jean from the grocery store had seemed to imply. If this was one of the top three must-sees, they needed better road maintenance.

"What was the name of the asylum, way back when?" Heidi tossed the question in Emma's direction to keep her occupied.

"Valley Heights Asylum. Founded in 1888 by Reginald Kramer."

"When did it close?"

"In 1927."

"Do you know *why* it closed?" Heidi slowed as an opening seemed to loom ahead. Dark and shadowed, with trees grown so tall and so thick that she couldn't make out a structure.

Emma didn't respond.

A nervous twinge bit at Heidi's stomach. She glanced at Emma. "Are you all right?"

Emma nodded.

Heidi rephrased the question. "Why did the asylum close?"

"It ran out of money."

Heidi slowed the car as the woods began to give way to a swath of open property. A rectangular building rose from the underbrush and thick overgrowth. Three stories with the eastern side crumbled and diminished to the foundation. Rows of windows, uniform in size, lined the remaining structure, some with glass still in them, but most broken and ragged from time.

An iron fence surrounded the grounds, portions of it bent and sagging inward, ready to collapse to the earth from years of neglect. There was a gap at the front where at one time a gate must have swung. Tall and ornate, Heidi imagined, with a lock perhaps to keep out unwanted visitors and keep in . . .

Well, asylums were their own form of prison after all, weren't they?

Heidi shifted the car into park and then turned to Emma. "Do you want to come with me?"

Emma had grown quieter. She stared out the passenger window at the asylum.

"Why don't you stay in the car." Heidi didn't want to suggest it for selfish reasons, but now she was full-on second-guessing, since her phone remained dark with no text from Connie. She couldn't even call her now. No signal was like a bad omen.

Emma shook her head. "No. I'll come."

She reached for the door handle and opened the door. Heidi followed suit. Within moments they stood at the asylum's gaping front entrance, staring up at the dilapidated brick structure.

Heidi entered the grounds silently. Emma followed close behind, her hands buried in her scarf and her eyes wide, taking in every nuance of the place. Beneath their feet, long grasses tangled and twisted. Some flattened by weather and time, others standing and struggling to find sunlight through the thick overgrowth of forest.

Heidi squatted, her hand pushing away the grass to flatten on a cobblestone. She looked up at Emma. "There was a stone walkway here, I'll bet you anything."

She stood and craned her neck toward the still-standing portion of the asylum. From here it seemed taller, darker, more Gothic in nature. If she closed her eyes, Heidi could almost imagine the forms of nurses in starched white with triangular caps passing behind the windowpanes. She could recreate the opening of the asylum entrance to a wide hall, with plain wood floors and whitewashed walls. Perhaps to the left, the first room would have been a visiting area, where people would come to see loved ones committed to this place. Or not. Maybe once here, the patient would have been forgotten. Ushered away into seclusion while the world outside carried on as if they no longer existed.

Maybe a person would have stood in the entryway, waiting for an aide to take them to meet with the registrant. To discuss admittance of a loved one, the long-term care options. Perhaps they would sit in a wooden chair with wide arms and a leather cushion. The solemn stillness of the place would be broken by a scream. A wild scream. Splitting the sterile silence with its anguished cry. Wailing . . . Rocking . . .

"Oh my gosh!" Heidi spun, snapping from her trancelike state.

Emma was on her knees behind her, jeans pressed into the grass and on the barely noticeable cobblestone walk. Her arms flailed in a circular motion, her eyes staring up at the third floor, wide and terrified.

"Emma!" Heidi hurried toward her, dropping beside her. Reaching out with her hand to lightly touch Emma's shoulder.

"No. No, no, no." Emma twisted away, still fixated on the upper-floor window.

"What happened? What's wrong?"

The more Heidi asked, the stronger Emma rocked, and every question agitated Emma further. She remembered the rubber ball Rhett had given Emma the night Ducie had been injured. She'd squeezed it. Deep breaths. Eye contact.

Oh, she was going to have a thousand penances to pay now!

Avoiding the regret that twisted at her, Heidi positioned herself in front of Emma, commanding her attention.

"Emma, breathe with me," she insisted. But even measured breaths refused to calm the young woman. A tear trickled down Emma's face.

Whatever had happened, whatever she'd seen, had petrified her.

"Emma?" Heidi was almost nose to nose with her, and Emma reared back, a wild look in her eyes. "Please, Emma. Do you want to go? We can go. I'll take you home."

"Home." Emma's voice warbled through tears.

"Yes. I'll take you home." Heidi reached for her, but Emma jerked away and skewered Heidi with a stern look.

"My brother. Get me my brother."

"Yes. Yes, we'll get Rhett." God help her, Rhett would hate her for this.

"Get me home," Emma insisted. "Away from her."

Heidi paused, not sure she'd heard her right. "Wait. Away from *her*?"

Emma shook her head, fresh tears trailing down her pretty face. Eyes turned upward again. She rocked back and forth, on her knees, her breaths coming in tight, short gasps.

"I don't want to see her again."

"Who, Emma?" Heidi urged, probably harder than she should.

"Misty Wayfair," Emma whispered, dropping her gaze to Heidi's, her lower lip trembling. "This is her home. Didn't you know?"

CHAPTER 17

This was more than eating humble pie. Heidi had made a mistake, and now it was time to face the full wrath and judgment of Rhett Crawford. He'd ignored her — completely — when she'd turned her car up the Crawford drive. Ignored her when he'd helped Emma from the vehicle, when he led her into the house, and also when he helped Emma snuggle on the floor next to Ducie. Even the dog had ignored Heidi as he nosed his mistress with concern, maneuvering himself so he could lay his head in Emma's lap, offering the sort of comfort it seemed no one else could.

But now? Now, Rhett Crawford was not ignoring her. With a jerk of his head in the direction of the kitchen, Heidi knew the clenched jaw and steel-gray eyes forecasted an ominous storm headed her way. Her insides curled and twisted. She'd tried calling Connie the moment her phone had a strong enough signal following their frantic exit from the asylum ruins. She should've called Connie to begin with — not texted her. Then she would have known it was a wrong number! She'd texted the wrong person for permission to take Emma out! When Heidi entered Connie's number in her phone's contacts, she'd made an error — off by one digit. The only option left was to call Rhett. A secondary emergency backup. And Heidi's judge and jury.

She wished Connie were here. At the moment, facing Emma's mother seemed far less daunting. Instead, the Hulk turned, drawing in a deep, controlled breath that testified to some very turbulent emotions. He braced his hands on the counter behind him.

Heidi crossed her arms. She could either give in to another anxiety attack or face him. She was used to facing condescension. This was still in her control. She tilted her head and waited him out. There was no way she was going to offer up the first word.

The standoff was entirely visual. Their eyes locked in a tug of war that dared the other to go first. Finally, Rhett blinked. She'd won.

"That was an idiot move."

Or maybe she hadn't won. She'd never let

him see it, but the words were cruel, and they hurt her. Heidi shrugged, her arms still crossed over her heather-green V-neck tee.

Shrugging was an immature response, but Heidi couldn't speak. Her throat was choked by tears. Her eyes burned as she blinked fast to push them away.

Rhett studied her for a moment, his hat jammed low over his forehead. He released the counter and matched her stance, crossing his arms. "You don't take a special-needs person out of their comfort zone. You don't leave without clearing it with their guardian."

He was right. Still, she had some defense. "I texted your mom."

"To the wrong number. And you didn't call her? Obviously, you weren't that concerned." Rhett's tone stated his doubt.

Heidi pursed her lips, straightening her shoulders. It was unfair to say she wasn't concerned. She was — she had been — she'd no desire to hurt Emma any worse than she already had. She swallowed back those irritating and pressing tears that were an enemy to her composure. What she intended to say, *I'm sorry, I never wanted to hurt Emma,* did not come out from her lips. Instead, Heidi heard herself defending, building up her wall, insisting on holding her ground.

"So, when she's home, your mom never takes Emma anywhere? They just stay here, never leave the house? That's not a realistic expectation."

"You're not Emma's mother."

The impasse was tense. Her defense was weak and shouldn't have been given. It was what she had always done. In lieu of the wrongs she believed her parents had bestowed on her with their legalism, she'd used that as justification for her misjudgment. She was doing it again. Only now she saw the truth of it, and it stung. She wasn't an innocent party to the problem.

The air was saturated with both of their frustration. Rhett's, rightfully so. Hers, born of the same anxiety a cornered, wild animal felt. Heidi tried again.

"I'm sorry. You're right. I should have called — I should have . . . but you need to stop treating your sister like a fragile human, Rhett. She's capable of so much more than you give her credit for."

Rhett's jaw muscle twitched. His eyes narrowed. "You've known us little more than a week. You've not earned the right to coach me on an entire lifetime with Emma."

Heidi tightened her arms around herself, willing her voice not to shake with feeling.

"I realize I still need to learn to understand Emma, but it's not like her life was in danger. I put her in no danger! I care about her. I did *try*! And I called you. I brought her home. Give me some credit for good intentions. She even asked to go! I was trying to give her an experience she'd enjoy."

"She asked to go?" Rhett raised an eyebrow.

"Yes!" Heidi insisted, even as her memory replayed the conversation.

"Really." He obviously didn't believe her.

Heidi's breath caught. Wait. No. Emma had *suggested* it, not asked. Heidi couldn't help the way her eyes flew up to meet Rhett's. "Emma offered the idea," she corrected weakly.

"Because she knew it was what you wanted." Rhett shook his head. "Why? Why not wait for my mom to get back to you? Why just *go* and hope for the best?"

"Because!" Heidi threw her hands in the air and let them fall with slaps against her jean-clad thighs.

"Because *why*?" Rhett insisted again.

Heidi looked away from his piercing stare. She didn't say anything. Couldn't say anything. A tear betrayed her and rolled down her cheek. She angrily swiped at it with her tattooed wrist.

Rhett uncrossed his arms and reached up, dragging his hat from his head. Heidi turned back toward him and was momentarily distracted by the thick mass of light brown hair that stuck up in a zillion directions. With a little grooming and that square jaw, the man would be remarkably handsome. But he intimidated her. Plain and simple. Rhett Crawford was an enigma of fierce loyalty and protection, and God save anyone who threatened his own. In a brief flash of irrational thought, Heidi wished she was his — his fiercely protected — instead of the one who threatened what he held close.

"What's in it for you?" He ran a hand through his hair, this time in an agitated motion, as though irritated by the fact he couldn't pinpoint Heidi's motivation for being in the Crawford home, let alone befriending Emma.

Well, she could be honest about one thing — even if it meant leaving out the reason for why she'd wanted to visit the asylum ruins. Heidi bit the inside of her upper lip, eyeing him with an extreme amount of caution. "I really like your sister. She's unique. I feel awful for hitting Ducie with my car. But, more than that . . ."

Was it wrong to even attempt to claim she

related to Emma in a small way? Would that be insulting? That Emma's anxiety, extreme as it might culminate, was a physical and visual reaction to what Heidi so often internally fought against? What she was warring against right now?

Rhett waited. He didn't say a word. He didn't look even a little bit swayed toward understanding.

Heidi drew in a short, shuddered breath. She couldn't look the man in the eyes. She stared at the floor. "That's — that's it," she muttered. "I just like your sister."

Rhett shoved off the counter and edged past her toward the door. He opened it and gave her a piercing look. "You're not being honest. You can leave now."

Heidi stared at him in disbelief. Not moving. She'd earned no right to be here, to demand acceptance, and yet she knew if she walked out that door she'd never come back. For some reason, the idea sent desperation coursing through her.

"No," she whispered.

"No?" Rhett gave her a distrustful smile. "You hurt my sister. More than once. I've talked to Brad and Vicki. I know about you."

Heidi stiffened. "What's that supposed to mean?"

Rhett's hand tightened on the doorknob

of the open front door. "You're all about yourself."

This time Heidi bit her cheek. The bad habit of biting the insides of her mouth was her war against the senselessness of panic. But this — this was worse. It was hearing the statement her parents, her sister, had drilled into her through her growing-up years as she rebelled against strong restrictions and battled against anxiety defined as lack of faith.

You're selfish.

You're not submissive.

You're only concerned about yourself.

You need to just realize everything is fine and get over it.

Heidi opened her mouth to respond, but her lower lip trembled. She bit down and cleared her throat, finally able to level her gaze on the man.

"You don't know what you're talking about," she whispered.

Rhett met her eyes. "No?"

"No." Heidi shook her head. "And you don't deserve to know. Not any of it."

Rhett gave his head a distinct nod toward the door. "Then you can go."

Heidi gave a swift glance over her shoulder. Toward the room where Emma rested with Ducie.

"I don't want to go." Heidi's voice shook.

"Why?" Rhett asked quietly, not even frustrated anymore, just challenging her for an adequate answer that she refused to provide him.

"Because —" Heidi shook her head, catching a glimpse of strands of her blue-dipped hair. She glanced at her wrist. *Fly free.* She should've tattooed *Fly Away* instead. "Never mind." She hurried to the kitchen table where she'd tossed her bag, snatched it up, and jerked the strap over her shoulder. Fleeing toward the door, she went to exit. But Rhett nudged the door just enough that there wasn't room for her to pass through.

"Why?" That Rhett was insisting on an answer instead of letting her leave when he'd just told her to confused her. He seemed to circle around her. Cautious, a bit threatening, but almost as if he knew something that she didn't. Something about herself.

His voice was low, calm. It tore through every part of her that lacked self-confidence. Every part that was afraid, wounded, torn apart. Rhett Crawford didn't belong in those places, and he hadn't earned the right to scale those walls with one word and a half-closed door.

Fine. She would give him an answer. If it

would make him back away, release her from the cornered trap she was in, and let her flee.

"Because with Emma — I actually feel like I belong." Heidi jerked the door against his grip and it opened. She slipped through the entrance and didn't look back.

She should be used to it. The never staying in one place. The always moving on. Only, for the first time in a very long time, she ached to look back.

It was a rash decision, but then she was known for them. Heidi parallel-parked her car on the main street that ran through Pleasant Valley. Most of the buildings were attached, with only a few having narrow alleys between them. They were two-story, flat-front buildings from the turn of the century, constructed of brick or wood. Some of them had been restored to their original vintage charm, while others were covered over with siding reminiscent of the 1970s.

Heidi ignored them as she hiked down the sidewalk, swiping at her face and praying the tears she'd let fall freely in the seclusion of her car hadn't left dried, salty trails down her cheeks. She could suck it up with the best of them, and she was doing it now. Her feelings spiraled from desperation to anger to offense because of Rhett Crawford. But, her path was clear. It was obvious — as it usually was.

There were only a few things to wrap up and then she'd leave. Leave Pleasant Valley and leave her mother, whose confusing letter seemed like a dance with an old woman's confusion rather than anything legitimately serious. She would leave Vicki and her brother-in-law behind — gladly. There would certainly be no love lost for the mysterious messages of implied madness. She was crazy? This place was crazy. Rhett Crawford included. Emma, the major exception.

She paused in front of the antique shop and looked up its brick face to the second story and darkened windows. Heidi held the photo album to her chest, drawing her gaze back to the picture window, its display creatively stocked with an old rocking chair with a quilt draped over its back. A Victorian side table with curved legs. A doily hanging over it and a porcelain vase displayed on its center. A rag rug on the floor along with a basket filled with dried bouquets of lavender.

It was charming. It was homey. It was peaceful.

Everything Pleasant Valley wasn't.

Heidi entered the small alcove and reached for the brass door handle. As she pulled it open, a tin bell announced her arrival.

Facing Connie Crawford would bring closure to a book Heidi had opened but barely started.

She wove through an array of old clocks, books, drawers of antique doorknobs and printing-press keys. While the room smelled a bit musty, there was a tiny hint of cinnamon wafting through the air. Something that hinted of orange and nutmeg too. Essential oils perhaps.

Connie was at the counter and lifted her head, her eyes growing serious, a slight thinning of her lips as she drew them tight.

Heidi didn't know if that was a bad or a good thing. She approached anyway, the photo album her only shield between herself and Emma's mother.

"Hello," Heidi ventured. She couldn't afford much more. Her veneer of self-confidence and proper reticence had been stretched thin and threatened to bust at any moment.

Connie's lips softened into a smile. One of gentle empathy. Something Heidi had not expected.

"I got a call from Rhett," Connie began.

Heidi stopped, the vintage bar counter a barrier between them. She gave a small nod. A tiny knot formed in her stomach. "I'm sure he more than filled you in. I wanted to apologize and return this."

At Connie's raised eyebrows, Heidi hurried to explain. "I don't need my money back, I'm just — I don't really want the album. And . . ." She set it on the counter and took a step back. "And I'm heading out. So . . ."

Connie nodded, placing her hands on the album's cover. "I see."

"Thank you for your hospitality. For allowing me to be Emma's friend — even for a short while. I'm truly very sorry for the chaos I've brought to your family." Heidi gave a chuckle that was more of a scoff — directed at herself. It was either that or cry. She was done with tears. Rhett had squeezed them all out of her. "Don't worry. I'll be out of everyone's way real soon."

Connie nodded. She ran a finger over the velveteen of the album, then looked at Heidi, holding her gaze. "Do you always run away like this?"

Heidi blinked. She cleared her throat and clutched at the leather strap of her bag that ran across her chest. "I'm not sure what you mean."

Connie tapped the book. "You came here a little more than, what, two weeks ago? And we discovered this curious and creepy photograph in the album. When you left that day, I immediately called Rhett and told him the strangest thing had just happened. And after I shared about you and the photograph, I told him that I bet you were the type to sink your teeth into something until you figured it out. You had that sense of intrigue in your eye. A bit of the devil-may-care about you."

"It's the hair and tattoos. An age-old stereotype." Heidi flicked her colored hair and offered a fake laugh, her lame attempt at dissolving the tension with humor.

Connie leaned forward, her arms cradling either side of the album, her palms pressed down on the counter. She tilted her head as if to study Heidi. "But you're afraid, aren't you?"

Connie's words of truth sliced through Heidi with the clean edge of a well-sharpened blade. She blinked, took another step back and toward the door. Yet if she excused herself now, it'd be a fulfillment of Connie's astute observation. That she ran. Ran away from things.

Well, yes, Connie Crawford. Yes. That was what she did. It was either that or be completely and totally enveloped in the belief that she was an unwanted after-thought, a disappointment, and a failure. It was either that or be consumed by a darkness — a weight — no one could understand or comprehend, because it was the demon that lived inside of her.

"Why did you take to my Emma so?" Connie's gentle question broke into Heidi's thoughts. "Circumstances haven't been particularly conducive to building an attach-ment, and yet even she has been drawn to you. I'm just curious. Why?"

Hadn't she just had a similar conversation with Rhett? The big *Why* question just wouldn't go away.

Heidi gave Connie a sad smile. "Your daughter is kind — she's a breath of fresh air. And, I like playing Risk," she added with a laugh.

"And that's all?"

Heidi winced and eyed the ceiling with desperation. It wasn't any help, so she looked back at Connie. "I'm sorry. I really am. I've always messed up since I was a kid. Nothing earth-shattering, just — you know — D's and C's in school. I didn't like church, and my dad was a pastor. I listened

261

to Fall Out Boy when my parents wanted me to listen to Steven Curtis Chapman. That type of thing."

Her answer had nothing to do with Emma.

Connie seemed to understand that. "And . . . ?"

Heidi glanced at the front door again.

"Listen to me, dear." Connie drew back from the counter and came around it. She then leaned back against the counter, like Rhett had in the Crawford kitchen just a few hours before. Connie's understanding smile was still there. Her graying hair framed her cheeks and her gray eyes — very much like Rhett's, only warmer — more sincere.

"Rhett is extremely protective of Emma. Sometimes more than he should be, really. But when you grow up in a small town with a special-needs sister, it can get claustrophobic. You hear everything everyone says and maybe what they think. That's made Rhett very sensitive."

Heidi blinked. *Sensitive* was not the word she would ascribe to the Incredible Hulk.

Connie ignored the raised eyebrow above Heidi's left eye. "My husband is a hunter. He took the kids out bowhunting with him when they were both old enough to walk. We learned something important about

Emma. Emma sees the world in blacks and whites. If you introduce grays, it's upsetting at a minimum, catastrophic at its worst. If there was a deer, she expected Murphy — my husband — to shoot it. She had no concept of distance or a clear shot. She'd get very upset when he'd let the deer walk away. So, we learned to construct life with black-and-white in mind and prepared ourselves to help her step through the inevitable grays. Through that, growing up and being the older brother, Rhett became a rescuer of sorts."

"A rescuer?" Heidi couldn't hide the skepticism in her voice.

"There was a specific time when he was thirteen and went hunting with Murphy. The yardage was perfect, the line of sight unencumbered, so Murphy released the arrow and, well, it was a bad shot. There wasn't much blood to track. It didn't seem like the deer was fatally wounded and yet it was difficult to tell. They had to wait a bit, because in some situations, if you try to find a wounded deer, it will keep running, and putting it out of its misery is not possible. Rhett didn't agree — he wanted to find the buck. But Murphy taught Rhett that day, that sometimes, when an animal is frightened or wounded, you need to pull back, give them space, maybe even let them go."

"That doesn't sound remotely like rescuing." Heidi swallowed against empathy for the poor deer.

"That's what Rhett thought too," Connie said. "They went back the next day and tried to track the buck. Unfortunately they didn't find any more signs of him or a blood trail. But here's the funny part to the story: Murphy has trail cameras in the woods. The next spring, they checked the images and guess what they saw?"

Heidi waited. Expectantly.

"The buck. He'd survived. Now, if they'd done what Rhett had wanted, they would have pushed him too fast. He might have been injured enough where he'd have bled out and never been found. A complete waste. But by being patient, the deer was able to bed down and heal."

Heidi nodded. "It's a strange story, Connie, but I'm not a hunter. I don't see —"

"We're not going to chase you, if you want to run. But it's always been Rhett's instinct to push forward and rescue the wounded. He sees that in you. That frightened, hurt look in your eyes. The same thing he sees in Emma when she's overwhelmed. It's why he pushed you so hard today. He wants you to admit there's more to your desire to be friends with my daughter. That it's deeper than you taking Emma to the asylum ruins, regardless of why you did it. That every time someone comes close and maybe could help you heal, you're skittish. You jump up and it reopens the wounds and something chaotic happens and you keep running."

Heidi could see the parallel now. She could sense it by the tightening in her stomach. She looked out past the rocking chair and through the front window.

Connie reached out and laid her hand on Heidi's elbow, drawing Heidi's attention back to her. "Rhett's a boorish, backwoods country boy with the conversational skills of a bear. But he's also a Crawford. We can spot someone who's been injured. We'll let you run if you need to, because keeping you here won't help if in your heart you don't want to stay."

The woman's motherly hand raised and cupped the side of Heidi's face. It was a foreign feeling. This nurturing gentleness. This forgiving care in spite of her horrendous error in judgment.

"Heidi," Connie's voice drew her in. "You love being with Emma because Emma accepts you for who you are. Just like she accepts herself. That girl has more confidence than some of us the world of science would deem 'neurotypical.' Without special needs. You must understand, Heidi, we're all okay if you make mistakes. Just don't run away. You came here to Pleasant Valley for a reason. Maybe it's the photograph in the book. Maybe it's whatever you thought you'd find at the asylum. Who knows? But I see purpose in you. A purpose your Creator designed in you. Let us help you find it."

Connie removed her palm from Heidi's cheek and stepped back. But there was pleading in her eyes.

"Please stay. We want you to stay. To try again." Connie shrugged and gave a small, apologetic chuckle. "You don't have to let Rhett in. Although he may kick down the door with the finesse of a lumberjack. But Emma really does have an innate judgment about people, and in an extremely brief period of time my black-and-white girl put all her black-and-white trust in you. And that, my dear" — Connie's words wrapped around Heidi's turbulent soul — "that's enough for us."

CHAPTER 18

THEA

The iron gate opened, soundless. Its height surpassed her by at least a head, and once Thea had stepped beyond it, walking in the footsteps of Simeon, she regretted her decision. Whatever Mr. Amos's investment in this small hospital hidden in the woods, no matter Simeon's compelling request to assist him, Thea knew that neither of those reasons were good enough for her to risk upsetting her own future. Yet she was hard pressed not to. Tempted by fate, perhaps, or more likely than not, the deep, compelling need to know why? Her mother had disappeared. Ragged hemline, bluish outline of a lithe and dark frame, and then dusky memories that, as Thea grew, became vague impressions that she questioned if they were even real.

There was no reason to assume with such certainty that entering the asylum would be

267

opening the musty tome of her own story. But there was a foreboding in Thea's soul, the living kind that refused to let go, but instead sank villainous claws of trepidation into her spirit. She knew. For no other reason than that ominous twist of one's stomach before truth was finally given a voice. She knew that, somehow, she was tied to this place. This place in the woods.

"Over here." Simeon's voice was low as he rounded the asylum, the wooden camera box clutched in his hand, the tripod in the other. Tree branches swayed over the roof. Oak trees that reached toward the attic gables, and a few thin, white trunks of poplar spearing their way toward the sky. Any pine was held to the boundaries outside the iron fence, as if unwelcome. A gardener's shed stood in the backyard of the asylum, and Simeon strode toward it. His steps were familiar and confident. He didn't seem afraid, and oddly, Thea sensed he was more at peace here than anytime she'd seen him before.

The shed's door opened quietly. He disappeared inside the darkness while Thea stayed behind. She wrapped her arms over her dress, drawing her crocheted shawl tighter around her body to ward off a chill that rose from within and matched the breeze rustling the leaves. She dared not look at the asylum. At its wide windows on both floors, geometrically in a row and measured identically. Thea was wary of what she would see inside — *who* she would see inside.

She could understand why family members ended up not paying a visit to the ones they'd left behind here. It wasn't a welcoming place. It was dark, even outside, and for certain the inside would be sterile and hollow of life. For the patients were, for all intents and purposes, all but dead.

Simeon exited the shed, a small burlap sack in his hand, the photographic equipment missing.

"Where is the camera?" Thea's heartbeat quickened. That was what they were here for, after all. Simeon had explained that while Dr. Ackerman had requested a photographic log of every patient, Simeon had managed to acquire only four. There were fifteen more patients, and it was laborious to take their photographs. They didn't understand how they must sit still and not move. Some rocked back and forth, moaning. Others stared into the distance in their chairs each day, but when moved from their routine they became violent. Striking out at anything new, anything strange.

Simeon hadn't answered her. Instead, Thea watched him walk away, the sack swinging from his hand. She shook herself from her position of pause, waiting for a response that wasn't forthcoming, and hurried after him. Mr. Amos was still teetering on the edge of getting better or turning for the worse. If for no one else but him, Thea pushed forward. Somehow the old man had won her loyalty in a brief time. Maybe it was the tiny squeeze he'd given her hand last night when she'd stopped to visit his convalescing bed.

Wayward pinecones littered the lawn. Sticks too, and Thea's shoes snapped one in half. The only noise in an otherwise silent, wooded island of grass. The wind picked up a bit, the branches swaying more, the leaves clamoring for attention. Simeon walked to the back corner of the property where there was another gate. Much smaller than the one in front and far less obtrusive. He opened it and disappeared through. Thea had almost caught up to him, and she hurried after where Simeon maneuvered down a craggy path composed of tree roots and half-buried rocks.

She stopped, catching herself by pressing her left palm against the scratchy bark of an oak tree. A small clearing became exposed.

Stones lay in a row. From what she could see, there were at least six in the first row, four behind it, and an awkward granite tower of a marker tilting in the back corner, alone.

A graveyard.

Simeon was kneeling at one of the stones, his back to her, suspenders stretched over his shoulders. Since it appeared he didn't intend to offer an explanation, Thea mustered the gumption to move forward.

"What are you doing?" Her voice, a mere whisper that was carried away by the breeze over the markers.

He gave her a quick glance but still did not speak. Simeon reached into his sack, and from it he removed a smooth stone. Much like those he'd taken from the river several nights before.

Curious, Thea stepped even closer as Simeon reached out and rested the stone alongside another oval one. The marker had been crudely chiseled.

Ethel Morgan
b. 1872 – d. 1907

But it was the words carved into the stones that captured Thea's attention.

"What do they mean?" Thea dared to ask the very silent, almost reverent Simeon.

He ran his thumb over the words on both stones, then drew back, rising to his feet. He shoved the bag into his coat pocket. Thea could hear more stones rattling together in the bag.

"It's who she should have been," he replied cryptically, still fixated on the stones around the deceased woman's name.

"I don't understand. Who was she? Was she a resident here?" Thea heard a bang. A door somewhere had shut wildly from the wind. She startled and looked over her shoulder, but all she could make out was the trail leading to the asylum, the woods, and glimpses of the third floor and its roof.

Simeon turned and brushed past her, the air around them growing thick with unspoken thoughts and questions. He started up the trail, and Thea hoisted her skirts in her hands and hurried after him.

This time, however, she was unwilling to let it go unanswered. "Simeon," she demanded.

He stopped and twisted to look at her, his gray eyes a certain type of haunted that burrowed deep into her soul.

"You've known such grief, haven't you?" Without thinking, she extended her hand, her fingertips. Maybe if he grasped them, she could pull him back to life.

Simeon didn't respond to her reach. He looked over her shoulder, at the cemetery. "I buried a few of them. I was alone."

The meaning of his observation cut through Thea. Alone. No minister. No grieving family. The patients had slipped into eternity, and when he'd arrived to work, their burials were on his task list.

"You immortalize them with words?" she ventured.

Simeon blinked. Then blinked again, coming back to the present moment, rather than wherever depths he'd been in his mind. He gave her a wan, crooked smile and nodded. "Words they should have been. The woman? Buried there? She rarely slept. She was never at peace. So I gift her with them now. Slumber and stillness."

"Forever," Thea acknowledged.

"Yes. Forever." Simeon turned back and headed up the trail.

Simeon had vanished through a doorway and left Thea standing in a back room of the asylum. She'd prepared herself to enter

273

through the front door. Perhaps be received in a waiting area, staring through the windows toward the road she'd come down. She'd expected there to be a room prepared, a nurse or two, to assist with the patients. She'd planned on setting up the photography equipment and reminding herself that these would be very different interactions than when she photographed someone who had already passed on.

But no. They'd entered through a back door meant for asylum staff, and she stood in what seemed to be a cloakroom for employees. Three women's cloaks hung on pegs. An extra pair of men's shoes rested on the floor beneath them. Three wooden chairs lined the opposite wall.

A long hall stretched through the doorway, with several doors on either side. Thea had no wish to try to find Simeon, assuming he'd return for her. Yet he hadn't. His wordless exit had left her feeling bereft, but perhaps he'd expected her to follow? And she hadn't. Now what should she do?

She waited for another minute or two. The insides of this place were gray and dull, but very quiet. Thea sniffed. The noise seemed loud and obtrusive.

Finally, footsteps!

Thea peered down the hall. A woman in a

dress, also gray, was walking toward her. A white apron covering most of her torso and draped over her dress. A triangular white hat perched on top of black hair.

"Rose!" Thea was surprised.

Rose's smile was gentle and welcoming. A relief after Simeon's silent vigil at the cemetery.

"Thea. I'm so sorry. Simeon makes assumptions . . ."

"I was supposed to follow him, wasn't I?" Thea offered a sheepish smile.

Rose's eyes seemed brighter today. She nodded. "Yes. But you didn't, and he gets lost in his thoughts and didn't notice until he was in the office. I've come to retrieve you. I can't blame you for staying here and not venturing forth."

Thea stifled a sigh of relief. Thankful that Rose understood her apprehension in wandering the halls of a mental asylum.

She followed closely this time, unwilling to lose sight of Rose — which seemed unlikely. Rose wasn't particularly chatty, but she was very aware of Thea's presence, offering her comforting looks over her shoulder as they traveled down the long hall, ignoring the closed doors.

They came into an open foyer, where daylight spread through the windows. The floors were worn but clean linoleum, not fancy or decorative. The walls in this room were whitewashed. There were no pictures, no extra décor that a patient could grab or launch or break. Only plain wooden chairs against the wall and a coat tree. The tall double doors of the front entrance made Thea realize that if she only had traversed the hall on her own, she would have wound up waiting in the place she'd originally envisioned.

Rose paused and turned. "Simeon has gone to prepare the room. I'm not certain you'll get more than one photograph today. The patients are kept on a routine and a schedule and . . ." Her voice waned, and Thea nodded.

"Simeon did explain that to me."

"Oh good." Rose ran her hands down her apron and lifted her eyes. "I suppose this surprises you."

"That you're a nurse? Yes," Thea admitted honestly. The other day, outside the asylum, she'd assumed by implication that Rose was here solely for Dr. Ackerman. That perhaps he was a beau.

"Oh, I'm not a nurse. I'm an aide. Only an aide. We've three nurses here. Two for the daytime, and one who works the night shift," Rose explained.

Thea thought it curious she'd not seen nurses in town, or that the townspeople rarely spoke of the asylum at all. Rose seemed to read the question in her eyes.

"It's a small hospital. We've only nineteen patients. The nurses dorm in the attic rooms. That way, in the case of an emergency at night, they can be summoned for extra help. I'm the aide who helps during the days, as well as Dr. Ackerman, and also another doctor from a town about eight miles from here. He visits frequently for additional support. We always have Simeon too, if things get really out of hand." Rose's eyes shadowed briefly. "That doesn't happen often, thankfully," she added.

It seemed woefully ill supplied with staff, but perhaps, Thea acknowledged, that was her own ignorance of the matter.

"We'll go upstairs now," Rose said, her tone dropping a notch. She captured Thea's gaze with a solemn expression. "It's very different upstairs. The patient quarters are there. Please. Don't be disturbed by anything they say or do. While you may be surprised by some things, be assured we are not. It's best to stay silent and let us work with the patients."

The small room had a lone window, four-paned, barred, and overlooking the front cobblestone walk. Simeon stood in the middle of the room, the Kodak box camera mounted on the tripod. How or when he'd retrieved it from the shed out back confused Thea, but then many things did that to her lately. She eyed the wooden chair against the white wall, natural light illuminating it. It would make for an easy photograph in terms of setting the camera to capture the image. Once taken, she would need to develop the plates in a darkroom. Simeon had explained that he and Mr. Amos had constructed such a room in the basement. It did not excite her to go into the basement of the asylum, but the negative plates would need proper attention, so she had little choice.

Simeon looked up as Thea entered with Rose, who quietly excused herself on pretense of collecting their patient.

"I'm sorry." His eyes reflected a transparent honesty.

"That's all right," Thea responded with a small smile.

Simeon moved aside, and Thea naturally took over the process, preparing the camera. It was what she was familiar with. What Mr. Mendelsohn had taught her to do. She could feel herself distancing from the moment, becoming mechanical as she prepared the plates. It was a blessing, really, to not feel. To insert herself behind the tool that would capture a moment forever, yet stand between her and the stark reality of death . . . or in this case, suspension between the here and the hereafter.

Footsteps drew her attention, and she looked up as a slight figure entered the room. Simeon stood to the side, his eyes sharp now, attending and kind. Thea instantly knew why Simeon needed assistance in lieu of Mr. Amos. He was the familiar, the camera the foreign. If he hid behind it, the patient would panic, but with Simeon methodically directing the moment, the other photographer became merely an extension of the camera. An object, rather than a person to be feared.

The woman's expression was distant. Her head tilted to the left, and she stared ahead as if seeing beyond the walls. A dress covered her, stained but clean, and too short for her already petite body. Her legs that peeked out below were scrawny and bruised. Her feet wore stockings. Thin ones that rose above her bony ankles and sagged behind to her heels. Her graying, dark hair had been pulled back into a low bun at the nape of her neck. It seemed, from the waist up, that someone had gone to great lengths to attempt to prepare her for the photograph.

Rose followed the woman, who must have been in her late forties. She didn't touch her but kept a careful radius, as if any physical contact might send her into a tantrum.

"This is Effie." Rose met Thea's eyes.

Thea offered a nervous smile. She couldn't deny that a little part of her was frightened by the tiny woman, who looked as if a slight breeze would lift her off the floor and carry her into the heavens.

"Hello, Effie," Thea offered.

Effie stopped in the middle of the barren room. Her eyes surveyed Thea, and for a moment Thea thought she saw a hint of awareness — realization, perhaps. And then it disappeared, and Effie's face returned to vacancy.

Simeon intervened and stood behind the chair. "Here, Effie. Please, sit."

Effie's feet shuffled across the floor. She followed the sound of Simeon's voice and lowered her body onto the chair. Now that she was facing Thea, Thea could see her pale skin was marred by bruises on her cheeks. She frowned, studying her as she did anyone whose picture she was about to capture.

Rose had come near Thea, and she leaned

in to whisper softly into Thea's ear, "Effie has horrible spells some days. She'll flail her body and hit things. She had one a few days ago. It's why she has bruises."

Spells. Thea tried not to interpret what that might signify. She'd heard Mrs. Mendelsohn speak once of a woman who had "spells." Some thought she was possessed by the devil himself, such a fit she would throw. Drooling from the mouth, eyes rolling, her body arching and then finally collapsing into an exhausted state. It was terrifying, Mrs. Mendelsohn admitted. She'd also mentioned how that woman had been committed to a hospital. Just like Effie.

Simeon squatted in front of Effie and captured her attention. "Effie, I'd like for you to recite me a poem."

Thea readied herself at the camera. She could tell that Simeon was preparing Effie for a photograph, and the opportunity to take one might be just a sliver of a moment.

"Can you, Effie?" he urged gently.

When she didn't respond, Thea sensed Rose shift beside her. "She likes that poem 'A Chilly Night.' The one by Christina Rossetti."

Simeon gave his sister a blank look.

Rose took in a small breath and began to quote softly:

"I rose at the dead of night
And went to the lattice alone
To look for my Mother's ghost
Where the ghostly moonlight shone."

Thea watched, transfixed, as Effie's head came up. Her eyes focused, and a tiny smile tilted her lips. She looked first at Rose, then Simeon, then back to Rose. A little nod and her body relaxed. Her lips moved as she continued the verse with a soft, reedy voice that sent shivers through Thea.

"My friends had failed one by one,
Middle-aged, young, and old,
Till the ghosts were warmer to me
Than my friends that had grown cold . . ."

Simeon stood, caution in his movement, so as not to bewilder Effie. He gave Thea a quick look, and she nodded, attempting to ignore Effie's recitation and instead take the photograph. She framed the potential image and made sure Effie was centered from the chest level and up.

"I looked, and I saw the ghosts
Dotting plain and mound:
They stood in the blank moonlight
But no shadow lay on the ground;

They spoke without a voice
And they leapt without a sound . . ."

Thea was ready. She gave Simeon a look. Effie needed to stop. Her lips were moving, and it was critical that nothing moved. Simeon tried to interrupt the woman, who sat hunched in the chair.

"Effie," he said.

She ignored him, her voice a continuation of the words that seemed as though etched in her mind.

"I called: 'O my Mother dear,' —
I sobbed: 'O my Mother kind,
Make a lonely bed for me
And shelter it from the wind . . .' "

Thea straightened, her eyes connected with Effie's. The woman blinked rapidly, softness absent from her face, the words of the poem frozen on pale lips. She stared at Thea.

"Please, stop," Thea breathed. The horror of the poem touching the places she'd tried to tamp down, the fears she harbored of this place. This prison.

Effie fixated on her. Her eyes wide, sincere. It seemed she was very aware of what she said and what it implied.

"My Mother raised her eyes,
They were blank and could not see;
Yet they held me with their stare
While they seemed to look at me.

She opened her mouth and spoke,
I could not hear a word
While my flesh crept on my bones
And every hair was stirred."

Thea stumbled back from the camera, but Effie's gaze speared her. Captured her and refused to let her move anywhere but back against the bare wall.

"Stop!" Thea cried out.

She vaguely saw Simeon scramble toward Effie.

Rose was but a blur in Thea's vision.

For a moment, Thea thought Effie would keep reciting, but she didn't. She stopped and stiffened, leaning forward. "You." The words, shaky and laced with shock, filtered through Effie's lips. "It's you."

Thea gave Simeon a bewildered look, and Rose moved quickly to Effie's side.

"Come, Effie." Rose motioned for Effie to rise. The woman did as she was beckoned to, yet her eyes remained focused on Thea.

Thea was shaking. Almost violently. A terror shot through her like a bullet fired from a gun held in Effie's own tremoring hand. The recognition in Effie's eyes. Her mother? Had Effie seen her mother in Thea's face? *Was* Effie her mother? Maybe the woman who had left Thea at the orphanage had indeed found her way to Valley Heights Asylum and Effie —

"Misty Wayfair . . ." Effie drew out the name in awe. As though she were transfixed by seeing the ghost herself in the room.

Coldness saturated Thea. Simeon's hand wrapped around her elbow, to steady her. Maybe she'd wobbled a bit on her feet at the name on Effie's tongue. Maybe she'd grown pale. Thea didn't know. All she knew was, Effie was staring at her, not in fear but in fascination.

"You've come back to me," Effie breathed. "You've come back."

CHAPTER 19

"What did she mean?"

Thea sat at a table in the downstairs kitchen. Simeon set a cup of tea in front of her, and she wrapped her cold fingers around it. Rose hadn't reappeared since she'd hurried Effie from the room.

"What was that horrific poem!" Mothers. Ghosts. It tore into her, the words like thorns sticking in her heart.

Simeon pulled out a chair, nodding his thanks to one of the hospital's cooks, who returned from making tea to chopping vegetables for making broth. The sound of the knife clomping against the wooden cutting board only increased Thea's anxiousness.

"Why would she say that to me?" Thea tried again.

Simeon's expression was wary. He'd been disturbed by it too. As well he should, considering the rumored ties of the mystical

Misty Wayfair to his own family. He folded his hands and lifted his eyes.

"I don't know, Thea. The poem is one that Rose reads to her. Effie loves poetry." Simeon glanced at the cook, who ignored them.

This was probably normal for her, to hear of strangeness and odd behavior.

Simeon continued. "The patients say things sometimes that often mean nothing, just a story in their own minds."

Thea noticed his shoulder jerk up toward his ear and his cheek twitch. The familiar signal he was not at peace.

"A story of Misty Wayfair?" Misty Wayfair whose spirit wandered the woods, spiteful and wicked.

Only she hadn't appeared wicked.

Thea recalled the vision of the woman in the street below her room. In the rain and fog, arms outstretched as if reveling in the beauty of the night. If anything, Misty Wayfair had turned from a peaceful dance into a terrified run from something . . .

"Do you believe in spirits?" Thea breathed.

Simeon blinked.

The cook dropped her knife. It clattered to the floor. She mumbled and bent to retrieve it, shooting them a hasty glance. "So sorry," she muttered.

Simeon gave her a wary look, then offered Thea a slight shake of his head. He pushed his chair back and stood, motioning for Thea to follow. He led her from the kitchen, and she could feel the cook's eyes burning into her back. They went down the same hallway she'd entered by, passing a nurse with a starched uniform and a rather stern face.

Soon Simeon had led Thea outdoors, where she drew in a deep breath, filling her lungs with air rife with the scent of pine and earth. There was an iron bench in the corner of the yard. Simeon took her to it and motioned for her to sit.

They were silent for a while. He kept his face averted, as he always seemed to, but Thea could still see his features twitch in the familiar tic. More apparent now and indicative of an internal heightened awareness of the situation.

Finally, he spoke. "I believe that people see what they want to see."

Thea remembered the apparition or the vision or whatever the woman was beneath her window. "But, if a person isn't looking for . . . if they're not superstitious and hoping to see something . . ."

Simeon raised his head. Hair fell over his forehead. His eyes were gentle, his mouth quirked at the corner, and his right shoulder rose on its own volition, then settled. He waited, allowing his body to regain control. "Misty Wayfair died in 1851, Thea. She is dead."

"But — Mary?"

"What about Mary? What has she to do with this?" Simeon stiffened. His features grew stern now.

Thea swallowed. Oh, she'd ventured into a place she had no right to go. "Never mind." She shook her head, hoping to gracefully back away from her question.

Simeon stared at her. Thea tried not to be distracted by his facial motion, however subtle it was. He wasn't going to stop leveling her with a look. He was more confident now than ever before. The mention of his dead sister's name had conjured up defenses in the timid man that Thea had not been prepared for.

"They say that Misty Wayfair . . . she makes appearances. Just before a Coyle passes away."

Simeon blinked.

Thea shifted on the bench. She twisted her hands around the cloth of her skirt, staring down at the sensible navy cotton. She cleared her throat. "They say she's wicked and spiteful and anyone —"

"If you prefer not to be near me — near us — you may leave."

"That isn't what I meant." A frantic urgency filled her. She wanted to disassociate herself from those in Pleasant Valley who had branded the Coyles as outcasts. She didn't want to unintentionally take sides with the origins of the original Kramer Logging baron and his feud with his daughter, Simeon's grandmother. She certainly didn't want to somehow tie herself to the likes of Mrs. Brummel or Edward Fortune, who simply carried on a family's bias into the third generation without good cause. A ridiculous prejudice based on status and perhaps religious affiliation.

But, she also didn't wish to remind insane patients of Misty Wayfair. To listen to words that practically spoke her nightmares and sometimes wishes aloud. Her mother, dead. Their ability to speak, to find resolution, impossible.

Thea wanted peace. For once, she just wanted to be at peace!

Simeon leaned over, elbows on his knees, staring with an empty expression beyond the garden shed and into the woods. It appeared he had closed her out. Instead, he waited until he had his features under control and could speak without a slur or lisp.

"My great-grandfather built this asylum, they say," he explained. A robin fluttered from a nearby oak and landed in the lawn in front of them. Thea and Simeon both fixated on it. She waited for him to speak again.

"There was good in him. But I remember my grandmother telling us how disappointed he was when she married my grandfather. Then how equally appalled he was when they discovered my grandfather's supposed — relations — with Misty Wayfair. My grandmother Mathilda stood by my grandfather Fergus for all those years. But I think, deep down, she also believed it was true."

The robin hopped closer to them, pecking at the ground, at some mysterious object neither Simeon nor Thea could see.

When Simeon said no more, Thea licked her lips as she gave him a hesitant look. "Did your grandmother ever say why they never resolved the conflicts between her and your great-grandfather? It seems an awful weight to bear and a sad dissolution of family legacy. For all of you." She didn't dare mention that it also had stolen their financial legacy — Kramer Logging.

Simeon waited as the robin tugged at a worm, pulling back and forth from the earth. When it succeeded, the bird flapped its wings, escaping their perusal with its dinner hanging from its beak.

"No. My grandmother was never one to explain anything." Simeon leaned back and smoothed the thighs of his pants with his palms. "Nor was my father." His voice had grown hard, as if certain unspoken memories lingered just beneath the surface.

Thea's anxiousness had begun to assuage since leaving the innards of the asylum. Still, Effie's outburst and the way Rose had rushed her from the room made Thea question, How would an insane woman know anything about Misty Wayfair? Was the story of her murder so infused into every recess of Pleasant Valley, its woods, and the asylum hidden in its depths that it had made its way even into the dark places of a disturbed woman's mind?

"Do you ever — ?" Thea stopped this time. She bit her tongue.

Simeon glanced at her. "Yes?"

Thea shook her head.

Simeon shrugged. "You may ask. I'm sure I've been asked worse."

Thea swallowed, but a tiny smile touched her lips. He had gotten his irritation under careful control, and in some way, while the tic at the edge of his mouth still made his left eye jerk, he didn't seem as resigned as he had earlier. For a moment, Simeon was just — honest.

"Do you ever wonder how Misty Wayfair actually died? And how she was tied to your family as a lingering haunting?"

Simeon folded his hands and tapped his thumbs together. "She was murdered."

"Yes, but why?" Thea asked.

Simeon turned then, settling his slate gray eyes on her face, studying her as if assessing whether to say what was on his mind or to remain vague. Finally, he turned back to staring into the distance. He breathed in deep and released the air through a resigned puff from his mouth.

"They say she was strangled and thrown into a well at the edge of Kramer Logging."

Thea didn't speak. She couldn't. She'd already heard that part. It was the details she wanted to know. She wanted to know because, no matter how she tried to excuse it, the fact that she reminded Effie of Misty Wayfair unsettled her. The fact that everything in this place seemed touched by a woman dead for more than fifty years was unnerving. The fact that no one could explain the *why* behind Misty Wayfair's death and subsequent "hauntings" was unsatisfactory.

Simeon tipped his head back and looked up as his sister opened the back door of the asylum, waving them in. He turned to Thea, piercing her with his steady gaze.

"Coyles never ask why. We're not allowed."

With that, he stood and walked away, his shoes making soft steps across the lawn. Thea watched him as he approached his sister. Two siblings, so alone, so ostracized, and almost as mysterious as Misty Wayfair herself.

Before they left the asylum, Rose had explained that Dr. Ackerman wished to speak to Thea. Simeon left her with his sister and disappeared to where he seemed most comfortable. Alone and outdoors, tending the grounds, ignoring the photographic potential of at least one more patient's picture. They'd both lost their interest for the day. Thea had no desire to return to the upper level of the asylum.

Instead, she followed Rose through another hall and to the first door on the left. She waited as Rose knocked, met Rose's twilight eyes and read the reassurance in them, then entered the office. She started a bit as the door closed behind her, and Rose left her alone.

Dr. Earl Ackerman appeared much the same as he had at Mary's funeral. His stature was lean and tall. He wore a similar suit, only this time the suit coat hung off a peg on the wall, and in its place he had on a medical frock that hung to his hips and was buttoned at the front. His tie was a deep green. His mustache was tended neatly, and the way he presented himself was enough to make Thea believe he was not only confident in his medical abilities, but also in his appearance.

Perhaps someday his would be the image a future young woman looked back on in a photograph and remarked at how handsome some men were back at the turn of the century. Thea blinked to snap her awareness back to the present and away from the distraction of imagery and imagination. Handsome, yes, but something about him made her uneasy. Perhaps because he assessed her almost as one might expect him to assess a patient's mental capabilities.

Thea didn't like to be read like that. She wasn't a book, nor was she in need of psychological care.

"I want to apologize." His voice was such a deep baritone that it filled the room. Thea jumped a little, and he waved her politely toward a chair opposite his desk. "Please. Have a seat."

She did so, but something inside her made her glance out the window. One of the few that didn't have bars on it. She saw Simeon outside, trimming a bush. Her eyes clung to him, wishing he'd look up and see her. And rescue her? Thea broke from her stare and returned her gaze to Dr. Ackerman. She didn't need rescuing. She was a guest here, not a new induction.

Dr. Ackerman was speaking. "When I asked Simeon if he would approach Mr. Amos about the possibility of assisting with photographing our residents, I'd no idea that he would seek an alternative in the event of Mr. Amos's recent troubles. I'd like you to know that in no way should you feel obligated to assist Simeon."

Thea waited, unsure of what to say. She wasn't certain if that was a veiled hint to not return or merely providing an escape for Thea to politely decline.

The doctor continued. His eye contact was so direct that Thea looked down at her hands folded in her lap.

"Simeon has worked here, along with Miss Coyle, his sister, for the last three years. I knew of his interest in photography and his mentorship by Mr. Amos. It was merely an opportunity for me to help patient records be more updated by adding a photograph. It certainly isn't a necessity. Although the patient records, while small, are abysmal."

Thea lifted her eyes. Images of her mother walking away from her returned with a vengeance. There must have been an unspoken question on her face, for Dr. Ackerman nodded.

"Yes. Valley Heights Asylum was opened by Reginald Kramer almost twenty years ago now, shortly before his death. While the space is limited, you can imagine the comings and goings of patients here. It is a peaceful place, and family who are forced to admit their loved ones need — assistance — will choose a place such as this so they can leave conscience-free."

Conscience-free. Like her mother had left her at the orphanage?

Thea swallowed. "Do they ever return to take a patient home?"

Dr. Ackerman's brows rose in surprise. "Take them home? No. No, unfortunately, there is no leaving a place such as this. Only by death, but then a patient may live decades here before that claims them."

Decades. If so, if her mother had indeed been here, then she'd either died relatively quick after being admitted or . . .

"And your records are not up to date?"

Dr. Ackerman strode to the window and looked out. Now he seemed to watch Simeon, as Thea had, before he turned back to her.

"Simeon and Miss Coyle joined my staff when I first arrived here at the hospital. The previous doctor passed away, and I accepted my station here. When I arrived, I discovered that while the patients did have minimal information recorded and medical logs had been kept, all was in a state of disarray."

"And so you wish to make that right?"

"Of course. But not at the expense of others. I will be sensitive to your delicacies, Miss Reed. I've no desire to subject you unwillingly to the . . . well, outbursts of the patients or other such sights."

"Do you have need of further record sorting?" Thea's question came before much thought. If Mr. Amos didn't recover soon, she felt obligated to keep up his appointments on his behalf. He had, after all, agreed to take her on at her arrival in Pleasant Valley. Yet the idea of having access to the asylum patients' records, even past records, intrigued her as well as frightened her. It would, perhaps, be an uncomplicated way to answer the question: Where had her mother gone?

Dr. Ackerman walked behind his desk and lowered himself onto his chair. "Are you saying you're interested in assisting beyond just photography?"

Thea warned herself to think before speaking. She compartmentalized her thoughts this time and proceeded carefully. "Well, I would see to Mr. Amos's accounts as my first priority. However" — there was no reason not to be completely honest — "I've reason to question whether my mother may have been here at Valley Heights at one time."

"As a nurse?" Dr. Ackerman leaned forward in his chair. "I could quickly find out for you."

"No." Thea winced. This was exactly what she was terrified to admit. But then he was a doctor of the mentally ill, after all. Surely there would be no shame in speaking the truth.

"As a patient," she heard herself say.

"Ahh, I see." Dr. Ackerman nodded. "We could look at those records we do have organized. What was her name?"

"All I know of her is, P. A. Reed."

The doctor nodded again. "She may be in our past records. We've no patient by that name now, I can assure you."

"I see." Thea was both relieved and disappointed at the same time. The image of Effie stood out starkly in her mind. The absent eyes, the awful words filling the room, and then the awareness, the recognition.

Misty Wayfair.

"What do you know of Misty Wayfair?" Thea asked with a compulsion.

"Yes. Effie. Rose told me what she said to you. Again, I apologize. If you are interested in assisting with records, I would engage your help, although I also do not expect you to continue to work with the patients."

"Why would a patient even know of that story? The story of Misty Wayfair? Surely not all patients here are from town, but rather transplanted from outside. So how would Effie know of her, let alone believe I reminded her of Misty?" The questions came tumbling from Thea. Questions she'd wanted to ask Simeon but was afraid to. Questions she probably had no right to ask of Dr. Ackerman, yet she did.

He reached for a letter opener on his desk and ran the dull blade between his thumb and forefinger. Then he set it down, folded his hands, and met Thea's questioning look with a direct expression that convinced her he wasn't being at all deceitful with his answer. Though afterward she wished he had been.

"The patients see all sorts of things, Miss Reed. *Hear* all sorts of stories from the outside from staffers who come and go. The story goes that Misty Wayfair's ghost even frequents the halls of this place — looking for someone, they say." Dr. Ackerman shook his head, and his lips thinned as he paused in thought. "Effie — *sees* things. Many things. It's one of her *conditions*. I'm sure she believes she's seen the spirit of Misty Wayfair, and for some reason — we'll never understand, I'm sure — she believes you're her."

"But I'm not!" Thea insisted. The idea was appalling. Unnerving.

Dr. Ackerman shrugged. "But to Effie, you are. And to Effie, that is all that matters."

CHAPTER 20

HEIDI

It was all or nothing now. Heidi had decided to remain, so with that decision she had to regain her reason for being here in the first place. Her equilibrium of sorts. Connie had sent her home with the counsel to rest for a day, then regroup. She was invited back to spend time with Emma. Connie had insinuated she'd like to understand what had brought Heidi to Pleasant Valley. It was really, honestly, perhaps the first time anyone had shown genuine interest in what mattered to Heidi.

She wasn't quite sure what to do with that.

Heidi slouched on the sofa in the living room, knees pulled up to rest on the cushion, with her mother's letter open before her, revealing the familiar handwriting in blue ink. She balanced an open can of Dr Pepper on her left knee. To her right lay the old photograph album, along with the

302

unsettling note she'd found under her windshield wiper.

Her eyes skimmed the letter she'd received only two months prior. Two months, and she'd ended up coming at the call of a mother she had to admit she still sought approval from.

Heidi . . .

She noted that there was no introduction of "dear" or "darling," with the use of her first name or the use of "Honey" or "Sweet pea," or some other ridiculous childhood nickname. It made the distance she'd known since childhood between mother and daughter all the more palpable and real.

There is much to say, but not in a letter. Since your father passed away, I've slowly sensed my own mind failing. I know dementia to be a wicked truth of age and genetics, but I wished it wouldn't come to this.

I am frightened. Not of losing myself into the shadows of my mind. I am frightened by all that is unseen, and yet has now come to visit. We did our best to protect you. But we lived in a house of ghosts. Unspoken voices. The past and the present colliding with such force, we could only survive by ignoring it.

Please come.

Heidi, you are the reason the voices are never heard.

But they are finding their voice and soon will no longer be silent.

Come.

Come quickly.

It was signed simply *Mom*. The chills the letter had first given her still traveled through Heidi's body even now. In spite of her gray yoga pants and fuzzy socks and bulky fisherman's sweater she'd donned to ward off the early-morning chill of summer in Wisconsin's Northwoods.

She set aside the letter and pulled the album toward her, opening it to the page marked with the note card that begged the question, *Are you as mad as I?* Heidi's eyes met those of her look-alike in the sepia-tone photograph.

"I don't know," she whispered to an antique version of herself. "Am I?"

Thank God that Connie Crawford had seen the photograph the first day and affirmed its likeness, or Heidi would be afraid that if someone else saw it, they'd see something totally different. A different woman even from the one Heidi saw.

She avoided looking up, avoided the instinct to glance out the window for fear this same woman would be peering in at her again. Vanishing. Like the ghosts in her mother's letter.

"Please don't spill that." Vicki's voice broke Heidi's intent silence.

She startled and grabbed for the Dr Pepper that wobbled on her knee.

"That's a sure way to make it happen." Heidi rolled her eyes at her older sister. "Scared the life out of me."

"Sounds as though you've already done an excellent job of that yourself this week. Frightening others?" Vicki dropped onto a chair opposite Heidi, crossing her leg over her knee.

Heidi eyed her sister. Sometimes silence was the best answer rather than taking the bait.

Vicki shook her head and sighed. "I'd hoped things would be different. It's been how many years since we've seen you? But you're still impulsive and reckless. You're lucky the Crawfords aren't more upset with you. Emma needs routine and —"

Heidi pushed her feet off the couch and leaned forward. "She agreed to come with me."

305

"Because she wanted to please you. Or maybe she didn't understand your intent," Vicki debated.

Heidi set the can of pop on the wooden coffee table. "Don't discredit Emma and talk about her like she's incapable of making her own decisions. She's very intelligent and independent in many ways."

"I don't get this devotion you've developed toward her." Vicki tapped her fingers on the arm of the chair, studying Heidi. "Not that it's bad, really, I just — you haven't shown your own family that much attention in forever. What about Mom? Why not invest in her?"

Heidi reached for the Dr Pepper and took a sip. It was easier than answering, because Vicki's question had merit. As she predicted, Vicki continued.

"I understand wanting to make up for hitting Emma's dog. I do." She was trying to anyway, Heidi could tell. Extending some sort of peace offering in Vicki's own backward way. "But — Heidi, I'm not even sure why you're here. I thought it was Mom at first, then to help me at the lodge, but it's like you've no purpose. No — direction."

Bingo!

But Heidi wasn't going to admit that her sister had pretty much nailed Heidi's entire life in one sentence. Instead, she twisted in her seat and reached for her mother's letter. What was there to lose really? She handed it to Vicki and watched her sister over the rim of the pop can.

For a moment, something flashed across Vicki's face, but then she drew the paper away and looked at Heidi. Vicki's eyes beneath her sideswept, dark blond hair were direct. "You realize Mom has no idea what she's saying when she says it."

Heidi mustered a casual shrug, even though part of her instantly fought the disappointment that coursed through her. She was hoping Vicki would at least empathize, if not try to unravel the contents.

"It sounded pretty sane to me," Heidi argued. "It's even well written."

"Mom wrote how many articles for the church newsletter, Heidi? She could compose entire segments in her sleep. This?" Vicki tossed the letter onto the coffee table. "It's nothing, Heidi. Just her mind going off into one of her many stories. Yesterday she was trying to convince me that Dad was out fishing on the lake and was bringing home an entire stringer of bass and bluegill to fillet and cook up for supper."

"And this?" Heidi handed Vicki the note card.

Vicki's confidence faltered. Heidi could see it in her body language, the way she seemed to tense up.

"Where'd you get this?"

"It was under my windshield wiper."

Vicki frowned. "Did you show it to the police?"

"Why would I?" Heidi countered. "There's no threat, no crime in leaving a note under someone's wiper."

"Yes, but it matches the break-in message on your mirror!" Vicki scooted to the edge of her chair. Her face was paler now, marked by worry.

Heidi gave a blithe smile. "And it matches what you used to call me. Other than Monkey. Or maybe that was *why* you called me Monkey? You thought I was 'crazy as a monkey'?"

Vicki blew air through her lips, lifting loose strands of hair around her face. "Really, Heidi."

"No. It's all right. I get it. I'm overemotional. I have an anxiety disorder — which has been verified by medical professionals now." Heidi waited to get satisfaction from seeing Vicki's surprise. There was none. Maybe she'd already assumed as much and had grown past the immature taunts of their younger years.

"Heidi . . ." Vicki's voice dropped. "I'm not sure what's going on. Mom's letter is nothing. But — the message on your mirror and that card? Your claiming you saw a woman looking at you in the window?"

"Oh, for all that's holy, I'm not losing my mind, Vicki!" Flabbergasted, Heidi's mouth dropped open. "You think I did that myself? Created some story just for the attention?"

Vicki leaned back in the chair and crossed her arms. "It wouldn't be the first time."

Heidi blinked. They locked eyes, a silent standoff.

Okay. Fine. She'd tried to get others' attention through various stunts in the past.

Heidi pursed her lips. "I wouldn't insult myself if I were that desperate for you to take notice of me."

Vicki nodded, doubtful. "You mean like the time you stole Dad's car and went dancing with your high-school boyfriend? Wearing a bikini top and a miniskirt? I'd say that was a bit self-deprecating." A tiny laugh followed.

Heidi bit back her own smile at the memory. She rolled her eyes. "Well, I was only sixteen. How was I to know you never wear a bikini top with a miniskirt?"

Vicki offered a chuckle, and then her smile disappeared.

Heidi smirked. "Look, I know I've done some dumb things. But this isn't one of them! I've nothing to gain by staging a break-in and leaving myself notes."

"Or claiming to see ghosts?" Vicki added.

"Exactly!" Heidi grinned for real this time. "What could I possibly gain from any of that?"

Vicki didn't answer. Instead, she heaved a sigh and looked down at her fingernails, picking at a chip in the mauve polish. Finally she met Heidi's gaze. "Attention, Heidi. You would gain attention. Even that letter from Mom. You like to have the world revolve around you. As if our family has ghosts!" She gave a derisive laugh. "And the messages, the woman in the window? All of that was with Rhett around. We all know how you like to . . ." She let her sentence hang.

A numbness washed over Heidi. Vicki didn't deserve an answer, yet Heidi still felt the need to defend herself. To justify herself to the demure and staid sister who capped her in years by a solid fifteen and had, in many ways, been more of a mother to her than her biological one.

Heidi hoisted the photo album from the sofa and slipped the photograph from its paper frame. She handed it to Vicki, who still held the mysterious note card in her other hand.

"What's this?" Vicki asked.

Heidi waved her hand. "Just look."

Her sister stared down at it. There was no shift in her expression, no look of shock, no quick lifting of her eyes. She flipped the photo over and read the penciled script on the back.

"Misty Wayfair," Heidi said, impatient for Vicki to say something — anything. To confirm to her sister that she wasn't on a desperate bid for attention.

Vicki swallowed. She nodded. "The woman looks like you."

Heidi scooted to the edge of her seat. "And she's dead."

"Of course she's dead. This was taken over a hundred years ago." Vicki shot her a weird look.

"No, look." Heidi stood and moved to position herself next to Vicki on the arm of her chair. "The body is held upright by a clamp. It's a metal frame of some sort. You can see it by her feet."

"Oh my —" Finally, a reaction. Vicki pulled the picture closer to her. "That's disgusting. Did they *sew* the body's eyes open, or did they just paint her eyes in after?"

"It looks like paint to me." Heidi leaned in closer as well.

Vicki's expression said she was appalled. She glanced at Heidi. "So, they photographed a dead woman."

"And she looks just like me," Heidi asserted, wanting Vicki to focus on the main point of the picture.

"Where'd you get this?" Vicki twisted to look at Heidi.

"At Connie's shop. The first day I came here. I found it, I bought the album, and the next morning" — Heidi tapped the face of the dead woman — "that woman was staring into my window."

Vicki flipped it over again. "Misty Wayfair," she murmured.

"Do I look like the Misty Wayfair they say haunts the woods and asylum?"

"Is that why you took Emma there?" Realization spread across Vicki's face.

Heidi nodded. Finally. It seemed Vicki was moving beyond her critical attitude and into the same realm Heidi was existing in.

"This can't be Misty Wayfair." Vicki shook her head, handing the photo back to Heidi. "According to what I know of the legend, they say she was murdered sometime in the 1800s, maybe a few decades before this photo was taken."

"Then why would someone write her name on the back?" Heidi insisted.

Vicki cleared her throat and pushed to her feet, leaving a whiff of lilac-vanilla perfume in her wake. "I don't know. I get why you've been unnerved, Heidi, but there's got to be an explanation. It's not like there's really a ghost, like some dead woman has come alive to target you specifically."

Heidi sank into the chair Vicki had abandoned. "Then how do you explain my look-alike in a photo album in a town our family has no connections to? The name on the back? The strange notes and messages? Mom's letter, for goodness' sake?"

Vicki shrugged, reaching behind her head to tighten her ponytail. "I told you — I don't know. But there are more important things to focus on right now. Real-life things. Like Mom. And not her letter full of fiction, but Mom as she is now. Today."

That stung. Disregarding everything meant disregarding her. Heidi wasn't even sure that Vicki knew she did it. It probably wasn't intended to be a dismissal, but it was all the same. Mom was important. The lodge was important. Vicki's life was important. Heidi was just chasing shadows and dreams like always.

Vicki walked off toward the kitchen, the

conversation apparently over for her.

Heidi stopped her. "Vicki?"

Her older sister turned. She looked so much like Mom. "Yeah?"

Heidi couldn't help it. She had to say it. "But all this — it proves I'm not nuts. It proves that something is happening here in Pleasant Valley. Whether you want to acknowledge it or not. Someone in the past looked exactly like me. Someone in the present wants to mess with my head. That's not important to you? Not important enough to dig into and figure out what the connection is?"

Vicki pursed her lips, and her chest rose and fell in a silent sigh. For a brief moment, she seemed conflicted. Then she leveled Heidi with a sisterly look. "I love you. I do. But, Heidi . . . I just — can't."

It was the lamest, most hurtful excuse Heidi had ever heard.

CHAPTER 21

Heidi waited at the front counter of the repair shop. A girl barely out of high school had greeted her and then, per Heidi's request, disappeared into the back to call for Brad. Vicki had asked Heidi to drop off his lunch on her way to see Mom. But, for Heidi, it was stop number one of three, not two. She was heading back to the asylum first. To explore more — without Emma this time — and see if she could uncover any clues. What she'd find in a run-down, abandoned hospital was yet to be seen. Probably nothing. She wasn't even sure what she was looking for.

The double doors to the shop opened, only it wasn't Brad who emerged. Heidi tensed as she met Rhett's uninterpretable expression. He wiped his hands on a blue cotton rag, his customary battered baseball cap rammed onto his head.

"Brad stepped out for lunch."

"Oh." Heidi set the insulated bag on the counter. "That's what I brought for him."

Rhett tossed the rag into a bucket by the door and crossed his arms. Waiting. For what?

Heidi offered him an impertinent grin. "Well, then, Dr. Banner, never mind."

"Who?"

Heidi blinked. Really? He didn't know? "Better brush up on your comic books, hero."

She turned on her heel and hiked out of the shop. That type of attempt at banter could only go nowhere good and fast. Opening the door to her car, she slipped in, then shrieked as the door was yanked from her hand when she tried to close it.

Rhett leaned over and peered in. Really. All he needed was green skin.

"The Hulk?" was all he said, phone in hand. She caught a glimpse of a Google page. He'd had to Google it?

She stifled a wry chuckle. Ohhhh, the backwoodsman had a weakness. He wasn't a comic fan. Heidi was willing to latch on to any chink in the man's hulking façade.

She put her hands on the steering wheel and stared up at him. She raised an eyebrow, hoping she was leveling him with a look equal to the one he was giving her.

"If the shoe fits," she shrugged. "Wait. The Hulk doesn't wear shoes." She gave him a mock look of empathy and glanced at his steel-toed boots.

Rhett's expression didn't change. He scanned her car. The photo album on the passenger seat. The blue note card from her windshield wiper. A paper map of the Pleasant Valley region, the river, and the side roads, because heaven knew GPS was worthless in the great up-north.

"Where're you going?" he growled.

Heidi tipped her head, refusing to be intimidated. Emma wasn't in her care.

"That's for me to know." She flipped the words at him like a rich man would blithely toss cash into the air. Heidi turned the key in the ignition.

Rhett didn't move. Didn't release the door.

Heidi reached for the door handle and gave a little tug. "Um, my door?"

"You're going to the asylum." It was a statement.

Heidi paused. "So?"

"I wouldn't go there alone." Again, a blink only. No smile, no raised brows, not even a change of inflection in his voice.

Heidi bit back a sigh. Irritation toward Rhett, and also annoyance that he'd somehow read her own internal hesitation. Going to the abandoned asylum alone posed no legitimate threat that she knew of, yet it still creeped her out. Especially after Emma's declaration when they were there. As if she'd seen a ghost — a ghost that did not exist.

She looked up to respond to Rhett, but he was gone.

Oh. Okay then.

Heidi pulled her door shut and yelped again as the passenger door yanked open and Rhett reached in, picking up the photo album and note card before squeezing his frame onto the seat.

"Excuse me?" Heidi glared at him.

Rhett reached behind him and set the items on the back seat. He shut the door and gave a wave of two fingers. "Let's go."

Heidi eyed him incredulously.

"No." She shook her head. "I'm going alone."

"No, you're not."

Ooooh, he was going to play the alpha-male card? Fine. Heidi killed the engine and removed the key from the ignition. "Then I'm not going." She was done trying to earn the man's respect. Trying to loosen him up or figure him out. Now he was downright under-her-skin annoying.

Rhett took the keys from her hand. "Good. I'll drive."

He pushed open the car door, and before Heidi could react, her driver's door was open and he was leaning in. "On second thought," he said, "we'll take my truck."

She had no intention of admitting it, but bouncing along in the passenger seat of Rhett's beater truck with Rüger the dog pressed against her leg and Archie the mangy cat doing an impressive balancing act on the dashboard was far more comforting than trying to maneuver this rutted road on her own. It had become a familiar jaunt, and since it was sunny out today, sunshine filtered through the leafy treetops. The woods were more inviting than when she'd been here with Emma.

The asylum hadn't changed — why would it? — yet somehow it seemed different today. Less imposing, and less haunting. Heidi walked ahead of Rhett, who seemed content to let her be, to explore on her own. Rüger pranced beside her, nose to the ground, his one-eyed furry face sniffing at traces of rabbit or squirrel, maybe even deer.

"What do you know about the asylum?" Heidi tossed the question over her shoulder. She stood at the front door that hung on a single hinge and was ajar. She could see in. Filthy linoleum flooring greeted her, along with severely cracked plaster walls, some sections revealing the lath framework behind.

"Not much." Rhett's baritone was practically in her ear.

Heidi whirled. "Stop sneaking up on me."

"I'm not." He shrugged.

She edged through the doorway into what once had been the foyer. Her eyes swept the room. There was no furniture, nothing really of any interest outside of the fact the place practically oozed untold history and felt like lingering souls floated in the corners.

Heidi shivered.

No. No wandering souls today.

Her footsteps were silent as she crossed to the middle of the old lobby. Rüger had slipped in and was nosing around in the corner. A mouse probably. Rhett stood in the doorway still, hands in his pockets, patiently waiting for her to do whatever it was she'd come here to do.

A narrow staircase with walls on both sides led up to the second floor. A long hallway ran to the right of the stairs, with a few doors on each side of it. Heidi looked farther down the hall and saw yet another door at the far end. This one appeared to open to the backyard of the asylum.

"Weird," she mumbled. Who would have thought to build a mental hospital deep in the woods, far away from civilization? Why not at the edge of town? Easier access, less — bizarre.

Heidi moved to the bottom of the stairs.

"Careful," Rhett admonished.

She cast him an exasperated look. "Listen," she said with a raised brow, "if you're going to hang out with me, I'm going to need more than just one-word sentences and military commands. Either stay here and leave me be, or come. But if you come, use your big-boy words."

His face darkened at her words.

Eek. Heidi winced inwardly. She sounded lofty and rude, like Vicki. She hefted a sigh and offered a gentler smile. "I'm sorry. It's just — I don't know why you're here. You don't even like me."

Rhett snapped his finger at Rüger. The dog was wandering down the abandoned hall.

Heidi repositioned her foot on the bottom step.

"It's not that I don't like you." Rhett reached down and gave Rüger a reassuring pat on the head. Then he lifted his gray eyes, a bit softer now. "I just don't trust you."

"I'm not hurting anyone today."

"Exactly my point." Rhett neared her, and she could smell the repair shop on his shirt. Grease and fresh air. "You're reckless."

"Ahh." There it was again. The presupposed insults. Heidi bit back a perturbed sigh.

"You're cute. Reckless is cute," Rhett stated blandly. "But it can cause a lot of trouble." He pushed past her, pounding his foot on the stairs to test their stability.

Did he just say she was *cute*?

Heidi stared after him, even as he was on the sixth step.

Rhett glanced over his shoulder. "Coming?"

"Yeah." Now who was speaking in one-word sentences?

The upstairs of the asylum felt spooky. Shafts of light escaped into the hallway from the two open doors in the long line of rooms, and also from the far end where the roof and side had caved in and lay open. Debris littered the hall, piles of leaves and sticks, with mud caked in the corners and thick cobwebs that swayed in the breeze.

Rhett went ahead of her, bouncing on the floorboards, testing the structure to ensure one of them didn't fall through and plummet to the first floor and break a leg, if not their necks. Heidi peered in the first room to the left. It wasn't much different from the foyer below. Wood floors instead of linoleum, but the same plastered walls with cracks creating their own road map on the wall. A long window with bars over it. *Bars.* That was different from downstairs.

"Do you think this is where the patients were housed?" she ventured.

Rüger padded into the room and looked around, his tail wagging, long fur brushing the air.

"Probably," Rhett replied.

Heidi nodded slowly. "Why is Misty Wayfair connected to the asylum?" She didn't ask the second part of her question. *Why did Emma seem to think Misty resided here?*

Rhett continued to pound his foot on the floorboards as he made his way to the next room. He stopped and braced his hand against the wall, his eyes scanning the space before him. "They say Misty Wayfair has been sighted on and off over the years. But most of the claims have been disproven. My uncle thought he saw her back in the seventies when he was hunting around here. Turned out to be a homeless woman."

That was perhaps the longest stretch of

words Rhett Crawford had ever spoken to her.

Heidi nodded. Maybe if she was quiet, he would talk more. She followed Rhett into the room, which was almost identical to the last one. She moved across the floor and grasped the bars at the window, tugging a bit. Funny. The bars were still solid, even though the patients' screams had long since drifted away.

"They also say Misty Wayfair was attached to someone who once lived here. No one knows who." Rhett stood next to her, and they stared beyond the bars to the front yard below. Heidi could see the truck, and Archie too, still curled up on the dash.

"No one ever cared to find out?" Heidi asked.

Rhett shrugged. "Why? The woman is dead."

"But she lived." Heidi turned a surprised gaze on him. "Why do people dismiss the dead so easily? Once you've passed, you're no longer important?"

Rhett eyed her.

So much for not talking and letting him talk.

"Do you even know who Misty Wayfair was?" she whispered.

Rhett met her stare. "No."

At least he was honest.

"And you don't care?"

Rhett was silent for a long moment. Finally he said, "If you care, then I care."

She was stunned. It didn't add up. Didn't make sense.

"But you don't even like me," she told him.

"I never said that."

"Yes, you did."

"Nope." He shook his head.

"You act as though you don't like me."

He nodded. "That's fair."

"What does that mean?"

"Because you hurt Emma." Rhett's eyes drilled into hers. Honest. Open. Confident.

"Yes," Heidi nodded, tearing her gaze away. "I said I was sorry."

"Then you hurt her again."

Gosh. He was relentless. But then she'd goaded him into this.

"So . . . about Misty Wayfair," Heidi said, hoping to distract him.

Rhett's elbow nudged hers. She met his eyes again.

"The difference between you and Misty Wayfair is that she's beyond saving. Whatever happened to her, whoever she was. But you're not."

An emotion Heidi couldn't explain awakened in her. The stunning kind that told her someone had, perhaps for the first time, read one of her fears correctly. In this particular case, that she was just like Misty Wayfair. Wandering, alone, misguided, and left to herself as though everyone were afraid to discover the real her. The real person behind the flippant, coy responses, the impulsiveness, and the deep-rooted anxiety buried beneath it all.

Heidi couldn't acknowledge his comment. It was too personal. Too frightening to let someone in. Someone who just moments before she'd compared to the Incredible Hulk.

A crash from below startled them both. Heidi ripped her eyes from his, and they both started for the door. Rüger let out a series of barks that said danger was near, and then the dog took off ahead of them.

"Rüger!" Rhett's command echoed through the empty building.

They both hurried toward the stairs, and just as Heidi moved to descend, Rhett put out his arm.

"Hold." His voice was quieter now. Rüger stood at the bottom of the stairs, the fur on his back standing up, a low growl coming from deep in his throat.

"What is it?" Heidi froze in compliance

with Rhett's command. Happy to let him control the situation. Well, at least she hoped he was in control.

Rüger took a tentative step forward, then launched out of sight. The wall blocked their vision. Rhett took deliberate steps down the stairs, and Heidi felt no shame in cowering behind his solid back. At the bottom, Rüger had disappeared. The foyer was silent.

"What was that crashing sound?" Heidi whispered.

Rhett held up his hand, demanding silence. He listened. Pointed.

Rüger came padding back into the room from the hallway.

Heidi looked down the hall to where he'd come from — the back door stood open, swaying in the wind, slamming against the doorjamb. "How'd that get open?" she asked.

Rhett didn't answer. Instead, he stepped slowly down the hallway, glanced into the rooms whose doors were open, and checked the closed ones. Arriving at the far end, they came to a door that opened into a back room. Old hooks hung from the walls, most likely where employees once hung their coats and jackets. An empty milk can lay overturned on the floor, but not recently, going by the dirt and leaves packed on top and around it. The windows here were filthy and hard to see through, some of the panes cracked or missing.

Heidi opened her mouth to speak, but Rhett's hand on her forearm stopped her. He squeezed and pointed with his other hand.

The wall opposite them, in the corner, was crumbling white-washed plaster. Red letters, fresh, dripped down the broken pieces of plaster and onto the floor, painted in haphazard swaths.

Forgotten in a place of madness.
You will be too.

CHAPTER 22

"All right. Let's get some warmth in us." Connie eased onto a chair opposite Heidi, pushing a hot cup of tea toward her. The kitchen table between them, Heidi had the album, the note, and a blank notepad in front of her. A mug of lukewarm coffee sat nearby, neglected. Heidi wrapped her hands around the fresh cup of tea and let her mind calculate the events that had unfolded since the fright at the asylum ruins.

Rhett hadn't been able to get a call out from the asylum to the police. So they'd made their way back to town and stopped at the station. They filed a report and were reassured that the police would be sending out officers to look at the vandalism. Maybe they'd find fingerprints or some DNA and match them with a name in their database. But it was all so ambiguous, Heidi wasn't holding out hope.

Rhett drove her back to the Crawfords',

where Heidi curled up on the couch next to Emma. She'd tried to hide her tremors, but as soon as Rhett left the room, Emma helped Ducie to stand and encouraged the dog to lie down on the floor next to Heidi. Emma had waited with expectation. It didn't take Heidi long to drop her hand and curl it into the fur of Ducie's neck. The dog nudged her arm. Sensing. Knowing. Emma settled on the floor beside her dog, just below where Heidi rested. Three comrades. Different struggles. Common hearts.

An hour later, Heidi heard the sound of a vehicle pulling up the Crawford drive. She peeked out the window to see Rhett — he'd returned her car. He still had her keys from when he'd swiped them earlier. It was a simple deed, but thoughtful. Still, she'd had no desire to return to Lane Lodge. To Vicki. To the room where the first blood-red message had appeared on her mirror.

Returning home about the same time, Connie rescued Heidi from just such a thing. She warmed up venison stew for supper and whipped up a batch of biscuits to go on the side. Never having eaten venison, Heidi hesitated. More trauma was not going to help her collect her wits and keep from an all-out panic attack. But, it was good — like beef — and Heidi sensed some awareness flooding through her internalized anxiety with the uplift of protein and her blood sugar.

Connie's husband, Murphy, came home too, but then he snatched up a plate of food with a grin, gave a quick peck to Connie's cheek, and escaped out the back door on his way to the workshop. With Rhett, Heidi supposed. Or maybe Rhett had gone back to his place? She assumed he had his own home and didn't live with his parents.

Nope. She was wrong. He was still here.

A soft, brushed-wool blanket settled over her shoulders, breaking her focus away from what had happened and returning her to the present. Casual, as if it were commonplace to do so, Rhett tucked the blanket around her neck and then pulled out a chair by his mom. Emma followed him and sat in the fourth chair. Heidi looked at each one of them, and they all met her eyes.

"Wh-what are you all doing?" Heidi didn't understand. The blanket. The three people opposite her. The photo album between them. The sense of . . . family.

Emma tilted her head and gave Heidi a smile. "We're going to help you."

It was so simple. So sincere.

Heidi gnawed at the inside of her lip. She glanced at Rhett, who reached for the album while nodding at Connie's gentle smile.

The older woman reached across the table and took Heidi's hand. "You're not alone, honey."

Heidi swiped away a rebel tear.

Not alone.

Vicki had walked away from this. From her. But the Crawfords had not. They were rallying, and she didn't deserve it.

She muffled a watery chuckle as even Ducie limped into the room, three-legged, tendering the one Heidi had inadvertently broken. The dog wrestled himself to the floor beside Emma, a groan escaping his jowls.

As they were all laughing at the sight, the back door opened and Murphy entered, his gray hair ruffled, his ginormous shoulders, so much like Rhett's, lifting the load of an antique trunk. Leather handles on both ends, he hefted it down to the floor.

He smiled, his beard tickling the collar of his flannel shirt. "Figured we may want to rustle through this thing too," he said and broke the silence as they all stared at him.

A smile broadened across Connie's face.

Murphy explained, "It's that trunk we bought at the estate sale. When we picked up that photo album. Haven't gone through it yet, but who knows? If you've a dead girl who looks like you in there" — he nodded toward the photo album — "maybe you got more stuff in here that'll help it make sense."

"Great idea!" Emma looked between her father and Heidi.

Rhett leaned back in his chair. Content, it seemed, though Heidi noted he gave her a few glances now and then as if doing some internal assessment to make sure she was truly okay.

She wasn't.

Not in the least.

Everything about today was foreign. Frightening. And now, enticing.

Heidi was on unfamiliar territory. Where the asylum had turned into a nightmare, the Crawfords were turning into a dream.

Either way, she would have to wake up at some point. And real life had already proven it held very little promise for her.

The trunk's contents were strewn across the Crawfords' kitchen floor. Emma sat in the corner, a vintage newspaper open, her finger tracing the lines as she read, her mouth moving silently in forming the words. A few newspaper clippings, yellowed with age, perched on her knee. She was lost in another world, set in 1908 Pleasant Valley.

Rhett was studying the photograph of Heidi's deceased doppelgänger.

Murphy sat in a chair nearby, his legs stretched out, work boots on, and a cup of coffee balanced in a brawny hand.

Connie lifted another item from the trunk as Heidi pulled the blanket Rhett had given her tighter around her shoulders. She tried to reconcile with today's events. Events that had sent her anxiety into full-fledged panic mode but now were counteracted by a calming peace. Regardless of cryptic words painted in blood-red on an asylum wall, despite that they matched messages which seemed to be pointed at Heidi, everything felt right.

Everything felt . . . safe.

Heidi chose to allow herself to relish it. For now. She knew it wouldn't last, but no matter. Tonight she would accept it.

"Interesting!" Connie opened the lid to an antique cigar box, its top embellished with a faded color image of a woman in a ball gown and a man in an evening suit and top hat. An envelope lay inside. Just one. Also faded and weathered-looking with its edges yellowed.

A name was scrawled on the front.

Dorothea Reed.

"That name sounds familiar," Heidi muttered.

Connie scrunched her lips in thought. "Hmmm, it does to me too." She flipped the envelope over and slid out its contents. "It's definitely a personal letter. I wonder why it was saved?"

"What's it say?" Murphy asked. He sounded like Rhett. Direct, almost commanding, and yet when Heidi gave him a hesitant look, she found warmth in his expression.

"Let me see if I can make it out," Connie answered. "The handwriting is very thin and cramped." She examined the page for a moment.

Emma discarded her newspaper and slid across the floor next to her mother. "I can read it," she stated plainly.

"Go ahead then," Connie laughed. "I can't make head nor tails of it."

Emma took time to carefully smooth the letter's edges and creases, handling it as a precious gem of history. She cleared her throat, and her voice was even as she read.

"Dear Thea,
You were twelve when we took you in. It was our Christian duty. Looking back, I'm uncertain as to whether it was a wise

decision, but as I lie on my deathbed, I find I must give you what little resolution I can. Mr. Mendelsohn will not be kind to you once I am gone. He is a brusque man. While he will not harm you physically, I fear he will become spiteful. You may wish to leave him. Please do not. In exchange for knowing you will care for my husband until he too passes into the hereafter, I will give you what I know of your history before you came to the orphanage."

"Well, that sounds menacing!" Connie inserted.

Murphy grunted his agreement. "Hope she left that Mendelsohn guy."

Heidi exchanged glances with Rhett while Emma waited, an impatient look on her face for having been interrupted. She dropped her gaze back to the letter and continued.

"All that is known of your parentage is your mother's name: P. A. Reed. You were left at the orphanage at four years of age. They told us your mother had traveled from the Pleasant Valley, Wisconsin area, which of course is significantly north of where we are currently. You were left with little belongings. A dress, a nightgown, and a knitted hat. You said few words for the first year and thereafter became a friendly child. That is, unfortunately, all I know. But perhaps a name and a place may be all the tools necessary to assuage any curiosity as to your parentage should you wish to appease it.

I regret that I was naught but a guardian to you. Mothering died when our child did, so many years before you.

I bid you and this world farewell.

Please remember your promise to me to care for my husband.

> With some affection,
> Margory Mendelsohn"

Silence filled the room. It was a sad letter, Heidi determined. And, somehow, she related to it as the words drew her into the life of this Dorothea Reed, as though the letter were written to her. Of course, she knew her parentage and roots, yet the feeling of being an afterthought, ostracized by way of not belonging, that was something Heidi knew all too well.

"Thea Reed." Rhett slid the photograph of the dead woman across the table toward Heidi.

She picked it up and gave him a questioning look.

"She's the photographer," he added.

"That's right!" Connie snapped her fingers.

Heidi lifted the picture. "Yes. That's where I've heard the name before."

"The trunk had *T. Reed* etched into the leather handle on its far side. Everything in it must belong to this Thea girl. That photo album musta been part of her belongings then." Murphy sat up and leaned on the table. "Makes sense. It was right next to the trunk at the sale. Fact, I think we bought them all together. The trunk and the album."

"Who was Dorothea — Thea Reed then?" Heidi ventured.

Emma broke into the conversation as she folded the letter back to its original form. "Dorothea Reed was the photographer apprentice who worked alongside Mr. Amos, the owner of Amos Brothers Photography, a portrait studio in Pleasant Valley. He suffered an attack of the heart in May of 1908, and Dorothea Reed and a Mr. Simeon Coyle assisted in retrieving medical attention for him."

They all stared at Emma.

She blinked back at them as if reciting historical facts was everyone's best talent.

338

"It was in that paper," she said, pointing to the vintage paper she'd left behind in the corner.

Murphy chuckled. "You do beat all, baby girl."

"Who is Simeon Coyle?" Connie asked Emma, as if somehow the girl would instinctively know.

And apparently she did.

"Simeon Coyle was descended from Reginald Kramer, founder of Kramer Logging. His grandmother Mathilda married Fergus Coyle, and Reginald Kramer disowned all her line afterward. His nephew, Edward Fortune, inherited the logging company, which is why today there are no Kramers there. Only Fortunes."

"Fortunes who have a fortune!" Murphy groused and took a sip of his coffee.

"I still don't see how any of this explains the woman in the picture who looks like me." Heidi's head was spinning.

Emma slipped the letter back into the envelope. "Maybe because you're a Coyle."

A dust particle landing on the tabletop could have been heard in the silence that followed.

Emma, oblivious, set the envelope back in the cigar box and replaced its lid. She returned her attention to them. "There's a sketch of Mary Coyle in one of the newspaper clippings from the trunk. Her obituary. It's the same woman as in your picture. She looks like you."

It was all so obvious to Emma.

Heidi frowned. Her eyes swept up to meet Rhett's, even as Connie lunged for one of the newspaper clippings Emma had been browsing earlier.

"But," Heidi protested, "we're not from around here. My family has no history in Pleasant Valley."

"Are you sure?" Rhett's eyes drilled into hers.

"I —" Heidi stopped. Of course she was. She'd been raised in a church in Minnesota. Her father was born and raised in Nebraska. He met her mother at college. Mom was from Wisconsin, only she said she'd been raised in Madison, which was several hours south of here.

Still. Heidi fingered the handle of her teacup. "If I were related to the Coyles . . ." She let her words trail as her hypothesis took her places she wasn't sure she wanted to go.

"Then Misty Wayfair will come for you," Emma finished. "Like the curse says she will."

"Legend has it Misty Wayfair was as ill as

the residents in that asylum," Murphy offered.

Connie laid her hand over her husband's. "Murph." Her voice held concern, and a quick glance was sent Heidi's way.

"It's all right, really." Heidi nodded. "I'm not a Coyle. We've no connection to Pleasant Valley at all."

But her eyes locked with those of the dead woman, Mary Coyle, in the photograph. Painted-on eyes or not, Mary's vapid expression told a different story. And yet it hadn't been Misty whom Heidi had seen in her bedroom window. It was Mary.

Even a fragment of the idea sent a shiver through Heidi. What were the odds there were two haunting spirits roaming the woods of Pleasant Valley? Both connected by a curse that seemed as though directed straight back to Heidi herself.

CHAPTER 23

THEA

Everything about the previous day was unsettling. She couldn't get Effie's poem recitation out of her mind, nor could she stop second-guessing the offer to sort through the old asylum records. As much as her spirit yearned to flee the asylum forever, it was as if an unseen hand held on to the hem of her dress and pulled her back. Making her stay. Like Thea recalled wishing she could do as a little girl when her mother's feet had carried her down the walkway and out of Thea's life.

During the night, Thea had wandered with restless unease to the window and peered down over the silent street. There was no woman dancing through the fog. No ghosts or visions or spirits. The dead had remained dead last night, even though Thea could hear Mr. Mendelsohn's troublesome voice deep in her mind.

"A wandering spirit is nothing to bandy about as nonsense."

The old photographer, with his skinny hands, would drum his fingers on the top of the table and stare across it at Thea. She'd never, in the years spent with him, grown accustomed to the cold superstitions that rested in his eyes.

"A gentleman whose son I photographed after a specific bout with the measles wrote to me later inquiring as to whether I'd seen his son's spirit in the photograph. Indeed, I had. Floating just up and to the right of his actual dead form. Of course, I denied it, for who was I to encourage the wanderings into the afterlife of a very healthy man? Still, a month later, his wife returned the photograph of the dead child to me. Her husband had taken his life one night after claiming he'd been stoking the fire and had turned around to see his son rise suddenly from a prostrate position on the couch — as if from inside a coffin."

Thea recalled his stories, spoken with such conviction that she too half believed them to be true. Half believed that Mr. Mendelsohn's teachings of the afterlife were as logical as the instructions of how to work his camera. But now? Mrs. Amos had indicated her faith in a Creator, with a vested interest in them — in Thea — and that idea was

343

much more welcoming. It would change the concept of the afterlife too. For wouldn't a Creator have a plan for the dead beyond just allowing their souls to wander aimlessly? That belief made Heaven seem possible, life seem purposeful, and the darkness lift, even if just a little bit, to allow light in.

Now, Thea buttoned her skirt at the side of her waist, inspecting herself and her dress in the mirror. Satisfied, she pinned a simple velvet hat to her hair and snatched her reticule from the desk. When she opened the door, she gasped as Mr. Fritz, the other boardinghouse guest, stood with his hand poised to knock. He blustered and wiped his hand over his mouth as he collected his wits. He seemed as surprised as she was.

"My apologies, Miss Reed. I didn't mean to intrude."

Thea eyed him as she drew her door shut behind her. "Yes?"

Mr. Fritz shifted his weight and tugged on his coat, regaining his proper confidence. "I was meaning to inquire — about the topic of conversation the other morning. I was hoping you might help me understand a bit more of the story surrounding Kramer Logging and this family, the Coyles."

Thea narrowed her eyes and took a few steps toward the stairwell that would take her to the front entrance of the boarding-house. The idea of escaping to Mr. Amos's studio was growing in its appeal. Not to mention, she wanted to visit him now that Mrs. Amos had sent her last message, with the doctor saying he was "out of the woods."

Mr. Fritz followed her.

Thea lifted her skirts as she descended the stairs. She answered him over her shoulder. "I don't believe I will be of much assistance, being new to Pleasant Valley my-self."

And quite unnerved by it all, she might have added. But she didn't.

She paused at the bottom and turned, leveling a censorious eye on the man. "Why do you wish to know?"

Mr. Fritz offered a small smile. The kind that tried to imply he posed no danger and insinuated he wasn't nosy — like Mrs. Brummel. He twisted his bowler hat in his hands. "I'll be frank with you."

"Please do," Thea encouraged, her eyes narrowing as she attempted to read beyond Mr. Fritz's platonic smile into the depths behind his rather normal brown eyes.

"Have you ever heard of Nellie Bly?" he asked.

Thea blinked. "I have not."

"No." Mr. Fritz shook his head. "No, I

don't suppose you have. Regardless, I'd like to speak with you further about your impressions of this community. Being new and all. Mrs. Brummel has implied that you've become rather — close — to Simeon Coyle. I know they are distantly related to the Fortunes, who own the logging company, who in turn are related to Reginald Kramer, the founder of Valley Heights Asylum."

Thea watched him pause, seem to collect his thoughts in the same cadence as he collected his breath. She glanced beyond them, toward the main lounge of the boardinghouse. It wouldn't surprise her if she were to see Mrs. Brummel's shadow stretched across the floor. Eavesdropping. Collecting hearsay that she could then twist and cajole into interesting stories for the rest of her boarders and town friends.

Mr. Fritz continued. "Nellie Bly is a journalist from New York. About twenty years ago, she committed herself into an asylum with the purpose of bringing to light the — ah — *travesties* of treatment, so one might put it, that the patients were subjected to."

Thea had no idea where this was going, but a restlessness inside her made her edge her way toward the door. Toward escape. But Mr. Fritz followed like a horsefly on a hot, muggy day.

Once on the sidewalk, Thea turned to him. "Mr. Fritz, I'm sure I'm not following why you've an interest in my opinions — which are merely that. Opinion. I daresay, you would be wise to leave it all alone."

She didn't know why she'd added the warning at the end. Whether to mimic Mrs. Brummel's insistence that indeed an accursed spirit of a murdered woman would haunt him, or more likely because something within her wished to protect Rose — to protect Simeon. Her heart warmed. She blushed. Wishing she hadn't.

Mr. Fritz noticed, his expression growing shrewd.

"I'm a newspaperman. I'm from Milwaukee and, considering Miss Bly's exposé, I'm not the first to be inspired to investigate the well-being of the patients at asylums such as Valley Heights. Yet here I find there is a much deeper story, or so it seems."

Thea wished she were brave enough to be rude, to turn on her heel and walk away. Yet, something held her. Mr. Fritz was as hypnotized by the mysteries of this town and its generational conditions as she was.

Mr. Fritz lowered his voice, glancing all directions before speaking again. "Mrs. Brummel stated you were assisting Mr.

Coyle in photographing the patients at the hospital. You have gained access to a very private institution. To areas of the hospital a mere visitor is not allowed to go. I was wondering if I could hire you to . . ." He paused, reading her face as if to determine whether she was even a tiny bit open to listening. What he saw must have encouraged him, for he cleared his throat and continued, "I would like to hire you to report to me the conditions of the patients. Their treatment. The staff's methods of helping during patient distresses."

"You wish for me to spy?" Thea was incredulous. The very idea of nosing around the hospital for the purpose of solving whether her own mother had been a patient there already had her in great turmoil. Reporting back to a newspaperman seemed unconscionable. Especially if it implicated Simeon and Rose in the process. By means of simply being the grandchildren — the *disowned* grandchildren — of Reginald Kramer.

"I wish for you to help me gather the information needed to give Valley Heights a positive report. Mental asylums are not particularly in good standing with most people. Communities are becoming suspicious of abuse and the mishandling of patients. Still, we know these places of care are necessary for certain individuals."

"Abuse? Mishandling?" Thea echoed.

"Yes." Mr. Fritz extended his elbow to silently communicate he would escort her to wherever she was headed. Thea tucked her hand in its crook for no other reason than she was uncomfortable discussing it in the middle of the boardwalk on Pleasant Valley's main street.

She started toward the portrait studio. Mr. Fritz fell into place beside her.

"It's a delicate subject, really, Miss Reed. And you should know . . . some of it might challenge your sensibilities."

Thea gave him a sideways glance that probably was more of a sneer. "I take photographs of corpses, Mr. Fritz. If my sensibilities were any more hardened, I'd exhume their bodies and practice surgical science on them. So, please, do continue."

He had the gallantry to blanch at her boldness. At her mention of the activity of dissecting cadavers to practice medical skills.

"Well then. Aside from rough-handling and the like, some hospitals have taken to . . ." He sidestepped horse droppings as they crossed the road to the other side. They hurried in front of a logger's wagon that was clambering toward them, the massive horses in front, the logger perched high on his seat. Riding along in the wagon bed sat a few more loggers. All of the men were covered in flannel and denim, on their way to Kramer Logging for a day's work.

Once they reached the other side of the road, Mr. Fritz went on with what he was saying. "Sterilization," he said in a rush.

Thea stopped on the sidewalk. "Pardon?"

Mr. Fritz shifted his feet. "Some doctors have subscribed to the practice of sterilizing their patients to avoid any reproduction of the genetic abnormalities."

Thea's heart pounded, and her breaths quickened. But she quickly composed herself. It had never occurred to her that a hospital committed to caring for those with troubled minds would resort to such inhumane care. Let alone . . . her imagination went wild. What exactly was sterilization anyway? She had no desire to ask Mr. Fritz to expound on it.

"Is that all?" she demanded.

Mr. Fritz ran his fingers over the brim of his hat, which he'd set on his head when they'd begun their walk. "No. There are other atrocities. I'm doubtful with a hospital as small as Valley Heights that they'd be applying experimental treatments to the patients' brains; however, in larger hospitals, this is a somewhat frequent practice. Accepted as well. But I find it —"

"Appalling." Thea's response was slightly louder than a whisper. She glanced toward the door of the portrait studio that they now stood facing. While she couldn't see through the door or through the walls to the river beyond, her mind could conjure the imagery there. The forest, the serene brick hospital set a ways off in the darkness, alone. And the small graveyard . . .

Mr. Fritz's declarations brought an entirely different story to her mind. A troubling one. One of a mother struggling, leaving her daughter behind, entering a facility claiming to be devoted to her care, and then . . . experimentation.

If indeed what Mr. Fritz said was true, where did Valley Heights fall on the scale of good and bad? Were Rose and Simeon aware of any mistreatment? Had Simeon buried the evidence of abuse under the silent covering of the woods?

"Yes." Thea heard the word escape her mouth before she could ponder further. Mr. Fritz's gaze flew to meet hers.

"You will assist me, then?"

Thea nodded, though her stomach felt sick at the idea. "Yes, but if — if there's anything untoward happening there . . ." She hesitated. But, no. It was a tale that must be told, if there was any truth to it. "Then I will tell you."

Mr. Fritz's mouth thinned into a smile that wasn't victorious or elated. More resigned. "Thank you, Miss Reed. My hopes are that you will indeed find nothing amiss."

"I have one condition," Thea added.

Mr. Fritz raised his brows. "Condition?"

"If you uncover more of the story of the Coyles — of Misty Wayfair, of Kramer Logging — you will tell me first."

Mr. Fritz cocked his head, suspicious. "Why? What interests you so about the Coyles?"

Thea's chest tightened. With emotion, perhaps, or trepidation. Or both. "I sense that both Simeon and his sister, Rose, are merely pawns in a line of unfortunate events. They are both employed at the hospital, and if something were to be exposed there, and more was brought to light of their family history, I feel it only a kindness to know of it and to —"

"To protect them?" Mr. Fritz supplied.

Perhaps, yes, that was what she was hoping. Thea nodded.

The newspaperman eyed her for a moment, then gave a short nod. "Very well.

However, I'm still uncertain as to why you have such a vested and loyal interest in them. They're of no consequence to you."

No consequence.

He was right.

But even though Simeon wasn't beside her, Thea could feel the depths of Simeon's shadowy eyes on her. The way his very frame drew her to him. As if, somehow, and for some reason, they were bound together, and they just didn't know why.

After a day at the studio, Thea determined to visit Mr. Amos. He would be pleased — she hoped — that she'd successfully completed a sitting with Mr. Fortune. The man had returned, quite wary, and with an air of being offended Mr. Amos had dared to have a heart attack. Even so, Mr. Fortune settled, and Thea had finally taken a photograph.

Mrs. Amos opened the door at Thea's knock, and a smile met her faded blue eyes.

"Oh, dear me. You've come for a visit! Bless you!"

Thea slipped inside the house, the warmth of the front room almost suffocating her. While her elders must be chilled, Thea missed the fresh air that had been shut out behind her.

"How is he?" she inquired politely.

Mrs. Amos looked over her shoulder, her lace cap dangling around her ears, with white wisps of hair framing her face as she returned her attention to Thea. "He's restless, to be sure. He wants to return to the studio and keeps grouching that he has appointments to fulfill. Whatever those may be. I ask" — Mrs. Amos put a conspiratorial hand on Thea's arm — "how many photographs can one man take in a town this size? I've no idea. He doesn't realize that if our children didn't wire us funds, we'd be most destitute."

Thea gave an empathetic smile to the old woman, not for the last time wondering what inspired Mr. Amos to stay in Pleasant Valley when it seemed his family had long left the town behind them.

"Come." Mrs. Amos led her through the front room to a bedroom in the back of the small two-story house. A well-worn carpet runner, which had seen better days, lined the hall.

The door to the bedroom stood open and was quite narrow, revealing a bed, wide enough for only one person, against the far wall. Thea also noted a single window with lace curtains, a small bureau cluttered with knickknacks, and an end table with a stack of books on top. Mr. Amos, propped against pillows, greeted her with a cranky frown.

"What are you doing here?" he grumbled.

His wife flustered around him, straightening his blankets, tugging on his shirtsleeve to pull it down to his wrist.

Mr. Amos gave her hand a light slap. "Stop your molly-coddling! I'm not dead."

"You were dead enough to see the Lord himself, I daresay," Mrs. Amos shot back, though her wrinkled face was still wreathed in a patient smile. "Dear Simeon brought you back to the land of the living."

Mr. Amos glowered at her. "I've not been resurrected. You exaggerate, old woman."

"And you grumble too much, old man." She gave him a pat on the shoulder and sidled past Thea. She gave a wink and whispered, "Enjoy yourself, my dear." Mrs. Amos then disappeared down the hall, leaving Thea standing there in the doorway.

"Well, now that you're here." Mr. Amos speared her with a look. "What is it you want?"

Thea drew a deep breath and entered the room, standing awkwardly over him until he pointed to a chair in the corner. She slid it over toward the bed and lowered herself onto it. Taking out Mr. Fortune's newly developed photograph, she handed it to him.

Mr. Amos took it from her, his eyes glossing over the picture. "He came back, eh?"

Thea nodded. "I'm quite proud of the photograph. He cooperated and didn't show me any disdain." She'd expected Mr. Fortune wouldn't want a woman photographing him. Mr. Amos raised an irritable brow. "I'd have denied him services if I had the resources to afford it. Can't stand the Fortunes. Highfalutin ninnies in a town of lessers, they are. So they think anyway." He handed the photograph back to her. "You should be proud of it. Figurin' as you take pictures of the dead, a live one is bound to look a lot better."

Thea bit back a smile. After years of following Mr. Mendelsohn around and always feeling rather assaulted under his elderly gaze that lingered too long, she thought Mr. Amos a welcome relief. He was grumpy. A harmless grump with an edge of grandfatherly fondness that laced his words by way of soft eyes.

"I want you to know, Mr. Amos, I've been keeping up with your appointments. All of them." Thea made sure she emphasized the word *all*. She didn't think he'd want her mentioning the asylum out loud.

Mr. Amos frowned. "Whaddya mean?"

"Well," Thea explained further, folding her

hands in her lap, "you will have no lost revenue from the appointments in your books. I will be sure to keep them and develop the photographs for you. As well as your — your other ventures."

"What other ventures? What're you talkin' about?"

Thea hesitated. Simeon had said he was working with Mr. Amos, hadn't he? Yes. It was Mr. Amos's camera equipment. The photo album of patients in the back room.

"I'm working with Simeon," she admitted, lowering her voice.

Mr. Amos's eyes widened. He braced himself on either side, his hands pressed against the mattress, raising himself into a sitting position. "Now, you listen here . . ." He glanced toward the door, as if someone might be standing there, listening. Thea looked too. There was no one. "You leave Simeon alone." Mr. Amos wagged his finger at her.

Thea tipped her head in correction. "Simeon requested I help him. It was at his behest."

Mr. Amos's scowl deepened. "Then he's just as crazy as — missy, that place ain't — you just best not," he struggled to finish his command.

"Whyever not?" she couldn't help but ask.

Mr. Amos eyed her. For a long moment, he said not a word. Finally he opened his mouth, bordered by unshaven gray whiskers that covered some of the gauntness in his cheeks. "I said I'd photograph the patients. Not more than a few weeks ago. The missus and I . . . well, money has been scarce lately."

Thea waited.

Mr. Amos adjusted the blanket around his waist.

"I've had a fondness for Simeon," he continued. "For years. The boy always shadowed my shop — back in the day when things were a bit brighter here in Pleasant Valley. Before . . . before Simeon's parents passed, and the darkness of those rumors started up again. But that place? That place isn't a place for you. You stay away from it. From Simeon. From the Coyles, you hear?"

"But why?" Thea pressed. Simeon was almost as timid as a man could be, and Rose was ethereal and lost in her grief, but fulfilled by her work at the hospital.

Mr. Amos shook his head. "You trust me, Miss Reed. Nothin' good comes from befriending a Coyle."

It wasn't the first time she'd heard that.

"I don't believe it," Thea argued.

Mr. Amos skewered her with a stern glare.

"Believe it. There's more to that family than meets the eye. The Kramers. The Coyles. Misty Wayfair."

"Do you know what it is?" Thea ventured, holding her breath.

Mr. Amos stared at her, then turned his head to look out the window.

"Seems strange, don't it, that a dead woman wouldn't lie in peace? That she'd haunt a family — a town — like a vengeful spirit?"

"If you believe that sort of thing," Thea responded. Mr. Mendelsohn's devoted superstitions quickened her heart.

"I don't believe that sort of thing!" Mr. Amos turned back to her. His eyes were direct. Firm. Convicted. "Yet, it keeps happenin'. Someone keeps taking them. One by one. There's no explanation for the Coyles dying, and their passings are too coincidental in my book. First their father, Mathilda Coyle herself, their mother, and now Mary? No. No, I don't believe that sort of thing. But there's got to be an explanation. God knows, as a man of faith, our eternal destination isn't limbo. I know where I'm going when I die, by the grace of God himself. And I know that Misty Wayfair is as dead now as she was fifty-odd years ago. So, if it's not Misty Wayfair, then who is it? I ain't never heard of that many people in one family passing away in such strange ways, you know?"

A coldness settled over Thea. She swallowed, but it seemed apprehension had lodged in her throat. Suddenly the concept of Misty Wayfair became far less ghostly, and far more human.

Mr. Amos nodded slowly. "Someone murdered Misty Wayfair way back when. They're all connected. And there are only two Coyles left, ya hear? Whoever wants to avenge Misty Wayfair all these years later? I don't think they're gonna stop with Mary. And if you're with them —"

"Then I'm just in the way," Thea finished.

Mr. Amos patted his heart. "This malady may be God's way of tellin' me to back off before they take me too. Poor Simeon and Rose. Thought I could help. Thought I could keep them safe, but — it's comin' for them." He met Thea's eyes. "And, whoever it is, they ain't going to stop until every Coyle is buried in the cold, hard ground."

CHAPTER 24

The river swept by with the persistent turbulence that imitated the tension lying just beneath the surface of Pleasant Valley.

Dinner with Mrs. Amos had been a kind gesture from the old woman, and Thea wanted to stay. Mrs. Amos had invited her to sit and read aloud the Scriptures, with Mr. Amos listening on with closed eyes. Thea hadn't been exposed much to the Word of God, and it bewildered her that while reading, a strange sense of peace came over her. Something in the Amos house was different. Yet it was less a ghostly spirit and more, as Mrs. Amos declared, the whispering Spirit of God. If so, then He made the unknowns less frightening. Dangerous, yes. Imposing, for certain. But terrifying? No. She could sense that even crotchety Mr. Amos believed God had not lost control, and while he vehemently urged her to stay out of the asylum and away from the Coyles, she could see Mr. Amos also questioned what her part was in it all. As though her Creator had some exceptional plan for her life.

It was a lovely thought, if one fancied pursuing the idea of a Creator. Thea might have sidestepped the notion a month ago, but now? Perhaps it had merit after all. Considering everything else she'd been taught left her spiraling in a whirlpool of confusion and aimlessness.

Now, Thea wandered down the street toward the boardinghouse. The summer sky was still alight. Townsfolk mingled about, collecting at the Methodist church for the evening's midweek prayer service. A couple of Kramer Logging wagons rolled through town at the end of the day. Thea took refuge in their distant company.

The river continued its endless journey. Thea considered it, debated, then chose to follow the river's course. She headed to the riverbank, peering into the depths of the less frantic pools, to the smooth stones beneath the water. Stones Simeon Coyle etched with words of what now-deceased patients might have been like — in another time, or place, or really, another life.

"Are you lonely?"

The simple question, voiced by someone

behind her, startled Thea. She jumped, twisting as she did so, her gaze colliding with the gray eyes of Simeon himself. He'd come out of nowhere. Like a ghost himself.

Was she lonely? Of course she was. But she dared not admit it to Simeon, who one moment she felt she could trust even with her deepest secrets, but in the next moment she realized with surety she really didn't know him well at all.

"Are you?" She turned her attention back to the waters. To the tiny whirlpool that swirled at the base of a boulder in the middle of the river.

Simeon edged his way out onto a slick-looking rock and squatted. Dipping his hands into the cool water, he let it stream through strong fingers. He appeared more relaxed in the evening light, the orange sky in the distance, with the woods silhouetted as a dark mass in the foreground.

"More often now, yes," he admitted, then plunged his arm up to his elbow, pulling forth a smooth, oval river stone. He wiped it on his pant leg and stood.

"What will you etch on it? And for whom?" Thea asked.

Simeon's face muscles jerked, causing his eye to close in an unbidden wink. He gave her a sideways glance, almost like he knew there would be one more twitch and then he could face her, his faculties in control once again.

"There was an older man who passed last year. He would sit at a window and stare out. He would cry. For no reason." Simeon balanced his way back to the rocky and jagged riverbank. He handed the stone to Thea. "I will carve the word *comfort* on it."

Thea rolled the stone in her hand. Its dampness leaving her palm cool. She could almost envision the word etched there. See the stone laid at the base of a grave marker in the lonesome burial ground of the hospital.

"You assume death brings comfort, then?" Thea handed it back to him.

Simeon's fingers grazed hers. He didn't react, but every nerve inside her tingled at the touch. As if something magnetic connected them. Opposites and yet replicas of each other. Lonesome. Awkward. Private. One driven to find answers, and one haunted by a story he seemed to ignore.

"Death brings no comfort. At least to those left behind." Simeon gave a small laugh. A dry one that resonated the undertones of grief. "Mr. Amos told me there is hope in the hereafter. That God provides a way to know Him. To experience peace."

He stopped, and their eyes met.

"Do you believe that?" Thea truly wanted to know, considering the direction her thoughts had taken during the Scripture reading at the Amos home.

Simeon narrowed his eyes. "There is reason in it, though some might argue it's a weak man's way of coping with life. But, I've also seen too much sorrow to believe God is happy with it — with us. I mean, if He created it all, then wouldn't He have a purpose for it? I think, as mankind, we have thoroughly ruined a good plan. Now, the Creator must fix it. One person at a time. It is no simple miracle."

"What if we don't let Him fix us? What if I don't believe I am broken?" But she did believe it. Circumstances taught her she was broken long before she ever contemplated if the Creator might have more merit in existing than a wayward spirit passed on in the afterlife. If it were true, then part of her wanted to believe that God really had created her, had a reason for her, and maybe even wanted her.

Simeon shrugged. "I'm no scholar. I just know . . ." He stared across the river. "When you see death face-to-face, you wish to know what lies after. I know one ghost exists. It is the ghost of my soul, suspended, with a choice to make. To acknowledge a Creator, or to acknowledge only myself and assume I am all I have."

"Maybe that's why we're lonely," Thea ventured. She was tired of being her only constant, her only source of strength. She was so tired.

"I believe it is so." Simeon met her eyes again.

Thea realized he'd stepped nearer to her. Perhaps to balance on the river's rugged edge. Perhaps because he felt the same tug toward her as she felt toward him.

The right side of his mouth twitched. Just enough to draw her eyes. She rested them there and, without thinking, raised her fingers and laid them over the corner of his mouth.

Simeon stilled.

She watched his lips, carved like a strong man's but set in the face of one whom life had beaten into submission with its violent whip of tragedy. "Has your face always . . ." Thea asked without finishing.

"No," he whispered, his lips moving beneath her fingers.

"When did it begin?" It was none of her business why his face would jerk, why his shoulder would suddenly seize upward toward his ear and pull his head down toward it as if latching together for seconds at a time.

He didn't answer. Perhaps because she'd not removed her fingertips from his mouth. Thea tried again. "Does it hurt?"

"No," Simeon responded.

Thea could feel him. His chest inches from hers. Not touching, and yet close enough to sense his very soul lifting and combining with hers.

"Then why?" Thea slowly withdrew her hand, but this time Simeon's lifted and clasped her wrist with a gentle but firm grip.

"My father — he was not a kind man."

"He hurt you?"

"Many times, yes."

"And Rose? Mary?"

"Often." A low response.

"And he damaged you? That's why your body —"

"He frightened me," Simeon admitted. "As a boy. Terrified me. When I am nervous, or unsettled, it becomes more pronounced. I don't know why."

Thea noticed his shoulder lift a bit, and Simeon struggled to right it.

"Are you afraid now?" she whispered.

He stepped closer, her wrist still held in his grip between them. Simeon lowered his face, compelling her to lift her eyes from his malady and to his gaze. Thea did.

"Yes," he answered.

"Of what?" Thea frowned, searching his face.

"Of you."

Thea froze as Simeon released her wrist, but he did not step away.

"I shouldn't frighten you," Thea argued, though her voice was hardly above a whisper. And her conviction was as much to convince herself as to convince Simeon.

His eyes narrowed, the right eye almost shutting in a wink. Twice, three times, four, and then it steadied. "You're like a sailor's siren, Thea. Dangerous. I don't know why, but you call me with a silent song. I'm afraid you will wreck me."

Thea's breath held, suspended between them. "I've done nothing to you," she breathed.

Simeon's fingertips lifted and grazed her cheek. "And that is why I fear you. Because you will. And that will be my undoing."

Sleep had become a taunt. Something Thea attempted to grasp but was left with an empty arm extended. She rose, washed her face in the porcelain basin on her bureau, dried it with a clean linen, then brushed through her long, honey-colored hair. She'd watched herself in the mirror, noted the shadows growing under her eyes, questioning all things.

To the right of the basin and its pitcher rested Mrs. Mendelsohn's letter. It was what had brought Thea to Pleasant Valley to begin with. To lay to rest — she'd hoped — the mystery that was her mother. Now? She stared at her reflection, wondering if her mother's story somehow held hands with the tragedy that seemed to surround Pleasant Valley like a shroud. Like the black crepe draped in a parlor room, covering mirrors and paintings, embracing a loved one's casket, casting a thin, see-through film over life. Just blurry enough to confuse, to darken, and to make one wonder.

Thea reached out and laid a palm against the mirror. Against her reflection.

Was this emptiness, this questioning, because she didn't know who she was? Because she had no belonging, no point of reference, no identity? Or was it deeper than that? Was it just a longing to know her Creator and the reason why she existed in the first place?

Regardless, Thea pulled her hand toward herself, her fingers toying with the ribbon at the V in her chemise that dipped over her breasts and created a shadow. She was Thea

Reed. She'd always believed she was capable, strong, and ached for her independence. Now that Mr. Mendelsohn was dead, she had found it. And she felt more imprisoned than ever . . .

Shaking her head as if to awaken from a trance, Thea tightened the ribbon and reached for her blouse. She would head to the asylum this morning. If she found something about her mother, about P. A. Reed, perhaps it would put to rest her personal restlessness.

Not long after, Thea left Pleasant Valley behind her. The quiet bustle of the early dawn beginning. A low fog settled around her ankles as the cool air from the night warred against the warmth of the spring morning. She cast a glance at the riverbank where she'd stood the night before with Simeon. But then she turned her attention to the bridge that crossed the waters. The woods loomed ahead, the road open yet dark beyond.

She entered, the trees rising around her. Really, it was a peaceful place. The deep blueish hues of the woods' shadows matching the evergreen depths of its biology. Valley Heights Asylum was not far, and Thea breathed deep of the air. It was rife with earth and moisture. That sort of perfume created by dirt and moss and leaves wet with dew.

A stick cracked.

The tiniest sound and yet, with that one snap, Thea's tentative peace dissipated.

She stopped in the middle of the road. Looking behind her, she saw no mode of transportation approaching her. Nor was Simeon or Rose following her, also on their way to work.

A crow swooped in front of her, its black wings beating the air, calling a repetitive *caw caw* that echoed down the road.

Thea collected her wits, adjusting the strap of the bag she'd slung over her shoulder, packed with a shawl, a handkerchief, and a small lunch Mrs. Brummel had provided.

There was nothing.

She was alone.

A few more moments, and this time the crack of a stick was definite and loud. Thea turned toward the sound. It came from deep in the forest.

She saw a flash of white.

Then a small laugh echoed through the woods. A chuckle that started in someone's throat and traveled into their chest. As if they knew something Thea didn't.

"Who's there?" Thea gripped the strap of

her bag until her knuckles were white.

Another twig snapped. This time on the opposite side of the road from where Thea was looking. She spun around.

Another chuckle floated through the air and the low-lying fog, carrying across the morning and wafting into the narrow shafts of sunlight that broke through the treetops.

"Misssss-ty . . ." a woman's voice called. Musical. Lilting. Taunting. "Misssss-ty."

"Come out!" Thea shouted. Yelling at whoever teased from the shadows. She turned a full circle in the road.

The crow swooped over the lane again, turning its head as it flew and leveling its beady black eyes on Thea.

The voice began to sing, a tremoring vibrato. The melody was both haunting and unfamiliar.

Thea's chin quivered as tears burned her eyes. She plowed forward, eyes fixed on the road ahead, wishing away whoever — whatever — mocked her from the darkness of the forest. The asylum was not far ahead. She would get there, then take refuge within its whitewashed walls.

But as she hurried, the voice seemed to parallel her. Minor tones. Eerie notes.

Thea began to run, her breath catching in small gasps.

There. The iron fence. The gate. The roof of the asylum. Thea stumbled over a root that rose in the lane. She catapulted forward, but as the ground surged up to meet her, she was hauled upward by hands that gripped her forearms and a body taking the brunt of her weight.

Simeon.

Thea reached up, grasping his shoulders. She looked wildly about her, in the woods, toward the asylum, into the shadows. Where was it? Where was *she*?

"Did you hear her?" Thea demanded, her eyes raking Simeon's face with a frantic urgency.

Simeon frowned. His face wasn't twitching. His body was firm. Confident.

He wasn't afraid.

Thea released him and stepped back, as if he were a stranger. Different. Somehow unaffected by the mockery that had followed her through the woods to the hospital.

"Did you hear her?" she asked again, her voice watery, rising with insistence.

"Who?" Simeon shook his head. "Hear who?"

Thea stopped. She could hear herself breathing, heavy and upset. The singing had vanished. The voice calling for Misty had disappeared.

The forest was still.

Even the sunshine had broken through, with the asylum and grassy grounds bathed in a beautiful warmth. Like a refuge in a dark, venomous world beyond.

"Misty. Misty Wayfair," Thea breathed. Only it couldn't have been her. Why would she call her own name? "She was singing," Thea reasoned aloud, trying to come to terms with what she'd heard — what she *thought* she'd heard.

"Singing?" Simeon responded.

"Yes." Thea nodded. Vehemently.

Then she looked up.

Looked into gray eyes. Saw his shoulder rise and fall, his head and mouth twitch repeatedly. Simeon backed away from her. His own chest rose and fell now. He turned, and with an uneasy sweep of his gaze through the woods, he gripped her hand and pulled her toward the hospital.

The iron gate slammed shut behind them.

He locked it, a ring of keys pulled from his belt hook.

But even as the key resonated and grated the lock into place, Thea knew. No iron fence, or gate, or brick building filled with the mentally insane would keep Misty Wayfair at bay.

CHAPTER 25

HEIDI

She laid the photograph in front of Brad and Vicki, sliding it across the counter. Its old edges were yellowed, but the photograph still stared up at them with a poignancy captured in time. The early dawn's light stretched through the window and onto the bar, where Brad poured his coffee and Vicki was already checking items off her to-do list for the lodge.

Vicki paused and stared at the image she'd seen before. "This picture again?"

Brad drew next to her and observed it, taking a sip of coffee. His dark brows rose up and under his damp mop of black curly hair. He shot Heidi a look. "Whoa. You're dead." He gave her a wink.

Heidi wasn't feeling humorous today.

Vicki pushed the photograph back to Heidi. "I already told you, I don't know anything about it."

"You gotta admit, that's a bit creepy, Vick," Brad inserted.

Vicki frowned. "What do you want me to say?"

Heidi tapped the face of the woman in the picture, then flipped it over. "It says 'Misty Wayfair' — right here." She showed the name to Brad and Vicki. "But this woman's name is Mary Coyle. Are we related to the Coyles? Is that what explains the physical similarities? What do I have — what do *we* have — to do with Pleasant Valley?"

"Nothing!" Vicki stepped back.

Brad took another sip of his coffee. As if he knew it would be dangerous to get between the two warring Lane sisters.

Vicki glowered and tugged her button-up plaid shirt down over her jeans. "I don't even know who Mary Coyle is. It's not like I have time to rummage through the town's history."

"But it's not chance I look identical to that woman in the picture." Heidi tossed it onto the counter between them.

Vicki rubbed her forehead with her palm and released a controlled sigh. "Heidi," she began. Slowly. As though speaking to a child. "It is possible that you could look a lot like someone. Even a dead woman."

"Vick." Brad's voice held a hint of warning. Vicki was getting snippy.

She slid off the barstool and stood, glaring up at Brad. "What? This is nonsense. It's been nonsense since Heidi arrived." Her voice clipped, and Heidi saw Vicki's throat bob with frustrated tears. "You've hardly helped out the last few weeks. The lodge was broken into. Half of our guests have left. And you've spent more time with Emma Crawford and — and *Rhett* — than with us *or* Mom. The asylum ruins? Now the cops are looking into that graffiti. Every time you're around, Heidi, every time, it's like getting hit by a hurricane. I'm sick of it."

Vicki slapped the counter with her hand. "Now it's some conspiracy theory that you're related to a dead woman in a photograph?" She raked her fingers through her loose blond hair. "No one cares about an old photograph!"

Vicki whirled and gripped the sink, her back to them. Heidi noticed her hand swipe at her face. A pang bit at Heidi. Her sister was crying. There was more to Vicki than she ever showed — ever shared. Heidi could see it, but she'd never bothered to try to open up her sister and see inside of her. They'd both allowed the wall to grow between them.

Brad reached for Vicki, but she shrugged him off.

"No. I'm not doing this." She turned on her heel and marched from the room.

Brad took another gulp of his coffee, probably nerves now rather than peaceful Monday-morning inspiration.

Heidi reached for the photograph, debating whether to follow her older sister, to find some common ground. Or whether to just ignore things, like she always did.

"It's been tough for Vicki." Brad's words grated on Heidi's raw hurt.

She noticed her hands were quivering as she held the photograph. Her antianxiety meds were going to have to really do their job today, she could tell.

"Yeah. Well, her and me both," Heidi muttered.

"Whatever happened between you two anyway?" Brad eased himself onto the barstool Vicki had vacated.

Heidi ran her thumb over the photographed woman's face. Mary Coyle, according to the paper clipping Emma had found, had died of melancholia. Depression. It was sort of ironic really, that she would have suffered from a form of anxiety just like Heidi. Of course, if in fact they were related . . . She tugged her attention back to Brad.

"We never got along, Brad. You know that."

"But why?" he pressed. "Vicki won't talk about much of anything. When she and your parents took over this place, I came along for the ride. To support her. To support them in their retirement from the church. But, Vicki and I had just married. It's like the entire first pre-married half of her life, she won't talk about."

"You dated her. You had to know our family is dysfunctional at best."

Brad gave her a wide-eyed, scrunched look over his mug. "But it's like something traumatic happened, and none of you want to talk about it."

"Yeah. Me. I was born. There's your trauma." Heidi leaned on the bar and gave him a sideways smirk, attempting to hide the fact she *needed* to lean on the bar. Her stomach was in knots. She was seeing tiny flecks in her eyes, and a sense of impending doom had settled over her like a thunderstorm. "That and the fact there were all these rules and expectations. Vicki tried to comply — I never did. You thought we were the healthy, Bible-believing family Dad and Mom made it out to be?"

Brad shrugged. "Sure. And you were. I mean, faith has been integral in your family."

"And legalism," Heidi added. "Try growing up in a house where the Backstreet Boys are akin to Satanic music."

Brad eyed her. "You're exaggerating."

"Maybe." Heidi slid a stool closer with her sock-covered toe and rested her foot on it. Blessed relief. Her knees were shaking. When she spoke, her voice gave her away. "It's tough having your faith measured. Jesus was supposed to be about grace when we fall short, but Mom and Dad twisted it so we had to reach some vague point of perfection before Jesus would have the time to look at us."

Brad studied her. So much so, Heidi knew he could see the anxiety she battled within — in the way her body had stiffened, in the way she swallowed repeatedly so she could digest the panic and make it go away.

"Vicki gets your anxiety issues more than you know." His tone was low. "You both handle it differently."

The frank honesty in his eyes told Heidi something about her sister she'd never realized. "No, I-I didn't know."

Brad nodded. "She's uptight, but I love her, Heidi. Vicki tries to be all things for all people."

"I gave up on that years ago," Heidi admitted. But then, somehow she still felt like a failure, so maybe that wasn't entirely true. Heidi looked down at the photograph. "So, what do *you* know about the Coyles of Pleasant Valley? The disowned heirs to Kramer Logging?"

Brad waited a moment before taking her cue to redirect. "Not much."

"And you don't think we could be related to them?" Heidi studied the face of the darker-haired woman. The one who appeared far more alive at the time of the photograph.

Brad set his empty mug on the bar. "I don't know. Maybe there are records somewhere that would help all this to make sense."

Heidi lifted her eyes to Brad's, irritated that tears were certainly reflected in her own. "Do you think — do you think my parents came to Pleasant Valley for a different reason? Other than taking over a church?"

Brad frowned. "What reason would that be?"

Heidi sniffed and flipped the unsettling photograph over so she couldn't see the woman's face. "Oh, I don't know. Maybe

381

you're right. Maybe there *was* something. Maybe they had secrets?"

The question hung between them.

Unanswerable.

Heidi lugged a laundry basket filled with soiled white towels into the lodge's laundry room. She started a load, hoping Vicki would take it as a white flag of peace when she returned home. The guests in Cabin 4 had left on Saturday, but for whatever reason, Vicki hadn't had an opportunity to clean it. Pouring in laundry detergent, Heidi shut the drawer and pushed the buttons. The washer flooded with water.

A good wipe down of the cabin's kitchen and she'd be done. While the cleaning had served the additional purpose of helping Heidi work through her nerves, she also wanted to prove something to both herself and Vicki. They were family. Dysfunction aside, they needed to stick together. Maybe that was what Vicki had been harping on about all along. Maybe Heidi did have some maturing to do.

She slipped her feet into a pair of ugly, beat-up blue Crocs and headed back toward Cabin 4. She stopped and answered a few questions from a guest about how long they could take the lodge-provided kayak out on the lake. But soon she was lost in her thoughts again, spraying Lysol on the kitchen counters, the stainless-steel sink, and the fronts of the nicked-and-scarred cupboards. Earbuds in her ears, she hummed to a classic hit by The Police. Nothing beat the classics.

Moving into the bedroom, she sprayed the exposed mattress with cleaner and wiped it down, its plastic cover wrinkling as she rubbed it dry. Heidi sniffed. The campfire smell that often accompanied the cabins from the fire pits outside seemed stronger today. She tossed the rag into the cleaning pail and entered the adjacent bathroom. A good, thorough spray down of everything and she went to work.

She wrinkled her nose. Strange that the campfire smell would be so strong in the bathroom, especially over the strong fumes of the cleaner. Heidi frowned as music belted in her ears, sung by Sting's smooth and raspy voice.

Setting down her cleaning rag, Heidi exited the bathroom. The smoke smell was enough now to cause her to tug an earbud from her ear. Nothing. No sound. Walking into the main living area, Heidi stopped.

A thin film of smoke filtered over the floor. It took a split second for Heidi to process it, but as soon as the reality slammed into her senses, she bolted for the front door off the galley-style kitchen.

Heidi yanked on the door while grabbing at her pocket for her phone. The other earbud ripped from her ear and fell to the floor as her phone disconnected from the cable. She hurried outside, and out of the corner of her eye, Heidi saw orange flames licking the side of the log cabin.

A guest of Cabin 2 across the gravel drive poked his head out the doorway and gaped at her.

"Call 911!" Heidi yelled at the man. His face blanched, a quick nod, and then he disappeared back inside.

Heidi sprinted for the lodge and burst into the foyer. She grappled for the fire extinguisher on the wall and yanked the pin from its mechanism. That there was already one inside the cabin was an afterthought as she raced back to the burning cabin. Her panic wasn't helping. She needed to stay calm, to think clearly in facing the emergency.

The fire had reached the roof, and she could see the curtains inside the cabin erupt into flame.

"They're on their way!" Cabin 2 man shouted at Heidi.

Heidi could barely hear him over the roar

of the fire. "Get everyone out of their cabins!" she hollered back.

Seconds later, she saw the man knock wildly on the door of Cabin 1. Hopefully, everyone was gone for the day, out exploring the great outdoors.

The fire was quickly getting out of hand. Heidi rushed to pull open the front door. But the door fought back and kept closing on its own. Dumb spring hinges! Heidi had no clue if she should target the outside of the cabin or the inside. Her mind was spinning, her breaths coming in short gasps. She was *not* the person you wanted in an emergency!

She had to think, to remain calm.

Heidi took a deep breath and opted for the inside.

With the extinguisher held out in front of her, she ran into the cabin and squeezed its trigger, pointing the nozzle at the corner of the living area where the fire had devoured the curtains and was starting to consume the couch. She swept the extinguisher from side to side.

A scream jerked her attention to the window where vintage Coke bottles once sat on the sill but now were scattered across the floor, crashed into smithereens. A hand pounded on the outside of the window.

The heat was horrific, and Heidi backed away, even as her eyes took in the sight of a woman. Her face a blur as the ash and soot on the windowpane clouded her features. The woman slapped her palm on the window again, and Heidi tried to wave her away.

Stupid lady! She was going to get herself severely burned!

Flames licked their way up the wall, spreading across the kitchen to the side of Heidi and toward the front door. Seeing that the extinguisher had run dry, Heidi decided it was time to escape.

The woman continued to bang on the window. Heidi backed toward the door, but once again it had closed. She reached for the doorknob. It was too hot for her to grab. Fear curdled in Heidi's throat as she saw the glow of flame outside the front window. All the linens were in the washer at the main lodge, so there was nothing to use to soak in water and open the door with!

She spun back toward the living room, engulfed now in flames. The window in the living room shattered. Heidi held her arm over her mouth and coughed as tears from the smoke trailed from her eyes. A bloodied arm reached in through the broken window, a lifesaving signal for Heidi to make her escape through the jagged remains of the glass. She jumped over the burning rug by the couch, smoke burning her nostrils and choking her throat. Heidi's eyes watered, and terror coiled her muscles into tight springs of adrenaline.

She grasped the hand, batting remnants of flaming curtains away from the window, ignoring the pain. The woman's grip was strong. She continued to shriek, her words unintelligible. Heidi braced her foot on the edge of the table the television was sitting on and yelled with exertion as she boosted herself upward, clutching the woman's hand for fear she would let go. Heidi's free hand wrapped around the window frame, shards of glass piercing her skin. Her knee braced on the sill and then she tumbled forward onto the ground. As the flames continued to shoot upward, the woman who'd shattered the window dragged Heidi away from the cabin to safety.

Heidi rolled onto her stomach, retching smoke from her suffocated lungs. She grappled for breath, her hands burnt and bleeding as she braced herself on the ground. Glancing up, her eyes squinting, she saw her. The woman from her first day here. The woman from the antique photograph.

"You!" Heidi's voice cracked.

She tried to wipe away tears with her forearm.

Sirens sounded as fire trucks sped up the drive.

Heidi reached up for assistance from the woman, but there was no hand this time. She got to her knees, crying out as she realized the knee she'd braced on the windowsill had been cut from the broken glass. Pushing herself off the ground with a groan, she stumbled farther away from the inferno.

She heard the firefighters shouting. Smoke blurred her eyes, disorienting her as she gagged again for air. Trying to clear her lungs, her mind.

Worried something had happened to the nameless woman, Heidi hurried toward a firefighter in full gear and already heading her direction. She grabbed his sleeve.

"A woman! She helped me out! I don't know where she is!"

Heidi pointed at the window, the frantic motion sending a trail of blood down her wrist and forearm.

"Heidi!"

The male voice from beneath the helmet gave a sharp holler.

"Where did she go?" Heidi shrugged him off and spun in a bewildered circle. A small gathering of guests stood far off to the side, allowing the firefighters space to work.

Water burst onto the cabin, droplets filling the air.

Arms encircled her waist to pull her back from the area of danger.

Heidi kicked at the air, clawing at the firefighter's grip. "A woman! She saved me! Where is she?"

She twisted and struggled as the rescuer hauled her toward a waiting ambulance. "Let me go!" Everything in Heidi fought now. Irrational and persistent. She couldn't formulate any clear thought other than the memory of the bloodied hand and arm reaching through the window, providing her with freedom.

"Stop it!" The firefighter's shout in her ear only incensed her further. She struggled harder.

"Knock it off!" He brought her to the ground and onto her back, straddling her, and shouted to a law enforcement officer, "We need to restrain her!"

The impact of the threat stunned Heidi. She stopped fighting. Her body went limp beneath his. She looked up at the firefighter, and her eyes collided with familiar, turbulent gray ones.

"Rhett?" She couldn't reconcile the image of him in full firefighting uniform with the greasy mechanic in flannel.

He pressed her shoulders to the ground, his weight held off her by his knees.

"Are you done?" Rhett barked.

Heidi nodded.

He flipped his leg over her and pulled her from the ground. Heidi wobbled on weakened legs as her muscles relaxed. The officer Rhett had waved over took her by the elbow and around her waist.

"Get her to the medics," Rhett instructed.

Then, with a nod from the officer, Rhett sprinted back to the chaos.

Heidi limped alongside the officer, scanning the faces of the people who had congregated. It hurt to breathe, to move, even to keep her eyes open. But she did. She had to. The woman who'd saved her was no ghost. She was flesh and blood, and just like before, she had vanished.

CHAPTER 26

It was more than the stitches in her knee and the bandage on her burned left hand that had Heidi limping with purpose toward the front entrance of the memory-care facility. It was the words Vicki had directed at Heidi this morning — the morning after the fire — that caused her to pack up her things, tuck the vintage photo album under her arm, and get into her car.

"Get out."

Two words that summarized the culmination of their familial relationship. As if she herself had started the fire. As if the police weren't investigating it as arson. As if her testimony and repeated insistence that a strange woman had saved her from the cabin fire meant absolutely nothing.

"More of that Misty Wayfair crud?" Vicki had said, glaring at her.

Of course not. No. This wasn't a legendary ghost, old-town folklore, or some random account people had all but forgotten in the annals of time. It was a real human being.

Still, it did all come back to the photograph, and a face which looked just like hers. It came back to Vicki, who acted like getting rid of Heidi would rid them of the chaos that trailed after. The one who'd upset the family. It came back to the twist of emotions on Vicki's face that told Heidi she warred against wanting to strike out and blame Heidi for everything, and also wanting to weep and wrap her arms around her little sister, thankful Heidi hadn't been killed. Heidi could see it now — the desire to give life to sisterly affection — but Vicki didn't act on that emotion.

"Get out."

The impact of the moment had left Heidi stunned but obedient. She had left immediately. Without a backward glance.

The only person who might make sense of it all was barely in control of her wits, let alone her mind. Her mother. The one who'd penned the mysterious letter that had brought Heidi to Pleasant Valley to begin with. The mad wanderings of a woman who'd lost herself in the heartbreaking passages of dementia.

Vicki's words of accusation as Heidi had

packed her things still curled into Heidi with the vicious attack they were meant to be.

"You're crazy, Heidi. You always have been, and you always will be."

It was a word people used often. *Crazy.* It was crazy how windy it was outside. Or, how crazy was it that the Green Bay Packers shut out the Minnesota Vikings in the last quarter? Or, if one didn't get more sunshine, they'd go crazy.

Crazy.

Crazy is as crazy does.

That was what it meant to Vicki. Crazy meant a state of mind and actions that defined a person. It wasn't a word that was bandied about loosely for the Lanes. No. It meant too much in their family.

Heidi was the crazy one. The girl who had locked herself in a closet when she was five and rocked back and forth as if she'd lost her mind. No matter that she was terrified — of what, she didn't know and never did find out — she was just horrifically and utterly alone.

Without comfort, or nurture, or even medical help, she'd coped as well as a child could. ADHD. An early diagnosis her parents refused to believe, later recalled, then reassigned as an anxiety disorder. No matter. Heidi could fix it. As she always had. But she couldn't stop to think. Because if she did, logic and emotion would war against each other, the world would spin, and that closet that kept her safe in a controlled environment would become ever so appealing once again.

No thinking.

Action only.

Curse the consequences.

And now here she was.

Heidi stared across the small dining room of the care center. Her mother sat at the corner table, her back to the wall. Her gray hair was bobbed around wrinkled, gaunt cheeks. She was four years away from eighty. For a moment, Heidi allowed herself to think of what it must have been like for her forty-six-year-old mother to have found out she was going to have a baby when her only child was already in high school and she was well on her way to independence from children. A stab of empathy, and then Heidi tasted the familiar bitterness that so quickly followed it. She only knew what it had been like to be the "accident," and the troubled one at that.

Stifling a sigh, again she shut down her thoughts. Heidi hadn't eaten lunch, her stomach already nauseated and upset. She didn't need to turn her mind over to the anxiety that always stood just outside the door, knocking, as persistent as Jesus.

Heidi gave an attendant a weak smile. It must have been the woman's cue, for she approached Heidi, straightening the hem of her scrubs shirt.

"Loretta has been doing all right today," she began.

Heidi nodded. Good. Maybe she'd be coherent enough to explain the letter crammed in the back pocket of Heidi's jeans.

"She just ate lunch," the aide continued, "so she'll probably do well for another hour or so, but then she usually needs to rest."

"For sure," Heidi agreed. An hour was enough.

She pulled out a chair and swiveled it so the chair was next to her mother. Loretta Lane's wheelchair was pushed up against the table. A small jigsaw puzzle had been dumped onto the table, and Loretta was fingering a puzzle piece.

"That's an edge, Mom." Heidi decided that maybe a little normalcy would help her mom relax. "Why don't we sort the edges from the middle pieces?"

It was what her mom had always done when putting together puzzles. Sort. Then construct the frame, then fill in the middle. Of course, this puzzle was maybe a hundred pieces, and each piece wasn't nearly as small as the five-thousand-piece puzzles Loretta used to do.

Loretta looked up at Heidi. A line drew between her brows, her eyes studying Heidi for a long moment before she looked back at the puzzle piece in her hand.

"Oh." A nod. "Yes. Let's do that," Loretta agreed.

They worked in silence for a slow five minutes more. Heidi reached into her pocket, took out the letter, and laid it between them. Folded but glaring up at them. Loretta focused on the puzzle. Each piece taking anywhere from twenty to thirty seconds to determine if it went in the edges or the middle-piece pile.

Finally, Heidi was done waiting. She slid the letter around the puzzle and in front of her mother.

Loretta stared at it, then raised her eyes. "Is that from your father?" she asked.

"Dad?" Heidi was taken aback for a second.

Loretta nodded, her eyes wide. "He hasn't come by in a while. Is he away on a trip?"

Heidi avoided blurting out that her dad had died a few years before. "Sure. Yeah, he

396

is." She nodded. Why make her mother revisit the grief? "But the letter isn't from Dad. You sent it to me."

Loretta drew back, her hand fluttering to her throat. "I did? I don't like writing letters."

No. No, she didn't. Another reason Heidi had found it so very odd when she'd received it.

"Should I read it to you?" Heidi offered.

"No, I can read," Loretta snapped. She lifted the paper and eyed her scrawling handwriting. Her eyes remained focused on her own words, and Heidi allowed her the time to take it in. To digest it. Hopefully, to remember it.

"Well, that's silliness." Loretta set it back on the table. She looked at Heidi with an earnestness Heidi wasn't prepared for. "Why would I write that?"

Heidi felt her hopes thud to the pit of her stomach. Exactly. Why? And her mother didn't remember. "I don't know, Mom. I was hoping you could explain it."

Loretta lifted a puzzle piece and tapped its one straight edge. "I don't believe I wrote it. It's stuff and nonsense, that's what it is."

Okay then. Heidi was just going to go for it. She picked up the letter and skimmed the words. "What did you mean by, 'we lived in a house of ghosts'?"

Loretta's lips thinned, and she gave Heidi a sideways look. "We don't believe in ghosts. Absent from the body is to be present with the Lord. You know that."

Yes. She'd heard that many times growing up, and Heidi had to admit she'd seen little evidence to support paranormal activity anyway. All right. So her mother hadn't meant real ghosts.

"Did you mean we lived in a house of *secrets*?" Heidi pressed. She didn't want to feed her mother answers, but at the same time, a nudge might help things along.

Loretta blinked a few times as if to clear her thoughts. She looked at Heidi. "Who are you again?"

Oh, Lord, have mercy.

Heidi could feel the impatience welling up within her.

"I'm your daughter," she answered.

Loretta's mouth quirked into a smile that insinuated Heidi was the one mixed up. "No, you're not."

Aggravated, Heidi reached up and tucked her hair behind her ears. She resettled in her seat. "Mom, I'm Heidi."

"Not Vicki," Loretta stated.

No. Not Vicki. It stung that her mother

didn't remember her, but she remembered Vicki.

"I'm your younger daughter. Heidi Loretta Lane." Maybe saying her full name would prompt her mom's memory.

Loretta's smile waned, and her eyebrows raised sternly. She wagged her index finger at Heidi. "No. You're not my daughter."

"You said I am the reason the stories are never told." Heidi pointed to the line in the letter. "Why is that?"

Loretta was quiet. Maybe remembering. Maybe just confused.

"You were never supposed to be."

The whisper was barely audible. Heidi leaned forward. To hear it from her mother's lips. The words that confirmed everything she'd ever felt.

"You didn't want me?" she asked blatantly.

Loretta pushed a puzzle piece over toward another. She reached out and pushed them together. They didn't fit. She pressed harder.

"Fudge," the woman mumbled. She separated the two pieces.

"Mom?" Heidi couldn't believe how fast the woman could exit the conversation. How her mind had become a prison of sorts, letting her out only momentarily to enjoy reality and then penning her back inside.

"Hmm?" Loretta lifted her head.

"Mom, what are your secrets?" Heidi asked. She had to push. She had to know.

Loretta dropped her gaze.

"Mom?" Heidi reached out and laid her hand over her mother's palm.

The woman looked at their hands, then flipped hers over and curled her fingers around Heidi's. They were cold, the skin paper thin, and Heidi could see the veins in them.

"You always had a mind of your own, you did." Loretta squeezed Heidi's hand. Their eyes met, and for a moment Heidi sensed her mother was back. That she recognized her. That she knew it was Heidi to whom she spoke.

Heidi held her breath. Afraid even a sound would break her mother's awareness.

Loretta continued. "When you died . . . all of me died with you."

No. She wasn't speaking of Heidi. But the clarity in her mother's eyes was startling nonetheless. Unsettling, really.

"Mom, I'm here. I'm not dead." Heidi leaned closer, trying to capture her mother's attention.

Loretta released Heidi's hand with a small smile. "No. No, you're not." She returned to the puzzle, lifting a piece and eyeing its shape. She mumbled as she placed it in the edges pile. "But, you might as well be."

CHAPTER 27

THEA

Unearthly screams filtered through the cast-iron ceiling vent. Thea dropped the stack of papers onto the desk already piled with records and other sundry hospital notations. She stared up at the vent, her raw nerves grating with every scream. There was nothing she could do. A series of thuds sounded in the room above. A struggle.

"No! No, no, no, no, no!" The patient's guttural shouts sent horrible shivers down Thea's spine. She wanted to ignore it. To pick up the stack of papers and escape to the backyard and sort them there. But, truth be told, she was as frightened to leave as she was to stay.

She could hear Dr. Ackerman's voice, muffled, giving strong direction to whoever was in the room with him. When the nurse responded, Thea could tell it was Rose.

More conversation, interspersed with

kicks to the floorboards.

Thea moved to the doorway. Mr. Fritz would want her to see firsthand what was happening. It was part of her bargain that she'd struck. She owed him information in return for whatever he could find on her mother.

Exiting the small office, she looked to the left, down the hallway toward the back door. Ignoring the temptation of escape, she forced herself toward the main lobby and the stairs that rose to the second level. Her feet took them with tentative steps. One at a time. Her hand on the rail until that ran out and she was ensconced on both sides by walls. Reaching the landing, she turned right, toward the room above her office — toward the screams.

She paused outside the doorway. It was a room that held four cots. One long window with security bars set over it. Her hand on the doorframe, Thea peered around it.

"Give me the bands." Dr. Ackerman's voice was urgent as he stretched his arm toward Rose. Another nurse was bustling about at the far end of the room, having herded two other occupants into the corner, distracting them with tiny cups of water.

Rose handed circular straps made of leather and buckles to the doctor. He went to work over the patient he had restrained in a chair. It was Effie. The woman's back arched with her head bent backward, her mouth open. He strapped the bands around her ankles.

Effie choked, and her feet raised in the air, then dropped to the floor.

"Blast it, woman!" Dr. Ackerman shouted. He held her down while waggling his fingers at Rose. She hurried toward him. He buckled the woman's right hand in a strap that was attached to the chair, and the chair was bolted to the floor. The patient struggled for her freedom, her one free arm clawing at the doctor's face. Clawing or slapping, Thea wasn't sure. In fact, she wasn't sure Effie was even aware of what she was doing. She wasn't fighting so much as thrashing uncontrollably.

"Restrain her!"

Rose followed the doctor's orders, strapping down Effie's left hand now.

The woman's head jerked forward, then slammed back against the chair. Her eyes rolled toward the ceiling. Spittle trailed from the corner of her mouth.

"Thea!"

Rose's surprised reaction broke through Thea's shock. She stood frozen in the doorway, fixated on the mental patient whose moans became muffled as Dr. Ackerman attached a leather muff over her mouth.

"What are you doing to her?" Thea couldn't weep. She couldn't be indignant. She was so taken aback by the sight that she had no compulsion to react either in distaste or in understanding.

"Get her out of here!" Dr. Ackerman commanded.

Rose hurried toward Thea, taking her by the arm. Thea caught a glimpse of the nurse in the corner, one of her patients having lain on the cold, wood floor, curled into a ball like a baby in a crib. The nurse gave her a cold glare that communicated well and good that Thea should not be here.

Rose guided Thea back down the stairs. As they neared Thea's office, she ushered her in and closed the door gently behind them. Her black hair was stuck out in wisps and strands from the struggle with the patient. She seemed to note her disarray, and Rose took a moment to untie her white apron, soiled by the day's work, and retie its bow.

"H-How could you?" Thea finally breathed, grasping for the chair by the desk and allowing her legs to collapse beneath her. She stared incredulously at Rose. "You harnessed a human being as one would a horse!"

Rose palmed the air in an effort to get Thea to lower her voice. "Sometimes — it is necessary."

"Necessary?" All Thea could see in her mind's eye was the blurred image of her mother. Had her mother lived here? Been restrained like the woman upstairs? Had she undergone being silenced by a leather muff forced over her mouth?

Rose knelt on the floor by Thea, resting her hands on Thea's knees. Her eyes were large and earnest. "Effie was having a spell. She was out of control, so we called for Dr. Ackerman. Sometimes, Thea, the patients leave us little choice but to restrain them."

Thea searched Rose's face. There was honesty in her countenance, but also sadness. Rose didn't enjoy it, she found no cold satisfaction in it. In fact, it seemed to pain her greatly. Rose bit her bottom lip.

"Not all patients are like her, Thea. Some are docile and sad. They stare for hours into the corners. But others . . ." Her voice waned.

Thea attempted to compose her shock that had quickly turned to outrage. Rose was correct. Thea didn't understand, but then, if she did, would she agree with their course of action?

"How long will she be restrained?"

Rose glanced up at the ceiling as though she could see through the floorboards and assess the patient above. "It depends. For as long as she needs to be until we can calm her. Sometimes an hour. Sometimes much longer than that."

"Isn't there medicine? Something to help her —"

"We do what we can, Thea." Something changed in Rose's expression. A desperation, some irritation, mingled with an edge of defensiveness. "You have to understand, if you're going to work here and assist Dr. Ackerman with the files and — photography when possible — that you will hear and maybe see things you don't understand. I know it's frightening. Horrific. All of it. It's why I hate this place, and why I keep coming back. The patients are not normal, Thea. They need help. They are —" Rose clipped her words as her tone had grown higher and more upset.

Thea could see her working hard to control it.

Rose took a deep breath and let it out through her lips. She blinked and regained her composure. "Mary was — she suffered greatly from melancholy. Dr. Ackerman suggested many times that she be committed here. To be nursed and cared for, as her frame of mind was not a pleasant one." Rose swiped at the corner of her eye.

Thea waited, unsure where Rose was taking her in the conversation. Afraid to follow but feeling it necessary to do so.

Rose ran her fingers on either side of her nose, over her mouth, and then dropped them to her sides. "There are so many people who should be committed here but aren't. Like Mary. My, how I miss my sister."

Thea winced at the grief in Rose's voice and the resignation in her eyes.

"But," Rose continued as she pushed to her feet, "God help them if they are. Hell cannot be much worse than being banished to a place such as this."

Thea stumbled into the sunlight that struggled to breach the canopy of trees. She'd combed through papers all day, putting them into smaller piles. Finding nothing on her mother, P. A. Reed, and nothing on the asylum that would support Mr. Fritz's suspicions of abuse — at least on paper. She tilted her head back, willing the sun to warm her face, begging the trees to pull back their branches and let its rays through.

There was no solace here. Not inside or outside. As she brought her eyes back toward the woods beyond the small yard, she noted the trail to the asylum's graveyard. Its narrow path, cluttered with rock half buried in the earth and tripped with roots rising from the ground as if to snare someone. It beckoned her. She had no desire to follow, to go blindly into the woods where only hours before the taunting voice and melody had sent her catapulting into the asylum. Perhaps she understood now. What Simeon had meant the night before by the river. The siren's song that beckoned, deceptively beautiful and intriguing, but in the end baring its fangs and pulling the wayfaring soul into ruin.

That was how it seemed to Thea as her feet navigated the rough trail. She had no choice but to follow the instinct that pulled her toward the little graveyard. Perhaps it was what Misty Wayfair wanted, when all was said and done. A willingness to walk to one's end. So, she didn't have to cajole, tempt, or deceive. Just a simple path into the forest where, eventually, one would disappear, and the world would continue knowing that Misty Wayfair's curse had claimed yet another. Her keening song the only vague remembrance.

Thea shook off the unwelcome dark feelings. Oddly, the sun had indeed broken through the thick treetops, and its warmth cast over the gravestones, their flat faces lifted to beg of it to stay. To lift them from the darkness of the grave and into an eternal hereafter. She paused, staring down at them, crossing her arms over her chest. Her shirt was bloused over the narrow waist of her skirt and was cotton thin. Thea should embrace the warmth of the sun as the markers did, and yet she couldn't.

She took a step forward, browsing the crowded plots with a wary eye. Thea knew she shouldn't be afraid of a cemetery. It held no threat, no ghosts that would push skeletal hands through the ground to grab at her feet. Still, Thea sidestepped so she didn't plant her feet directly atop where these souls had been laid to rest. Out of respect, but also out of fear.

In the far corner, the four-sided white stone rose alone. The keeper over all the others. Its sides were worn smooth by the weather and the passage of time. Green lichen and moss grew in crevices, around the lettering carved in the face. Thea walked toward it, tiptoeing around a stone that stared up at her, an unfamiliar name with a rock Simeon had left, bearing the declaration *Free* on it.

Free.

Thea had never stopped to consider that she felt imprisoned. But perhaps it was as true for her as the patients in the asylum or for Simeon and Rose. Trapped by the legacies left them by their parents and grandparents. Unsolved stories, and in Thea's case, a wandering that kept her from being rooted. She didn't know who she was. Not really. *Reed* was a surname left to her by a nameless mother. *Mendelsohn* was a name never adopted but with memories attached to it that wrote scarring tales and conflicting theology on her heart. She was just . . . Thea. More lost now than before coming to Pleasant Valley.

She fingered the letters on the front of the four-sided pillar. The name was difficult to read. The years scrolled a date from long ago. *Robert.* Robert something. Thea drew in a deep breath. The years had not been kind to the memory of this man. Even the birds had defecated on his name, leaving stains and markings behind.

Thea moved to the side farthest from the woods. It struck Thea as strange that with as much care as Simeon had given the cemetery, this stone would be so marred from animals, weather, and lack of care. She ran her palm over the lettering, chipping away at the stiff lichen that had built up over the name.

Maybe the action of cleaning the name soothed her, but Thea lost track of time. This side of the stone was particularly worn. The letters so weathered that some of the etching had melded into the face.

Thea's fingernail caught on the lichen, pulling it away from the first few letters of the surname.

She halted.

Narrowing her eyes, Thea wiped her hand over the letters.

Way . . .

She knew what it would say before she finished clearing the name.

Misty Wayfair's name stared back at her. So real, so definitive, that for a moment Thea could only stare back.

Misty Wayfair
Died April 1851

Nothing more. No birth date. No epitaph. Not even a middle name.

It was stark.

So lonely.

So . . . .

"You found her."

Simeon's voice made Thea jump. She cast startled eyes toward him, then swallowed her initial fear and turned back to the marker.

"Why didn't you tell me?"

Simeon moved around the marker to the other side. He began to clear off whatever name was there, as if, now discovered, there was no reason to keep it hidden.

"Why did you keep it secret?" Thea insisted, running her index finger over the *M* in Misty's name.

"It wasn't a secret," Simeon said.

Thea noted how his mouth jerked, as though being pulled up into a tight smile and then released. He focused on the stone.

"She's truly buried here?"

"She was the first," he affirmed.

"I didn't think the asylum has been here that long. And Mrs. Brummel said she was — murdered. Not a ward of the asylum."

"All of it is true. She was buried before the asylum was built."

Thea could sense her frustration growing. Simeon seemed so vulnerable at times, yet now he was standoffish and tight-lipped. Certainly his family history was none of her business, although it was no secret that the

413

Coyles were intertwined in scandal with Misty Wayfair. It was like a murky river where, at first, things seemed clear, and then when one approached, you couldn't see to the bottom for the silt that clouded its clarity.

"Simeon." Her voice was firm, demanding that he look at her.

He did. His hair askew, his eyes guarded, his face shadowed by whiskers and secrets.

"Is it true, what they say? That Misty Wayfair had — a relationship with your grandfather?"

Simeon's face contorted. He was aggravated. Thea could almost feel his irritation at his malady as he tried to control it.

"N-No." The facial tic made him stutter. He drew in a deep breath and then let it out, slow and controlled, through his nose. "My grandfather was faithful."

Thea had nothing to lose. Misty Wayfair's legendary hauntings were affecting her too now, as evidenced by the dance with dark melody in the woods that morning. "Who killed Misty Wayfair?"

Simeon blinked. There was honesty in his eyes. "No one knows."

"Why does she hate the Coyles? Even now? Over fifty years later?"

Simeon dug into his pocket and pulled

out a handkerchief. He used it to scrub at the lettering on his side of the marker.

"Simeon?" Thea refused to accept his silence.

"Because." He slapped the stone. His eyes were brewing when he leveled them upon her. Gone was the timid Simeon, the awkward Simeon, the soft-spoken Simeon. In his place stood a man who battled against his inability to protect his family, and his ineptness to dispel the rumors and division that had kept the Coyles ostracized by the people of Pleasant Valley.

She waited.

Finally, the words came as though dragged from his mouth. "*She* is dead, Thea. There is no Misty Wayfair haunting the woods. There is no ghost. No curse."

Thea drew back at the vehemence in his tone. "Then how do you explain it? Who was in the woods this morning, taunting me?"

He raised his eyes to the sky in barely veiled exasperation. "I don't explain it. I can't explain it. My family continues to pass away, one by one, and the songs are sung, and Misty is *seen*. Our cousins, the Fortunes, continue to ignore us as chattel and live in the legacy my great-grandfather began. Oust the Coyles, the Irish Catholics,

415

and Fergus the unwelcome son-in-law. My grandmother suffered because of her father; she suffered because of Misty Wayfair. We suffer still!"

The force of his words echoed through the woods.

They stared at each other, the pillar gravestones between them. Thea's palm pressed against Misty's name, and Simeon's against the gravestone on his side.

"Don't you want to know, to find out, to understand what happened?" Thea breathed.

Simeon reached forward, and his hand snagged hers. The warmth of his callused fingers shot a thrill through her, and then he pulled her toward him. She stumbled at the tug, grasping at his coat to steady herself. But there was no warmth in his eyes as he made her turn, made her look at the carving he'd cleaned with his hands.

His breath was hot on her ear as he leaned in and replied, "Don't you want to know? To find out? To understand? Or are you like me, weary of trying."

Thea focused on the name.

Simeon continued. "We are the descendants of a greater tragedy. Bigger than ourselves, Thea. When you unleash the monsters, they *will* find us. They will find *you.*"

She didn't know how to respond. Not as her eyes took in the name of her mother.

Penelope Alice Reed Wayfair

The woman she'd been trying for so long to find was dead. As Thea had wished it to be. And there was no taking back wishes once they'd been given life.

CHAPTER 28

HEIDI

She'd ended up at the Crawford home. She shouldn't be surprised. Heidi was drawn to them like a moth to a flame, a bee to pollen, a bear to honey, or whatever appropriate cliché someone wanted to associate with it. It was more than the random text from Connie, inviting her to a homemade dinner — Connie knew Heidi's welcome was outlived at Brad and Vicki's — it was the idea of family. Heidi had to remind herself that she couldn't expect to simply insert herself into a functional family unit, and yet here she was, leaning back in an overstuffed chair and playing Risk with Emma.

Venison steaks off the grill consumed, along with a spinach and strawberry vinaigrette salad, followed up with a slice of rhubarb pie. It was all so . . . homespun. Especially since Murphy was out in the yard, putzing around with an old chainsaw

418

he'd picked up at a garage sale, and Connie was doing a crossword puzzle on the sofa just to the right of Heidi and Emma. It was the opposite of Heidi's life. She was edgy, her burns and cuts stung, her mother's words echoed in her ears, and the questions plagued her with dogged persistence.

Couldn't she ignore it all for one night? One night of blissful peace? Just pretend that she was — somehow — a Crawford, and the hardest obstacle ahead of her was how to overtake the territory of Western Europe. And how to ignore Rhett. Firefighter Rhett. *Volunteer* firefighter.

He was like the proverbial hero. Brawny, grouchy, earthy, and . . . fireman-y. But for all his Hulk-smashing, the green skin was wearing off and he was becoming a man. Just — a man. That was perhaps even more dangerous. Heidi wasn't in the right emotional state to ward off dangerous. It was good he was outside and not sulking in the corner. Good that the ball he was throwing to Rüger just beyond the window was green and reminded her of his grumpy side. Good that he had stopped and looked at her through the window and . . .

Heidi tore her eyes away.

Emma stared at her, a questioning look in her eyes. "It's your turn."

Connie glanced up.

Heidi cleared her throat. "Yes." She picked up a die. "I'll roll one and attack Western Europe."

Emma gave her a smile of satisfaction that the game was on.

She lost the attack.

Heidi sighed. *Figures.*

"Heidi." Rhett's voice cut through the room. Heidi started, and a few of her armies tipped over. Emma reached to right them.

"Yeah?" Heidi eyed him, very aware that Connie was looking between them.

There was a weird tension in the air, as though something had shifted. She didn't know what or why. But for some reason, she saw him differently now. Maybe that was it. He had calmed her after the spray-painted ominous message at the asylum ruins, and he'd tackled her during the fire, and somehow his force had shown her he had more control over the situation than she did. Why did she like that? She'd no desire to be dominated. No. It wasn't domination. Far from it. It was that he was logical and capable of handling such moments when she clearly wasn't. When she was jumpy and on the verge of tears. The yin to her yang.

"Come outside," he said. Another directive, but spoken in his no-nonsense voice that communicated nothing other than a suggestion but without the extra words.

Heidi looked to Emma, who smiled. "It's okay," Emma said.

She didn't seem disturbed by the fact they were leaving the game unfinished. Probably because it was Rhett. Heidi was learning that Emma would make just about any adjustment for Rhett. He was her safe person.

Heidi studied Rhett's broad back as she followed him outside. She frowned at herself. She wanted a safe person too.

She always had.

They rounded the house to the backyard that was bordered by woods. A square block with five black circles on it sat at the edge of the woods, with a few hay bales piled behind it. Rhett paused about twenty yards away, and Heidi noticed two hooks jammed into the ground, bows hanging from them.

She gave Rhett a raised eyebrow. "Are you going hunting?"

Rhett leaned over and lifted one of the bows from its hanger. It was black with neon-pink strings, an arrow already mounted on it, wrapped with neon-pink wraps.

"Target practice." He ran a thumb over

the pink fletching on the arrow. "It's how I de-stress."

"De-stress," Heidi echoed. Shoot things with a bow and arrow. Yes. This was the Northwoods of Wisconsin.

Rhett met her eyes. His gaze was frank and open. "You need to unwind."

That was obvious. Heidi rolled her eyes and gave him a silly smile. "You think?"

She wanted to cry.

Rhett glossed over her retort and the underlying emotion. He looked down at the bow. "This is Emma's. She's okay with you using it. It's set to pull back forty pounds. Let's see if you can."

Heidi blinked incredulously. The man was serious. "I've no clue how to shoot an arrow."

"I know." Rhett extended the bow toward her.

She stepped back. "My hand." Waving it toward him, her hand bandaged from the, thankfully, minor burns she'd received from the fire.

"The grip rests between your thumb and forefinger. You don't have to strangle it." He demonstrated and then handed her the bow.

Heidi took the bow by its grip and steadied herself, surprised by the fact it wasn't as heavy as she'd expected. He was right. It balanced remarkably well, and she didn't need to grasp it with the full embrace of her hand.

"Give me your right hand." Again with the commands.

Heidi held out her hand, and her palm instantly warmed when Rhett took it and slipped a black — thingy — over her wrist. It had a metal clasp that dangled from it.

"This is the release," he explained, buckling it around her wrist like a watchband. "Pull back on the trigger here with your thumb and clip onto the D-loop on the bowstring. It might rub your burn a bit when you do this, 'cause you have to hold the grip tighter. Raise the bow and don't throttle the grip. The arrow's in the rest, so when ready, see if you can pull back the string."

"Just like that?" Heidi had no idea what he was talking about. "There's got to be a better way to do this."

A tiny smile quirked the corner of his mouth. "There is. But you don't have the patience for it."

She tilted her head and glowered at him. "Really?"

"Just pull it back." He neared her, the bow between them, and he positioned himself, like he was ready to grab her forearm and

423

help her pull back the string.

But he didn't.

Heidi pulled. Nothing happened. She gave him a doubtful look. "It won't move."

Rhett gave her a gray stare. "You need to really pull it."

"I am!" She argued, half laughing, half whining.

Rhett shook his head. "It uses a distinct set of muscles to pull back a bowstring. But you should be able to pull back forty pounds."

"How would you know?" Heidi retorted.

Rhett's eyebrows creased inward. "Because I had to pin you down outside the cabin when it was on fire, and you just about clocked me with a right hook. So, *pull* it back."

"Fine." Heidi refocused, and this time she pulled the string back. Her arm quivered. She couldn't get the string over the crux of the pull.

"Too hard?" he asked. It was a sincere question, not taunting. He reached toward her arm to assist, but paused when Heidi gave her head a stubborn shake.

"No." Heidi put a few more grunts into her tug until the string was all the way back. "Holy wow! This is hard to hold."

Rhett was intent on the bow and her form.

Or what little form she had.

"Yeah," he agreed. "Forty pounds might be too hard since you're not used to it. The draw length should be good, though. You're about Emma's arm span."

"Okay, fine. What do I do now?" Heidi gasped, her arm shaking from the exertion of holding back the string.

"Look through the peep, line up the first pin in the sight, and release it. At the block."

"What?" Heidi half hollered at him. Did he think she knew something — anything — about archery? Because she didn't.

"Aim and release," he barked.

She closed an eye and saw some glowing green pin in a round thing, aimed her arrow, and released the trigger. The string instantly let go. The arrow shot through the dusk and cleared the target, sticking instead into a hay bale behind it.

Heidi spun, the bow in hand, and gave a well-deserved slap to Rhett's shoulder with her other hand. "You're horrid." She was peeved, and added to that, mortified and embarrassed.

Rhett reached for the bow.

Heidi swapped it to her right hand, as her burns were starting to sting. She pulled it away from him and leveled him with a glare. "No. I don't need to be made a fool of. Not today. Not ever."

"You're not a fool." Rhett sidestepped her and tugged the bow from her grip.

"Then what was this? A lesson in how to look stupid?"

"Nope." Rhett hung the bow on its stand. "C'mon." He hiked toward the hay bale.

Heidi chased after him. "This is no destressor, if that's what you're thinking. My arm hurts! Not to mention, I doubt anyone learns how to use a bow without a good lesson on the *parts of a bow*!" She hissed the last words. "You even said there was an easier way!"

Rhett was at the hay bale now. He reached up and pushed his left hand against it as he yanked the arrow from the hay with his right.

"You're right." He turned and stared down at her, holding the arrow against his leg. "There is. It's called a *lesson*."

Heidi was suddenly aware of how tall he was. She opened her mouth to argue, then snapped it shut.

"But this is how you do life." His words pierced her like the arrow. "You're obstinate. You don't want to be taught."

"What do you mean?" Fine. He had some overarching point he wanted to make?

Then go ahead, Rhett Crawford, make it.

426

"You just do stuff — without first thinking it through."

"Whatever." Heidi was finished with this conversation. She spun on her heel to stalk back to the house. It was annoying how perceptive he was — oh, and that he was right.

"Then you ignore it and walk away," he added.

Heidi stopped, her back to him.

"You've got to stop, Heidi. Just stop."

She heard him come up behind her. There it was. The hand on her arm, turning her toward him. Darn it. Heidi dropped her gaze to the grass beneath their feet. Her eyes burned with tears. It was what her family had always told her, and yet for some reason it sounded different coming from Rhett.

"The same way you won't learn how to shoot with a bow by just doing it, you won't figure out what's going on here — in Pleasant Valley — with your family by jumping in and being reckless. When you get hurt, you shut down. But if you'd just slow down, if you'd let people help you, if you'd . . ." He stopped, almost as if the words took too much energy to spit out.

Heidi looked up.

Rhett's expression was intense. She couldn't look away. For the first time, for real, she saw what Connie had meant when she said he'd muscle his way in like a bear, but that he really, truly wanted to rescue.

"Let me help you," he finished, a sigh following his declaration, as though his words were lame.

But they weren't lame. Heidi felt her chin quiver. She pressed her lips together and looked past him at the hay bale and archery target. Tears escaped, and she wrapped her arms around herself.

"No one wants me," she whispered. Aware she almost sounded like a wounded toddler who'd lost her way in a supermarket. "I saw a woman — at the fire, Rhett. I really did, whether anyone believes me or not." Heidi lifted her eyes, not trying to hide the tears this time. "She pulled me out. She looks like that old picture in the album. I tried to talk to my mom. She's completely losing it and thinks I'm dead. Maybe I am — to her. I don't know. And Vicki thinks I'm nuts. Heck, *I* think I'm nuts. I can't do it anymore. I don't know where I belong, I don't know who I am — who my family is. I'm a mess, Rhett. I'm such a mess!"

Her last words released in a choked sob.

Rhett drew her toward him. She stumbled, resisting at first. He gave another tug, the arrow dropping to the ground at his feet.

Then her face was buried in his chest.

And, he was safe.

CHAPTER 29

This was new. Sitting beside Rhett at the police station, Heidi gave him a sideways glance. It was very *different* having someone accompanying her for no other reason than to be supportive. She was sort of afraid to look at him for fear he'd evaporate and she'd slip back into her normal state of self-reliance. It was an anomaly she struggled to comprehend. Being an independent woman by nature and by sheer circumstance of life, the element of having someone on her team was comforting. Maybe too much so. She didn't want to get used to it, and as she'd guarded herself with the Crawfords before, one moment of face-planting in Rhett's chest didn't mean he was her cohort in life forever.

Footsteps on the hard linoleum floor of the station drew her attention. Detective Davidson came toward them from down the hall, wearing a polite smile, a flicker of interest in his eyes. He was nice too, Heidi remembered from the night of the lodge break-in . . . but he wasn't Rhett.

Oh man. She needed to quit this right now. She was already getting too soft toward the giant.

"Why don't you come in here?" Detective Davidson waved them toward a tiny room with a table and chairs.

They each took a seat. Heidi drew her hair back into a ponytail, then released it, letting the blue-blond strands fall over her shoulders. She drew in a sigh. To calm herself. A familiar weight settled on her chest. Unsolved questions. A vivid image of a woman slamming her hand on the window, screaming at her, and then vanishing afterward.

"All right." Detective Davidson leaned forward on the table, folding his hands together. "I'll get straight to it. We confirmed that the fire at the lodge was arson. I've already met with Vicki and Brad." He shot Heidi a hesitant look. "I guess you're staying at the Crawfords' for now?"

A raised eyebrow.

For sure, he'd want to deduce any strife between family. Motives. Possible interpersonal reasons for striking at each other.

Heidi nodded. Connie had extended the offer, she'd taken it, and probably had the best sleep in her life last night, camped out in their guest room. Rhett had gone back to his place not long after her meltdown, and she'd ended up sipping hot cocoa with Connie until midnight. Talking. Just . . . talking.

"Okay." The detective rolled his lips together in thought. "So, what we know is, between the original break-in and the message on your mirror, the graffiti at the asylum ruins, and now the fire, all this really does seem to be targeting you, Heidi. Your sister mentioned a note card left under your windshield wiper too?"

Vicki was thorough. Heidi nodded. While she didn't miss the fast glance Rhett tossed her, she decided to ignore it.

"It wasn't too unlike the message on the mirror. Basically implying I am mad or insane."

"Do you still have the note?" Detective Davidson asked.

Now she felt stupid for not reporting it. "Yes."

He smiled. "We'll need to get that from you, Heidi. We haven't turned up much for fingerprints or evidence. But your sister seems to think" — he looked at Rhett — "maybe you have someone from your past or even present who might have it in for you?"

Heidi bit back an irritated response. She swallowed.

Rhett spoke before she could say anything. "Mike, there's more to this that you need to know."

Mike? First-name basis. Small town. Heidi let Rhett talk. Let him help her, he'd asked. Okay. She'd try to do that.

Mike leaned back in his chair and crossed his arms, frowning. "Oooookay?"

Rhett ran his fingers over the brim of his greasy cap. "Heidi told me a woman helped pull her from the flames. It wasn't a guest of the lodge either. When we accounted for everyone after the fire, there was no such woman."

Mike glanced between them. "Yeah, I heard about that."

"I believe her," Rhett stated.

Heidi blinked and stared at him. The three words were simple. But they were ginormous. The act of believing what she said . . . Heidi bit the inside of her cheek.

"Also," Rhett continued, firmness lacing his voice, "the woman who pulled Heidi from the cabin was the same woman she saw looking in her window the day of the break-in."

"Really?" Mike was interested now. He leaned forward again.

Rhett nodded. "Where it gets strange is that this woman looks exactly like someone in a photograph my parents found in an old album at a sale. And both women look just like Heidi."

Mike blinked, not saying anything.

Heidi squirmed in her chair, but she noted Rhett sat there casually as though he hadn't sounded just a tad off himself.

"Next, you're going to tell me it's Misty Wayfair." A wry smile teased Mike's mouth.

Rhett responded with a small grin himself. It transformed his face from grumpy to rustic-handsome. "It's not, no. But the photograph does have her name penciled on the back of it."

Mike chuckled. His expression was disbelief and interest all rolled into one. "So . . . Misty Wayfair has returned, eh? After, what, a hundred and fifty years?"

"She's more interesting than Paul Bunyan," Rhett retorted.

"She's still just a legend."

"With some credibility." Rhett's words put a final exclamation point on the banter.

Mike nodded. "Fair enough. She was murdered in these parts, they say, but her ghost? Are you saying you believe in a ghost story?"

"No." Rhett shook his head.

"Okay, I give up." Mike palmed the air. "What *are* you saying?"

Rhett looked at Heidi. She tried to read his face but couldn't decipher if he wanted her to talk now that he'd used his quota of words for the day, or if he wanted her permission to explore ideas. Heidi opted for the latter and gave him a nod of encouragement. She was shocked when he tossed her back an almost imperceptible wink.

"I think Heidi is connected to Misty Wayfair. I think Heidi might be a descendent of the Coyles, who were rumored to play a part in the murder. Heidi coming here now seems to have exposed some old local history. Could be there are relations in the area who are protective of that story."

"Why do you think she's related to the Coyles?"

Heidi could tell Mike's brain was trying to wrap around the theory. She wasn't sure she understood it herself, but then added, "The woman in the old photograph was identified as Mary Coyle. If I look exactly like her, it's possible I'm —"

"Related to her," Mike finished. "Got it. But you're not from around here?"

"Not that I know of." Heidi shook her head.

Mike frowned. "Have you talked to Vicki

about this possible family connection?"

Heidi's shoulders sagged. "I did ask her about our family history, and she's clueless."

"Okay." Mike braced his palms on the tabletop. "Here's where we need to start. Let me do some investigating around town. See if there's anyone still in the area with some odd vested interest in this whole *legend*. Especially anyone connected to it who might also have reason to want to see you hurt. Heidi, you dig into your family history some more and either confirm the link to the Coyles or eliminate it. I need to see a solid connection, and right now it's a stretch. But if you think it's valid," Mike said, tipping his head at Rhett, "then I don't mind looking into it."

Heidi couldn't squelch the gratefulness that swelled within her. She tried not to let it show but had a feeling her emotions were splayed all over her face when she met Rhett's eyes.

Rhett turned back to Mike. "Thanks," he said and then stood.

Mike stopped him. "Wait. I need to see this picture. For real. Heidi, if you have a doppelgänger from the turn of the century, and one running around town starting fires and leaving odd messages, there's something really strange going on. And we need to get to the bottom of it."

An understatement if she'd ever heard one. But, Heidi had to admit, it was nice to finally be heard.

Heidi gave the memory-care facility a hesitant look. Rhett put the truck into park, rolled down his window a few inches, and reached up onto the dash to give Archie the complimentary scratch behind the ears. The cat trilled and nudged his hand. Heidi could only assume when it got significantly warmer out, Rhett would finally leave Archie at his place. But for now, the dash of his truck seemed to be the cat's happy place during the day. They had left Rüger at the Crawford home, leaving a gaping space between her and Rhett on the truck's front seat.

"What are we doing here?" she asked.

He shut his door and came around to meet her. He eyed her with his common-sense stare.

"I just saw my mom two days ago," Heidi added.

"Yep." Rhett stepped to the side, motioning for her to step out of the truck.

She did, but she didn't take any further steps toward the facility. Instead, she rolled the hem of her shirt between her fingers, the navy blue material soft in her hand. "My mom isn't going to help us. She can't remember things, and she — she doesn't know me at all."

Another major understatement. She thought Heidi was dead. Their conversation returned so vividly in Heidi's memory, her stomach turned.

"Let me see it." Rhett held out his hand.

"See what?" Heidi countered.

"Vicki said you came here 'cause your mom sent you a letter. I'd like to see it." His hand remained outstretched.

Heidi raised an eyebrow while nervously scratching the tattoo on her left wrist. "And you think I have it with me?"

Rhett just stared at her and waited.

"Okay fine." Heidi scrounged in her military green bag, pulled out the crinkled letter, and gave it to him. Impatience welled inside her. It was nice having him help, but it was also intrusive. Every step she let him in was one less brick in her protective wall.

He skimmed the letter, then folded it and handed it back to her. "What did your mom say about it?"

Heidi made a pretense of carefully tucking the letter back into her bag. "Oh, not much, other than insist I didn't exist." Heidi zipped the bag shut. She waved her hand toward the home. "Can we just go in, then?"

Rhett didn't budge. His eyes narrowed.

"What?" Heidi pressed.

"Did you ask Vicki what your mom meant?"

"Since the fire, Vicki won't talk to me. She didn't want to talk much before it either."

Rhett gave a grunt and turned toward the home. Heidi followed, lagging just a few paces behind him. An aide buzzed them into the locked-down facility. Within moments, they were in a lounge area and standing over Loretta Lane, who stared off into the corner. Her eyes empty.

Heidi wasn't sure what Rhett's intentions were. Getting any more details out of her mother seemed miraculous at best. She flopped onto a chair, as if they were here simply to eat cookies and watch TV with the old woman. Her mother. Her vacant, sad mother. If she thought too long about it, Heidi knew her emotions would twist into fits.

Rhett eased onto a chair beside Loretta, swiping his hat off his head. His hair stood up in bunches, a thick mess, but he somehow seemed more vulnerable. More approachable.

"That's better," her mother stated baldly.

She still stared into the corner. "That hat has seen its time, Rhett Crawford."

Heidi's mouth dropped open in disbelief — and hurt, if she were being honest. Her mother remembered who Rhett was? But not her own daughter? She blinked fast to shoo away the scalding tears that sprang to her eyes.

Rhett gazed into the same spot Loretta did. "I like my hat."

"Always did." Loretta's hand lifted and settled down atop of Rhett's larger one.

"Got a question for you," he stated. No dancing around the conversation — he was diving straight in.

Heidi bit the inside of her lip.

"All right then." Loretta nodded. Her eyes were so cloudy, so unclear, it was odd that she spoke with such precision.

"Are you a Coyle?" Rhett asked.

Heidi shot forward, stopping herself when Rhett lifted a finger toward her. She leaned on her knees, her breaths coming fast. Just like that? He thought he was going to just ask and Loretta would tell him? It couldn't be that easy. It wouldn't be. It was obvious that —

"Why, yes. Yes, I am." Loretta's face transfigured into a vague smile. She turned her head and met Rhett's eyes. "Are you?"

"No, I'm a Crawford," Rhett responded. His eyes met Heidi's. She knew her expression was one of wounded incredulity.

How had her mom given that up without question, without even a blink? Heidi leaned forward, her elbows on her knees. Maybe her mother's fragile mental state had loosened the locks on the secrets she held. But when Heidi asked, her mother spoke only riddles in return.

Somehow, Loretta Lane knew Rhett, and trusted him, more than she did her own daughter. The pang of that truth stung Heidi.

Rhett addressed Loretta again. "Was Coyle your maiden name?"

Loretta gave a slight nod. She raised a tremoring hand and pushed a strand of hair from her eyes. She searched Rhett's face, her furrowed brows pulling even tighter together. It seemed she was thinking, remembering — or trying to.

"Coyle. Yes. I was a Coyle." Her tone made it sound more like a question than a statement.

Again Rhett exchanged looks with Heidi.

"Do you remember anything about being a Coyle?" he asked.

Heidi could see where he was going, making sure there were memories, even vague ones to back up Loretta's hurried agreement. To provide proof that she wasn't entertaining a random question as fact.

Loretta nodded. "My schoolgirl friend called me Lorrie Coyle. Yes."

Rhett nodded but didn't speak.

Loretta tapped her fingers on the arm of her chair. "My father changed it, though — when I was twelve. Too much stuff and nonsense being a Coyle in these parts. All those old ghosts that trail after us, even after all these years."

Heidi ran her palm over her neck. Agitated, she leaned back in the chair, then forward again. She wanted to interrupt. To ply her mother with questions, but for some reason, Loretta trusted Rhett. She found her voice, her memories . . . with Rhett.

"Is that why you moved back to Pleasant Valley?" Rhett asked.

Loretta gave a tiny shrug. "Ohhh, I don't know . . ." Her voice trailed, and she shifted her attention back to the high corner of the room. "My husband took a pastorate here. It seemed — good to come home. No one remembered me, though. We left when I was twelve. No reason to remember the Coyles. And I wasn't one anymore. We were the last of them, you know?" She smiled.

Rhett shook his head. "No, I didn't know."

"Yes," Loretta nodded. "We were." She twisted in her chair to eye him. "Now, there was a young woman here. She kept saying she was my daughter. She's not. My daughter died."

"When did she die?" Rhett shot Heidi a warning glance. Any interruption now could be detrimental.

Loretta frowned. She reached up and, with a shaky hand, pushed her hair behind her ear. "Who?"

"Your daughter," Rhett replied. "When did she die?"

"Oh." Loretta shook her head. "No, no, Vicki is fine."

She was leaving them again. Fading into a world of disordered thoughts trapped deep inside the vanishing memories of an old woman.

Rhett pressed his lips together in a kind smile and gave Loretta's shoulder a squeeze. "You take it easy, Mrs. Lane."

"Oh, I will," she smiled.

Rhett stood and motioned for Heidi to follow. She dogged his steps, biting her tongue until they had left the facility.

Heidi sucked in the warm spring breeze as they started across the parking lot. Rhett mashed his baseball cap back on his head.

"What was that?" Heidi strained to keep

up with his purposeful strides. "How did you — ? My mother knew you! How? Wha— ?"

Rhett clicked the locks and opened Heidi's door in the old-fashioned gesture of a gentleman.

"Your dad was my pastor. Before he passed away."

Heidi stared at him. "He what?" The reminder of her dad and his funeral that she'd not attended . . . no wonder Vicki hated her. Heidi always had a reason, and that week, well, there really hadn't been a good enough one, so she'd opted to say she had a stomach flu. She couldn't face her mom and Vicki. Not when she spent the weekend curled up in a recliner, watching movies and digging her fingers into kinetic sand trying to cope with her nerves. The dark, apocalyptic pall that settled over her the minute she'd gotten the call from Vicki about Dad.

Rhett continued explaining as he rounded the truck and opened his door. Heidi dragged herself back from her guilt trip. "That's how I got to know Vicki and Brad. Offered Brad a job at my shop about five years ago. Your family used to have Sunday dinner with us sometimes."

"Why didn't I know this?" Heidi blurted

without thinking.

Rhett raised an eyebrow. The kind that told her she'd have no way to argue against him, because he was going to respond with sheer, annoying logic.

"Because you never came to visit."

There it was. The truth. She turned to look out the truck window and away from Rhett, who had climbed into the driver's seat.

"And my mother is a Coyle? Why didn't I know that?"

Rhett tilted his head. "Maybe because you never knew to ask before. Referencing her letter gave your mom no details. Nothing to spark a memory. She can't recall why she wrote it. But, asking about a specific name? Apparently the detail jarred her."

"I wonder if she would have told me if I'd asked her today instead of you?" It was a murmured question. Not one Heidi really wanted an answer to.

Inserting the key into the truck's ignition, Rhett stopped and gave her a long look. "Maybe."

Again. A one-word answer. It didn't make her feel any better. Not at all.

CHAPTER 30

THEA

"Thea." Simeon's voice broke through her frantic thumbing through a pile of loose papers scrawled with inked handwriting. Names, medical information, random paragraphs of random observations.

Thea ignored him. He had known. All along he'd known her mother was dead and buried at the asylum. She'd admitted to him she was afraid of finding her mother here. She'd taken on the duty of rifling through the haphazard records to find out if it was even possible. And, Simeon had already known.

"Thea, stop." Simeon's words echoed in the small office. His hand closed over her wrist.

Thea froze. She eyed it. She shook him off. Turning, she skewered him with her hurt, ignoring the way his face twisted and jerked. He was upset too. He should be. He

446

was a liar. He was a deceiver.

"Why didn't you tell me? You let me come here, and all the time — all the time you knew Misty and my mother were buried here. Why at the asylum? Is my mother really a Wayfair? How is this possible?"

The questions came along with tears. There was no closure in finding her mother's grave. It had only opened and exhumed a chasm of unanswered questions.

"I didn't tell you because . . ." Simeon hesitated. He appeared to will his features to be calm. A deep breath through his nose, and then he released it. "Because I don't know the answers, Thea. I didn't know how to explain it to you."

"This is why Mr. Amos didn't want me here, isn't it?" He'd known too.

Simeon's jaw set. His eyes were clear. Strong. They drilled into hers as he flipped the edges of some of the hospital records. "No one knows why your mother was here. No one knows why Misty is buried here. The asylum wasn't built when she was buried. Those of us closest to it don't know what to do with it all, so we try our best to ignore it. Right or wrong. That's what we do."

Thea studied his expression. Her emotions began to calm. "The asylum was built around her grave?"

Simeon nodded. "And until you came, with your mother's initials and the surname of Reed, no one knew you existed."

Thea licked her lips and bit the corner. "Misty Wayfair . . . is she my grandmother?" Visions of the woman in the street below her room replayed through Thea's memory. Had the connection she'd felt to the eerie sight been that of a granddaughter to her grandmother? The thought was unnerving, and it gave Thea pause.

Simeon shook his head. "I don't know."

"Do I have a father?"

Simeon's look was pained and apologetic.

"You don't know," Thea concluded. She returned to the desk, lifting a stack of documents. She slammed them on the desktop in front of Simeon. "Start looking."

Their eyes locked. She recognized something familiar in his. Something she detested but understood all too well. There was fear there. The monsters he'd mentioned, being loosed. The stories they might uncover. None of it would be welcomed. None of it would be pleasant.

Thea tamped down her hurt at Simeon's actions. In a roundabout way, he'd been trying to protect her, just as Mr. Amos had. Maybe protect himself and Rose too. But it was time. Misty Wayfair had cursed these woods for far too long. Cursed the Coyles for too long. She had whispered death over them, avenging her own, and now she had touched Thea's life.

Perhaps Thea had been spared by growing up in the orphanage and in the care of the Mendelsohns. Maybe it was that distance that gave her the courage Simeon didn't have. Could she blame him? His father had abused and almost ruined him. His mother and sister had both passed without compelling causes. The town looked at him as an outcast.

But it was time.

Thea lifted her hand and touched Simeon's bare forearm lightly, his shirtsleeve rolled back. He glanced down at her fingertips as if she'd pressed into his skin with a branding iron.

"Simeon, it's time."

He moved his arm until his hand wrapped around hers. Their fingers closed in a desperate grasp. Not friends. Not lovers. Not family. Not enemies. But two lost people, weary and desolate, and each without purpose in a life that never embraced them.

A small knock on Thea's door brought her

attention from the window and view over Pleasant Valley and the river. The fact it was night and the moon was full meant the world seemed half awake still, even at midnight. But she'd not expected the knock. The boardinghouse didn't allow visitors into the living quarters, let alone in the middle of the night.

She leaned her shoulder against the door. "Who is it?"

"Mr. Fritz."

Thea pulled back and frowned. It was highly inappropriate for him to be here just outside her door. Opening the door would make it even more so. Yet the gnawing curiosity of why he'd come, along with the shared intrigue surrounding the asylum, made her reach for the knob.

She opened it a few inches, mustering a stern frown.

The older man's hand was already up, palm facing toward her to detour any conversation about etiquette and propriety. His balding head reflected a shaft of moonlight as it brushed across Thea's room and into the hall.

"I apologize. But I must speak with you."

"Now?" Thea glanced down the hallway. If Mrs. Brummel were to see them . . .

"Come downstairs to the parlor." Mr.

Fritz's directive would only partially make the situation less controversial, but he turned on his heel and slunk away.

She shut her door and made swift work of changing out of her nightclothes. Skirt, shirtwaist, and a knitted sweater for extra covering. Pulling her long hair back, she twisted it fast and pinned it. No need to add a wanton appearance to this travesty of a midnight meeting.

Within moments, Thea tiptoed down the hall, snuck step by step down the narrow staircase, skirted the dining room and found her way into the front parlor. Mr. Fritz stood by the window, and he turned when she entered.

There was nothing but urgency in his expression. He motioned her toward him, and as she came, he looked past her to be sure she'd not been followed or seen.

"Mr. Fritz, what is so critical that you must beckon me in the middle of the night?" Thea drew her sweater tightly around her.

The man crossed his arms over his chest. He was fully dressed and had the vague scent of fresh air about him that made her wonder if he'd just come in after being outside. His eyes were wide behind spectacles, and he lowered his voice.

"I've *seen* her now!"

"Who?" Thea asked, though she already knew. Suddenly her sweater didn't feel like enough covering.

"Misty Wayfair!" Mr. Fritz wheezed between clenched teeth. He took two steps toward the window and peered up and down the street before saying over his shoulder, "She's out there tonight. Wandering. I saw her."

Thea glanced into the dark corners of the parlor. Not that she expected to see Misty Wayfair materialize in one of them, yet that feeling she often got when Mr. Mendelsohn spoke of spirits as if they truly existed wrapped its chilling embrace around her.

"Where?" Thea's voice had a slight shake to it. The morning's interlude on the way to the asylum, the tormenting song, was all so real yet. But now? The image of Misty Wayfair and the possible link to her mother caused Thea to shiver.

Mr. Fritz turned from the window, his expression still intense. "She was by the river. Mrs. Brummel said she was wicked, and I daresay she's right. The creature chased after me. Arms outstretched as if she were going to take flight! She stumbled and weaved. If she were alive, I would daresay she'd been imbibing, but as a spirit, it was haunting."

Thea sank onto a nearby settee, her legs weakening. She stared up at Mr. Fritz. "Did she sing?"

"Sing?" Mr. Fritz shook his head. "No. She appeared — desperate almost. She knows." He scratched with nervous energy at his shoulder. "Dear heaven, she knows!"

"Knows what?" Thea whispered.

Mr. Fritz looked out the window again. He appeared anxious that Misty Wayfair had followed him. That she would breeze through the wall and wrap her bony fingers around his throat, strangling life from him as had once happened to her.

"She knows I found out." He noticed the curtains drawn back on either side of the window. Reaching out, Mr. Fritz began to loosen the tie on one side, letting the filmy lace drop in front of the glass like a shield. "I believe I've inadvertently found more clues as to how — and why — she died."

Thea stilled.

He let the other curtain fall before hurrying to her side, dropping onto a chair only inches from Thea's settee. Leaning forward, Mr. Fritz captured her gaze with his frantic, wide eyes.

"I had no idea what I was investigating! When I came here to research the hospital. When I asked you to — oh, Miss Reed!"

He drew back. "You must not go back to that place. I have put you in grave danger. Promise me you won't go back!"

Thea narrowed her eyes. "Mr. Fritz, tell me what you have uncovered. I must know."

He drummed his fingers on his knee as if reconsidering why he'd asked her to the parlor in the first place. She could see the questions splaying across his face. Was he putting her in more danger? Would it sic Misty Wayfair onto Thea as it appeared she had come after him?

"Tell me, please," Thea coaxed.

"I was researching when the hospital was first constructed. I wanted to uncover its purpose — its origins, as a part of my story. Why build an asylum in the woods? This isn't a populated area, Miss Reed. The demand for a place such as Valley Heights seemed unwarranted at best."

Thea stayed silent, afraid that if she responded, Mr. Fritz would cease talking.

He licked his lips and glanced toward the doorway. "It's believed that Mr. Kramer of the logging company built it. Really no more than twenty years ago. That's not that long ago, Miss Reed. Not long at all. So why is there already a second doctor on staff, the first having left no more than a few years ago? Word of patients having passed? Mental patients often live out long lives in hospitals run properly — even improperly, for that matter. How is it there are death records on file of several patients? That piqued my interest, as you must imagine. But then . . ."

Mr. Fritz's pause made Thea desperate. She clasped her fingers together to keep from throttling the man with his dramatic glances at the lace-shrouded window. The shadows it cast made the parlor eerie. Ghostly.

"Then?" Thea pressed.

"Then —" Mr. Fritz drew in a shuddered breath — "there was another name on the register for the asylum construction. Fortune. Mr. Edward Fortune."

It had far less of an impact on Thea than it had on Mr. Fritz. She frowned. It stood to reason Mr. Fortune's name would appear on the paper work. He had, after all, been Mathilda Coyle's cousin, Mr. Kramer's nephew. He had become the heir appointed after Mathilda's very public family ousting.

Mr. Fritz continued. "Edward Fortune was already in his sixties when the hospital was built. Think of the arithmetic, Miss Reed! Mr. Kramer would have been in his nineties. *Nineties!* How invested would a

455

man nearing a century have truly been in constructing an asylum? Very little, I'd imagine! Therefore, it leads me to believe the driving force behind the establishment was not, as it was made to appear, Mr. Kramer at all. But rather, Mr. Fortune."

Thea blinked, still trying to comprehend the implications that seemed very apparent to Mr. Fritz.

He studied her face. "You're not following."

Thea shook her head. "No. Well, I am. But I don't see —"

"Why it is important?" Mr. Fritz gave her a nervous smile. "It was built over the well, Miss Reed."

She frowned again.

"The well," he insisted again. "The well they found Misty Wayfair's body in. Strangled. Pale and gruesome in her death. A moldy stone well covered in moss and disregarded, as the old homestead it was on had been long abandoned. There was no newspaper here when she died, but with a little digging, it wasn't hard to uncover who found Misty Wayfair after she'd passed."

"Who?" Thea breathed.

Mr. Fritz swallowed hard. Thea saw his Adam's apple bob in his throat. "Mathilda Coyle."

It started to make sense. A little. Thea calculated the additional information. Edward Fortune, building an asylum over the place of Misty Wayfair's death. Mathilda Coyle, the one who discovered the body of Misty Wayfair.

"I can only continue to wonder why Misty Wayfair haunts the Coyles but not the Fortunes as well," Mr. Fritz mused, tossing another furtive glance at the window.

"Are you saying you believe Mr. Fortune or Mathilda Coyle were responsible for —" Thea stopped. She couldn't say it. Didn't want to say it.

"Did they kill her themselves?" Mr. Fritz choked out, as if the words were dragged from his throat. "I have to believe there's more to it we don't yet understand, Miss Reed. It's not by chance there is still a rift between the families today. And a rift over an unapproved marriage for religious purposes? Perhaps in a place such as Milwaukee, but here? In the Northwoods of Wisconsin? People cannot afford to be that biased for that long. No, something darker divided them. Something far darker."

"What?" Thea breathed, though she needn't have asked the question.

"Murder," Mr. Fritz rasped. "Murder — and sickness. Sickness of the mind, Miss

Reed. Someone was very, very ill."

Thea stared at him. The impact of his suspicions taking root in her mind.

Mr. Fritz surged to his feet, startling her. He strode over to the window and pushed back the curtain. "Misty Wayfair has come back now. Her tale is coming to light, and she *will* have it told." He turned back to Thea. "She will avenge her death. I'm quite afraid that I — *we* — have not seen the last of her."

CHAPTER 31

"She's very ill."

Rose's words of worry greeted Thea as she neared the office of the asylum. She had all but sprinted down the road to the asylum that morning, frightened she would encounter Misty Wayfair. Terrified she would hear singing. Mr. Fritz's superstitions had been awakened with the sighting of her the night before. It crowded out Thea's intentions of helping Simeon take another photograph of a resident. Even sifting through the disorganized office and its records gave Thea the feeling she was drowning in little bits of a deeper story that didn't fit together.

She paused outside of the doorway. Eavesdropping.

Dr. Ackerman's deep voice rumbled in response to Rose. "We knew she wasn't doing well."

"Yes, but —" Rose argued.

"But we are doing all we can," Dr. Ackerman affirmed.

"Does she have any family? Anyone we should notify?" Rose's voice was breathy with concern.

"Effie is alone, from what I know. When I came here last year, I was told she was one of the few who had no family."

Effie? The poor woman they'd tied to a chair? The woman who, in her delusion, had linked Thea to Misty Wayfair.

Thea tilted her head and closed her eyes at the realization. What had seemed like the macabre exclamation of a madwoman now took on some merit in Thea's mind. Her mother — assuming P. A. Reed equated to Penelope Alice Reed Wayfair — was connected to Misty Wayfair, and in turn so was Thea. The inclination that Effie knew more than she credited her for made Thea look at the ceiling as if she could see through the floor into the rooms above. She had no desire to revisit Effie. Ever again, truth be told. But if Effie knew something . . .

Thea heard Dr. Ackerman's shoes on the floorboards. He was walking toward the door. She composed herself so it appeared she was just arriving. Taking a few steps, Thea met him at the door of the office. She saw Rose's concerned face behind him.

"Miss Reed. Simeon said you would be in

today for another portrait sitting."

"Yes," she replied, unwilling to let her wild and racing thoughts show on her face.

Rose stepped closer to the doctor and placed a hand on his arm. "Excuse me, I shall go see to her," she murmured.

Dr. Ackerman looked down at Rose's hand.

She dropped it.

"Yes," he nodded. "I would recommend trying to get sustenance in her. If she can keep it down."

"Certainly." Rose gave Thea a weak smile.

It reminded Thea of the first day she'd met Rose. Her blue eyes were shadowed again, her face dropped with the inevitable weight of impending grief. If Effie was seriously that ill, if she was dying even . . .

Thea met Dr. Ackerman's studious expression. "Is everything all right?" she inquired, pretending she'd heard nothing.

"Yes, Miss Reed." Dr. Ackerman gave her a stiff nod and exited the room.

Thea stared after him. What had Mr. Fritz said? Dr. Ackerman was the second doctor to offer services at Valley Heights Asylum.

She hurried into the office, dropping her things on a chair and eyeing the mounds of unfiled paper work. Who was the first doctor, then? And why did patients seem to have a habit of dying so quickly here at the asylum hidden in the woods?

Simeon placed the camera in its housing as a nurse led a stooped-over man from the room. The patient had been more than co-operative, for he hadn't spoken, hadn't moved at all. The unearthly stare of his eyes ruffled Thea's already troubled nerves. Simeon had kept the man at ease until Thea exposed the lens of the camera and the portrait was captured on the plates.

"I can develop the negative plates," Simeon offered. He avoided looking at her.

They were alone in the empty room, captured by the bars on the window and the closed door. Tension separated them. Thea wished to eliminate it, and yet she wondered if it was safer to leave it be.

Simeon moved to pass her, camera box in hand.

Thea reached out and touched his sleeve. He paused, lifting his eyes. He was guarded, almost as if she had been the one to keep secrets from him. Or, more accurately, maybe because he was accustomed to being pushed away.

"I need you." The words drifted from her lips before she could truly consider whether it was wise to speak them aloud.

Simeon didn't react.

"We can't live, Simeon, without knowing the truth."

It was the other part of why her emotions were so turbulent. If Simeon's grandfather, Fergus Coyle, had truly been as the rumors claimed — the lover of Misty Wayfair — and if Misty was indeed Thea's grandmother, then it was possible she and Simeon shared the same grandfather.

An indefinable part of her rebelled at the thought. Yes, she and Simeon seemed drawn together, linked by something or someone greater than them. But a part of her — an unexplored part of her — wished it to be also because . . .

"I know." Simeon's admission broke into her thoughts. His eyes searched hers, and Thea could read in them the same unspoken apprehension. His free hand rose, hesitated, then lightly settled on her cheek. She wanted to lean into it. To ignore the obstacles, the secrets, and to find, for just a moment, a sense of belonging.

But she dare not.

Thea pulled back. "Who was the doctor who ran the hospital before Dr. Ackerman?"

A line creased between Simeon's eyes. "Dr. Ingles."

She had the man's name. Thea would give

it to Mr. Fritz. Perhaps he could uncover more, and she uncover documents, and maybe then it would become clear what had happened here at Valley Heights. What had happened, even, to Misty Wayfair.

"I need to see Effie," Thea said, lowering her voice so it didn't filter through the cast-iron floor vents.

Simeon cocked his head, his brows furrowing. For now, his features were relaxed. Thea took a small comfort that he wasn't upset with her.

"Why?"

"Because." Thea looked at the door. It was still closed. She stepped closer to Simeon, avoiding the increased pace of her heart, and whispered into his ear, "She thought I was Misty Wayfair. What if she knows something?"

Simeon didn't turn his head, but Thea could feel his breath on her ear as he whispered back, "She's just a patient."

Thea nodded. "Yes, but — not all patients are really that mad, are they?" She ignored the vision of Effie's convulsing body before she'd been buckled to a chair.

Simeon didn't reply. For a moment, Thea was worried, but then he gave a short tip of his head. "All right. But you'll have to be stealthy. Rose is at lunch downstairs in the kitchen. The nurses will be doing their rounds. Effie is down the hall in seclusion. Last room on the left."

"Thank you," Thea whispered.

Simeon turned his face then. They were inches apart. His gaze dropped to her mouth, then rose back to her eyes. "Misty Wayfair has never been safe, Thea. Be careful. Even with Effie. Speak in low tones. Gentle. Don't be forceful or Effie will startle. Even sick, she could react violently."

Thea nodded.

Simeon's chest rose and fell. He shook his head, as if sparring against his own thoughts, and backed away a step. "Be careful," he said again.

And then he was gone.

Thea turned the doorknob to Effie's room. The upper hall of the asylum was deserted. She knew at any second one of the day nurses in her starched white apron and hat could appear. She would have no good reason to explain why she was here in Effie's room. Absolutely none.

She slipped in, shutting the door quietly, leaving her hand in the crack between the door and its frame. Drawing a deep breath, Thea faced the room. It was bright. Daylight shafting through the barred windows. The whitewashed walls almost glowing, the floors painted gray, and the bed covered in white linens.

Effie lay beneath a sheet and a blanket. Her face was pale, her cheeks gaunt. Thea moved next to the bed, finding her seat on a wooden chair by the window. She leaned over, looking into Effie's resting face. The woman's eyes were closed. Her dark hair unwashed and lying in strands around her shoulders.

"Effie?" Thea whispered. She reached out and touched the woman's shoulder.

Effie's eyes startled open. She took in Thea, the room, the window, and then settled back on Thea. She said nothing. Her lips were dry and cracked.

"Would you like some water?" Thea offered.

Effie only blinked.

Thea rose and moved across the room to a stand that held a basin, a cup, a pitcher of water, and a stack of linens. She poured a cup with water and returned to Effie.

"Can you sit up?" A question one might ask a sane person. She noted a metal pan on the floor. A vague scent of vomit wafted to her nostrils. Poor Effie. They eyed each other.

"Can you sit up?" Thea repeated.

Effie blinked. A slight shake of her head.

"I will help you." Thea leaned over Effie and slid her arms beneath the patient's. She hoisted Effie up at an angle, then propped her pillow behind her, folding it in half for extra fullness. She reached for the cup of water and brought it to Effie's lips.

The woman raised her hand, fingers shaking, and touched the cup. Her eyes never left Thea's face, never roved the room, or ventured to look out the window.

After a small sip, Thea withdrew the cup from Effie's lips. "You are very ill, aren't you?" she whispered, stating the obvious.

Effie didn't answer.

Thea eyed the pan and hoped the woman wouldn't lose the little water she'd taken in.

Effie's hand shot out and clamped around Thea's wrist.

Thea stifled a squeal and sucked in her breath.

Though most assuredly ill, Effie had not lost all her strength. Not yet. Her fingers bit into Thea's skin. Her eyes came alive. Her voice was hoarse as she whispered.

"Misty?"

"No." Thea looked at the fingers gripping her wrist. "No, I'm Thea."

"Don't let them come." Effie's voice was small, shaking. She fixed her eyes on Thea.

"I don't want them here. Please. Make them go away."

"Who?" Thea leaned forward, telling herself to remember this was a madwoman who had been here for years.

"The nurses. They all think I'm insane."

Thea couldn't hide the frown. Effie *was* insane. Her occupancy here at the hospital proved it. The thrashing she'd witnessed was also evidence that all was not right with Effie. But she would entertain Effie's fancies.

"Why do you think I'm Misty Wayfair?" Thea diverted.

Fear reflected in Effie's face. She licked her dry lips, biting down on the bottom one until it drew a tiny drop of blood.

"You look like her."

Effie's admission curled around Thea's nerves.

"Have you seen her? Her ghost?" Thea breathed.

A small wrinkle appeared between Effie's eyes, like she was confused. It disappeared. "No. There is no ghost. Misty Wayfair is dead."

Thea nodded. She glanced at the door, aware her time with Effie should be kept short. Or worse, could be cut short by one of the nurses Effie so feared.

"Then why?" Thea asked again. Trusting a

468

madwoman was as ridiculous as it sounded. Yet, Thea couldn't avoid the nagging feeling that something was very wrong. When she looked deep into Effie's eyes, she saw an awareness there, in the depths of them. It stunned her.

"I saw her picture." Effie drug out the words. "A tintype. You are just like her."

"Where?" Thea couldn't veil the excitement in her voice. "Where did you see this?"

"A woman had it." Effie looked beyond Thea, as if recalling. "She — lived here. And then she died. She was — my friend."

"Who was she?" Thea knew. Oh, how she knew the answer already!

"Penelope." Effie's chapped lips lifted in a vague smile. "She was like me."

Thea waited. Tears collecting in her eyes at the sound of her mother's name.

Effie stared at Thea. "Strange things happen to us. I don't remember what. But we would awaken. She with black eyes. Sometimes I will bite my tongue so hard I will bleed. They act like we don't know, but we do. It's as if we become ghosts, and we chase them for a while until we return our bodies and then . . ." Her hoarse voice wavered. She closed her eyes, then opened them. "Then we are strapped down. Well, I am. Penelope is free now. Sometimes I am free, but I have nowhere to go . . . ." Her voice trailed away, and she closed her eyes once more.

Thea sat in silence, watching Effie's chest rise and fall, slumber having overtaken her. That was it then. It had to be. She looked like Misty Wayfair. She had to be her granddaughter, and Penelope her mother. Penelope a patient here. Penelope tied to a chair. Restrained. Alone. Trapped.

She moved to rise when Effie's eyes flew open. She reached for Thea's hand and gripped it. "The portrait. Penelope hid it — in a crack in the wall. At the bottom of the stairwell."

"How do you know this?" Thea frowned. Patients weren't allowed downstairs. Their living quarters, the main room, was all upstairs.

Effie gave a tiny smile. "Sometimes we were free."

CHAPTER 32

Thea closed the door carefully. Effie had drifted into a fitful sleep. It was time to leave before she got into trouble.

"What are you doing in Effie's room?"

Rose's hoarse whisper pierced the hallway.

Thea whirled. Her hand flew to her mouth. At least it was Rose and not one of the nurses, or Dr. Ackerman.

"I-I wanted to . . . I'm sorry, I . . ."

Her fumbling for words was rescued by Rose. The other woman looked over her shoulder to be sure they were alone. She balanced a teapot in one hand and an empty cup in the other. She strode over to Thea. "You must be careful. Dr. Ackerman doesn't like — he doesn't want people with the patients."

Thea nodded. "Of course." She edged past Rose. "I should go down to the office. I've filing to do."

"Yes. And hurry. I'm here to give Effie

some tea for sustenance. The other nurses are in the far ward. If you go now, you'll avoid detection." Rose moved toward Effie's door, then stopped, turned and gave Thea a stern eye. "Thea, don't do this again. It is very frowned upon."

Thea hurried away, her feet taking her down the enclosed staircase, until it opened at the bottom into the main foyer. She surveyed it quickly. It was empty. Kneeling at the bottom step, Thea rushed to check the steps and nearby wall, looking for a crack.

There.

She saw a gap between the wall and the bottom step. Thea reached toward it. Her finger barely squeezed into the tight space. She could feel the smooth edge of something wedged between the step and the wall. Working to push it toward the opening so she could grip it, Thea rejoiced when the edge of the tintype made its appearance.

"Did you drop something?"

Dr. Ackerman's question drifted down from above her. Thea scrambled to stand, slipping the tintype into the pocket of her skirt, unnoticed.

"No. I just — lost my footing."

His eyebrow raised, and his handsome features considered her words. He seemed to accept them and moved beyond her to go up the staircase. "Very well then. Be careful next time."

"Yes." Thea nodded, watching him ascend. "I will."

She hurried down the long hallway to the office. Entering, she shut the door behind her, leaning against it, her breaths coming fast as if she'd been in a footrace. Closing her eyes, Thea collected her wits before reaching into her pocket and withdrawing the tintype.

The resemblance was staggering.

Misty Wayfair was most assuredly her grandmother. There was no denying it now. Her cheekbones were high, as were Thea's, with lips the same shape, and her features the same as what Thea saw every morning in the mirror at Mrs. Brummel's boardinghouse. Misty's dress was dark, cut simple with a lace collar. The skirt was voluminous but not hooped as a wealthier woman during the time of the War Between the States would have worn. Her hair was parted in the middle and rolled on the sides to the back. On her lap . . .

"Mother," Thea breathed.

A little girl, no more than two, perched on Misty Wayfair's lap. Her dress was cut similarly to her mother's, slightly offset at the shoulders. A small ribbon encircled the child's neck. An inexpensive accessory to mark her as a female child. Curls sprung up on her head and at her neckline.

Thea stared at it a moment longer, then slipped it back into her pocket, considering all she knew. Edward Fortune had built the asylum here. Mathilda Coyle had found Misty in the well. Penelope had been admitted here, but by whom? Obviously, it was after a grown Penelope had left Thea on the steps of an orphanage much farther south, not to be given a family and a home until the Mendelsohns arrived some years later. And Effie . . . she spoke of their freedom, and yet the fear that hid behind her words was palpable.

Mr. Fritz was right. Something more horrible than just Misty Wayfair's death had occurred in this place.

It was another night without sleep. Thea had found nothing helpful that afternoon. She'd returned to the portrait studio to fulfill a sitting obligation Mr. Amos had in his appointment book. After which Thea had visited the Amos home, pleased to find him mostly recovered, with Mrs. Amos scurrying around him with the agitation of a woman who looked forward to the day her crotchety husband returned to work.

Now, she lay on the bed staring at the portrait, the lantern on the bedside table casting a soft glow over the faces captured on tin. Thea pondered the woman in the picture and compared it to the woman she'd seen that night, when she'd first come to Pleasant Valley. Had it been her grandmother or merely an illusion? A deep ache filled her, causing a tear to escape the corner of her eye and trail its way onto the pillowcase.

Simeon was right. Misty Wayfair was dead. Whether her spirit still roamed the woods, looking for peace or avenging herself against the Coyles for some unknown reason, Thea couldn't explain it. But her ties to Misty, to her mother, had been broken long ago by death. She would never have them back, no matter how hard she looked or what she uncovered. For uncovering more of her roots had left Thea feeling as unfulfilled as the moment she'd stepped into Pleasant Valley and photographed Mary's dead body.

There had to be more.

She rose from her bed. Still dressed, Thea reached for her sweater, its dark-green wool soft against her as she pulled it on. She slipped the tintype into her sweater pocket. Soon she'd traveled down the stairs of the boardinghouse and had eased the front door open quietly.

The night air was cool, and she could hear the river in the distance. It beckoned to Thea as though, were she to jump in, its current would sweep her away toward something meaningful. Toward purpose. Toward an explanation of why she even existed in the first place.

Thea reached the riverbank and saw his silhouette. The moon was still large and round, shining down on the water and making it sparkle like a million diamonds. The woods beyond the river were dark shadows of blue. But Simeon sat there, on the bank, silent.

She'd not had a premonition that he would be here. Yet it appeared the same place called to them equally. Sinking to the earth beside him, Thea said nothing.

Simeon gave her a sideways glance. His body was calm again. It had been calmer of late, she realized. His face less contorted. As the intensity of the circumstances increased, for some reason, Simeon seemed more at peace.

Thea pulled the tintype from her pocket and held it toward him. His fingers brushed hers as he took it. It was difficult to make out the details, the woman's features under the night sky, but she saw Simeon lift it close to his face. She noted the lines that creased between his eyes.

Simeon handed the portrait back to her. "Misty Wayfair and your mother."

"How did you know?" she asked, slipping it back into her sweater pocket.

Simeon stared out over the river. His jawline clenched, whether from his perpetual tic or because he was biting down, Thea wasn't certain.

"Even in the darkness I can see the resemblance between you and Misty. It's no wonder Effie thought you were her."

"Effie knew my mother."

Simeon looked at her, the moonlight casting shadows across his face, illuminating the stubble along his chin.

Thea searched to put her thoughts into words, to explain to Simeon what she'd found out from Effie. To try to identify which questions still floated unanswered, and of them which ones haunted her the most.

"Simeon . . ." She hesitated. He didn't know of Mr. Fritz, of her agreement with him. The deception gnawed at Thea's conscience. "I've spoken to a newspaperman. He's been seeking out information about the hospital, about the treatment of patients there."

Simeon waited, his gaze fixed on her.

Thea hurried on, "While I've told him nothing is amiss, he also has been looking into the asylum's history. It wasn't your great-grandfather Kramer who founded the hospital. It was Edward Fortune — he built it over the well your grandmother found Misty Wayfair's body in."

She waited. Watching. His face would begin to twitch soon, and his shoulder would follow suit soon after. But nothing happened. Simeon narrowed his eyes.

"Edward Fortune" was all Simeon said. Then he nodded, as if it somehow made sense.

"How do you remain so calm?" Thea asked. Her voice drifted over the waters. "I have this urgency in me. I can't quench it. I feel as though so much is amiss, and it is all about to explode like a gunshot and wound more than the past already has!"

Simeon picked up a stick and snapped off the tip. He tossed it over the bank into the river. "I am making peace with myself."

His answer was so simple. Thea envied him.

"How?"

Simeon snapped off another piece of the

stick and flicked it from between his fingers. It flipped into the air and disappeared into the darkness. "Something Mr. Amos told me once. I've pondered it. I believe I'm finding it to be true."

"And that is?" she asked, pulling the sleeves of her sweater over her hands until only her fingertips peeked out.

"That while the past — the consequences of the past — might have a dire effect on me, it still doesn't change who I am. We weren't created to find our identity in life. We were created to discover our Creator. In doing so, our identity is defined."

The depth of his words rolled over Thea. She'd been pondering much the same since the time they'd last spoken of such things. A Creator. She questioned His existence as she questioned Misty Wayfair's. Yet a blind man could see they all didn't just come from nothing. Perhaps one might wish to discredit God someday and say they did, but Thea couldn't believe that. It would be like throwing her photographic chemicals and plates into the air and suddenly a beautiful picture came into being. No. It took thought, creativity, an investment.

Simeon's stick snapped again. Another flick. Another piece falling silent into the river.

"I remember my grandmother Mathilda. She hated my father, for what he did to us children. My mother never fought him. She waited until he was finished with the strap or the back of his hand and then she would comfort us. But there was something in the eye of my grandmother. Something dark." Simeon tossed the rest of the stick into the water. "I never wanted to think about it. But if I can focus on the Creator then, perhaps the mistakes and carelessness of those around me don't define me. He does."

The ache in Simeon's voice frightened Thea. She turned to search his face, but his profile was without expression. He simply stared over the water in the direction of the asylum.

"I don't believe Misty Wayfair haunts these woods, Thea. Your grandmother was laid to rest when she died. Your mother, years later. There is no curse, except that of mortal sin."

Thea was scared to reach for him. To touch him. She waited.

Simeon shrugged as if she'd asked him a question, or perhaps his tic was returning. "My grandmother said something once. She told me that to protect one's family, sometimes grave choices must be made."

Thea waited.

Simeon turned to face her.

She could see his eyes, sad, and his voice was resigned.

"No matter what my grandmother Mathilda claimed publicly, she believed my grandfather had been with Misty."

His statement was simple, but it was heavy with meaning.

Thea drew in a soft breath. "Do you think she — ?"

"I don't know." Simeon shook his head. "But, Mathilda Coyle did find Misty's body . . . and who but the killer would think to look in a well?"

CHAPTER 33

HEIDI

Heidi was raging. Ten calls to Vicki between the memory-care facility and the Crawford home. Ten ignored calls. And she knew they were ignored, because they only rang once and then went to voicemail, and the last six calls went straight to voicemail. Vicki was snubbing her.

She hopped out of the truck before Rhett had even pulled it to a complete stop.

"Hey!" he shouted at her as she marched toward the house. Heidi heard his door slam and his footsteps close behind her. "Heidi, you need to calm down."

Calm down. Sure. If the heartache of her mother recognizing Rhett and sharing personal history with him wasn't enough, Vicki's direct refusal to take her calls had tipped her over the edge. She couldn't even find out *who* she was if Vicki didn't at least talk to her! According to their mom, they *were* Coyles! They *did* have history here in Pleasant Valley. Vicki had to know more — she *had* to!

"Heidi." Rhett was directly behind her shoulder, catching up to her with long strides. "Stop and look at me."

Enough with the directives!

Heidi turned but kept walking backward, giving her hands a haphazard wave. "No. I don't need to *obey* you. Go ahead. Kick me out! Send me packing! Join the club, 'cause I'm used to it!"

Rhett's face darkened.

Heidi turned back toward the house. She yelped when he sidestepped around her, and his body blocked her from continuing toward the house. She almost rammed her nose into his chest.

Rearing back, she glared at him. "Just leave me alone."

He touched her arm, applying a bit of pressure, like he instinctively did with Emma to calm her. "Come with me. Please," he added for good measure.

Heidi stumbled backward. "No. I don't *need* you." She jabbed her finger at him, annoyed at the water in her voice. "I don't need — need *them,*" she said and waved toward the Crawford house and Emma. "I don't need my mom, or Brad, or-or *Vicki*!"

She ended with a shout. An emotional, dramatic yell, and her fingertip rammed into Rhett's chest.

She gave him a stony scowl.

"You all can take that and — and shove it." Heidi spun and stalked toward her car.

"Heidi!" Rhett shouted after her.

She ignored him and hauled her car door open.

"Heidi!" This time a sharp command.

Whatever. She'd never listened to anyone before — and for good reason — and there was no way she was going to start now.

She dared a look through the windshield at Rhett's thunderous expression. A moment of misgiving stabbed her. A few weeks and she could see through his Hulkish exterior. He was worried — about her. Protective. But she didn't need protecting. No one ever had anyway, and really, if she were honest, she knew no one ever would. At least not for the long haul.

The little dive on the main street of Pleasant Valley was quaint and rustic. A typical Wisconsin Northwoods bar and grill, it was family atmosphere colliding with an old western saloon. The main room served pizza and opened to a narrower galley-style bar that opened again at the far end to a small stage. It was early evening, and a few families sat enjoying their pepperoni and cheese pizzas. Some couples ate hamburgers across from the bar. The bartender was busy pouring Mountain Dew, Orange Crush soda, and popping the tops off bottles of beer — right or wrong — in true Wisconsin style.

At the stage, the karaoke speakers were muffled, with half-blown woofers and a treble that sounded like it was being played through tinfoil. Heidi sat at a corner table. She'd hide here — in the corner — until she figured out what to do next. She'd listen to karaoke and try to pretend the corner's shadows were the old closet she used to huddle in. It was numbing. She didn't even need alcohol. In fact, her large Dr Pepper with ice, held in her left hand, was proof of that.

"Ironic." A college-aged girl smiled at the karaoke DJ.

He grinned. "Alanis Morrisette. Atta girl."

The singer stepped onto the stage. A few couples sat at tall, round tables, their smiles of encouragement welcoming. No one was intoxicated here. It was just small-town fun well before sunset.

Heidi shrank further back into her corner, eyeing the carefree expression of the girl who balanced the mic in her hands. The music started. Heidi closed her eyes. They were depressing lyrics. But oddly it fit, and the girl singing wasn't half bad.

The music continued. A few hoots of approval from enthusiastic onlookers. Heidi took a sip of Dr Pepper. The scraping sound of a chair against the hardwood floor made her eyes fly open.

Rhett caught her gaze. Heidi took another long drink of Dr Pepper, not looking away, daring him to stay — and if he did, challenging him to understand her.

Rhett held out his hand.

A tear escaped her eye.

The background track continued to play, and the girl warbled on the minor-keyed melody.

"Please, come with me." A small flick of his fingers, encouraging Heidi to take his hand.

He said please.

Heidi was helpless to ignore that. She stood. He followed, and together they exited the bar and grill.

They stepped onto the sidewalk. The evening air assaulted Heidi's senses. The smell of the grill's deep fryers mixed with the scents of the nearby river and woods. It was as close to Heaven as she'd ever gotten.

She hated the fact she'd fallen for this place. She wouldn't even think about how she felt about Rhett.

She started as she felt Rhett's fingers graze hers, and then the callused palm fold around her hand. Heidi was in step with him as Rhett continued to walk, not saying a word. Finally, she twisted her hand so that she held his back. It was a small gesture from them both. His indication of being more sensitive. Hers of releasing some of her stubborn hurt so she could listen to reason.

They walked in silence. Heidi jogged alongside him as they crossed the road. Followed him down a gravel trail, then stopped on the embankment of the river that cut between town and the woods where the asylum lay in ruins.

Heidi let go of Rhett's hand and wiped her eyes with the heels of her palms.

"I'm sorry."

Rhett didn't say anything. He stared out across the water and watched it take its rolling course over rocks and boulders, cutting the earth away a little bit at a time with its momentum.

Heidi flattened her lips as she followed his gaze. "I need to talk to Vicki — if she'll acknowledge me. But I — I don't have a good feeling about this. About where this is going."

Rhett nodded.

Heidi gave him a glance from the corner of her eye. He squatted down and picked up a flat, round stone and sent it out over the water. It skipped a few times before disappearing into the depths.

"You don't have anything profound to say?" Heidi quirked her eyebrow and curled her lip in sheepish hope.

"Nope," Rhett replied.

"Still don't like karaoke, huh?" she quipped. Trying to infuse humor. Anything to stop the nauseating swirl in her stomach or lighten the weight on her chest.

"Never did," he answered.

Heidi nodded. She drew in a deep breath — cool, fresh air surrounded by water and woods that helped to calm her nerves.

"I can't stop thinking about Thea Reed's trunk of stuff. About Misty Wayfair. My mom. Misty Wayfair was real, you know? And all that's left to define her tragic life is a ghost story. What kind of legacy is that? Is that all it is? Do what we can while we're alive, and then die and let the ones left behind define who we were?"

She jammed her hands into her jeans' pockets and kicked the toe of her mint-green Converse shoe against a pebble. She didn't expect a response.

Rhett launched another stone into the water. His motion sent a whiff of grease and spice in her direction. It was a musky smell, the collision of work and men's deodorant. And it was weirdly comforting.

"You're looking at life all wrong."

"Oh really?" Heidi turned toward him.

Rhett glanced down his shoulder at her. "Yeah. You're all worried about yourself."

Heidi blinked fast as tears threatened again.

"Remember when I had you shoot with the bow and arrow?"

She couldn't forget it. Heidi nodded.

Rhett shrugged. "First thing I tell a new hunter, if they're listening . . ."

Heidi rolled her eyes.

He continued. "I tell them when you aim, you try to keep both eyes open. You line up the sight with the target. You fix your focus. You shoot."

"Makes sense," Heidi said.

"You don't look at any of the other pins in the sight. Just the one that lines you up straight. You don't worry about the arrow either. You align yourself with the target, and you focus on it."

"So, what's my target then?" Heidi wasn't

quite following. "My family history? Who's trying to burn me alive or accuse me of insanity?"

Rhett shook his head. "It's *Who* made you. 'Cause everything else around us? It's gonna fall. It's broken. Your target is what you're aiming for. Security. Purpose. Strength. Your Creator."

"A foundation," Heidi whispered. The roots of her Christian upbringing starting to shed light on where Rhett was leading her.

"Yep." He turned back to the river.

"That's sort of a cliché, isn't it? Find yourself in God and forget about your circumstances?" Heidi was goading him.

Rhett eyed her. "Have you ever seen anyone really live that way?" It was a challenge.

She contemplated the question. Yes. She had. A few people she knew when growing up had seemed well grounded. Less concerned about rules and legalities and more passionate about a relationship with their Creator. She'd discounted them at the time, but then . . . Heidi met Rhett's eyes. Maybe that was exactly what she loved so much about the Crawfords in the few short weeks she'd come to know them.

"I envy Emma, you know?" she whispered.

"I don't mean that to sound insulting or insensitive. But, she's so — content with who she is. Your family is content with who she is."

"There've been tough times," Rhett admitted.

"Yes, but would you change her? Would you wish her to be anything other than who she is?" Heidi ventured. She worried she might sound crass. Maybe disparaging unintentionally, but she asked anyway.

"No." Rhett's eyes softened at the thought of his sister.

Heidi's brows furrowed as emotion welled in her throat. "See? That's what I've always longed for. That kind of acceptance."

Rhett gave a slight smile, but his eyes lit with understanding, even under that blasted greasy baseball cap.

"Emma knows who she is. She's not dependent on me or our parents for her identity."

Heidi bit her bottom lip. Rhett's eyes followed the motion. He took a step closer, then stopped. His hand came up, and his fingertips touched Heidi's cheek.

"Mom always told Emma she was 'beautifully and wonderfully made.' No exceptions."

"No exceptions?" Heidi asked, her voice

hitching. The idea of focusing on a Creator instead of herself was terrifying. It didn't make sense. It went against everything society taught. And yet . . .

"No exceptions." Rhett's affirmation was firm, his strength undeniable.

There was more than Heidi Lane, misfit and unwanted. There was Heidi Lane, created and wanted. She just needed to chase after the Creator.

"What happens when you focus on the target and release the arrow?" she wanted to know.

Rhett smiled. "The arrow follows your aim."

"So, fix your eyes on the target, the rest will follow?" Heidi reworded.

"He promises it will." Rhett nodded. Then he bent, picked up another stone, aimed, and threw it.

Heidi watched the stone fly and land in the water. Engulfed by the river — cold, refreshing, clean — the stone dropped below the water's surface and disappeared.

CHAPTER 34

THEA

She stared at the document in her hand. A plain sheet of paper, ink-stained from wayward drops from the pen that once had drafted the words onto the page. She reread the name at the top with its looping letters and slanted handwriting.

Penelope Alice Reed Wayfair

The first evidence — beside the gravestone — that her mother had indeed been a resident here. Thea skimmed down the page to the doctor's signature at the bottom. Not Dr. Ackerman, but the original doctor. Dr. Thomas Ingles.

Date of Admittance: January 28, 1889

Thea drew in a sharp breath. Not long after Thea had been left at the orphanage. Just mere months later, her mother was committed to the newly constructed Valley Heights Asylum. Never to leave again, but in death.

Female. White. Unmarried. Shows evidence of unpredictable seizing of the body, followed by prolonged periods of stupidity. She remains not speaking nor addressing anyone. If spoken to, it is with great difficulty she replies with a monosyllable. She is stubborn. Willful. At times shows hallucinative effects. Cries for a child it has been purported she never birthed.

Thea dropped onto her chair. Her hand shook, and the paper rattled as she stared at the handwriting. The child she never birthed. Unmarried. Was it possible that Penelope had been like her mother, Misty Wayfair? Secret relations with others? Thea would never know her father — there was no one to claim her. Had Penelope secreted Thea away to the orphanage before whoever committed her to the institution was able to discover where Thea was? Or that she existed?

She read the rest of the page. More statements of her mother's medical condition. A schedule for routine testing. The word gave Thea pause.

Testing.

She didn't know of any specific testing that Dr. Ackerman currently practiced on his patients. Constraints, yes. Medications, of course. But . . .

A chill settled over her. The kind that confirmed what Mr. Fritz had eluded to: abuse, experimentation . . . Had all of this occurred, not recently, but when Penelope and Effie were younger? Under Dr. Ingles's supervision? It might account for the gravestones in the woods.

Thea laid the page on the desk and began sifting through the remaining loose-leaf papers. The quivering in her hands matched the urgency rising within her. She felt that at any moment Dr. Ingles himself would enter the office and condemn her for searching the files. Staring at her with emotionless, heartless eyes as if assessing her own mental stability.

Effie exhibited very similar symptoms to the records on Penelope. If it were possible that Penelope had been sane enough to whisk Thea away to an orphanage, then there was merit in considering that Effie might not be as insane as perhaps thought. That argument would not be well received, yet Thea couldn't ignore it as she skimmed another page.

The office door opened. Thea shrieked, spinning to face the newcomer, clutching loose documents to her chest.

Rose froze in the doorway. Her eyes wide, her black hair swooping up and under her triangular cap. Tea, from the cup in her hand, sloshed over the side and landed with a splash on the floor.

"Rose!" Thea gasped. "You frightened me."

Rose stared at her with some disbelief. She held out the cup in a tentative gesture. "I brought you tea. You seemed upset this morning when you arrived."

Thea lowered the papers and arranged them in a subtle gesture on the desktop with the others. She reached for the cup and sipped the tea, relishing the warmth that trailed down her throat.

Rose stepped forward and touched Thea's hand, concern in her eyes. "You're very pale, Thea. What is it?" Rose tilted her head.

Thea took another sip of the tea before setting it on the desk. "It's my mother." She lifted the signed document and held it toward Rose. "She was a patient here. Did you know that?"

Rose's expression translated surprise. Her eyes flew from their glancing at the document to meet Thea's. "Oh, my heavens. I

496

had no idea."

Thea nodded. "My mother was admitted here, and Effie knew her." She turned back to the desk, reaching for the papers she'd put there on Rose's abrupt entry. "I'm afraid to know what happened to them. To all the patients who passed away here."

Rose ran a finger over the other pages littering the desktop. "Patients are unwell, Thea. They don't always live as long as those who have good health."

"Yes, but *testing*? They experimented on my mother, Rose. Are you aware of any trials that Dr. Ackerman performs on the patients here?"

Rose's eyes dimmed. She shook her head. "No. But I've heard stories. Dr. Ackerman has mentioned his distaste for some of Dr. Ingles's previous methods. I don't know which ones he incorporated. Some of the larger hospitals have tried electricity. Even surgical procedures on the brain to try to —"

Thea clapped her hand over her mouth. She shook her head. "That's awful."

Rose drew in an anxious breath, glancing toward the closed door. She took a step toward Thea. "It *is* awful. But, perhaps necessary? The patients have no lives. They have been left here to die, and what if we have a cure for them? For Effie to cease thrashing and seizing and to be normal?"

"Normal?" Thea whispered. "Who defines what normal is?"

Rose blinked. "There are treatments . . ." Her words waned as Thea stared at her.

"Do you believe that?" Thea asked. "If Mary, your sister, had been admitted here because she was — she was *sad* — would you condone their using electricity on her to make her happy again?"

Rose stumbled backward. Her hands flew to her chest, and she clenched them there. Her eyes darkened. "You don't know what you're saying."

"No. No, I don't!" Thea swiped a tear from her cheek. "But my mother was here, Rose. She died here. These *tests* might have even been the cause, yet I'll never know for certain."

Rose swallowed hard, pressed her hands flat against her apron, smoothing it over her skirt and seeming to compose her own emotions. Nodding toward the tea, she offered Thea a small smile. "It is horrible. This place — the people in it — it is all very sad. But it is here. Now, drink your tea, take deep breaths, and then carry on. It's what I do. Every day, Thea. We carry on."

■ ■ ■ ■

Mr. Fritz met her on the porch of the boardinghouse. Dinner had concluded. The pot roast and potatoes Thea consumed adding to her already increasing nausea. She'd found no more records on her mother, nor on Effie, but already some things were becoming clearer. If not now, then in the not-so-distant past, Valley Heights Asylum had been a place of experimentation. Once she knew what to look for, Thea began to peruse other patients' records, five years and older. Always the words *testing, procedure,* or in a few cases, *surgery* were mentioned. She referenced the small cemetery's logbook, and many, if not most, of the names were written there as well.

"You've uncovered something?" The newspaperman asked eagerly.

Thea nodded. "But it is from the past. Dr. Ackerman appears to be genuinely concerned for the welfare of his patients." She summarized her findings for the man, who listened intently.

"This is consistent with what I've uncovered at other hospitals. Slowly the care seems to be improving for the patients, but there's much yet to be done."

Thea eyed him as he took a step toward the porch rail and looked out onto the street.

"This is a strange town, Thea Reed. I've no regrets in saying I will be glad to leave it behind me."

"You're finished with your story, then?" Thea drew her shawl tighter around her shoulders.

Mr. Fritz gave her a quick nod. "After the other night? Yes. I've no wish to aggravate the ghost of Misty Wayfair any further. If you've discovered nothing untoward at the hospital, I will be pleased to take what you've given me as foundation for my story about institutional care and leave it at that."

Thea hesitated. She had no way to hold him to it, but she had to ask regardless. "And you will not mention the Coyles? Or Misty Wayfair? Because their story has no bearing or impact on patient care at the hospital."

Mr. Fritz turned to face her directly. "The Coyles? No. You are correct. But the history of that place! To think that Edward Fortune constructed the hospital where he did. That's a story in and of itself."

"A small story," Thea stated, hoping that Mr. Fritz saw no sensation in its retelling.

"Not small, really. Still, it *is* all conjecture."

Thea was confused. "I thought you confirmed Mr. Fortune had built the hospital?" What conjecture could there be if the land deeds and records were there at the town hall?

Mr. Fritz raised an eyebrow and gave her a look that communicated more untold details. He scratched the side of his head about his ear, as if debating whether he should divulge them to her. Thea tipped her head, catching his eyes and not looking away.

"All right then." Mr. Fritz gave his head a little shake, like he'd lost an argument neither of them had verbalized. "I did inquire of some of the older, longtime citizens of Pleasant Valley. They don't share much, mostly because it might speak ill of Mr. Fortune, and the town needs him and his company to keep it alive economically. Even our dear Mrs. Brummel here bites her tongue about those slanderous tales. It took some cajoling to get the snippets I did. Cajoling and bribery too, I must admit."

Mr. Fritz tapped the porch rail with his left hand. "So, not long after Misty Wayfair was found murdered, it seems Edward Fortune and his new wife became benefactors for a young girl. A waif. No more than a few years of age. No one knew where she came from, and no one asked. The child grew up in the Fortune home but moved away once she reached adulthood. A few years later, she mysteriously returned. Shortly after that, Mr. Fortune began construction of the asylum."

Thea stared at the newspaperman. "Do you know this woman's name?"

Mr. Fritz eyed Thea. "Therein lies the mystery. All the years she lived with the Fortunes, they never brought her to town. In fact, even now, some question whether she existed at all. They only heard that her name was Penelope."

Thea turned swiftly away, her breaths coming fast. The motion made the porch spin around her, and for a moment Thea felt as if she might faint. She grabbed for the rail as the world closed in and went dark.

"Miss Reed?" Mr. Fritz's concerned voice heralded her from the blackness.

Thea squeezed her eyes tight and then opened them. Clarity returned then, and she looked at the newspaperman. "Where did she go after the asylum was built?" Though Thea already knew the answer, she wanted to hear the story as known by the town.

Mr. Fritz shrugged. "A few say she traveled south and disappeared. Others say Mr. Fortune built the hospital *for* her. But no one really knows for certain. The Fortunes never spoke of her again, and there was never any sign of their providing for another person other than the children they'd had of their own. As I said, not a small story, but there's just too much conjecture overall. I'm not comfortable publishing it."

Thea's breath caught in her chest. "So, you won't write it?"

Mr. Fritz waved her off. "I don't have enough facts, not to mention I've no desire to flirt with a spirit such as Misty Wayfair's. There are too many loose threads, and somehow she seems to weave in and out of them all. Besides, I cannot forget her face. That awful, hollow expression. It chills me even now to think of it."

Her face. Thea still clutched the porch rail, her knees weak, nausea creeping into her throat. When she'd witnessed Misty Wayfair dancing near the boardinghouse in the street below, she saw no distinguishable features. Of course, the night and the fog hadn't allowed for much detail.

"What did she look like?" Thea asked.

Mr. Fritz patted the hair he'd combed across his balding spot. He grimaced and shook his head. "She looked like death. Pale, her hair dark and stringy, with eyes set deep in her head. Her cheeks were so thin, the cheekbones reminded me of razors. Miss Reed, it still grants me nightmares. The way she wove and leaned, as if she could not walk on bare feet, and yet, in some ways, it was like she floated."

"Did she float?" Thea couldn't help but ask.

"No," Mr. Fritz answered, "but it seemed so. And the words she spoke were horrifying. I shall never forget them."

"What words? What did she say?" Thea had only heard her sing and call out her own name, taunting.

"It was poetry." He drew a deep breath, as though it frightened him to remember.

"My Mother raised her eyes,
They were blank and could not see;
Yet they held me with their stare
While they seemed to look at me."

Thea gaped at Mr. Fritz in dumbfounded shock. The words. The recitation. She could still hear her voice. The thin, wispy tone of Effie as she muttered the verse while posing for her portrait. The haunting words before her declaration, which still replayed in

Thea's head.
You've come back.

CHAPTER 35

HEIDI

She was a Coyle. It wouldn't have meant much to her, even a month ago. The Coyles weren't a link to some famous ancestry. It wasn't like she'd uncovered she was a descendent of JFK or something. But here? In Pleasant Valley? The Coyles were a legend, apparently. A legend that had, in the end, chased the remaining Coyles from town and resulted in a legal name change.

Emma was sitting at the Crawfords' kitchen table when Heidi came down for breakfast. It had been a fitful sleep, in spite of her conversation with Rhett at the river. She poured coffee, noting how Emma leaned into the laptop in front of her, wrapped into a vivid story. Only it wasn't a story.

Heidi moved behind Emma and studied the screen. Lines, tiny leaves, people's names, and links. Emma finally seemed to

506

notice Heidi. She drew back from her computer, adjusting the purple infinity scarf around her neck.

"What are you studying?" Heidi could only assume Rhett had put Emma on the trail of more information.

The younger woman gave Heidi a smile. "Dorothea Reed. The photographer of Mary Coyle's portrait."

"Ahh." Heidi took a sip of her coffee. She was going to refrain from plying Emma with questions. The information would be forthcoming without them, and Emma would remain relaxed and not feel interrogated.

Heidi went to a different chair and slipped onto it. Her yoga pants kept her legs warm from the chill of the glossy wood. Someone had opened the windows, and the cool morning breeze filtered in, bringing with it the aroma of pine.

The front door opened. Rhett entered, Rüger pushing past him to nose Ducie, who lay under the kitchen table.

"Morning," Emma stated.

"Hey, baby girl." Rhett reached out and squeezed her shoulder as he beelined for the coffeepot. The man might have his own place, but he should save the money and move back home. After all, he seemed to spend every spare moment here.

Heidi eyed him. His jeans, his customary flannel shirt over a T-shirt, and that cap of his. The man never changed.

A *meow* startled her, and she glanced at her feet. Archie rubbed against her leg while both dogs ignored the yellow cat.

"Where'd you come from?" Heidi crooned, leaning over to lift the cat onto her lap.

"Gonna be too warm today," Rhett answered for the cat.

Well, good. The man was considerate and realized living in the cab of a truck wasn't always healthy for a cat. Not to mention, where was the litter box? Heidi ignored the random question as Rhett asked a more important one of Emma.

"What'd you find?" Rhett leaned over his sister's shoulder.

Emma wasted no time in getting down to business.

"Dorothea Reed, also known as Thea, came to Pleasant Valley in 1908. She worked at Amos Brothers Photography. There isn't much known about her."

"Huh." Rhett sipped his coffee. "What's her ancestry?"

Emma shook her head. "There isn't any."

"What about the Coyles?" he inquired.

"There are lots of Coyles." Emma's response was confident.

"Is my mother listed in the lineage?" Heidi inserted.

Emma nodded. "Yes."

It figured. All this time, some of her ancestral history was only a mouse click away. Of course, not knowing her mother had her name legally changed as a child put a curb in that. But now . . .

Heidi exchanged glances with Rhett. It seemed he read her thoughts.

"What about Loretta's children? Is Heidi listed?" he asked.

Emma shook her head. "No. There are no more records after Loretta."

Back to square one.

"What about using my mom's legal name?"

Emma nodded. "I found her. You. Vicki."

Heidi sagged back in her chair, clutching her coffee mug. Thea Reed had turned up empty. Her mother's family tree was linked to the Coyles, but that was it. No dead daughter. No ghosts, outside of the Misty Wayfair story.

"Did you look up Misty Wayfair, Emma?" Rhett slid into a chair opposite Heidi. It creaked beneath his bulk.

"Misty Wayfair was killed in 1851. There are no newspaper articles, but there is a death certificate."

"May I see it?" Heidi moved closer to Emma, who tilted her laptop so that Heidi could view the screen.

The old document image popped up, scrolling cursive in ink across yellowed paper. Very straightforward and unimpressive.

"What about the old trunk? Thea Reed's trunk?" Heidi set her mug on the table. "There could be more clues in there."

"Wouldn't hurt to look again. Now that we know you're a Coyle." Rhett stood and tugged his ball cap down onto his forehead. "I'm going to work. I'll let Mike know we confirmed your background."

Heidi couldn't help the twinge of disappointment that he wasn't sticking around for the day. That he was going to work and leaving her to fend for herself. She had to be realistic. She was safe — for now — with no imminent danger hanging over her head.

"I'll help you." Emma's soft words interrupted Heidi's embarrassingly long gaze at Rhett as she watched him through the window. Archie shifted on her lap, his purr growing louder at the attention of Heidi's hand. She realized with a start, the one-eyed Rüger was at her feet, much like Ducie was at Emma's.

It seemed Rhett had left a part of him with her after all.

Dumb.

That was a dumb idea.

Still, Heidi found herself holding on to it as she followed Emma from the room, two attentive pets on her heels.

She'd learned not to talk a lot, especially when Emma was in deep concentration. Heidi paged through an old bread tin filled with doilies, strips of hand-tatted lace, handkerchiefs with embroidered flowers, and even a few linen towels. It seemed, for all their searching, they had uncovered Thea Reed's linen collection.

Heidi released a sigh and folded a handkerchief, laying it back on top of the other linens. Emma's computer had been traded in for an iPad. She had it balanced on her lap, comparing public records to newspaper articles she'd discovered. But they were of the First World War. Nothing that pertained to Misty Wayfair, the deceased Mary Coyle look-alike, or Heidi's family.

Emma put down the newspaper article and turned her attention to Heidi. "Simeon Coyle fought in the war."

"Who?" Heidi raised an eyebrow.

Emma handed her the news clipping.

"Simeon Coyle. According to the ancestry site, he is Mary Coyle's older brother. They also had a sister, Rose."

"Huh." Heidi skimmed the clipping.

Emma browsed the family tree on her tablet. "Simeon Coyle is your great-grandfather."

"What!" The news article dropped from her hand. "He's my mom's grandpa?"

Emma studied Heidi's surprised face. Heidi scolded herself for reacting so exuberantly. Emma gave a quick nod, assessing Heidi's control and seeing that things weren't going to explode into chaos.

"Your mother was born in 1943. Simeon Coyle had two sons. One of them, Peter, was your mother's father."

"Right. Grandpa. He died shortly after I turned four, so I never really knew him. Who was Simeon married to?" Heidi looked over Emma's shoulder at the family tree on-screen.

Emma squinted. She fingered the screen, scrolling up. "Alice Fortune."

"Wait." Heidi worked hard to quell the energy surging through her. She wanted to launch herself toward her phone that sat on the coffee table a few yards away and call Rhett. She tempered her reaction, not wanting to upset Emma.

Emma eyed her.

Heidi waggled her fingers with nervous energy. "Okay, okay. Hold on here." She eased away and reached for her phone, then scooted back next to Emma. Pulling up a note app, she started to type. Making notes herself would help her comprehend the mixed-up family tree.

"So, Reginald Kramer was Mathilda Coyle's father and Simeon's grandfather."

"Yes." Emma nodded.

"Okay. So technically" — the thought occurred to Heidi — "I'm a descendant of Pleasant Valley's lumber mogul, either way you spin it. Simeon Coyle was the grandson of the founder of Kramer Logging, Reginald Kramer. Then, Simeon ends up married to Edward Fortune's heir, Alice? Who was the heir to Kramer Logging?"

"Yes," Emma affirmed.

"My brain is whirling right now." Heidi blinked, staring at her app. "So, because Reginald Kramer disowned his daughter Mathilda for marrying a Coyle, he willed his company to his nephew, and it came under the ownership of the Fortunes. So technically, by Fortune or by Coyle, in a different set of circumstances, my family could have inherited Kramer Logging."

Heidi bit at her fingernail. Were the Fortunes of today upset about Heidi coming to town? Was their lineage somehow in question — or their rights to the logging company? No. It couldn't be that. They'd have no reason to try to burn down a cabin, or write crazy messages aimed at Heidi, when the law would be clearly on their side by way of written wills and inheritance. It wasn't a monarchy where a lost prince returned home to claim the throne.

She drew her finger back as her teeth bit too deep into the skin beneath her nail. The family tree was threaded and a bit confusing, but it didn't lend to any direct aim at her.

Emma spoke up, her finger stroking the iPad. "Edward Fortune, Alice's father, wasn't Reginald Kramer's direct nephew. He was Reginald's wife's nephew from her first marriage."

"So, no blood relation to Simeon?" Heidi ventured.

"None," Emma replied.

"That means he was cousin to Alice by name only."

"True."

"Well, there's a plus." Heidi's mind continued to spin. What a mess this was!

She stood. Rüger jumped up next to her, wagging his tail and sharing her pent-up energy. Archie eyed them from his spot on the couch while Ducie lifted his head briefly before lowering it between his paws with a puff of air that flapped his jowls.

Heidi crossed her arms and turned to stare out the window, over the Crawfords' mowed lawn and the small flower garden that circled the mailbox at the end of the drive. Musing, she fixated on the salmon pink blossoms of the geraniums. If she was in the direct line of the Kramer-Fortune logging enterprise of Pleasant Valley, then the age-old curse of Misty Wayfair became even more interlinked. They were all descendants in one way or another. The primary common denominator that connected them beyond the logging business was the murder of Misty Wayfair. How was it, after the big rift when Mathilda Kramer married Fergus Coyle, that Simeon, their grandson, spun around and remarried back into the Kramer-Fortune family?

It didn't make sense.

Not with the curse of Misty Wayfair lingering over the Coyles, determined to bury them all. No one who believed it was real would have allowed Simeon Coyle back into their family tree.

Heidi tugged her phone from her pocket and shot off a quick text. Within seconds, her phone chimed in response. She thumbed the screen and read the text from Connie.

Sure. Go ahead. Emma should enjoy some history sleuthing. Please keep it straightforward.

Heidi smiled. She met Emma's inquiring gaze. "How about we take a trip to Kramer Logging?"

Emma's eyes brightened. "Dad works there!"

"Yes." Heidi nodded and eyed her friend. "Emma, what if the whole story about Misty Wayfair was actually solved — years ago?"

Emma looked up at her and frowned in confusion.

Heidi attempted to explain. "If Misty Wayfair was put to rest for good, and that enabled Simeon to reconcile with his family and remarry indirectly, then it really was just a story. There was no ghost."

Emma furrowed her brows at Heidi. She might as well have said *No duh,* but she didn't. "There was never a ghost."

Heidi met Emma's frank look. "But even you — you said you saw her. When we were at the asylum ruins."

Emma shook her head. "No. I said it was Misty Wayfair's home."

Heidi tried to understand her. She was literal. Very literal. So, Emma would have said she saw Misty Wayfair if in fact she had seen her.

"What do you mean it was her home?" Heidi asked.

Emma shrugged. "The legend says it was. After she died. She haunted it." The young woman twisted her scarf around her neck, straightening it.

Heidi let out a small laugh of bewilderment. "But — so then — why did you — ?" She needed to tiptoe around her words. Emma required precise, clear questions. "What made you scared that day?"

Emma's eyes grew wide, remembering. "The woman. In the upstairs window. She scared me."

Heidi knelt next to Emma. She refrained from the instinct to grab her hand. "Emma, what woman?"

Emma gave her a quizzical look, as if Heidi should know. "The woman who looks like you."

CHAPTER 36

THEA

Thea tried to calm her nerves as she gripped the desk in the asylum office. She held her hand over her stomach that still swirled darkly. Last night had been restless, and she'd lost the contents of her stomach twice. Today, even the walk to the asylum seemed laborious. A walk she normally half ran after her unsettling interlude with whoever had taunted her from the woods.

She lifted a cup of tea Rose had given her. Even the nurturing Rose had noticed Thea wasn't feeling well, but Thea had no intentions of letting Rose know it was emotional angst. Or at least she thought it was. She certainly wasn't going to announce to Rose that Simeon had suspicions their grandmother had killed Misty Wayfair in a jealous fit. That Edward Fortune had later built an asylum by Misty's grave in what seemed to be a gesture for the mentally ill daughter

Misty had left behind. Thea's mother.

By no means did she intend on saying anything about her suspicions that Effie — *Effie!* — was the mystical Misty Wayfair who haunted the woods of Pleasant Valley, who somehow escaped from the asylum in bouts of freedom. And if it was Effie, then more than likely it was also Penelope, when she'd been alive.

Thea dropped onto her chair, holding her head in her hands as the room swirled. Had Penelope been the first "ghost" sighting? An asylum patient snuck from her prison in the dark of night, haunting the home of the Coyles?

Only Effie would know the answer to that — if Effie was well enough to tell. Or sane enough.

Thea stood, stumbling into the desk. She righted herself. Now was not the time to be falling ill. She peeked into the asylum hallway, hoping to avoid Dr. Ackerman or one of the nurses. She had no idea if she would be able to make it upstairs unde-tected, let alone to Effie's room. But she had to try.

Her steps were purposeful, in spite of how heavy her legs felt. She reached the top of the stairs and paused. She could hear voices to the right, down the hallway toward the dormitories and the commons room. A nerve-wracking howl from a patient. Nurses' footsteps as they hurried to calm them.

Thea turned to the left. The hallway was empty. She hurried down it, reached Effie's door, and pushed it open. She darted inside and shut the door behind her.

Effie lay pale and listless on the bed. If possible, even more gaunt and ill than before. But her eyes were open. She moved her mouth on sight of Thea. Her words barely above a whisper.

"You came back."

Thea hurried to her side, kneeling by the bed and grasping Effie's hand. The room whirled for a moment, and Thea blinked fast to clear her focus.

"I'm here."

"I can see Death. It's knocking on my door." Effie coughed, squeezing her eyes shut.

"No. No, it can't be." Thea gripped Effie's hand. "Effie?"

The older woman opened her eyes and stared at Thea. "I saw you, in the window of the boardinghouse, that night."

It *had* been Effie. Thea remembered seeing the woman dancing, free and unfettered, down the street. She hadn't imagined her. But, she was not Misty Wayfair's ghost. She was real, and hopeful, and longing for a different life.

"Yes." Thea nodded.

Effie closed her eyes and whispered hoarsely, "Penelope always hoped you would come back. I wish she were here to see you."

Thea swallowed hard, squeezing Effie's hand tighter. "Did my mother — did she know how to escape this place too?"

Effie offered a weak nod. "Through the basement. It's simple to sneak past the night nurse. And it's often forgotten to lock the basement hatch from the outside."

"Why do you come back here? When you're free? Why did my mother come back here to die — to be tested and experimented on?" Thea swiped at a tear that trailed down her face.

Effie smiled in resignation. "We had nowhere else to go. She couldn't go back to the Fortunes. They'd left her here to be cared for."

"Why? Why did Edward Fortune take my mother in as a child? Why did he create this place for her? A place of torment and a — a prison?" Thea blinked a few times in succession as the room grew blurry and then cleared.

Effie seemed to be fading. Drained and

tired. She opened her eyes. Tired eyes that had lost their will to fight but had regained some clarity in the wake of Thea's arrival.

"Edward Fortune was her father, and Misty Wayfair her mother. He made it look as though it were Fergus Coyle who'd spawned a love child, but it wasn't him. He was innocent. Mathilda Coyle killed Misty for no reason, and Edward Fortune kept her secret. Penelope never forgave Mathilda — even though she'd been lied to. She would watch their house at night. She would sing to calm herself when she longed to scream at the woman who killed Misty — Penelope's mother — in a jealous fit."

Thea's breath shook as she drew it in, attempting to steady herself. Her suspicions were all being confirmed. She was a Fortune. A non-blood-related distant cousin to Simeon. The lofty, entitled Edward Fortune's granddaughter. He had directed her to move a plant during his portrait, stared down his nose at her as she provided photographic services in the wake of Mr. Amos's attack. If Effie could see her striking resemblance to Misty Wayfair, then so must Edward Fortune! Yet he'd said nothing. *Done* nothing!

Thea rose from beside Effie's bed. The woman had slipped into a deep sleep. She laid Effie's hand over her stomach and brushed the woman's graying hair from her forehead.

"Sleep, Effie. Rest," she whispered.

The hallways were empty again. Thea hurried toward the stairs, her head feeling as if it were too heavy to hold up. Her heart pounding from the shock of the revelation. She was a Fortune! Effie and Penelope were the elusive ghost of Misty Wayfair!

But then who had taunted Thea from the woods outside the asylum? Certainly not Effie, not in the middle of the morning! And why had the Coyles died, one by one, so suspiciously? Penelope could not have been responsible for all that. She couldn't have! Thea reminded herself that her mother had passed away well before Mary Coyle. Even so, she couldn't avoid the niggling sense of worry. She would need to revisit the dates of Simeon's parents' passings and Mathilda Coyle herself. If her mother, Penelope, had been bitter enough to hover in the woods and watch the Coyles every night she could escape her prison, who was to say she hadn't?

Thea palmed the wall as she took a step down the stairs. She choked back nausea, holding her hand to her mouth. The stairwell seemed to narrow and then expand.

Thea squinted, attempting to see the next stair, when movement at the bottom captured her attention.

Simeon.

He stared up at her, an inquisitive look on his face. Then he cried her name as blackness swamped her vision and Thea sensed her foot slip.

The world built around Misty Wayfair's cursed life went dark.

HEIDI

Kramer Logging. The place where it had all started so many years before. It looked like a modern-day logging company. Warehouses for lumber. A lumberyard. Dump trucks, front-end loaders, trailers, and other strange trucks that Heidi didn't even know the names of. Men and women were scattered about, busy at their various tasks. The whole place smelled like fresh-cut wood. Heidi hiked toward the central office, Emma by her side. She wasn't sure where Murphy, Emma's father, worked, but Emma seemed to be keeping an eye out for him.

The door opened, and a bright office greeted them. The front desk resembled a doctor's reception area, and an older man sat behind it, eyeglasses perched on the end of his nose as he finger-punched a computer keyboard. He looked up. Smiled.

"Help you?"

"Yes." Heidi nodded. "I was wondering if I could speak with Mr. Fortune."

The man choked. "Mr. Fortune? You must mean *Ms.* Fortune. She runs the company, but uh, well, you realize she doesn't work from here?"

"Oh." Heidi's resolve sank.

"She works out of the head office in Wausau."

The reference to the closest city, about two hours away, pretty much sealed Heidi's intention of outright confronting the Fortunes with historical facts and lineage and asking them if they had any idea about their family. She had a tough time reconciling that Kramer Logging would be behind the recent incidents.

"Are there any of the Fortune family here I could speak with?" she asked.

The man hesitated a moment before answering, "Well, there's Bonnie."

"All right." Heidi nodded.

He blinked. "Can I tell her who's here?"

"Heidi Lane, please, and Emma Crawford."

The man groused as he got to his feet. "Be right back."

Apparently, they didn't have an interoffice

phone system. Or more than likely, he just didn't know how to use it.

He returned a few minutes later, accompanied by a tall woman with a kind smile on her face. Her graying hair was pulled back in a ponytail. Her dress was stylish but simple. She extended her hand.

"Hello, I'm Bonnie Fortune Pierce. Vice President of Kramer Logging. My older sister is the president, so I apologize she's not here to meet with you."

"Oh — I didn't have an appointment," Heidi admitted.

"Well then." Bonnie Fortune looked between them. "What can I help you with?"

Suddenly, Heidi was at a loss for words. She'd been so intent on coming here, the revelation of family history. But now . . .

"Heidi is your relative." Emma broke the awkwardness.

"Oh!" Bonnie's voice rose in high-pitched surprise. "Perhaps we should go into the conference room." She led them to a quiet room just off the lobby. "Please. Have a seat."

Once seated around a small table, the door closed, Bonnie's face grew a bit sterner. "I will admit, we've heard this before. Many people would like to find ties to the Kramer-Fortune legacy."

Heidi ducked her head. Barging in and declaring a direct-line relation probably hadn't been the smartest thing to do. She could almost see Rhett's expression of mildly entertained disbelief if he were here with her.

Emma filled the silence for Heidi. "Heidi's great-grandfather was Simeon Coyle. Who married Alice Fortune. In 1911."

Bonnie blinked.

Emma continued. "They had children. Their eldest son had a daughter, Loretta, who is Heidi's mother."

Bonnie brightened. "Oh! Loretta! You're Loretta's daughter?"

Heidi drew back, surprised at the instant recognition and friendliness. She nodded. "I am. Her youngest."

"Oh my," Bonnie nodded. "Yes. I've known Loretta for some time now. Several years ago, she came to me and introduced herself. Obviously, she wasn't after any part of the company, and legally we're protected anyway, but it was an interesting conversation. To say the least."

Heidi glanced at Emma, who adjusted her infinity scarf. She cleared her throat. "I didn't realize my mother had spoken to you."

"Oh, yes." Bonnie tapped the table with

527

her fingers. "She did. In fact, your sister — Vicki? Yes, she was with your mother during our meeting."

Heidi stiffened. Vicki? Her sister who had denied knowing anything about their family heritage? A twinge of betrayal resurfaced. Heidi bit the inside of her cheek.

"Such a fascinating history," Bonnie went on, "and all of it tied to that story of Misty Wayfair. What a sad story. And what a pity she's been sensationalized so. Her tale — the stories of our families — is quite unfortunate."

"You know what happened to her? To Misty Wayfair and the Coyles?" Heidi tilted her head in confusion.

Bonnie gave her a questioning look. "Didn't your family tell you?"

Heidi shook her head. "No." She opted for honesty. "Mom is unwell, and my sister and I aren't close."

"Ahh, I see." Bonnie seemed to consider her words now. Caution flickered in her eyes. "Well, I know some of it. I know they long ago uncovered who killed Misty Wayfair. I believe it was — well, they say anyway — Mathilda Coyle. In a jealous fit." Bonnie gave Heidi a regretful look. "Sadly, it wasn't anything she should have been jealous about."

528

"What do you mean?" Heidi asked.

"According to the story as my family tells it, Mathilda found out the day of her wedding to Fergus Coyle that Misty Wayfair had an illegitimate child. A daughter who was already a toddler. Because Mr. Kramer, Mathilda's father, believed an affair had gone on between Fergus and Misty, his telling Mathilda might have been a last-ditch effort to stop the marriage. But Mathilda married Fergus anyway. Although apparently her plan was already sealed with intent to kill her rival, Misty.

"But, it wasn't a Coyle who had fathered Misty Wayfair's child. Mathilda had no reason to be jealous. None. Unfortunately, it was a Fortune. Your mother's and our mutual great-great grandfather, Edward."

"A child? And Edward?" Heidi raised an eyebrow. "How do you know this?"

Bonnie gave a small shrug. "Edward kept a diary. Our family hasn't published it, of course. The town has fun with Misty Wayfair *sightings* and — well, frankly it does add a bit of pizzazz for the tourists. Old legends die hard, anyway. Besides, everyone except the very superstitious knows Misty isn't real. She never was — well, not after she died. But her child was. Her child was very real. Penelope Wayfair. If you investigate the historical records of the asylum, you'll find more of her story. Regardless, it's a sad chapter in the Fortune history that we share."

"And telling it was never an option?" Heidi tried to control the irritation in her voice. Had the truth been told, the Coyles would have finally had the stigma removed from them as cursed and ostracized. The Fortunes, in all reality, would have a century-old scandal that very few currently would care about. It seemed unfair that Bonnie and her family had let the legend continue uninterrupted.

Bonnie gave her a look of surprise. "Well, I suppose we could. But it's messy and old and irrelevant."

"Or not irrelevant," Heidi offered. The message on her mirror, the note card, the arson, but more so, the strange woman both she and Emma had seen. "I've had — sightings," Heidi began, knowing she sounded rather delusional herself.

"Yes?" Bonnie waited.

Heidi glanced at Emma. The young woman met her gaze, expecting Heidi to continue. "There was an arson fire at Lane Lodge recently. One of the cabins. A woman, she pulled me from the fire. She looked exactly like me, and she strongly resembled a photograph I found in an old album. A photograph of Mary Coyle, Simeon Coyle's sister."

Bonnie's expression grew serious. She looked down at her hands folded on the table and clicked her tongue against the roof of her mouth. "I . . ." She searched for words. "Listen, I know we're distant relations. And after your mother and sister visited me, well, let's just say I carefully vet my potential relations. In doing so, I discover many things. Private investigators are quite nosy, you know? I would suggest strongly that you speak with your sister."

Heidi frowned.

Bonnie gave her a sympathetic look. "Sometimes we search all over for answers when really they're very close to home."

Vicki.

She'd known all along then. Whatever the truth was.

Heidi pushed back her chair, attempting to tamp down her fury, her betrayal, and once again that horrific panic that twisted her stomach into knots.

"So you'll say nothing more?" Heidi offered up a weak challenge.

Bonnie drew a sigh in through her nose and let it out with a regretful shake of her head. "I'm truly sorry, Ms. Lane, but it isn't my place."

Heidi nodded. "Thank you for meeting with us, Ms. Fortune." There was an edge to her voice. Bonnie Fortune was kind, in a distant way, but not in a way that indicated she would offer any reconciliation or closure to the past.

Bonnie graced her with a parting smile. "If you ever need anything . . . I mean, I know the Fortunes may not be known for their past benevolence, still, you *are* family — no matter how distant. And I honor family."

Heidi managed a smile in return.

If only Vicki honored it too.

CHAPTER 37

HEIDI

Emma's cries jolted Heidi into a full-on charge through the Crawford kitchen. She left her phone on the table, ignoring the fact she'd just texted Rhett to see if he'd go with her to Brad and Vicki's when he got off work. It was time to meet with her sister face-to-face. But now Emma's wailing distracted her from waiting for his reply.

The family room TV had been muted. Murphy was kneeling on the floor in front of Emma, who sat on the couch rocking back and forth. Tears stained her face. Ducie had sidled up to his mistress, his broad nose resting on her knee. Connie rocked with her, holding her tight, whispering consoling words.

Connie glanced up in dismay as Heidi entered the room and skidded to a halt. The concern on Heidi's face must have been enough to garner an answer.

"She lost her Ducie scarf." Connie's explanation meant nothing to Heidi, yet she was aware how losing a precious item would affect Emma.

Emma released another sob. Her lack of words sent an empathetic ache through Heidi. She eased carefully onto the floor by Murphy, hoping Emma hadn't taken on her own anxiety after they left Kramer Logging. She'd tried to remain calm, to hold in her mounting hurt and betrayal. Emma had seemed fine. But — a scarf? There was still one around her neck.

"Where did you last see it?" Connie asked gently of her daughter.

Emma blinked and swiped at her eyes. Her rocking increased, and Connie adjusted her hold on her daughter, applying comforting pressure to help ease the anxiety.

"I saw it around my neck." Emma's chin quivered.

"Okay. That's good, Emma." Connie nodded. "When did you see it there?"

Emma sucked in a watery gulp. "When we went to the asylum."

Heidi wished she could forget that day when she'd upset Emma by taking her out of her routine. When she'd incensed Rhett.

"I'll go look there," Heidi stated.

Connie gave her a quick glance. "It's

almost seven."

"It's okay." Heidi stood. "I can get there and back before dark."

The recollection that Emma claimed to have seen the woman who'd pulled Heidi from the fire came to mind. She quelled the unease at the idea. Emma needed her. She needed her Ducie scarf.

Connie nodded. "The scarf is patterned with dogs. She doesn't wear it all the time, but when she wants it, it is always hanging on the pink hanger in her closet. Emma went to get it tonight, and the scarf was missing. There's no coming back from a missing favorite item."

Heidi gave Emma an empathetic smile. "It'll be all right." She hurried back through the kitchen, snatching up her car keys and phone from the table.

Far be it for the ghost of Misty Wayfair to keep Emma's dog-patterned scarf from the woman. Heidi owed Emma one. She owed the Crawfords too. She owed them every-thing.

Heidi's car slowed to a stop in front of the asylum ruins. Dusk was fast approaching, and for any other reason, there was nothing that would've inspired Heidi to come here alone. She glanced up at the line of windows on the remains of the second floor. Emma had seen the woman in one of those windows. The dead Mary Coyle? The ghost of Misty Wayfair? Or someone who needed more explanation, specifically from Vicki?

She wanted to interrogate her sister. That would come in time. Rhett had texted Heidi that they'd talk when he stopped by his parents' place. Before she'd lost a signal, Heidi had sent back a quick *OK*. Rhett would know what was going on soon enough.

Heidi got out of her car, phone clutched in her hand. Lot of good it would do if she needed it, but the flashlight app was helpful at least. Heidi flicked it on and held up the phone. Though there was still plenty of light, the woods didn't help any with their ever-deepening shadows. Heck, she had to be honest with herself. The flashlight just made her feel better.

Heidi revisited the events of the afternoon she'd visited here with Emma. Neither she nor Emma had gone inside the asylum. In fact, Heidi had returned later with Rhett. She would have thought, if the scarf had been dropped at the asylum, it would be lying on the old cobblestone walk. Why had Emma removed the scarf to begin with? A pointless question now. Maybe Heidi would return to the Crawfords' empty-handed, and the scarf would show up elsewhere. But Heidi had to do something.

She stood on the cobblestone walk, trying to ignore the asylum and the breeze that whistled through the crumbling roof. If, theoretically, the scarf had fallen on the walk, the breeze could have easily blown it somewhere. Heidi began searching the nearby undergrowth, the bushes, and along the fence line.

Some of the cast-iron fence still stood, leaning out from the asylum as if the years had made it tired. She weaved back and forth across the old hospital yard toward the side of the asylum and finally to the back. Heidi stopped. This was ridiculous. The scarf wasn't here. She held the flashlight up and sent the beam toward the woods at the back of the asylum. There was no way the scarf would have blown back there. No way at . . .

A flutter in the far bushes caught Heidi's eye. Her insides gave a jolt. Nervous energy and hope all wrapped into one. She glanced behind her to see if someone was following her. That prickly sensation she'd read about in books? Yeah. She was feeling it now.

Heidi hurried toward the flutter. "Ah ha!" Weird. The scarf was looped around a fence post, like someone had picked it up and draped it there. She reached for it and paused. The remnants of a trail led beyond the fence. It was more than a deer trail, or any other trail made by animals. It had the appearance of once having been often traversed. Perhaps by patients or staff of the asylum.

She pushed through some shrubs, detaching a branch with thorns on it from her sleeve. Raising her flashlight, Heidi noted a small opening. Without giving it much thought, she shoved down the trail, maneuvering around branches and another thornbush.

"What the —" Her whisper drifting into the woods. Unanswered except by the chatter of a squirrel.

Heidi stared at the rows of gravestones. Mostly half buried by the earth now, but a taller pillar stood out in the far corner. She ran the toe of her Converse over one of the markers. The name was all but lost now, with weather and time having eaten away at the carvings that must not have been deep to begin with.

An asylum graveyard.

Heidi shivered and tiptoed around the stones toward the taller one in the back. One peek and then she was getting out of here. The unsettling feeling had become thicker now, especially since dusk seemed to be waving its farewell far too quickly for Heidi's taste. Rhett would have a fit if he knew she'd come here alone.

She ran her hand over the face of the gravestone. A name of a man she'd never heard of. The next side.

Penelope Alice Reed Wayfair

Wayfair. Alice? Was this Simeon Coyle's Alice?

The next side was guarded by an evergreen that had grown up against it, its branches scraping the side of the stone. Heidi shouldered her way in and lifted her phone. The shaft of light touched the first name, and Heidi sucked in a breath.

Misty Wayfair

Nope. She was not doing this in the near-dark, outside of the asylum ruins. Time to grab the scarf and get the heck outta Dodge.

Heidi spun toward the asylum, hurrying her way as speedily as she could along the abandoned path. She focused on the dim outline of the fence. The post with the scarf.

The scarf.

Heidi stopped. She lifted the light.

Where was the scarf?

It had been there just minutes before. There was no doubt.

She searched the darkness frantically, but her phone's flashlight was only so bright and didn't cast a beam very far.

"C'mon!" Heidi hissed in creeped-out exasperation. She needed to get out of here. Away from this place. But she couldn't leave without Emma's scarf.

Or maybe she should.

A heavy sense of danger settled over her. The kind that warned her no scarf was worth this. Emma would have to work through her anxiety. At this point — Heidi passed the fence and darted a look toward the far corner of the yard — at this point she needed to leave.

She took another step, and without warning the scarf settled around her neck, yanking her back. Heidi choked out a scream, and her phone dropped to the ground, the light aiming away from her. Her hands flew up to grab at the scarf that dug against her windpipe.

The body Heidi stumbled backward against was no ghost.

It was very real. It was a woman. She could tell by the strands of long hair that wafted over Heidi's face as she fought against the cold hands that clutched the scarf.

"Don't fight," the woman's voice crooned. It shook a bit. As if she were unsure of her own actions.

Heidi tried to spin, but as she did, the scarf twisted and tightened around her throat. She tripped and fell, gagging as the Ducie scarf cut into her neck.

"No!" The woman's voice was urgent. Worried. Heidi felt the woman drop to her knees behind her. The scarf loosened, and the woman's arms came around Heidi's neck instead, dragging her back against her chest.

A hand came up and stroked the side of Heidi's face, flattening her hair.

"Shhhhh," the woman crooned. "It's okay, baby. Momma's here."

THEA

She groaned, turning her head on the pillow, only to endure the throbbing pain that made the light from the windows feel like a thousand knives burrowing into her skull. A hand clamped over her forehead. It was cool and gentle. Thea heard the murmur of voices, first Rose's, then Simeon's. She opened her eyes in small slits, just enough to see Rose exit the bedroom and Simeon sitting vigil by her side.

"Thea." Simeon edged closer when he saw she'd awakened. His familiar features were blurry. Thea tried to open her eyes wider, but it hurt too much. Her stomach still rolled with nauseating persistence.

"What happened?" Thea muttered.

"You fell down the stairs at the asylum. You're at our house. Rose has been tending you through the night. Mrs. Amos insisted we take you there, but they have no spare room for you."

Thea tried to journey through the fog of her mind. It was thick. But Effie's face revived in her memory, and then her story. Thea struggled to sit, but she fell back against her pillow as Simeon's hand pressed against her shoulder.

"Don't try to move." His fingers smoothed back her hair.

The weight of what she knew crashed in on her conscious mind.

"Edward Fortune!" Thea gasped.

"What?" Simeon leaned closer.

She felt as though she were speaking so loudly she was screaming, but perhaps she was only whispering. Thea couldn't tell.

"He's my grandfather."

Simeon's eyes widened. His mouth

twitched.

Thea tried to push words past her dry mouth and thick tongue. "He fathered my mother with Misty Wayfair. He knew your grandmother Mathilda had killed Misty, and he — allowed it. Took the blame and put it on Fergus, so Edward would bear no shame."

Simeon's face darkened. Thea watched his shoulders stiffen as the truth barreled into him.

"The Fortunes took my mother in and raised her as a waif." Thea's words tumbled over each other, on a dash to escape before she forgot the details entirely. "She left them and must have birthed me. Before she returned to Pleasant Valley, she left me at the orphanage."

Simeon's gray eyes were turbulent, and again his hand brushed her forehead. "Shhh, Thea. You must rest."

"No!" Thea blinked rapidly to avoid the feeling she might lose consciousness. "Mr. Fortune needs to answer for this. For my mother. She used to haunt your family, escaping the asylum at night to watch you. All of you."

Simeon didn't respond. The implications were there, and yet Thea thought she saw him calculating by the way his lips moved silently.

"She could not have been behind the deaths of my family," he said, more to himself than to her. "At least not my mother or Mary. Penelope had already been dead herself. And, they died of melancholy." Simeon dropped his gaze back to Thea. It was clear in his eyes that he no longer believed that. "Was it Effie?"

"No," Thea whispered. "Not Effie. She hasn't the mind or a reason to — to be a cause of your family's deaths."

"So, did . . . ?" The chair scraped on the floor as Simeon jolted to his feet, awareness flooding his features. "Edward Fortune. Did he kill my family? Did he allow the story of Misty Wayfair to propagate in order to drive away the Coyles from Pleasant Valley?"

Simeon stalked to the door, a purpose in his stride Thea had never seen before. As if Simeon had been awakened from a stupor of aimless wandering and hopeless resignation and now wished for closure. Once and for all.

"Simeon," Thea begged. No. He didn't understand. Mr. Fortune had no reason to make the Coyles his vendetta of death. He'd already had his purposes fulfilled. Mathilda Coyle had done so when she'd murdered

Misty Wayfair in a misplaced jealous attack.

But Simeon didn't seem to hear Thea. He looked over his shoulder at her, their eyes locking. Hers, attempting to plead for him to stay, and his, resolute that the truth of his family's deaths might finally be uncovered.

"This will end. Today. The curse of Misty Wayfair will be over."

The door closed firmly behind him.

CHAPTER 38

HEIDI

Headlights illuminated the woods around the asylum. A squad car's red-and-blue lights flashed. The woman gripping Heidi hissed with a worried expression into Heidi's ear.

"No. No more cops."

She released Heidi, who scrambled to her feet. The loosened grip also released the gag around Heidi's throat. Emma's Ducie scarf fell limp around her neck. She surged toward the woman, pulling her back to the ground with a grunt.

"Let me go!" the woman shouted. She clawed at the earth, dragging herself toward the woods. Trying to escape. To the endless forest beyond and the graves that marked the very ghost Heidi had once considered might exist.

Heidi grappled for the waistline of the woman's jeans, wrapping her fingers around

546

it and tugging her backward.

A man shouted.

Flashlights flooded the backyard.

"Heidi!" Rhett's voice broke through her frantic subconscious.

But no. This was her fight. This was her story.

Heidi straddled the woman's legs, grabbing at her shoulders and forcing the woman to face her. In the darkness, aided by Detective Davidson's light as he came upon them, Heidi stared into the eyes of the woman who had first peered into her room. A woman who, at first glance, was so like the dead Mary Coyle of the photo album. A woman who was the older version of Heidi.

"Please, Heidi!" the woman cried in desperation. "Let me go. Let me run."

"Who are you?" Heidi half screamed into her face. She knew she was crying. She knew the truth even before the woman admitted it.

Detective Davidson had his gun drawn.

Officer Tate was behind Heidi, and she could vaguely hear him commanding her to back away.

Rhett stood off to the side. She could almost feel his censure that she'd come here to the asylum alone in search of Emma's scarf. Censure born from protection. It wouldn't be safe. Not after the arson fire.

"Who are you?" Heidi gave the woman a shake.

Graying blond hair flopped over the woman's face. There was fear in her eyes, and an emptiness Heidi couldn't quite place.

"Let me go!" she wailed again.

Detective Davidson demanded something, but Heidi didn't register it. She leaned down into her doppelgänger's face and growled, "Tell me who you are!"

A moment.

A pause.

"I'm your mother, Heidi. Your mother."

Heidi rolled off the woman whose claims seemed so asinine, they almost had to be true. The police moved in. Rhett helped her to her feet. She stared at her look-alike.

Suddenly everything the dementia-riddled Loretta Lane said made sense. Ghosts in their family. Mistaking Heidi for the daughter who might as well have been dead to them. Worst of all, Heidi now understood why she had always been a misfit in her own family. She was their daily reminder of a daughter they wished to forget.

THEA

Thea watched Rose as she wrung out a cloth after helping Thea clean up. She didn't

548

feel much better. In fact, she was certain she was worse. Her mind seemed even more cloudy than before. She wondered if she had imagined Effie, the asylum, and the odd story of a ghost.

"Here." Rose's gentle voice awakened Thea to the present. She observed the woman's blue eyes, framed by dark brows, and her black hair swooped in its typical nursing roll on the back of her head. Rose ran the cool cloth down Thea's neck and ears.

"You'll feel a bit better now that you're clean."

She didn't. Not really.

Rose moved across the room to a bureau. Thea followed her with her eyes. Simeon had been upset when he'd left. She couldn't recall exactly why. But Rose wasn't upset. She was very calm.

Thea watched Rose return, a cup in her hand. Another kind smile.

"Can you sip this? It should help keep you hydrated."

Thea struggled to sit up in the bed. Rose held the teacup to her lips, and the lukewarm liquid trailed down Thea's throat, a momentary comfort.

She lay back against her pillows again.

"Where is Simeon?" she asked.

Rose shook her head, and her eyes shadowed. "He didn't tell me." She still held the cup as if she intended to ask Thea to sip again. But her voice was distant. Considering. "He always tells me where he's going."

Thea nodded. A memory returned to her. Fortune.

"Edward Fortune," Thea breathed.

Rose tilted her head. "What?"

"He was going to Edward Fortune's, I believe. My mother. Misty Wayfair."

Rose stared at her for a long moment. The ticking of a clock filled the silence, and then Rose offered another, smaller smile. "Sip?"

Thea eyed the cup. She'd never been a fan of tea. What had ever made her start drinking it? She recalled the first day she set foot in the Coyle home. Mary. She was dead. Yes. Thea remembered now. She'd taken their picture, sisters, Rose and Mary, and then had tea.

Effie had had tea.

And Thea, at the asylum.

"No, thank you." Thea tried to put her thoughts into order. "How did your mother die?" she asked Rose abruptly.

Rose's hand stilled, a little bit of tea sloshing over the side of the cup. "She . . . passed of melancholia."

"Like Mary?" Thea frowned. She knew

550

this. Her mind was so foggy.

"Yes." Rose nodded. "It runs in our family."

Thea struggled to maintain her focus. "Melancholy doesn't kill. Has no one told you that?" She didn't mean to sound rude, but she couldn't formulate anything other than her blunt thought.

"I know," Rose nodded. She set the teacup on the nightstand.

"Did you . . . give Mary tea?" Thea asked.

Rose studied her for a moment and then nodded. "She liked tea. She liked lots of tea. It made her feel better."

"And your mother?"

"Yes." Rose offered a vague smile, her blue eyes looking out the window across the room. "Mother liked tea as well."

Thea's breaths came a bit faster now. The intensity of the truth in that moment sent an awareness through her. "Your grandmother . . ."

"No." Rose shook her head. "She didn't like tea. But she taught me how to make it. It helps people who are sad, Thea. Like my mother and like Mary. Dr. Ackerman wanted Mary to live at the asylum. It's a horrible place. My sister didn't deserve to live there. My mother didn't deserve to suffer in her regrets. After Father died, she wallowed in her doubts. But she couldn't help it — she couldn't have stopped him if she'd tried. So, I gave Mama tea. It saved her. She isn't sad anymore."

Thea tried to move her legs. They were heavy, and her arms were hard to lift too. The realization she'd been drinking Rose's poisoned tea shot through her with the alarming awareness that Rose somehow saw herself as savior. To the ill, to the weak members of her family.

"Your father?" Thea gasped, choking as nausea rose in her throat.

Rose slowly lowered herself onto the chair Simeon had originally sat on. "I was simply trying to stop him. I was a child. We were in the loft, and he was angry. So, so angry. When he went to strike at me, I struck back, and he tripped and fell out the window. And then he was dead." Rose gave Thea a wide-eyed stare. "My grandmother Mathilda said, 'Sometimes to protect your family, a person must make grave decisions.' She told me that she had done so once herself." Rose's eyes filled with a fierce loyalty, an obsessive protection. "I only do what's best for the suffering."

Thea swallowed the nausea again. The room grew blurry. She closed her eyes as consciousness faded. Fighting against it,

Thea opened her mouth, gasping out, "Did you know my mother . . . ?"

Rose's voice echoed in Thea's ear, and her gentle hand brushed Thea's cheek. "I knew only Misty Wayfair's ghost. But when she came, when I would see her outside, staring up at our home, singing so softly, I knew it was time. She wanted them to come to her. So I helped them. I helped my mother and Mary, and now Effie and you. Effie speaks lies, and she is suffering because of them. I tried to warn you — to frighten you — in the woods that day outside the hospital. You needn't concern yourself with these things. They'll only make you unhappy. I just wanted you to be happy, Thea." Rose reached out and stroked Thea's hair away from her forehead. "But you're so brave. Even after I pretended to be Misty's ghost — to scare you — you still came to the hospital. So brave. But you needed to stop asking questions. They will make you sad. It's too painful. So, I'm helping you."

"I don't want any more tea," Thea argued weakly, trying to push away Rose's hand.

But the woman's soft voice filled the room. "Just a little more, and then everything will be all right."

HEIDI

She watched them lead her mother — Betsy Lane, they had identified her as — down the hall of the police station. The front door burst open, stealing Heidi's attention from Betsy and transferring it to the pale, wild-eyed expression of Vicki. Brad followed her, and it was his look that collided with Heidi's. Sheepish, sorry, and filled with a familiar expression of surprise. He hadn't known.

Rhett's hand curled around hers. Heidi took it for what it was. A silent warning not to overreact. Not to launch into a tirade against her sister. Heidi didn't agree. Every particle in her being wanted to cry and seethe at the same time.

"Where is she?" Vicki demanded of Detective Davidson, who came down the hall toward them, his shoes clicking on the linoleum floor.

He gave both Vicki and Heidi a quick glance. "She's in holding for now. We'll process her. She'll need medical attention."

"She must be off her meds," Vicki muttered.

Detective Davidson nodded. "More than likely. We've got a call in to her probation officer in Minnesota. Why don't you all come into the front room here? I'm guessing you need to talk."

He was right. They did.

Heidi refused to release Rhett's hand, even though he tugged it away, trying to give her family privacy. He followed, and in a few minutes, the four of them were seated around the table.

A loaded silence filled the room after Detective Davidson closed the door.

Brad sniffed.

Rhett kept quiet.

Vicki picked at a fingernail.

Heidi had no intention of leaving the stillness alone. She'd waited too long to understand.

"Why did you never tell me? After everything — especially now. The fire? You blamed me! The message on the mirror? Betsy admitted to it all! To get my attention! What is that about? I'd say trying to burn me alive and then saving me is a bit of an extreme way to do that! What's wrong with her?" Heidi's questions exploded like rapid-fire bullets in her sister's direction.

Vicki raked her hands through her hair and turned tired, sad eyes in her direction.

"She's my older sister. Your mother. She has schizophrenia. Half the time she doesn't know what she's doing. She's supposed to be in Minnesota the last we heard, in a hospital there. She was sentenced to serve time, but she received an insanity plea." Vicki's eyes filled with tears.

"An insanity plea?" Heidi shoved to her feet. "I'm thirty years old! How long has Betsy been locked up?"

Vicki bit her bottom lip and shot a look at Brad. His hand moved to cover hers. She swallowed, drawing in a deep breath. When she met Heidi's accusing glare, Vicki seemed to lose her last vestige of cold guardedness.

"Betsy got messed up with a really bad crowd out of high school. She ended up — well, her boyfriend ended up dead. Maybe an overdose, but Betsy was pinned for it. For dealing. After she served her time at the institution, she went right back to drugs and went off her medications. So, she was brought up on random theft charges, more dealing, et cetera. She's been doing time, Heidi. All her life." Vicki blinked fast, but tears escaped anyway. "Mom and Dad wanted to protect you from her."

Heidi sagged in her chair. Her chest rose and fell with pent-up emotions that twisted between shock, panic, and outright betrayal. Her *sister* — no, her *aunt* — had kept the secret all these years, along with her parents!

She'd released Rhett's hand when they sat down, but now she wished she hadn't.

Somehow, his perception was on high alert, and Heidi felt Rhett's hand settle on her knee beneath the table. He gave a comforting squeeze, then lifted his hand.

"Heidi," Vicki started, then stopped, looking at the ceiling as she rolled her lips against the emotion choking her voice. She dropped her gaze back down and locked it with Heidi's. "You were a prison baby, Heidi. Betsy went to jail pregnant with you, after her boyfriend — your father — wound up dead. Mom and Dad adopted you, protected you from it all. Maybe we should have told you years ago. I *know* I should have said something when this all started here, but it's ingrained in me not to. Mom said, 'Never tell!' And when you started having anxiety and panic as a kid, they thought the worst. That maybe you — you were like Betsy."

"I'm not like her," Heidi argued, hoarse from suppressed tears. But God knew she could possibly relate in a small way to her mother. Held at arm's length. Different.

Vicki reached across the table. Heidi ignored the gesture, even though for the first time honesty showed in Vicki's eyes. Regret and a plea for Heidi to forgive. Heidi didn't want to, and yet, in a way, she could see the twisted logic. Protect the innocent baby.

The one who should never grow up in the shadows cast by Betsy's own struggles and failures. But they'd abandoned Betsy and, in doing so, abandoned Heidi too.

"So," Heidi choked out, "you just *left* my — mother — on her own? In the system? And tried a do-over with me?"

"Please, Heidi! No, it's not like that!" Vicki begged, holding out her hands further. "Please. Mom and Dad tried. They did. Dad visited Betsy as often as he could. Mom wrote her letters. But Betsy — she knew you existed and we needed to keep you safe. Then Betsy stopped responding. No more letters. And she wouldn't come to see Dad when he visited her. After a few years, you graduated high school, you went off to college and — never came around anymore. And Betsy was a ghost of a memory."

"Is that why Mom and Dad moved here? To Mom's childhood hometown."

Vicki shrugged. "I guess? There was a pastorate. Mom wanted to get away from the years of memories in Minnesota, but she wanted somewhere familiar."

"Pleasant Valley." Heidi could hear the resignation in her voice. She could sense Loretta Lane's pain more than she wished to admit. Being guarded all those years. No wonder they'd tried to make Heidi tow the line! To stay in control of the offspring of the daughter they'd essentially lost! Coming back to Pleasant Valley must have been a last-ditch effort on Loretta's part to gain some control over an entire life that had never quite measured up. Like Heidi.

Heidi sucked in a sob that escaped her. She clapped her hand over her mouth. "Mom understood me."

"More than you know," Vicki whispered. Tears rolled down her cheeks. "When she really started failing a few months ago, she knew she was losing any last threads of normalcy she may have regained."

"And that's when Mom wrote to me." Awareness flooded Heidi. "She wanted to tell me before she lost her memory."

Vicki gave a watery nod. "It must be." And then she added, as though a massive weight she'd carried for years had lifted, "Finally."

Heidi reached out, hesitant. Vicki clasped her hands across the table and licked at the tears that rolled over her lips.

"We may not have done the right thing, Heidi. But, we did it because we loved you. Because we loved Betsy, and she couldn't — she couldn't be your mother. She couldn't care for herself. Please. Please forgive us."

Heidi knew forgiveness could not be given in a nod or in words. Nor was she sure it could even come. It would take time to process who she was, what decisions her family had made over the years in spite of her — *for* her.

She glanced at Rhett. His features were solid. His eyes met hers. In them she saw his confidence.

"Fix your eyes on the target and let the arrow fly."

"The rest will follow."

For the first time, Heidi accepted she could not charge ahead, nor could she run away. She had to choose to trust a greater purpose, one she didn't understand, and maybe didn't even like. But really, wasn't that what faith was?

CHAPTER 39

THEA

She wasn't dead. Thea sat in the bed, propped up by luxurious pillows and covered in a velveteen quilt. She was in the Fortunes' home, and the poisons that had wracked her body were vanishing. Health returning.

The sequence of events that had brought her to this place still bewildered her. But Mrs. Amos had told her the story on her last visit. How Simeon had beckoned the older woman to go to the Coyle home later that afternoon to relieve Rose, as he had to confront Mr. Fortune. How Mr. Amos had insisted on accompanying Simeon and the confrontation that ensued. How Mrs. Amos had finally arrived at the house to assist Rose, only to have the men, along with Mr. Fortune, arrive almost simultaneously. Mr. Fortune had been frantic to get to Thea. He'd been suspicious but not convinced she

561

was his granddaughter, but once Simeon revealed it to him, the arrogance had faded into distress.

She wouldn't be safe at the Coyle home, he'd argued. Something wicked lay inside. He'd suspected it for years, ever since he'd confronted Mathilda with his suspicions of her own darkness and she had admitted to him that she'd killed Misty Wayfair.

It was Simeon who arrived at the startling realization that Rose was the only unaccounted for factor. They'd all come upon Thea's room as Rose had admitted to Thea her deluded and misguided horrors.

A knock on the door brought Thea's attention off the events that had happened while she lay unconscious. It opened a crack, and Mr. Fortune peeked through.

"May I come in?"

Thea nodded.

He entered, the self-confidence back in place on his face. The commanding presence and a slightly lessened air of entitlement. He was, after all, still a Fortune.

Mr. Fortune lowered himself onto a chair. He gave Thea a small smile. "Your mother, Penelope, named you Alice."

"Then you knew about me," she replied.

This man, this stranger, had been so deviant himself. Perhaps now he wished to pay penance for his sins. Perhaps that was why he and his wife had taken in his illegitimate child with Misty Wayfair.

He cleared his throat. "She told us of you, when she returned home and was unwell. Penelope had been gone from our care for several years by then. I'm not sure of her story or how you even came to be. But she said you existed and she knew she wasn't well. She told me she didn't want me to have you, so she left you at an orphanage somewhere. I don't even know *why* she told me of you, yet she begged me to leave you be, away from this wretched town. She gave you a new name, she said. You were no longer Alice Fortune."

"Dorothea Reed," Thea responded.

"Yes." Mr. Fortune nodded. "That was my mother's name."

Thea tried to comprehend. Her name was not even her own. She was Alice Fortune. Not in Mr. Fortune's direct line of inheritance, due to the illegitimacy of her mother, but his granddaughter nonetheless.

"How did you not immediately know who I was? When I took your photograph?" Thea had to ask, to understand why he'd been so silent.

Mr. Fortune shifted in his chair. The look he gave Thea appeared more that he wished to unburden himself rather than seek for-giveness.

"As I said, I suspected. I didn't know for sure."

Thea nodded, but his words stung. It wasn't until her life was potentially in danger and he was cornered by Simeon and Mr. Amos that he'd come to face the truth about her.

Mr. Fortune cleared his throat. "I didn't know Mathilda Coyle killed Misty until years later. Truly, I didn't. I suspected. It ate at me. I couldn't tell my wife. In the end" — he looked down at his hand — "I allowed the story of her husband, Fergus, and the suspicions that he was Misty's lover to be believed. It cleared me of my trans-gressions. But you must know, I had no intention of it becoming this — this *legend-ary.* Of Misty being concocted into a ghost story! It all became so much larger than it was ever supposed to be."

Thea waited. She watched her grandfather drag his hand over his eyes as he took in a breath to continue.

"Mathilda already had a falling-out with her father, my uncle Reginald Kramer. The Coyles never would have become his heirs because my uncle disapproved of Fergus. After Misty was found, I . . . . I went to the . . . I went to where she stayed. One of the ladies there was caring for your mother, Penelope. I offered to take her in and be her benefactor. They didn't ask questions."

Thea blinked but said nothing. Let the old man confess and come clean, if he must. The only balm to Thea's soul was knowing the truth, as painful as it was.

Mr. Fortune continued. "I tried to take care of Penelope as best I could. My wife didn't know until years later that Penelope was really my child and not just a recipient of our good graces."

"And yet you put her in an asylum." Thea's throat choked, though she didn't break her stare from her grandfather's face. "You let them *experiment* on your own daughter."

Mr. Fortune lurched from his chair and stalked across the room. He looked out the window, his coat pushed back as he rested his hands at his waist. Thea watched his shoulders, stiff and unyielding, at last sag in defeat.

When he spoke, his voice bounced off the windowpanes. "I built the asylum to get Penelope the help she needed. What did I know of proper medical care for her? She would pitch and roll. Foam at the mouth." Mr. Fortune turned, and Thea could see genuine agony in his expression. "My daughter needed help. Dr. Ingles said such things would . . . help her."

And so many others had also been told the same. Thea recalled Mr. Fritz's story of other asylums. Other abuses. It was nothing new to mental institutions, and only recently had such practices been exposed.

"What will become of Rose?" She skirted her grandfather's explanation.

He blinked, surprised she had nothing to say. What could she say? Her grandfather had committed no crimes. He'd been selfish. He'd been underhanded and manipulative. He'd tried to atone for this by caring for her mother as a child and then as an ill woman. His attempts were a sad extension of a man who knew nothing but his own ambition to save his good name.

"Rose will answer for her crimes." He gave Thea a nod. "She's been taken to a hospital farther south until then. To be treated. She is very . . . unwell."

Yes. Thea nodded.

"But, I will monitor her care," Mr. Fortune added quickly. His mustache twitched as he sniffed. "She won't suffer what —" he stopped and met Thea's eyes — "she won't suffer what your mother suffered."

Thea gave her grandfather a small nod,

resolution filling her. She would not look for herself in this house. She would take whatever time was needed to make peace with the history that had wrapped its ugly, sinful grip around her family, and Simeon's family too.

For the first time, Thea breathed a prayer as she studied the old man at the window. She saw the wrinkles at the corners of his eyes, and the concocted air of superiority that kept his jaw straight and rigid.

Her prayer was to her Creator. Finding herself here was not satisfying. But she had been given life, after all. So there was a reason for her existence.

Maybe Simeon was right. That ceasing to uncover one's purpose, but instead finding out who one's Creator was, would be the most satisfying story of all to uncover. A bigger story than her own. A story of creation and of meaning, which was so much larger than a fallen family, and the whisper of a ghost's memory who, in a way, would forever haunt them all.

HEIDI

Heidi slipped the Ducie scarf over Emma's head and leveled it around her neck. The morning had brought with it a measure of hope. Only a little, but with it came the promise that it might grow, that healing was possible. Emma gifted Heidi with an enormous smile, her hands stroking the beloved scarf. Even Ducie struggled to his feet, tendering his leg still cast in plaster, and nosed Heidi's hand.

Connie laughed and reached out, embracing Heidi. They held each other for a long moment. No words were necessary, for really, what could anyone say? The revealing of Heidi's past, of her family, of their local ties, and the secrets were more than an empathic statement could account for.

When Heidi pulled back, Connie grasped her shoulders, looked deep into her eyes, and gave her a firm little shake. "You won't run, Heidi."

Heidi mustered a smile. "No. I won't." She drew in a long sigh. She'd wanted to run, multiple times during the night, as she lay in fitful rest in the guest room at the Crawfords'. But this time she also wasn't alone anymore, and in a strange way, she was starting to see who she was.

"And your mother — Betsy?" Connie asked.

Heidi shook her head. "I don't know. Vicki texted me and wants me to come with her today and help figure it out. Together." That was a new idea Heidi wasn't sure how to process. "But, we'll make sure she gets back on her medications, and then see what happens. Vicki seems to think — well, maybe we can get Betsy institutionalized again, but in a place that offers effective treatment. Depending on what obligations on her record she still has to meet, we may try to search out a faith-based hospital."

Connie offered a reassuring smile and drew Heidi in for another hug. She pulled back. "Let this be a time of healing. For all of you. For Loretta too."

Heidi nodded. "I'm not sure if we'll tell her about Betsy."

"All in good time." Connie stepped back and glanced out the window. "But for now, Rhett's here." Connie gave her a nudge toward the front door. Rhett was waiting outside in his truck, the engine running.

As Heidi climbed into the truck, Rüger nosed her leg, and she buried her fingers in his familiar fur. Archie yowled at her from the dash while Rhett maneuvered the stick shift into gear.

The trees whizzed by along the country road. Heidi contemplated today, the implications, and the brand-new journey in front of her. She considered the photograph of Mary Coyle, the story of her brother Simeon who married Alice Fortune, and the foggy legend of Misty Wayfair that really was never fully explained. She even considered Thea Reed's trunk and wondered how the local photographer had ended up with Coyle keepsakes.

And then there was Rhett.

Heidi didn't bother to hide the fact she was studying his features as she looked at him. His jawline, his greasy cap, his gray eyes, his expressionless face. The man had hardly uttered a word since last night, but as Heidi approached her newly revealed family secrets with trepidation, a different worry gnawed at her.

She continued to eye him, yet he remained impassive.

Well, Rhett sure wasn't going to say anything.

Heidi raised her eyebrow as he cast her a glance. He looked back at the road.

"So?" she asked.

Rhett braked as a turkey bobbed across the road in front of the truck. "So, what?"

Heidi bit the inside of her cheek. Fine. She was just going to ask. "So, was I just another one of your rescues? Like Archie, or Rüger?"

Rhett's brows furrowed. He shot her another glance.

Heidi tried a different approach. "You've

— you've been here for me. But now that I've uncovered what I needed to, I was just wondering if — well, if you'd still be around?"

A slight smile quirked the side of his mouth. "I wasn't planning on moving."

Heidi rolled her eyes and delivered a soft punch to his arm. "Come on. You like to rescue things — *people.* Your mom told me. She said you're a softie."

Rhett frowned.

Heidi pressed on. "I just didn't know if I'm just your latest rescue."

The turkey had crossed into the field on the driver's side. Rhett put on his turn signal and pulled the truck onto the shoulder. He shifted it into first gear, then shut off the engine. Twisting in his seat, he pushed Rüger to the floor. The dog lay on top of Heidi's feet with a grunt as Rhett slid over.

He leaned forward and studied her, his moody eyes roving her face.

Rhett didn't say anything.

Heidi was almost afraid he would.

Finally, he did.

"You never needed rescuing, Heidi. You just needed help aiming."

She smiled. Rhett and his archery references. She sort of liked it. Sort of liked him.

Well, *sort of* was an understatement.

Rhett's eyes narrowed, and he studied her briefly. Then he shook his head. "I told you before that I thought you were cute."

Heidi gave him a quizzical look.

He shrugged and waved his hand at Archie and then at Rüger. His voice lowered, and before Heidi could move, Rhett leaned forward and pressed his lips against her temple. "I have a habit of adopting cute creatures."

Heidi couldn't move away. Surprise and a funny swirling sensation filled her. Only this time, it wasn't panic.

She offered him a silly grin. "I'm not a creature. Sorry."

Rhett's face relaxed with humor, and he gave her a crooked smile in return. "No. You're much cuter." He pulled back, pushed down on the clutch, and started the engine.

Heidi leaned her head back against the seat and drew in a deep breath. Like a prayer. A promise.

"Ready?" Rhett asked.

Heidi nodded. "Yeah."

She had let the arrow fly. Now she would see where God would take it — take *her*. It was time to go meet her mom.

They sat by the river, evening fast approaching. Their walk from the Amos home to the riverbank was more peaceful tonight. The story between them known. She had left the Fortunes as soon as she was well. Thea knew she'd never truly be one of them, even though she'd discovered she was legally named Alice Fortune.

The river rolled on, its current the same habitual fervor as every night before. Simeon gazed out over it in his usual quiet fashion. His features were calm. He was at peace.

"How is Effie?" Thea ventured.

Simeon's mouth flattened, and he gave a thoughtful nod. "She's better. Dr. Ackerman was able to get her nourished. She did have an episode yesterday, I heard, and has been a bit catatonic since. But that was expected."

"Yes." Thea was grateful she needn't worry anymore that Dr. Ackerman would do anything but restrain Effie. She'd spoken to him at length, and while she felt his tactics somewhat extreme, there were no "experimentations" in Effie's future, or in the futures of any other patients. Nothing that would infringe on Effie's overall health. She would live out her life at the asylum.

God willing, a full life.

Thea had no intention of abandoning the woman who had been her mother's confidante.

"And — Rose?" Thea asked.

Rose. The unspoken between them. The one neither would forget. The sister Simeon grieved over as much as he had Mary, and the woman Thea wished had received more nurturing and guidance instead of becoming so disillusioned.

Simeon tossed a stone into the river. "I'll visit her. When she stands trial, I will be there." His voice was resolute.

Thea nodded. "I will be there too."

He searched her face. Simeon's eyes were turbulent. She wondered if he would ever truly find happiness. But then perhaps sometimes one's life wasn't about happiness, but rather about finding contentment in spite of one's circumstances.

A distant expression filtered across his face. "How did I not know? How did I not even see a hint of the signs? I shouldn't have been so blind to Rose. I was suspicious of my grandmother, yes, but I had no idea Rose would — my mother, and Mary . . ."

Thea reached out and rested her hand on his elbow. "You weren't blind, Simeon. You love Rose. She's your sister. You didn't want to believe that of her."

He gave a curt nod. "I didn't want to believe it of my grandmother either."

Thea left her hand on his elbow. He didn't seem to mind, and she wanted to touch him, to feel his tenuous strength.

"I don't understand why Rose didn't try to —" Simeon cut off his words.

"Try to what?" Thea pressed.

Simeon's gray eyes were rife with emotion. "Why didn't she try to take my life too? To *save me,* as she saw it?"

Thea squeezed her eyes shut. Against the pain on his face, the strain in his voice. When she opened them, he was staring back over the water. His jaw was set, his face calm regardless of recent events.

Thea knew why Rose had spared her brother. It was obvious to her.

"Because you are strong, Simeon. Rose didn't feel she needed to rescue you. You didn't need saving."

His hand clasped hers at his elbow. He worked his jaw back and forth. "I don't feel strong. I never did."

Thea moved closer to him. "Strength isn't a feeling," she whispered. "It's the will to forge ahead regardless of circumstances."

A tiny smile touched Simeon's mouth, and he chuckled. "That sounds a bit like faith."

Thea matched his bittersweet smile. "Yes. I suppose it does."

Simeon turned toward her, drawing her hand from his elbow and gripping it in his own.

She waited. Knowing how he felt, because she felt it too.

"I'm not certain where to go from here, Thea." Simeon moved as if to touch her cheek, his fingertips hovering just above her skin. His eyes narrowed. "But, I believe we were meant to find each other. I'm unwilling to be defined by the people around me. I always have been. And yet I cannot reconcile that you came here by accident — by happenstance."

Thea reached up and placed her hand over Simeon's and pushed his palm to her cheek. His eyes closed at the feel of her skin. She turned her face, and her lips pressed into the heart of his hand. She heard him breathe deeply, and she looked up at him.

"Do you believe — is it foolish to believe that, regardless of the tragedies, of the sorrow, there is a design to our lives?"

Simeon's eyes opened. His thumb stroked a light path over her lips. His eye twitched ever so slightly, and he shook his head. "I don't believe it's foolish. No more foolish than believing we simply exist and then we die."

Thea nodded, relieved that Simeon didn't scoff at her fledgling faith in a Creator. In a God who had seen fit to craft her into being. Her life had taken a defined path, steered by choices of her family in the past, herself, and the results that followed. But also directed by her own growing belief that life catapulted a soul toward the Creator, whether the person acknowledged it or not. The evidence of the fingerprints of design were on her life. On Simeon's life. Of the gifts amid the darkness. People like Mr. and Mrs. Amos, who were there when no one else was. Effie, whose loyalty to a friend from long ago had brought resolution to Thea's questions. Even Dr. Ackerman, whose care for his patients would be a small step in correcting the misinformed perspectives on those who struggled to find peace in their mental illnesses.

Thea drew back, tracing her fingers down the column of Simeon's neck.

"I need to know more," she whispered. "I need to understand why He formed me into who I am. I — I need to know *Him*."

Simeon released her and bent, picking up a river stone and feeling it in his hand. Thea laid hers over it so that their hands fully engulfed the stone.

"If I were to carve words into this for this moment" — Simeon stepped closer to her, the stone clasped between them — "I would etch the words *In spite of.*"

"In spite of?" Thea watched as Simeon's forehead moved nearer and rested against hers. They both opened their hands and studied the rather plain-looking river rock.

Simeon's words hovered between them. "In spite of the darkness, in spite of the crushing weight, this is not the last page. *We* are not finished, Thea. This place — this life — *will* break us. But from above, our Creator reaches into the depths, and He will carve into us something new."

Thea raised her eyes and met Simeon's. So close, so deep, so unguarded and honest she had to ask, just one more time. "You truly, truly believe that? That God will begin to bring restoration?"

"He has already started." Simeon closed the inches between them, a quiet confidence in his voice as he brushed her lips with a tender caress.

Thea could sense Simeon's belief in his kiss, his care, and his faith for more than their eyes could see. She could sense his soul melding into her soul, traveling a path with her, fragile but tipped in promise.

She drew in a deep breath of anticipation. Every creation was intended for a purpose. In broken places, beauty could be found. In beauty, she would find the Creator's perfect story. A story that didn't need to be rewritten, because it already was. Her story. She was Dorothea Reed. She was Alice Fortune. She was . . . created. And being created was no small thing.

AUTHOR'S NOTE

Regardless of "good intentions," humanity has a history of imprisoning sectors of individuals who miss the mark on the measurement of normalized society. While history speaks loudly of this in the present, we are often deaf to their ghostly cries.

God's tapestry of human experiences born from sin, suffering, joy, and triumph separate each of us into our own story. A spine with an embossed title that tells of our individualized blessings and curses. These stories mesh into a library of human need, which all returns to its Author, desperate to be understood. To be healed. To find the elusive strength one can never truly find within oneself.

He is the writer of your story. Every story has twists, trials, and victories. When we take up the pen to edit, that is when our stories run awry. Your tale, your life, has a purpose. A story of need, of brokenness, of salvation, and of beauty. As it is written. As it was intended to be.

May you lift the book that tells your story, change none of its pages, but instead may you find within its loose ends, its mystery, its tragedy, and its joy, your Author. The Finisher of your faith. Your Rescuer. The Writer who has composed your ending with a glorious sequel in mind.

QUESTIONS FOR DISCUSSION

1. Both Heidi and Thea struggle with understanding their personal identities and how this factors into their lives' purpose. How have you struggled to "find yourself"? Where are you now in that personal journey?

2. Hospitals for individuals suffering with mental illness were prevalent in the nineteenth and twentieth centuries. However, many people were admitted for undefined conditions such as epilepsy, prolonged grief, and even widowhood. What significant improvements has modern medicine made in helping individuals to deal with weaknesses of the human body and spirit? Which maladies today has our society been poor at offering support to hurting individuals?

3. Rhett and his family point Heidi toward

her Creator and help her to see beyond a clouded, internal focus. Who has played a pivotal part in your journey, both in your faith and in your formation as a person?

4. As you contemplate the story and the themes of identity and life purpose, how do you feel the legend of Misty Wayfair paralleled the lessons Heidi and Thea needed to learn?

5. Emma is a key influence, not only in solving the mystery of Misty Wayfair but also in bringing life back to Heidi. All too often, individuals with special needs are disregarded, but they have so much to offer us. Has someone with special needs enriched your life in some way? What lessons has this person taught you?

6. Heidi discovers an antique photo album filled with pictures over a century old. What is your favorite vintage find? Why?

7. Thea's career as a traveling photographer, serving those with a deceased family member through postmortem photography, is morbid to us today. But in the Victorian and early Edwardian eras, this was a widespread practice, and the photo-

graphs became treasured memorabilia. How do you or others you know memorialize a loved one today?

8. The romance in both stories is subtle; however, Rhett and Simeon each brought a unique perspective that resulted in Heidi and Thea beginning new journeys to know their Creator more deeply. Who challenges you on a regular basis to view life from a different perspective? Can you recall a specific instance when that challenge was a special help to you?

ACKNOWLEDGMENTS

This novel was far more difficult to write than any I've attempted before. The elements of mental illness, of special needs, of anxiety disorders all required sensitivity and a delicate touch. While I have my own personal journey within these elements, agonies and blessings, I also must thank:

Mary Jane Lines, who is a heroine of motherhood. And to her son, whose intelligence, creativity, love, and devotion to his family far outweigh the stigma of autism and bring to light a beautiful picture of God working out a good thing in our lives. Thank you, MJ, for opening your soul to me. For allowing me to see your struggles, your pain, and your precious, precious love for your son. I pray I have adequately represented an individual with autism. Any misrepresentations are entirely my own fault, and I will continue to study, to learn, and to defend the value of those with autism. They are a vital part of our community and of our hearts.

Tracee Chu. I didn't quite get a character named after you, but you're threaded through this novel anyway. From the dark elements, the sarcasm, and even the glimpses into the world of autism. You are another heroic mother whose son I adore, and whose simple bravery and humble friendship I thank you for.

Debra Penzkover. For entrusting your son to me that day of sixth grade youth group. For allowing him to teach me how to enter his world and see all the vibrant creations within it. I fell in love with your boy, and he has taught me many, many things. I am so proud of the man he has become.

Natalie and Kiana. We walk this journey together, our hearts intertwined because of inexpressible understanding. It was no mistake we found each other. In the darkness, beauty is discovered.

My family — my parents, my pirate, my littles, and my sisters — thank you for never judging me, for loving me in spite of me.

To all of us who struggle with anxiety, depression, panic, mental illness, learning disorders, special needs, and so much more . . . we were created with a purpose! The world is broken, and yet the Creator has a beautiful redemptive way of taking those broken pieces and crafting something precious and beautiful. Never forget that you are beautifully and wonderfully made. That is your identity. Search no further.

ABOUT THE AUTHOR

Jaime Jo Wright is the author of the acclaimed novels *The Reckoning at Gossamer Pond* and *The House on Foster Hill,* which won the Daphne du Maurier Award for Excellence in Inspirational Romantic Mystery/Suspense. She's also the *Publishers Weekly* and ECPA bestselling author of three novellas. Jaime works as a human resources director in Wisconsin, where she lives with her husband and two children. To learn more, visit jaimewrightbooks.com.

The employees of Thorndike Press hope you have enjoyed this Large Print book. All our Thorndike, Wheeler, and Kennebec Large Print titles are designed for easy reading, and all our books are made to last. Other Thorndike Press Large Print books are available at your library, through selected bookstores, or directly from us.

For information about titles, please call:
  (800) 223-1244

or visit our website at:
  gale.com/thorndike

To share your comments, please write:
  Publisher
  Thorndike Press
  10 Water St., Suite 310
  Waterville, ME 04901